A PLUME BOOK

WHAT HAS BECOME OF YOU

JAN ELIZABETH WATSON received her MFA from Columbia University. She lives in Maine.

Praise for *What Has Become of You*

"Watson develops [Vera and Jensen's] relationship with such subtle skill that it's hard to tell exactly when things start to go terribly, tragically wrong." —*The New York Times Book Review*

"Stylistically the book soars with smart, well-structured sentences that tantalize the literary senses." —Bookreporter.com

"Watson is working multiple shifts here, creating a coming-of-age story and a series of grim murder mysteries; probing the psyche of two characters who are alike, yet different; and introducing a cast of distinctive supporting roles. . . . Watson navigates among these twisty venues with ease, achieving that elusive goal—the page-turner." —*The Portland Press Herald* (Maine)

"Part gloss on *The Catcher in the Rye* and part millennial *The Prime of Miss Jean Brodie*, *What Has Become of You* is that rare beast: a page-turner that asks dark, difficult questions about the state of contemporary American society." —Joanne Smith Rakoff, author of *A Fortunate Age*

"Watson's twisty plot speeds with page-turner momentum, but what's likely to stick with you are the complex characters of Vera and Jensen, who are, by turns, vulnerable, flawed, and surprising, bravely struggling to rewrite the stories of their lives." —*Publishers Weekly* (starred review)

"Readers will soon want more from Watson." —*Library Journal*

What Has Become of You

Jan Elizabeth Watson

A PLUME BOOK

PLUME
Published by the Penguin Group
Penguin Group (USA) LLC
375 Hudson Street
New York, New York 10014

USA | Canada | UK | Ireland | Australia | New Zealand | India | South Africa | China
penguin.com
A Penguin Random House Company

First published in the United States of America by Dutton,
a member of Penguin Group (USA) LLC, 2014
First Plume Printing 2015

THE LIBRARY OF CONGRESS HAS CATALOGED THE DUTTON EDITION AS FOLLOWS:
Watson, Jan Elizabeth, 1972–
What has become of you / Jan Elizabeth Watson.
pages cm
ISBN 978-0-525-95437-8 (hc.)
ISBN 978-0-14-218191-1 (pbk.)
1. Substitute teachers—Fiction. 2. Girl's schools—Fiction. 3. Students—Crimes against.
4. Missing persons—Fiction. 5. Bildungsromans. I. Title.
PS3623.A87245
813'.6—dc23 2013029362

Printed in the United States of America
1 3 5 7 9 10 8 6 4 2

Set in Fairfield LT Std
Original hardcover design by Alissa Rose Theodor

This book is for Eric.

What Has
Become of You

Chapter One

Standing amid the library stacks, Vera Lundy thumbed through an anthology of contemporary essays, stopping at one of her favorites—"Goodbye to All That," by Joan Didion—and read the first line, which she already knew by heart: "It is easy to see the beginning of things, and harder to see the ends." *A neat, pat sentence,* Vera thought, *but not entirely true.* Sometimes beginnings are less clear-cut than endings; sometimes, when speaking of significant events, their points of origin are not so easy to locate. She wondered if she might be able to elaborate on this idea in a future lesson plan, putting it in a real-world context that her students could relate to. The recent arrest of a local man named Ritchie Ouelette for the killing of an eleven-year-old girl, for example—would this be considered a beginning or an ending? She supposed that would depend on whom you asked.

She was about to put the book back in its proper place when the librarian with the wobbly-wheeled book cart stopped her, saying: "Please don't reshelve that. Return any unwanted items to the circulation desk."

As though apprehended in the middle of a far more serious offense, Vera froze, holding the book at upper shelf level. "Oh, I'm *sorry,*" she said, taking stock of the librarian, whom she saw on at least a twice-weekly basis: crisp iron-gray hair; black horn-rimmed glasses; turtleneck under a shapeless denim jumper that seemed to be the unofficial, no-nonsense uniform of all New England librarians over a certain age. "I *was* putting it back in the right spot, if that makes it any better."

The librarian's expression grew frostier, and she reiterated "We ask that all unwanted items be returned to the circulation desk" with such grim finality that Vera felt chastened.

The librarian steered her rumbling cart in the other direction. Vera was sure the woman knew her by sight, knew her to be a respectful library patron—a *regular,* even, who returned her books well before their due dates—but she always regarded her with the same lack of recognition. Perhaps that was just her way. But Vera was sure that this librarian was dismissive of her because of her choice in reading materials. She was always requesting true-crime books from interlibrary loan—the more lurid in content, the better—though this all fell within the framework of research: Vera was writing a manuscript of her own, an account of a homicide dating back to her freshman year in high school.

The other possibility was that the librarian mistook her for a kid. Vera was petite and round-faced, with certain demure, girlish qualities and a bit of teenage insouciance thrown in to further muddy the picture. In reality, however, she was nearly forty years old—a fact she kept from everyone but her immediate family, who already knew the truth. It did no harm, she reasoned, to tell everyone else that she was thirty-five. Thirty-five seemed a good age to stick with for a while.

She pored over the new arrivals on the library shelf one last time, contemplating the possibility of adding a fifth book to her haul, but decided to restrict it to four this week: the copy of *The Catcher in the Rye* that had been the purpose of her trip, two true-crime books about cannibal killers, and an obscure but promising novel about a Victorian poisoner. Four was a good number, to her thinking. She'd once read that in some cultures the number four is regarded as unlucky—superstitiously avoided as the number thirteen is avoided in the Western world—but Vera's superstitions were selective at best.

Stuffing the newly borrowed books into her tote bag, she stepped outside and was pleased to find the weather had improved since she'd first set out; the bank sign next door read 48 degrees, which would make for an unusually temperate walk home. In Vera's mind, a world where the temperature constantly read 48 degrees would be all but perfect: just cool enough to necessitate a thick coat and a hat, but warm enough to keep her from shivering. The thick coat and hat were important, Vera thought, because they offered her a camouflage or subterfuge she didn't have in the warmer days of spring and summer; she liked being covered up, and she liked knowing she could run errands with uncombed hair or the same dirty T-shirt she'd slept in without anyone being the wiser.

In such a state, Vera could almost blend in with certain denizens of her town, for Dorset, Maine, was a place where liberal-minded college kids coexisted with the toothless and the unwashed; the hip small businesses and chichi restaurants flourished on the same blocks as pawn shops and bodegas in such disrepair that the hipster kids didn't dare wander into them. Self-satisfied middle-class people who owned or rented historic brownstones lived alongside those in housing projects. In truth, Vera felt she had little in common with any of Dorset's residents, yet it was Dorset where she had made her home after a failed attempt to make peace with her hometown of Bond Brook.

Reaching her apartment building, she unlocked the door, climbed three flights, and let herself into her studio apartment. Vera thought of it as a bed-sit—one room, and a small one at that—yet the kitchenette, which she never used for cooking, offered enough room for her to fit a little computer table and her laptop. The shelves near the refrigerator, ostensibly installed for the purpose of holding dry goods or cookbooks, stored school-related files with her students' papers in them, transforming the kitchenette into a serviceable study. As for the main area, most of its space was taken up by a full mattress. Vera's mother had cajoled her to consider getting a futon—something she could roll up to look like a couch during the day so that she might entertain guests—but Vera had scoffed at this idea. She knew she would not be *entertaining guests*. She would rather have it be just herself, alone in her studio, sleeping on a comfortable mattress.

When Vera had moved to Dorset from Bond Brook two years earlier, she had in her possession only that mattress, some trash bags full of clothes, and a few boxes of books she had carefully picked out from the rest she left behind. She had tried not to feel discouraged by the fact that, at her age, she was starting over again: *After this, everything will be easier,* she told herself. *Everything else I might need will come in its own time, just as things always do.*

Vera unpacked her tote bag and set her library books on the floor next to her mattress and box spring. She pulled out the dining room chair that was pushed into her desk, sat down, and opened her laptop. Still in her coat and hat, she logged into her personal email account—nothing there except for some junk mail and spam—and then into her soon-to-be-defunct faculty email at Dorset Community College. There was not much in this in-box, either: a message telling faculty to let students know of half-price tickets to see the Sea Dogs play in Portland; a weekly email from the IT department called "Technology Tip," which Vera never bothered to look at; a call for submissions to *Writ Large*, the student literary magazine. There was one email from an unknown sender, with no subject. Jensen Willard was the name in the message queue. Vera opened it and, by force of habit, read it quickly; Vera read everything quickly, as though text itself were something that might try to run away if she didn't pin it down.

To: velundy@dcc.edu
From: jawillard@thewallaceschool.edu

Hello.

My name is Jensen Willard, as you probably have deduced. I guess you're going to be substituting for Mrs. Belisle (this is for the tenth-grade English course, Autobiographical Writing: Personal Connections). I heard you taught at DCC, so I looked you up in the faculty directory there. Mrs. Belisle said we're going to get started on *The Catcher in the Rye* once you get here. I have my own personal copy that I wanted to use—the one with the original cover, not the maroon "serial killer" version that got issued to everybody in class. My version has notes in it, but I will use the other copy if that'd be easier for class discussions. Thank you in advance for any insight. I look forward to meeting you.

Sincerely,
Jensen Willard

Vera leaned more closely toward the computer monitor—she was painfully nearsighted, even with contact lenses—and reread the message more slowly. She suppressed a smile of bemusement. This Jensen Willard—a girl, no doubt, though the name had the trendy unisex character of so many young people's names nowadays, like Taylor or Maddox or Jordan—showed a funny mixture of earnestness and reserve in this informal writing sample. Earnestness in that she had taken the initiative to locate her new substitute teacher and ask her about class preparation; reserve in some of her diction ("Thank you in advance for any insight"). Vera thought certain phrases even hinted at wit. Most striking of all, the email was written in complete sentences, which was more than she could say for some of her college students' emails ("Ms Lundy i cant come 2 class 2day. im sick & puking" was a not-atypical email entry from a Dorset Community College freshman). She hit the REPLY button and started to type a response to Jensen Willard, then thought better of it. She would be seeing her in class tomorrow. Whatever she needed to know could wait until then.

Thank you in advance for any insight, Vera mouthed to herself, then thought, rather wildly: *What* insight? She did have what some people might call significant teaching experience: Prior to relocating to Dorset, she had taught as an adjunct at the University of Maine at Bond Brook, and even before *that* she had spent her early thirties earning a master's degree at Princeton, where she'd been awarded a teaching fellowship after a rigorous screening and application process. This appointment surprised no one more than it had surprised Vera. She had not been outspoken in her graduate workshops and seminars. She did not like to call attention to herself in that self-aggrandizing, showy way that her peers did—most of whom were more moneyed, more successful, more youthful than she was. It was hard to imagine her commanding any student's attention, but somehow, over time, she had learned to do it. And after a few devastating weeks of feeling as though she might bolt from the front of the classroom, Vera had come to appreciate certain aspects of teaching—had begun, finally, to think it might be the vocation she would stick with, or, as she joked to her few friends, "what I might like to be when I grow up, if being a police detective isn't in the cards."

Her most recent job—a six-week stint as a Dorset Community College instructor that had ended early when she quit to begin work at Wallace—had officially wrapped up the day before, two months before the spring semester ended, which she'd felt guilty about, though she knew her pupils were left in the hands of a good replacement. She had liked the range of students that she encountered, liked that the DCC student population included everyone from eighteen-year-olds fresh out of high school to sixty-year-olds looking to start new careers after retirement. More than anything, she'd been grateful to have a job.

But the adjunct teaching pay was not something she could continue to live off—not with her student loan creditors calling her night and day, wanting their due from her fellowship-free undergraduate days and leaving chilling computerized messages on her voicemail. These phone calls were too reminiscent of an earlier time—a time before answering machines, when the phone in her childhood home would ring and ring and Vera could do nothing but crouch in the corner with her hands clapped over her ears, knowing the threats and the vitriol that awaited her on the other end of the line.

When she saw the ad for the long-term substitute teaching position at the Wallace School, a private high school in Dorset's affluent west end, she had tossed an application their way, thinking she hadn't a chance in hell, even with her interesting credentials. She had nothing in the way of high school teaching experience. High school, she knew, was a different animal from college. But then Sue MacMasters, head of their English department, had contacted her. And even after Vera had bluffed and blundered her way through a series of interviews, Sue went ahead and granted her a position to start in February, covering someone's maternity leave, with the hint of continuing in September when the new term started up.

Vera was fearful and a little skeptical of the Wallace School, for it was one of those well-to-do college preparatory schools—one of the few that was still all-female, not coed—that allowed students to design their own curriculum and offered English courses with titles that were varied and pointedly politically correct: The Literature of Genocide, The Working Woman in Fiction. The name of the course she would be teaching—Autobiographical Writing: Personal Connections—had been a great source of mirth among her colleagues at DCC when they heard about it. *I'm going to think of it in the E. M. Forster "only connect" kind of way,* Vera had said, *and overlook that frightful* personal *part.* Most of her students would be fifteen and sixteen years old, but precocious for their ages, she imagined. Driven little overachievers all.

Vera had many different thoughts about this—about these *driven* fifteen- and sixteen-year-old girls she had not met.

She herself had not enjoyed being that age. On the contrary, those had easily been the worst years of her life. They had been the years of being ostracized, of being heartbroken, of being *hunted down.*

Vera's telephone, which she always kept on vibrate, buzzed from inside the handbag she'd slung over her chair. She winced, extracted the phone, and looked at the number of the incoming call: not the telltale 1-800 number of one of the bill collectors she was dodging, for once.

She opened the phone with relief. "Hi, Mom."

Her mother's thin voice came through the phone. She was smoking a cigarette; Vera could tell by the ragged way she breathed into receiver. "Hello, my loverly dotter," she said—her customary salutation. "I was just thinking of you."

"Aw, that's nice, Mom. I was thinking of calling *you* earlier."

"How are you feeling about tomorrow? Any better?"

"I feel out of my element," Vera confessed. "We're supposed to start reading *The Catcher in the Rye.* I had to get a copy from the library today; isn't that stupid? Somehow I have to link the novel to the idea of *personal connections*. I suppose I could talk about how Holden relates to Salinger, or how *Catcher* captures the sort of voice one sees in strong autobiographical writing. I'm just glad they already read *Macbeth* so I don't have to deal with *that*." Vera was babbling. She pressed her tongue up against the roof of her mouth and held it there.

"I'm sure you'll do fine, darling."

"Well, I put my clothes out for tomorrow, all ready to go. So I can't say I'm completely unprepared. And now I've got *Catcher*. What else could I need?"

"Just your own self," her mother said comfortably. "I don't want to take up all your phone minutes, but I *do* miss you. When are you going to have some time off to visit?"

Vera winced again. "I don't know, Mom. I'll have to sort out what my new schedule will be like." Though her mother lived only an hour and a half away, Vera did not have a driver's license—another source of embarrassment for her. It had all been very well and good to be without a driver's license while living in New York City, but Maine was a different matter—not having a driver's license was as much of an oddity and certainly as much of a handicap as having three heads.

"Well, let me know when you can," her mother said. "You could stay here in the guest room, and we could watch TV and get pizza. Big doings. By the way, are you remembering to eat?"

"Of course. I eat a lot. Mom, you don't have to keep asking if I *eat*. That stuff was *years* ago."

"Now that I don't believe. But me, I am getting a *gut*. It's the most obscene thing you ever . . . Oh! I knew I had some gossip for you, but I couldn't remember what it was. Your brother Ben ran into Peter at Home Depot the other day. He was with a woman. Great big, tall blond gal with a pretty face. Peter introduced her as his fiancée, but Ben can't think of her name."

"Good for Peter," Vera said sourly. "Really, I don't care what he's up to. I hope he *does* have a girlfriend or fiancée or whatever now. I hope he has a fiancée and is *happy*."

Peter was Vera's ex-fiancé. Their separation, which had been Vera's idea, had precipitated her move to Dorset. For all the whining he had done about the split, all the difficulties he had created and the fear he'd attempted to instill in her—all the *you're the only one for me*s, the *I can't live without you*s, even the *you won't survive without me*s—it certainly hadn't taken him all that long to recover, she thought.

"Mom," Vera said, "I'm glad you called. But I really do only have a few minutes left on my phone card. I'm sorry we can't talk longer. I promise, if this school gig turns out to extend till fall and become something steadier, I'll get a real phone again and can talk to you as much as you'd like."

"I'd love that. You know, when I was visiting the other day with Edna and Marvita . . ."

For another ten minutes Vera listened to her mother go on about her friends from the neighborhood and how they got to see their daughters and sons at least once a week. It was hard to get her mother off the phone once she got started; Vera knew she was lonely, living in Bond Brook by herself since Vera's father had died four years ago. She knew her two older brothers checked in from time to time, but as the only daughter, Vera knew that a certain responsibility fell to her. She also knew that she was shirking it. *A son is a son till he takes a wife, but a daughter's a daughter all of her life,* her mother had always been fond of saying. The responsibility implied in that statement had never been lost on Vera.

When she was finally able to hang up the phone, she sank back down at her table. She looked at the cashmere sweater and the skirt she'd hung from the hook outside her closet door. A pair of black tights hung there, too—the shoes she planned to wear would conceal the holes in the toes—and a bra and underpants so that she could wake up first thing in the morning and hop into all her clothes with no forethought. The large wheeled suitcase that she used for transporting schoolbooks and papers was also there, handle pulled out as though just waiting to be noisily dragged around the streets of Dorset. Vera unzipped the bag and took out the three folders that were used for each of her three new classes. Each had one sheet of paper in it—an attendance roster meticulously printed out by Vera the day before. She looked again at the names of the students for her first class, which would meet at eight o'clock in the morning:

Ahmed, Sufia

Arsenault, Katherine

Cutler, Chelsea

Friedman, Jamie

Fullerton, Autumn

Garippa, Louisa

Hamada, Agatsuki

Phelps, Harmony

Smith, Kelsey

St. Aubrey, Cecily-Anne

True, Martha

Willard, Jensen

Names. Just names. Vera knew from experience that a name tells one little about a person apart from the aesthetic preferences of the parents who named her. Still, she tried to imagine a face to go with each girl on her list. Knowing their names gave her much-needed power, standing before a roomful of strangers on her first day. She viewed it as a private embarrassment that such power was even necessary—that after nearly eight years of off-and-on teaching experience, she still had to summon her every last ounce of composure to not fall apart in front of her students, mortified by the eyes and attention on her, or, worse, the downcast eyes and the *lack* of attentiveness. She wished she didn't feel so fraudulent sometimes. She wished she were one of those brazen teachers who was comfortable in her own skin and loved the performative aspect of being up in front of a classroom—always glad not only to teach a class but also to put on a *show*. Instead, she forced her way through lectures and discussions, all the while thinking: *They see through me. They know what I am.*

Vera was strategically the first person in her classroom the following morning. She had shown up early not only to set up what she'd need for the class but also to get the lay of the land. After she had wrestled with all the chairs that were placed on the tables and set them right side up—the custodian must put the chairs up to sweep at night, she thought—she paced back and forth at the head of the classroom, skimming her fingers over the whiteboard tray, picturing the students who would fill up the long, empty tables and chairs in front of her. Near the whiteboard was a computer that one could use for teaching purposes with the aid of an overhead projector; though the computer was an older model, Vera turned it on and found that it worked. She did not have a proper desk, but another small table and chair up front seemed to be designated for the teacher. After some consideration, Vera pulled her table back a few inches from the first row of seating.

She imagined that whoever sat nearest the table would appreciate not having the teacher right on top of her, so to speak.

She placed her things on the table in the approximate order that she'd need them: her notebook of lesson plans, the stack of syllabi she'd photocopied, and her library copy of *The Catcher in the Rye*—the paperback version with the plain oxblood cover and mustard lettering. *The serial killer cover.*

The halls were quiet. Eventually she heard footfalls, and she looked up as the sound came closer. A fellow teacher, most likely. Teachers' walks always sounded different from students' walks.

A woman stopped short in the doorway of Vera's class. "You must be the new long-term sub," she said.

"I am." Vera stood up and approached the woman, extending her hand. She vaguely remembered having read that in ancient times, the handshake evolved when people were trying to find a way to show strangers that they weren't holding weapons in their hands. *Look, Ma, no gun.* "I'm Vera Lundy."

"Welcome," said the woman, looking down at Vera's hand before shaking it. "I'm Karen Provencher. I teach eleventh-grade English—various classes." The woman was wearing jeans and a crew-neck sweater. *Not in a million years,* thought Vera, *would I dare teach a class wearing jeans.* "Good luck to you, Vera," she said in a manner that seemed fraught with meaning, as though she thought luck alone might save her. "I'm sure I'll be seeing you around. Don't hesitate to ask me any questions about anything."

"Thank you," Vera said, "I appreciate that, I really do," and then the woman was gone. She hated the fact that she had not been able to keep the shy, deferential note out of her voice in this brief exchange. Karen Provencher was probably close to her age, but Vera could not help thinking of herself as being younger than every other professional person out there—a perception that became more absurd as the years went on.

More sounds were coming from the end of the hallway. Vera imagined students marching toward her classroom, crashing through the door, blocking off the entrance, leaving her trapped in the classroom with no way out.

An old memory, fragmented and flashbulb quick, came to her: the angry, insistent fists pounding on the windows of her childhood home; the muffled voices exhorting her to *come out from hiding, you weird bitch*; and Vera herself, suddenly much smaller and cowering on the floor in the corner with all the lights turned off so no one could see where she hid. *This is what it feels like to be under siege,* she had thought way back then. Astonishing, the powers that old memories held . . .

But now, when two girls entered the classroom, they took their seats without so much as a glance at Vera.

"Hello," she said to both of them at once, and then added inanely, "Are you here for English?"

One of the girls nodded. Vera noted that they looked very much alike—both with light-brown hair parted in the middle, both wearing hooded sweatshirts and garish printed pajama pants. Both buxom, with the sort of overripe figures that many local teenagers seemed to have. "Who are you?" Vera asked. "I mean—what are your names?"

"I'm Kelsey," the girl who had nodded said.

"Chelsea," chimed in the second girl.

Two more girls came into the classroom as the first two were still shifting around in their seats and unloading their backpacks. Did all high school girls travel in pairs? Vera acknowledged the latest arrivals with a diffident nod. Hesitating, she got up and wrote "Vera Lundy, Tenth Grade, Personal Connections" on the whiteboard. "Lest there be any confusion," she said aloud, hoping the girls might find this qualification humorous. No one laughed.

"You're the new teacher?" one of the newer arrivals said, tossing her hair. She had the kind of cascading blond hairstyle that was so perfectly layered and highlighted that it required a great deal of tossing in order to call more attention to it. She was impossibly tall, to Vera's thinking—model-tall, at least five eleven. The girl beside her was equally Amazonian—a brunette, olive-skinned, willowy, with a long, elegant face like a model in a Modigliani painting.

"I *am*," Vera said, trying to inject enthusiasm into her voice, as though being the new teacher were some sort of delightful accident.

More girls filed in, a steady stream of them now. The hallways outside the classroom echoed and reverberated with sound. Three minutes to start of class time. Too early to take attendance? Vera felt awkward, not knowing what to say in those crucial first few minutes. She waited a little longer. She felt she should be saying something, making polite chatter to put the girls at ease. But the girls were quiet. Quiet was something she had not expected. She had expected them to be talking among themselves, dismantling and filling up the silence. At last she counted heads—eleven in all—and said, "It looks like almost everyone is here. I'll start to take attendance. Please correct me if I mispronounce any of your names, or if you prefer to be called by a nickname."

Some of the girls' identities were not so hard to guess. Sufia Ahmed was a beautiful Somali girl wearing a hijab. Agatsuki Hamada, the only other nonwhite girl in the classroom, shyly told her that she preferred to be called Aggie. Between Chelsea and Kelsey and Sufia and Aggie, Vera had memorized four names—one-third of the class's identity was mastered. The tall blond was Autumn Fullerton, and the tall, long-faced brunette was Cecily-Anne St. Aubrey. "Do you like to be called Cecily-Anne?" Vera asked, thinking she might prefer a diminutive, like Cee Cee—but the girl wrinkled her nose and nodded as though not only was the answer obvious but the question was distasteful, too. When Vera ticked off Louisa Garippa's name, the girl called out, "I prefer to be called Lou."

"Lou," Vera repeated, starting to make the adjustment in her roster.

"I spell it *L-o-o*."

Vera looked at Loo, wondering if the girl knew she had fashioned her nickname after a British toilet. Loo had a nose ring and hair dyed a bright eggplant color. It was possible. "L-o-o," she said. "Got it."

The girls on the whole did not look as Vera had expected they might look. Of course, she had not visualized a prep-school-girl stereotype—plaid skirts, blazers with crests on them—but she had not expected most of them to look as though they had just rolled out of bed, either. Vera knew from her experience at Princeton that sometimes the richer a teenage girl was, the more shabbily she dressed. In contrast, at the community college where she'd taught, the freshman girls—buoyed by the presence of lusty farmer boys in the classroom, probably—sometimes wore full makeup and tight, low-cut tops.

"I'll try to learn your names as quickly as possible," Vera said. "And as for me"—here she tapped her own name on the whiteboard—"I'm Vera Lundy, your replacement for Mrs. Belisle. It may seem weird to you to have me coming in so late in the game. But I think with a little collaboration we can make the rest of the school year a good one, don't you?" The faces looked unconvinced. Vera wished for all the world that she could take back that cloying *don't you*? She hated hearing the strain in her voice already.

"I know you all know each other at this point," she said, "but since *I* don't know you yet, it would be helpful to have a little info about you before we get started today. So what I'd like to have you do is pair up with someone. Pair up with the person you're sitting next to; that would be easiest. I realize we have an odd number of students right now, so can we have someone be a group of three? Maybe you three up front?"

Begrudgingly, the girls looked at one another. Some of them smirked. Some moved their notebooks a little closer together. "I'm going to give you five minutes to interview the person next to you," Vera said. "You can ask her anything—about her family, her likes and dislikes, her favorite foods or TV shows, her favorite class . . . basically, anything that she'd be willing to share with the rest of us. You can jot down her answers in your notebooks so you don't forget them. When five minutes are up, I will ask you to switch off, and the person you've just interviewed will interview you. When we're done, you'll be introducing your partner to me."

There was some buzzing, a possible threat of resistance, before the girls bowed heads and gamely went about the activity. In teaching terms, what Vera had asked them to do was known as an icebreaker exercise, designed to make students comfortable with one another on the first day of class. But these students were already comfortable with one another. It was Vera who was uncomfortable. She wondered if they could see through her transparent tactic to buy some time for herself—to put *herself* at ease. Based on the smirks, she suspected some of them did.

She walked rather ineffectually up and down the rows of tables, pretending to take note of what the students were writing down. Most didn't seem to be interviewing each other; she heard a girl in one pair say, "I called Ryan last night. He wasn't expecting that at *all*," but she didn't chide her. At least the girls were talking and weren't silently in revolt.

The minutes passed. A little later than she perhaps should have—

the girls had devolved into relaxed chatter about topics blatantly having nothing to do with their interviews—Vera raised her voice over everyone else's and said, "Let's regroup. Who'd like to start by introducing her partner?"

Mercifully, a girl with short, curly auburn hair raised a chubby hand. "I'm Jamie Friedman, and I interviewed Harmony Phelps," she said, gesturing to a broad-shouldered girl with a knitted cap pulled down over her eyebrows. Vera thought about asking the girl to remove her cap. She decided it wasn't worth it. "Harmony is a sophomore at the Wallace School," Jamie went on. The other girls tittered. "She's fifteen. She'll be sixteen next month. She's a Taurus. She lives with her mom and dad and her brother and sister and her dog, Bella. She likes watching CNN and C-SPAN. Her favorite food is vegetarian stir-fry. She doesn't eat meat. Her favorite subjects are political science and women's studies."

She probably has a sister named Liberty, Vera thought, *and a brother named Leaf.* She nodded and listened, going up and down the rows, taking mental notes to help set each student apart in her mind. There was Aggie Hamada, for example, who seemed somehow more all-American than anyone else in the class—she radiated cleanliness, like an ad for Noxzema—and had won trophies for horse jumping. Then there was Martha True, a peer leader in a church youth group; Vera, who had no religious feelings of her own, worried that the girl would come to find her morally objectionable in some way. As they were nearly finished, Vera gave a start—there was a twelfth girl seated, a girl she hadn't noticed before. "Ah. We've got a dirty dozen, after all. You must be"—she checked her roster—"Jensen Willard."

The girl sitting at the desk was small, with wispy dark hair cut in no particular style. She was wearing a charcoal-colored dress that looked like something someone's grandmother had donated to Goodwill; it was made of a crinkly fabric, with a floppy, withered bow at the neck. The dress was accessorized with mud-caked combat boots, the long laces wound around her calves several times. Vera couldn't help thinking that the girl's style suited her. But how had she managed to creep in so quietly wearing those heavy boots?

"We were just finishing up introductions of each other," Vera said to her, "mostly for my benefit. Is there anything you'd like to tell me about yourself?"

"Not really."

Vera gave a tight smile. "Okay then. I suppose it's only fair if I tell you all a little about me, and then we'll talk a bit about what we're going to be doing the rest of the school year."

Vera abhorred talking about herself, but she did her best. She skipped the ignominy of her twenties (her acquisition of a flimsy undergraduate arts degree that netted her a succession of demeaning, low-paying jobs and inspired her decision to apply to graduate school) and bulldozed straight ahead to Princeton and the teaching fellowship and her job working for literary agent Christopher Sime. She tried to explain what a literary agent did, what the duties of a literary agent's assistant were; she did not mention that the job had paid so poorly that she had had to move back to Maine, back into the arms of a high school sweetheart who had promised some financial security. She made a calculated mention of her experience teaching college English, neglecting to mention that she had never taught high school students before. Wondering how to wrap things up, she added lamely, "I live right here in Dorset—it's just me, by myself. I'm working on a book based on a true-crime case, which I anticipate I'll have completed within the year."

The part about the book based on a real murder might have been best left unsaid. She had thirty-two rough manuscript pages written—not exactly what one might call a work in progress in the true sense of the word *progress*. She hoped none of the girls would inquire further about this point. But of course one hand shot up. It was Loo Garippa's. "What true-crime case are you writing about?" she asked.

"Well," Vera demurred, "I don't like to tell too much about an unfinished project. I worry that it'll jinx things. But I promise, when there's more to tell, you'll all be among the first to know. "

"Is it about that murder that happened here last month?" Loo persisted. "Angela from the middle school?"

"She was Finister's niece," Harmony Phelps said. "I mean, his niece by marriage."

"Who is Finister?" Vera asked.

"The *dean*," several of the girls chorused. Vera could almost read their minds: *Who is this woman, this so-called* teacher, *who doesn't even know who our dean is?*

"Oh, of course. Dean Finister. I knew that."

The girls seemed truly engaged now, sitting up straighter, eyes lighting up as though someone had snapped the cord of the shade that had obscured them. "My aunt works with the police force," Chelsea Cutler said, puffing out her full chest by another inch or two. "She worked on the Angela Galvez case. She helped arrest the guy who did it."

"This is an older case I'm writing about," Vera said. *Sit* down, she told herself. *Look casual.* She stopped in her tracks and lowered her behind onto the table at the front of the room; as she attempted to cross her legs, the table pitched forward an inch, almost depositing Vera on the floor. Recovering as the table steadied itself, she pulled her skirt down lower over her knees and said, "But isn't that a shame, what happened to that little girl?"

Some of the students nodded, and she felt that they wanted to talk about this; she saw this as her first possible point of connection, her first opportunity to get through to them.

"She was strangled," Aggie Hamada said soberly.

"Yes, I'm afraid that's so. I read all about that."

"I heard the guy they've got in jail now might not be the one who did it," Harmony Phelps said. "There's this guy who drives around town trying to pick up girls in his car so he can rape them. But nobody's caught *him* yet."

Chelsea turned to face the girl in the row behind her. "Are you saying my aunt got the wrong person?"

"I'm not singling her out. But you have to admit, the police can be pretty sketchy."

Vera could see that Harmony's retort was about to take this tangent to a potentially uglier place. She quickly got off the table and reached for a stack of handouts; she tried to ignore the dejection on the students' faces as she cleared her throat and distributed the lesson plan that covered the remaining twelve weeks of the school year.

"Getting back to business," she said, "I understand you've just finished *Macbeth*. As Mrs. Belisle must have told you, the next few weeks are largely going to be spent reading *The Catcher in the Rye*. Does anyone happen to have her copy of *Catcher* with her today? Please forgive me; I tend to refer to it as *Catcher* just as shorthand." None of the girls said a word, though Vera saw copies of the books on several girls' desks. She picked up the copy on the desk of the girl nearest her—Kelsey Smith—and held it up for all to see. The book trembled a little in Vera's hand. "This is *Catcher*," she said, "and you should definitely all have it with you in class tomorrow. Has anybody read it before?"

Two hands went up: Jensen Willard's and that of one of the tall modelesque girls—Autumn Fullerton, Vera confirmed, sneaking a glance at her roster again. "Autumn," she said, returning the copy of Salinger's novel to its owner and moving toward the tall girl's seat, "if

I asked you to tell the class what the book is about, in just a few words, what would you tell us?"

"Um," Autumn said. "It's about a boy? I think he's sixteen? The book was written a long time ago, I guess, and the book is mostly just him talking."

Vera glanced at Jensen Willard in the third row. She could have sworn she saw the girl give an eye roll, but when she saw Vera looking at her, she glued her eyes to the desk. Vera had been about to ask her to put in her own two cents about Holden Caulfield, but something in the girl's demeanor made her think better of it.

Vera turned around and wrote the words NARRATIVE VOICE on the whiteboard in large letters. "Narrative voice," she said. "Did Mrs. Belisle talk to you about what this is?"

"A narrative is a story," Jamie Friedman offered.

"That's right. It's a story. And what does *voice* mean, in terms of writing? What is a writer's voice? Could you define *that*?"

Vera felt as if the students were already growing tired of her. She could practically read their minds; if she wasn't going to talk about something interesting like homicide, then they wished she would just present a lecture and quit bugging them with questions. "Let's think of it in terms of singers," Vera went on doggedly. "If I asked you to listen to snippet of a song by, say, Mick Jagger"—*Jesus, I hope they know who Mick Jagger is,* Vera thought, *and why do I have to use words like* snippet?—"chances are you would be able to recognize him right away. His voice is that unique and that distinctive. It is as individual as a fingerprint. It has a . . . well, a classic rock swagger to it. One of the first swaggering rockers of that particular type, really. Each of you probably has your own singing voice, good or bad. You have your own unique *writing* voice as well."

Vera went on, trying to explain and illustrate the concept of narrative voice and why it is important. Most of the girls seemed to be actually listening, which emboldened her a little. Then Harmony Phelps's hand went up again. "Mrs. . . ." She looked at the board. "Lundy?"

"I'm a *Miss*. Yes, Harmony?"

"Why do we have to read a narrative about a teenage boy? We're all females here. I think it would be more valuable for us to read about a girl. We already just read about a bunch of guys, in *Macbeth*."

"Lady Macbeth wasn't a guy," one of the girls said.

"Well, the whole thing felt very masculine. It was all about masculinity," Harmony said, and then added virtuously, as though this explained it all, "It was *Shakespeare*."

"Yet as I understand it, the writing assignments you did in relation to *Macbeth* were about yourself." Vera was pacing the room now, her arms wrapped around her rib cage as though she were cold. "You wrote journals and personal essays about subjects like rivalry and ambition and the tragic hero, and you applied these themes to your own life. It will be much the same with *Catcher*, though the themes will be different, of course. I'm going to ask you to work on your first journal entry tonight after you read the first four chapters of the book. In general, unless I specify otherwise, I will be collecting your *Catcher* journals every Friday. We'll be taking breaks with other readings, too, so when the subject of the journals changes, I will let you know in advance."

The inevitable peevish riot of questions followed. *How long does each entry have to be? What is it supposed to be about? Does it have to be typed?* When Vera said that the journals could be about "anything," some of the students seemed pleased while others looked deeply unhappy. Glancing at the clock, Vera saw there was a little extra time left in the class—maybe seven minutes. Panicking a little, she picked up her copy of *The Catcher in the Rye* and said, "Let me read the beginning bit from the first chapter aloud. If you have your books with you, you can read along silently. This first paragraph alone sets the tone and establishes the voice. It'll give you a flavor of what's to come."

And then, at last, the class was over. Before Vera had even finished reading, the room began to fill with the decisive sound of book bags being repacked and girls pushing their chairs back from the tables. Jamie Friedman smiled at Vera as she headed out—Jamie Friedman, she thought, was a wise, calculating girl, knowing how to cater to adults. Such a girl might be useful to have in the classroom. The two model-y girls lingered behind, conferring with each other about something, and Jensen, who had showed up in class last, was also last to make any signs of leaving it, slowly packing her school things into a large army knapsack that had symbols written all over it with a Sharpie. Coming over to the girl's seat, Vera said, "Jensen, I got your email. I'm sorry I didn't respond, as I saw it kind of late. It's fine for you to use that other edition of *Catcher.* Thank you, though, for checking in."

"Oh," Jensen said. "You're welcome."

"Maybe you'll find it to your advantage that you've already read the novel."

The girl looked her in the eyes briefly. Her eyes were not a dark brown, as Vera had guessed they would be, but a dark amber color. The amber-colored eyes, along with her dark hair and pale, lightly freckled skin, made a pretty contrast, though Jensen wasn't what most people would consider pretty. "Maybe," she said, and she hoisted her knapsack over her shoulder. Then, without looking at Vera: "Do you mind if I ask you a question? It doesn't have to do with the homework."

"Shoot."

"You said you're writing a book. How do you do that—I mean, how do you go about writing a book?"

With a self-deprecating little laugh, Vera said, "Oh, I'm afraid that would take days to explain, if not weeks or months."

"I guess I mean . . . how do you go about writing a *crime* book? What made you decide to do that?"

Vera twisted her mouth, thinking. Unconsciously, she began rubbing the fat pads of her thumb and forefinger with her other hand. "Well," she said, "I don't know if I can speak to writing technique or method here, but I can speak to the *why*. It's because of my rather idealistic desire to see things end as happily as they can. To see justice done. To see the bad guys caught and the good guys cleared and the victims' families given the peace of mind that they deserve."

"No other reason?" Jensen asked.

Vera looked at her again. Was there something owlish in the girl's gaze—some hint that at any moment she might cock her head, spread her impressive wingspan, and swoop? *No,* thought Vera, looking again into her placid, amber-colored eyes. *She's a sweet girl, that's all. A sweet, albeit strange girl—not that there's anything wrong with* strange. "There are always other reasons," she said.

"I thought so," Jensen said. "Thank you for answering. I'll see you in class tomorrow."

Alone again and feeling nettled for reasons she couldn't explain, Vera shook her head and sighed. Jensen was a peculiar sort of girl, but she would surely not be the only peculiar girl she'd meet today, Vera thought. There were two more sections to teach before her day was over—essentially a repeat of the morning's performance. She hadn't had a spectacular start, but it hadn't been terrible, either, she thought, trying to view it in a glass-half-full kind of way. She should be thrilled that it had not been worse.

Nevertheless, she felt a flutter of disappointment she had not expected to feel, and it took her a moment to place where this disappointment came from. She had hoped to get a sense that the girls might like her. She had not really gotten this sense. Surprising, to realize this hurt a little.

Chapter Two

Having completed her first day of teaching—having reviewed, critiqued, and second-guessed it dozens of times—Vera found the early-morning class was stuck in her mind. She thought of the two willowy girls, Autumn and Cecily-Anne, their swan-like necks bent toward each other; of contentious and political-minded Harmony scowling under her knitted cap; of quiet Sufia Ahmed with her great, dark, liquid eyes; and of Aggie Hamada with her dimpled, radiant face. She thought of Jensen Willard, who was somehow both dignified and vulnerable in her wrinkled dress and mud-caked boots. The whole group together, all twelve of them, had been the wild cards, the girls she couldn't have prepared for.

The midmorning and afternoon sections of Autobiographical Writing: Personal Connections had been more along the lines of what she'd expected: girls who seemed friendly with one another, who talked to one another when Vera was talking; girls who tried to slip out their cell phones to send a text when they thought Vera wasn't looking and even when they knew she was; girls who looked at her shrewdly when they wanted to give off the impression of being good, of paying attention. They had none of the morning class's quiet sense of expectancy.

There was something to be said for students who came in with no expectations.

Though the students in her second and third classes were a less interesting mix than her first, Vera had become progressively more comfortable in how she presented herself—honing and retooling the aspects of the discussion that hadn't gone so well the first time around, keeping her topics on track, and even managing a few jokes that had made the girls in the later sections smile. Indulgent smiles, a small sop to Vera, but smiles nonetheless. The morning class, she thought, was never going to see her at her best; they were always going to be her trial run for the day. She couldn't help but feel sorry for them, guinea pigs that they were.

At home Vera sat at her worktable and scrawled a few illegible notes about the first four chapters of *The Catcher in the Rye*. She typed up a list of discussion questions, a handout for the students; since the handout was a last-minute idea, she would have to go to school even earlier the next morning to make the photocopies. *Really,* Vera scolded herself, *you need to plan better in advance.* Again, the feeling of fraudulence nagged at her. A real teacher would be better prepared. Disconsolate at this thought, she tried to cheer herself with a bit of mindless TV, flipping between a reality show about brides and a reality show about people who were hiding in bunkers because they believed a deadly apocalypse was coming.

She picked up the remote again and paused at a local news station when the mug shot of a familiar face appeared in the upper corner of the screen. "As the date for the trial of the Angela Galvez murder draws closer, twenty-five-year-old Ritchie Ouelette of Biddeford, Maine, has changed his plea from guilty to innocent," the news anchor said in liquid tones that barely masked her broad Maine vowels, but Vera was concentrating more on Ouelette's mug shot. The young man had an elongated face, prematurely thinning hair, and an expression so incredulous, so seemingly without guile, that his picture was hard to look at. Vera had known he would come around to pleading innocent. Seeing this mug shot anew, she was even more convinced of her earlier hunch that he was, in fact, as innocent as he now claimed.

Vera prided herself in knowing a great deal about the criminal mind and considered herself intuitive when it came to determining a suspect's guilt. Local serial killer Ivan Schlosser was a prime example—there had never been any doubt in her mind of *his* culpability. But Ouelette was young and nervous, the sort who could easily be coerced into his initial false confession, especially in light of the mounting circumstantial evidence against him—the carpet fiber from the trunk of his Ford found on the girl's body, the unspecified DNA (blood, Vera imagined) that had been found on the vehicle's front seat. There were some who also falsely confessed because they thought it would give them their fifteen minutes of fame, but Ritchie Ouelette didn't strike her as that type. In all the news footage Vera had seen of him, he hunched his tall frame as though he wished to disappear into himself.

She thought again of her early morning class and what they had had to say about Angela Galvez. She supposed she shouldn't be surprised that Dorset, ordinarily so complacent, was still shaken by the crime that had occurred a few months before. The Dorset murder had, in fact, had some influence on her decision to relocate to that town. Still in Bond Brook when the story broke, she had started collecting news clippings about the Galvez murder, comparing her findings to other true-crime cases that bore some similarity to the case. She had even come up with a little psychological profiling of the culprit: He was a solitary figure, she'd decided. Probably someone who still lived with his parents. Past convictions might include minor charges for being a Peeping Tom or some other minor voyeuristic offense. He was someone who liked to watch people, and that desire to watch had escalated into a desire to touch, to control, to possess.

As it had turned out, Ouelette did not fit this profile. He was a young number cruncher with an associate's degree in accounting, and he was raising his teenage brother by himself; he had once been charged with a DUI, but the criminal history ended there. Vera was sure that the person who fit *her* profile would damn well try to make use of his victim sexually before disposing of her body, yet there had been no discernible attempt to violate Angela Galvez, whose body had been found in a Dumpster behind a neighborhood Laundromat.

The news broadcast ended, and Vera sat in a stupor, watching the next two shows that followed. By the time evening had settled—another unseasonably warm evening, with the temperature holding fast—Vera became restless. To go out or not to go out? She decided it would do no harm to walk to one of her favorite bars for a solo congratulatory drink or two, a pick-me-up for having survived her first day at the Wallace School.

The bar she chose, a place called Pearl's, was comfortable and dimly lit, with dark wooden fixtures and nooks where one could make oneself inconspicuous if one wanted to. Tonight she sat up at the bar, on a seat as distant from everyone as she could find; it was true that some men might notice her and try to strike up a conversation, but she trusted her ability to steer them away politely. Though she liked the validation of being thought attractive enough to single out in a bar—and found it hilarious that those who did ranged in age from twenty-two to sixty-two—it was the three-dollar well drink specials, and not the men, who drew her there.

An hour passed, then two. Vera enjoyed the music that was playing from the jukebox and even, in her own masochistic way, began to enjoy the banal conversations she could overhear from nearby tables.

"I might have gone out with him a second time," she heard one girl with a piping voice say to another, "but my ferret hated him. She hates all men. I think one time a man did something bad to her. You know, like a gerbil-type deal." Her intention of leaving after two drinks somehow got cast aside, and as she was on her third drink, a man asked if he could take the bar stool next to her. "I guess so," she said.

The man who'd taken the seat next to her ordered a bottled beer and introduced himself as Sam—or was it Stan? Hard to make out over the jukebox, not that it mattered to Vera. He might have been in his late forties but wore a boyish-looking athletic jersey; even after all these years, Vera never ceased to be surprised when athletically inclined men paid attention to her. She thought herself too intelligent-looking to warrant a second glace from them. Perhaps the memories of high school jocks jeering at her in the halls had helped her to formulate this opinion. She could only conclude, then, that some men didn't look at her very closely or were not very picky.

"Let me guess," the man in the athletic jersey said. "You're a dancer, right? You have a dancer's body."

Vera looked askance at him; she had heard this one before. "No," she said. "I'm a *teacher*."

"What grade?"

"I've taught college English."

"You look young to be teaching college."

"I'm a writer, too," Vera said carelessly, draining her drink. This was something she simply never said to other adults. They never believed it, for one thing.

"Yeah? Whaddaya write—I mean, nonfiction or fiction or what?"

Vera wondered if he knew the difference between the two, never mind the *or what*. "It's about Ivan Schlosser. He was what I guess you could call a minor serial killer from the late 1970s to the late 1980s.

He killed a preteen girl in Vermont, a teenage girl in New Hampshire, and a teenage girl right here in Maine, in my own hometown. There may have been other victims, but those were the only ones they pinned on him. I'm afraid his crimes were eclipsed by the much more publicized crimes of Ted Bundy."

"Whatever gave a little lady like you an idea to write a book about a thing like that?" the man asked, seeming genuinely perplexed.

A little lady like you. This struck Vera as rich. "Well, for one thing, the crimes really happened. And I personally find Schlosser very interesting." Vera realized she was having a hard time saying the word *Schlosser.* Her next drink had arrived, and she took a long pull from her straw. "For another thing, crime itself is interesting."

The man named Sam or Stan said, "You oughta write one about that little girl they found choked to death. Now that's a story right there."

"Funny, you're not the first person to suggest that to me recently," Vera said. "However, I suspect that story isn't finished yet. Despite what the public seems to think, I don't think they've arrested the right guy. I could be wrong, and I hope, for the sake of all the other little girls out there, that I am. Do you want to know what I think?" She leaned in a little closer to the man—not trying to be provocative, exactly, but wanting to be sure he heard her.

"Sure, honey," he said. "Who do you think did it?"

"Well, that I don't know. I was just going to tell you an idea that I've often thought about. See, sometimes I think it's a fine line between being a writer and being a serial killer. It's all about creation versus anticreation. Building versus destroying. They both require a lot of energy, don't they? The difference between the two vocations might as well be arrived at by a coin toss. Two roads diverged in a wood, and I took the one more likely to keep me out of jail."

The man named Sam or Stan processed this for a second or two. Then he muttered something about needing to excuse himself to go to the restroom. She knew he would not be returning to his seat near her. She was terribly tickled with herself. Nearing the bottom of her fourth gin and tonic, she wondered why the drinks were hitting her so hard; rummaging around in her recent memory, she recalled that all she had eaten that day was a small ham sandwich, consumed at six in the morning. The air around her was beginning to feel soft and muted and velvety, which wasn't unpleasant; it was, however, a sure signal that she should leave soon.

Once outside the bar, she found that a bitter wind had unexpectedly picked up—the first wintry night in more than a week—and as she drew her coat closer around her and ducked her head, a couple of frat-boy types rounding the corner and heading toward the bar shouted, "You're going the wrong way, baby!" She smiled at them, head still held low. Was she supposed to act offended? She never knew how to negotiate such things.

The more she walked, the more evident her excesses became. She felt as if she were swimming through the streets of Dorset with the purpose and precision of a shark, yet she somehow also felt as though she were seeing herself at a great distance, hurrying home, trying to look sober and dignified and, yes, *driven*, while the real Vera floated fuzzily overhead. Her bladder strained with fullness. On one of her more recent late-night walks home from the bar, when no one else was out on the streets to witness this, she had not been able to make it home before her bladder let go—her tights and shoes were soaked by the time she let herself into her apartment, and she'd felt morbidly ashamed. The last thing she needed was to become one of those drunks who soiled herself.

Five blocks away from her apartment, she became aware of an even greater cause for concern than her straining bladder. She could hear footsteps behind her, and although it was too dark for shadows, she almost thought she could feel a shadow in front of her, cupping her like a cool hand—and she knew that such shadows didn't stay silent and passive for long, the way shadows were supposed to. She knew that some shadows gathered and grew, becoming a whole coven of shadows, an unkindness of them—a mob.

Hey, Vera, where are you going? Are you going to cast some more witchy spells? Are you going to wish for some more people to die? Death is just a part of life, right, Vera? You weird fucking bitch. You wanted *that to happen to Heidi, didn't you?*

This shadow had footfalls. This shadow was a certainty now. She tried to gauge its distance or nearness without turning around—no, she couldn't turn around, for if she turned around she might freeze on the spot, just as one always did in nightmares. And the last time that had happened . . . well, the last time that had happened, all those years ago, it had ended very badly for Vera.

Keep going, she told herself sternly. *Don't panic.* She sped up her steps, clutching the strap of the purse she had slung, *bandolero* style, across her body in the manner she'd learned from living in New York City. She withdrew her apartment keys from the zippered sleeve of her purse, holding them so that the point jutted out between her fingers—a makeshift weapon suitable for stabbing an assailant in the eye, if it came to that. And then she was on the steps of her apartment, practically tripping in her haste to get up them and into the safety of indoors. She let herself in and turned around just long enough to see a man tramping down the street, away from her and toward whatever destination he'd had in mind all along.

She closed the front door behind her. *You're a paranoid fool,* Vera thought, now doubled over in front of the door to her studio, tears smarting in her eyes as she turned the key in the lock. In the battle between terror and her bladder, the urgency of her bladder now took precedence.

After hobbling to the bathroom to relieve herself, she chucked herself onto her mattress, fully clothed, and fell asleep within minutes—a dreamless, stagnant sleep.

Next morning came early—even earlier than planned, due to the last-minute decision to photocopy the handout—and Vera felt weak and bleary as she prepared for her first class. She had a horrible suspicion that she still stank of gin, though she had given her teeth and tongue a thorough brushing before she left for work. She waited as the girls from her first section began to turn up, in pairs and sometimes in trios; she smiled wanly at each and wondered if she should make small talk, but doing so seemed too forced and pitiful. Better to sit and look busy with paperwork. She adjusted what few notes she'd written on the day's assigned reading and stacked and restacked her pile of handouts as though the success of the class depended on their alignment.

When the last girl had come in—Jensen Willard, loping a little from the weight of her giant army knapsack—Vera said, "All right, let's get started. You all have *Catcher* with you, I hope. I ended yesterday's class by reading a short excerpt from the first chapter. To put us in the mood of the novel, and because I think it bears hearing one more time, I would like to read the novel's introductory paragraph again."

Vera knew she should probably ask a volunteer to read aloud, but she wasn't sure she could stand to hear Salinger's narrative butchered by a faltering amateur reader. Vera knew that she read well. Her voice was one of her strong suits, capable of producing many tones and emphasizing nuances of meaning through its inflections. And indeed, the girls all seemed to pay attention when she read, even though they had heard the exact same excerpt the day before. When she was finished reading, Vera stuck her bookmark in her copy of the novel and squarely faced the students. She wished she had thought to bring a bottle of water to class. Her mouth was so dry.

"Now," she said, working her way down the first row of tables, pausing again for effect as she moved down the second row, "Holden starts off by saying that what readers probably would want to know about him is 'that David Copperfield kind of crap'—in other words, the basic biographical details that writers often provide for their characters at the beginning of a novel. Who he is, where he's from, what his parents do for a living, what his grandparents did before that. But what's interesting is that he does not, in fact, go on to tell the readers 'that David Copperfield kind of crap.' Do you think Holden is cheating readers of what they really want to know? Is it what *you* would really want to know, when first 'meeting' a new character?"

"Depends on the character," Jamie Friedman said promptly.

Vera gave Jamie a small, approving nod. "Why do you say that? Why would it depend?"

Jamie went blank. She had shot her wad too quickly and was now overthinking it, Vera could see. "Anyone else want to hazard a guess? An opinion as to why it might depend on the character?"

"Well, with some characters," one girl said—Martha True, a bespectacled girl with a sharp little chin and a wobbly, nasal voice—"their background is important to the plot. With others, you don't really need to know all that stuff to be able to understand them."

"Sometimes having all that background stuff gets boring," Loo Garippa said. "Some stories start off talking about somebody's great-grandfather or something, and who cares? It doesn't really have anything to do with what happens later."

Vera was already pleased with the direction the class was taking. These girls were sharper, sad to say, than some of her community college students had been. They were certainly more responsive. She uncapped one of her whiteboard markers and drew an uneven triangle on the board. For the next ten minutes she spoke about rising actions and climaxes (there was no giggling when she said "climax," as she had expected there might be) and conflict and plot structure.

"Holden Caulfield says things really *funny*," Kelsey said out of the blue, making Vera wonder if she had been paying attention to any of what came before. "When is this book set again?"

"I'd be happy to refresh your memory." Though this hadn't been on her day's agenda, Vera began to talk about the 1940s and the life of the author who'd written *The Catcher in the Rye*. Inspired, she pulled down the movie projector screen and downloaded Internet pictures of young Jerome David Salinger himself as well as various quaint-looking pictures of New York City back in the day. She called this "providing sociohistorical context." "Because of the different time period, it's possible some of you might not feel a connection to Holden; things may seem quite different to you now. But many readers over the decades have found that the thoughts and emotions Holden has are universal and timeless. As we read further in the novel, I'd like for you to be especially mindful of his thoughts and emotions and whether or not you think they reflect what it's like to be a person close to your age. These are issues you can explore in your journals as well.

"That's about all we have time for today," Vera said. "I appreciate your attentiveness. Please don't leave before you take this handout. It's a list of discussion questions pertaining to chapters five through seven, which is your reading assignment for tonight. Please write answers to these questions—complete sentences, *please*—and bring them with you tomorrow."

There were a couple of audible sighs and groans as the girls gathered up their books. Vera felt a little dazed. The class had been a slight improvement over the day before, she thought—at least she'd looked more self-possessed, hangover and all—but she wished she had engineered a more *focused* discussion. There were so many things she had wanted to cover. She watched the students departing and observed that once again Jensen Willard seemed to be in her own little world, still working on the buckles of her knapsack when all the other girls were making their way toward the door.

Then she raised her head, looking Vera dead in the eye. "Did you get my email?" she asked.

"Your email? You mean from the other day?"

"No, I sent you one last night. A new one. I sent it to your email account here."

It was all Vera could do not to blush. She hadn't even figured out how to log into her new Wallace School email account yet. "I haven't had a chance. What was the upshot of it?"

"I sent you some pages of my journal. If you get a chance to read it early, maybe you could let me know if it is what you're looking for, or if you want me to do them differently for Friday. I brought a hard copy, too." Jensen handed Vera a rather substantial number of pages with a cover page on top, all clamped together with a binder clip.

Vera, who still hadn't become accustomed to the ways of high school overachievers, covered up her surprise quickly enough to say, "Goodness. I'm sure it's just fine. But I'll tell you what. I'll try very hard to look at these pages tonight, and if I feel they need to be reworked a little, I can let you know tomorrow."

"Thanks." Jensen finally managed to fasten her knapsack shut, and said, as though speaking to its buckles, "I like writing."

"That's wonderful," Vera said sincerely. "I figured you must, based on what we talked about yesterday after class."

"Your bookmark is nice," Jensen said, looking Vera in the eye again. Her vacillations between indirectness and boldness had a disquieting effect . . . the eye contact that would hold fast for an instant and break away, as though the girl were sneaking little snapshots of things.

"My bookmark? Ah—my bookmark." Vera took out the bookmark she was using for *The Catcher in the Rye*; incongruously, its photograph featured a famous picture of F. Scott and Zelda Fitzgerald posing at the bumper of one of their cars. Maybe Jensen had read *Gatsby*?

"I don't really like Fitzgerald's writing," Jensen said in the same tone of voice someone might say *I hate onions*. "Scott's, I mean—I haven't read anything by Zelda. I just think it's interesting how he basically drank himself to death, and she burned to death in a nuthouse. That makes me kind of like them."

"Me, too," Vera said. She couldn't restrain her smile—grin, really. The grin disappeared just as quickly. She was betraying too much about her own morbid inclinations by responding with too much warmth, too much approval. She gave another one of her little nods to the girl and turned away, busying herself again. "Well," she said, "we'll see you tomorrow, won't we?"

That evening at home, Vera struggled to activate her Wallace School email account. She gave up after her fourth attempt and allowed herself some diversions on the Internet—cleaning out the spam in her personal email account, reading an email from her old grad school friend Elliott, and then turning to the true-crime discussion boards she sometimes lurked (but never posted) on, one of whose topic du jour was the Black Dahlia murder of 1947. A particularly rabid poster was trying to catapult the theory that Elizabeth Short, the bisected murder victim, had been slain by a big-name Hollywood executive.

Amateur stuff, Vera thought, *and* completely *unoriginal.* Bored, she closed the browser window and then Googled her ex-fiancé, Peter, as she sometimes could not resist doing.

There were several hits—mostly links to articles published in the *Bond Brook Gazette*, all related to Peter Mercier's small business—and then something new, an engagement announcement from that same publication. There was no photo, but the announcement described his betrothal to a florist named Betsy Gillingwater. A second Google hit led her to a wedding registry, presumably set up by the fiancée; she couldn't imagine Peter bothering with something so fussy. Feeling like a consummate stalker, Vera looked at the items Betsy wanted for the marital home—percale sheets, Ralph Lauren towels, and all manner of cookware, including such extras as garlic presses and lemon zesters and something called ramekins, whatever those were. *So she's a domestic type—a cook,* Vera thought. *Peter must be loving this.* The one time Peter had made the mistake of asking Vera to bake something for his company potluck, she had had to run out and buy a disposable tinfoil pan at the dollar store. *Well, more power to you, Betsy. More power to both of you.*

There had been a time when the thought of Peter with any woman who wasn't her would have driven her into a rage that knew no bounds—the sort of obsessive rage that would cause her to fixate on poor Betsy, to imagine terrible things befalling the hapless woman—but now she felt almost nothing. *You're getting soft in your old age, girl,* she told herself.

She closed her laptop and got up to pour a herself a generous glass of wine—the cheapest, most vinegary wine she had been able to find in the corner bodega—and, thus fortified, started digging around in her wheeled suitcase until she produced the folder for her morning class; email or no email, she could give the hard copy of Jensen Willard's journal a look. She lay down on her bed on her side, glass of wine resting on the floor next to her—would students be appalled to know that teachers read their writing in bed sometimes?—and began to read. Her eyebrow lifted as she saw the title on the cover page for the first time. It was as though the girl had foreseen the subject of that day's lecture—though, she supposed, it wouldn't take the Amazing Kreskin to predict the direction Vera had taken.

That David Copperfield Kind of Crap: Journal Entry #1, by Jensen Willard

I have to admit, I'm a little confused. Do you want to know about me in this journal or do you want to know about Holden Caulfield? Or do you want to know about me in relation to Holden? (Now I'm doing what you do—asking questions.) I'll start with me, I guess, and move on to Holden as needed, or at your say-so.

With every journal I write I feel the need to reintroduce myself in case the previous journal gets lost and leaves the reader with no backstory—no David Copperfield kind of crap—whatsoever. After all, I'm no Anne Frank. I haven't got an Otto Frank in my life to recover my journal from the enemy and share my story with the world. Not that I'm comparing myself to Anne Frank in any way . . . well, I guess I just did, but I know it's not a good comparison. A comparison like that could piss a lot of people off.

My name is Jensen Willard. My namesake aunt is dead now, from a brain tumor. She already had the brain tumor when my mom got pregnant with me, so my mom got to feeling noble and promised her dying sister that she'd name her unborn child after her in some way, shape, or form. But my mom didn't have an ultrasound—she was so convinced she was going to have a boy. After I was born, and after my mother inspected my body, searching in vain for a penis, imagine how screwed she must have felt. She didn't like her sister's first name, Nora. I don't know why. To me, Nora is the name of a girl in an English or Irish novel who has roses in her cheeks and gets the shock of her life when she leaves the provincial lands and is taken advantage of by a cad. (I like that kind of story. Does that surprise you?) Jensen, my aunt's married name, now used as a first name, calls to mind a pretentious, twerpy guy with a pipe in his mouth. Maybe a butler.

I am fifteen years old—I turned fifteen in October. My mother says I have the mental maturity of a forty-year-old and the emotional maturity of an eight-year-old, and that's pretty spot-on, I have to admit.

For the longest time I've felt older than everyone else around me. The social climate at school only makes this contrast more obvious. It seems like all my classmates ever talk about is who's going out with who or what outfit so-and-so got at the mall. I could name names, if you wanted me to, from our very own class.

Cecily-Anne St. Aubrey and Autumn Fullerton have fathers who are partnered in a law firm. They are both terrible people and also happen to be cokeheads, but all the teachers here at Wallace adore them to pieces. Kelsey Smith and Chelsea Cutler are both jocks who live for softball and field hockey. They're actually as stupid as they come, but their slavish study habits will guarantee their entrance into good colleges later on down the line. Loo Garippa is the biggest poser I have ever met in my life. She wants everyone to think she's all edgy and punk, but she's really this closet happy person who has a new boyfriend every week. Aggie Hamada has never had a tough day in her life, although it's rumored that one time in eighth grade she got an A-minus in science class and got grounded for two months because it wasn't an A. Jamie Friedman has a new stepmother and is always talking about how much she hates her, but then in the same breath she'll brag about the new designer outfit her stepmother bought her or how her stepmother is taking her on a skiing trip to Switzerland.

They're all pretty contemptible. All of them yammering on blithely about stupid stuff while the world around them wells up with death and heartache and existential crises, which they don't see or they don't care *to see. They don't understand how easy it would be for their lives to be over in a minute.*

This is a fact: From the time I was a little girl, I always knew life was more about sadness than anything else.

How did I know this? You mentioned music in class the other day. Something about Mick Jagger. When I was little, I used to cry at sad songs coming out of my parents' CD player. I couldn't make sense of most of the lyrics back then, but I could tell sadness from the way singers sang. The minor chords always give it away. I even knew when songs were secretly sad—songs that seemed upbeat enough on the surface but hid a sorrow that maybe even the songwriter didn't want you to know about. I knew other things, too. I knew that most grown-ups really don't know much more than children, though they pretend otherwise, and that it's impolite to let on that you know this when you're a child. From the day I was born, I saw far too much for my own good. I suppose you could say I had the curse of seeing the world in a clear-eyed way while having the manners to keep what I saw to myself.

In some ways I was childlike back then, and in other ways I wasn't. I played with Annabel Francoeur, a girl my age who lived a few houses up the street from me, because I knew that every child was supposed to have at least one friend. We would play our games—girl-games she would dictate, ranging from soap operatic Barbie doll plotlines (Ken sleeps with Barbie's sister Skipper) to games of "house" where I was always The Boy—but instead of feeling as though I were playing a game, I felt as though I were playing the role of a child playing a game and doing a shitty job of it. I've gotten better at playing roles since then, I guess.

Sure, I had fun sometimes as a kid; I can remember certain moments, certain silly and meaningless moments, like lying in Annabel's backyard after sundown, the two of us side by side on our backs in the grass, and me thinking: For the rest of my life I will remember what it feels like to lie in this grass. I will remember this dark sky. *And once I told myself I would remember, I never forgot. Not even now, long after Annabel has stopped wanting to associate with me.*

When I was about nine years old, I had an epiphany. I was sitting on the embankment of my elementary school playground—alone, like always, because Annabel went to the Catholic school—and a thought occurred to me (or maybe more a premonition than a thought): Life is never going to be better than it is now. After this, it'll just be one disappointment after another. Like I've been trying to say, if something is true, I can feel *how true it is. So that's something that's changed me. Once you know something's never going to get any better, you never have to waste energy on false hopes again. It's kind of freeing, really.*

And you wonder why a cheery soul like me doesn't have any friends. Well, except maybe for one, if a boyfriend counts as a friend; I do have a boyfriend, sort of. A little later on I suppose I'll have to tell you how I ended up with one of those.

It feels like I'm just getting warmed up—I swear you will be sorry you assigned me this journal—but I am being called down for dinner. It's meat loaf, which means it's going to be another bowl-of-cereal night for me. This journal entry ends on an anticlimax. This reminds me of something—having read all of Catcher *(see, I do the shorthand, too), I have to ask if Holden's mother ever cooked him meat loaf? Maybe that was part of Holden's problem, not having a mother who made meat loaf and offered the standby option of a bowl of cereal. Just some food for thought, if you can excuse the bad pun. And P.S., I don't think* The Catcher in the Rye *is all that great of a book, to be honest, but I know you have to teach it. I like* The Bell Jar *better.*

Her arm completely asleep from resting her weight on it, Vera turned the last page of the journal as though expecting more, then looked again at the cover page. She was impressed with what she had just read. She thought, *I must warn her about discussing other students in her journal entries.* Then she thought: *Who am I kidding?* She found the observations too engrossing and too informative to censor. Vera already found herself recognizing the lens through which Jensen Willard saw the world.

Chapter Three

Around four o'clock every morning, when the last of Dorset's barflies had simmered down and the farmers were not yet awake, Vera often found herself driven out of bed in an attenuated state of alertness. She liked having this small window available to her just before dawn, when the hour was hers and hers alone to claim, and she frequently used this time for writing and researching. On this particular morning she was reading some of her files and transcripts relating to Ivan Schlosser, reviewing his confession of the murder of Heidi Duplessis, the high school girl from Bond Brook.

Why would someone deliver a voluntary confession? was the question Vera had written at the top of her notebook page. Was there some kind of reward involved, real or imagined, in owning up to a crime that hadn't been traced to him? Had Schlosser simply wanted to boast—to take credit for every one of his misdeeds? Looking over the transcripts of his interviews with Detective Leo Vachon, Vera could see no hint of remorse.

SCHLOSSER: I didn't know I was going to stab her until my knife was at her throat [LAUGHTER], but once I started I knew it was the right thing to do. Didn't expect her to scratch up my arms like she did, though. She was a solid little thing. Big boobs, big shoulders. It took a few minutes before she went still. Then I took her into the bathtub and cut her up . . .

VACHON: What did you cut her up with?

SCHLOSSER: A tree saw.

VACHON: This was a tree saw you already had or one that you bought?

SCHLOSSER: It was one that was in the basement of my apartment. I think maybe it was the landlord's. I never saw nobody use it. I know I never cut up a tree in my damn life. Just people.

Vera kept turning pages of the transcript, dropping them on the floor in haphazard piles that she would neaten up later. She read more details about the deaths of Schlosser's two other young victims. They had not died exactly the way Heidi had died.

Vera had been only fourteen years old when Heidi Duplessis, a sophomore from her own school, had been forced out of the home where she was babysitting and murdered hours later in the woods. In the hierarchy of high school cliques, Heidi had been a moderately popular girl—a girl who wore expensive, preppy clothes and had a head full of spiral-permed curls. She was known for a ready smile filled with short, white, square teeth that flashed in the middle of her deeply tanned face. Heidi Duplessis, age fifteen: friendly, well liked, unthreatening, but still not someone who would have deigned to speak to Vera, even if their paths had crossed directly.

Heidi had been strangled to unconsciousness before she was stabbed, though one stab wound was ruled as her ultimate cause of death; with Schlosser's other two victims, Margot Pooler and Rosemary Trang, he had skipped the preamble and gone straight to the stabbing. Though Vera knew that killers sometimes switched up their modus operandi, she also couldn't lose sight of the fact that serial killers tended to like the consistency of patterns and that each new mode of killing had its reasons.

Vera also knew the strangler and the stabber had something in common. They didn't mind demonstrating a sense of intimacy toward their victims. They were not afraid to get close. She thought about the papers she had just reviewed and dropped down on her hands and knees, sorting through the pile until she found the page with the passage she wanted to read again.

VACHON: What else can you tell us about the murder of Heidi Duplessis?
SCHLOSSER: Well, what do you want to know? It started with choking, like I said. I was holding her throat, and I moved in real close, so if you were looking at us from far away, you'd have thought it's just a man and a woman about to kiss. But my intent was just to get a real good look in her eyes so I could see the life go out of them bit by bit.

Vera copied these exact words into her notebook and studied them, thinking. *Now this,* she told herself, *might really mean something. This might be put to good use somewhere in my Schlosser book.* But she was beginning to lose steam, now that the sun was threatening to come up. Two more hours before she had to leave for school, not enough to go back to bed but just long enough to grow weary before her workday even began.

She placed her head on her table, on top of her folded arms, and closed her eyes, still thinking of Schlosser's confession. The words *just a man and a woman about to kiss* floated through her mind in the disembodied way that thoughts did when she was close to sleep. *I could make something of this,* she thought from this far-off place, but she knew she would not—not on this morning, at least. The hours never worked in her favor. And even if they did—even if there were finally time enough to begin to write what she wanted to write—something always got in the way of it. Her unfinished schoolwork waiting to be graded. Her lesson plans waiting to be drafted and finalized. Her own fears and doubts causing her to look at the reality of Schlosser like a child peeping through her fingers at something—something she knew she shouldn't see but wanted to.

Vera considered herself a creature of habit—someone who came into her own once she'd carved out a routine for herself.

By the time three weeks of teaching at the Wallace School had passed, she felt as though she had begun to get her footing in her three classes and had developed an innate sense of the rhythm and pace she could expect from each set of girls. More important, she had a better handle on each girl as a result of reading her journal entries; she had seen each girl's whole *being* emerge more vividly on the page, though some, of course, presented themselves with more powers of articulation than others. She had hoped that this would happen—that she would come to know them better and that they would come to trust her more, as the exchange of entries and comments grew.

What she hadn't expected is that she would become the keeper of their secrets. That they would feel safe confiding in her.

Who would have guessed, Vera thought, that the beautiful Cecily-Anne St. Aubrey had been in two foster homes before being permanently adopted by a wealthy couple just three years before? And who would imagine that Aggie Hamada, who seemed to have a picture-perfect life, was tormented by her parents' recent split—especially since her father had left her mother to take up with her baby brother's nanny? Even Loo Garippa, so outwardly rebellious with her piercings and her eggplant-colored hair, confessed to taking mail-order diet pills that left her with headaches. (Vera had directed her to the school nurse, who was better equipped to handle this problem than she.) Although Vera knew as well as anyone that things were not always what they seemed, she still felt surprised by each new revelation, surprised that the girls would want to share such things with *her.*

She felt she owed her girls something, and she tried to repay their confidences by breaking up the boyish voice of Holden Caulfield with readings that offered a slightly more relatable (she hoped) female perspective; she assigned Katherine Mansfield's "The Doll's House," excerpts from *The Pillow Book*, and Marge Piercy's poem "Barbie Doll." And when responding to students' writing, she made it a point to scrawl a few kind words on each girl's writing exercise—the simple acknowledgment that told them someone was listening.

The exception to this was Jensen Willard, who had yet to receive any written feedback from Vera. Though Jensen's follow-up journal entries had been less disclosive than her first, they'd been no less revealing, in their own funny way; following her assigned reading of the essay "Hateful Things," Jensen had written her own list of hateful things that beautifully spoofed the complaint list written by Sei Shonagon, the famed, opinionated courtesan of Japan's Heian period. ("When you are about to make an astute point in class, and somebody else raises her hand to put out the obvious and takes the discussion in a stupid direction from which there is no return, that is hateful indeed.") Vera had come to enjoy her contributions from week to week, but had not felt there'd been enough time to write the lengthy response she wanted to. A simple, supportive scrawl did not seem acknowledgment enough for Jensen Willard.

By the time the Monday of her fourth week of teaching rolled around, Vera's classes had a decidedly different feel to them—the difference of attacking her days with a plan instead of flip-flopping between several possible ideas and instinctively choosing the one that felt right in the moment. On this particular Monday, she decided to start her morning class with a ten-minute freewrite on the subject of themes in *The Catcher in the Rye*.

"Now, theme," she reminded them, stalking up and down the rows as the students opened their notebooks and rooted around for their pens, "is not always easy to identify before you've read a novel in its entirety. Still, I think what you've read from *Catcher* should have already provided at least a few hints about the book's main idea. Take a stab at it. Any guesses are fair guesses."

Minutes later, as Vera collected the freewrite exercises—waiting patiently as many of the girls took time to take the fringes off their notebook sheets, piece by scraggly piece—she began to talk about theme as it pertained to the novel they were reading. She spoke of loneliness, alienation, the desire for closeness to another human being, the preoccupation with what is real versus what is false—pausing to scribble each item on the board as she mentioned it. She felt she could not get her words out fast enough, could not write fast enough; what she really wanted was to hear what the girls had to say and to see the machinations of their minds.

"I thought one of the themes was about what happens when he doesn't do well in school," Kelsey Smith said. "How he goes down a *slippery slope*."

"How *who* doesn't do well in school? Make sure your pronoun references are clear."

"Holden."

"Thank you. I wouldn't say that's a theme exactly, but it's an important plot point. What else? Any other ideas?"

Harmony Phelps raised her hand. "Guys are assholes. That could be a theme."

"Is that a universal truth, though?" Vera asked. Some of the girls laughed, as though to say yes. "Don't answer that just yet. I definitely do want to come back to the question of whether you think Holden is, well, an asshole, especially when we get to some of the later chapters. It may come down to a matter of opinion."

"Some people might say that Holden is . . . what Harmony said he is . . ." Jamie Friedman said, "but others might think that it's okay. Because he's smart, so that makes up for it."

"There's different kinds of smart," Martha True said timidly, from the back row.

It was all Vera could do not to look at Jensen Willard. She had a feeling the girl had no shortage of opinions on this subject. Vera's eyes skimmed over her, resting at last on Martha in the back. "Do you think he's smart, Martha?"

"I'd say he's clever."

Loo Garippa raised her hand. "I have a question. It might be kinda off topic."

"Okay."

"What is it with Holden and serial killers? I was looking on the Internet, and I guess serial killers really get into this book. I thought maybe you'd know the answer, with the book you're writing and all."

Vera could have sworn Jensen Willard was smiling demurely, eyes locked on the table. She was wearing another moth-eaten dress that had most likely been a rich black at one time but had dulled to the same charcoal color Vera had seen her wearing before. Over that, she wore an army coat that, by the looks of it, had once belonged to a fellow three times the girl's size.

"That's a bit of a misconception," Vera said, "thanks to Mark David Chapman, the man who shot John Lennon, and John Hinckley Jr., who attempted to assassinate President Reagan in the 1980s. Neither of whom was a serial killer, by the way—I suppose you'd call them assassins, or would-be assassins—but both of whom happened to like the book a lot."

"But why?" Loo asked.

"It's probably because Holden talks about wearing a people-shooting hat," Chelsea Cutler said. "That's kind of weird, isn't it? He has this funny hat, and he's running around his room telling his roommate or whoever that he shoots people in that hat."

"He doesn't mean it," Jamie said, in the sort of indulgent tone a mother might use to excuse a toddler with a biting problem.

Autumn Fullerton was stroking her hair as though bored. "He *might* mean it. You never know. Maybe later on, after the book ends, he *could* go on to kill someone." Vera recalled that Autumn had read the entire book. This told her all she needed to know of what the girl thought of Holden.

"I know this might be controversial of me to say, but I'd submit that anyone could kill someone," Vera said. "Anyone is *capable*. The only reason why most people don't do it is because they'd feel guilt or shame if they did, and rightly so. The people who kill are those who have no guilt or shame. Personally, I think Holden has both. That's why it's unlikely he'd be capable of any serious violence. As you read more, you just might decide that he's a kind person who's capable of love."

"Really? I don't think he loves anyone but *himself*," Harmony Phelps sniffed.

A flurry of responses rose over that, with several girls trying to outtalk one another—Autumn, Cecily-Anne, and Harmony the loudest of them all. Seeing that she'd opened the floodgates of healthy debate pleased Vera; the fact that some of the quieter girls in the class had jumped into the fray felt like a success of sorts, even if the discussion had steered toward dangerous waters. Vera wondered if she had been wrong to say what she had said—that *anyone* could kill someone. It seemed like one of those glib comments that wouldn't hold up under logical scrutiny or, more distressing still, could be taken out of context: *Hey, Mom, do you know what my English sub said today? She said we all could be murderers!* Try as she might, she couldn't seem to keep her interest in true crime out of the English classroom. But Loo Garippa had started it, not she.

At the end of class, Vera practically had to yell over the girls: "Please note the reading assignment on the board. And don't forget, I'm collecting journals on Friday—at least two entries from each of you."

Every class, Vera knew, had its regular latecomers and those who were slow to leave at its close. She had come to expect to see Jensen lagging behind the others, but Sufia Ahmed, who was usually eager to get on her cell phone and out the door as soon as class was dismissed, was not one who tended to stay behind. On this day, however, she remained in her seat, hands folded, studying Vera with her large, grave, liquid eyes while the other girls gathered their things and left. The class was empty except for her and Vera and, of course, Jensen, who was bent over tying her bootlace, the muddy sole propped against the chair where she'd sat.

"Miss Lundy, I would like to speak to you," Sufia Ahmed said in her soft voice. Vera had to step close to her just to hear her.

"Yes, Sufia, what is it?"

"What you said today? I do not think it is right."

Here it is, Vera thought—*a moral dissenter at last.* "Are you referring to my comment that anyone can murder someone?" Vera asked gently.

"Yes," Sufia said. "And I do not think such things are right to talk about in class."

"I absolutely don't mean to be offensive to anyone. Please bear in mind that my opinions are just my opinions; you're encouraged to think critically, to question what I say. But what is right and wrong for *me* to bring up in class is my determination to make."

"I am here to learn about the literature of America and of Europe, the great literature of all the world. I am not here to learn about killing. Killing was one of the reasons my parents fled their country."

Vera nodded, shutting her eyes for just a fraction of a second. She could not help but feel a pang in her heart, hearing Sufia's words. "I understand what you're saying," she said after a moment's pause. "But the dark side of human nature is something that is represented in much of the great literature you will read. You really can't escape it."

Sufia shook her head slowly from side to side, her large eyes sad. "I do not think you understand. You say you do, but I don't think you do. These things you say in class—maybe I will ask Dean Finister if it is okay for you to speak of such things."

"Oh, Sufia. I'm so sorry you feel this way, I really am. Do you have some time to talk this through? I don't have another class for a while yet."

"I have my American foreign policy class now."

"Can we schedule some time to talk later, then?"

"I will think about this," Sufia said, and she turned and seemed to float out of the room, as she always did, with her light, precise walk and the hem of her traditional Somali dress rippling behind her.

Vera rubbed her eyes as though to clear them of something she wanted to be rid of. *Well, now you've done it,* she thought, and tried not to think about the greater implications of this encounter with her student. Surely Sufia would forget all the day's class discussion before she could even think of reporting it. Vera knew how mercurial kids were, changing their moods and whims on a dime. But what if she didn't forget? What if Vera's careless comments made their way back to the dean?

Vera wondered if Jensen Willard, who was finally moseying toward the door, had been listening to the whole exchange. If so, she decided not to let on that she knew. There were other matters to discuss, long overdue. She closed her eyes again and counted to ten, knowing that the girl would still not have passed through the door by the time she had recollected herself. "Jensen?" she said. "Could I speak to you for just a minute, please, before you go?"

The girl came and stood by her chair with about the same gusto with which one might approach a firing squad. Leaning in toward her and speaking in a near whisper, Vera said, "I've been meaning to tell you for a few days now—there's a reason I haven't returned any of your journal entries. I want to hang on to them a little longer so I can write some decent comments on them—give them the response they really deserve. But on the whole, I'm impressed with them. Really impressed."

"Thanks," Jensen said, looking a little surprised. Surprise was the first glimmer of any emotion that Vera had ever seen her display.

"While you're not writing *exactly* what I had in the mind for a *Catcher* journal, I want you to keep doing what you're doing."

"I can make it more about the book if you want. More of a literary analysis."

"If you can work in a bit more analysis, that'd be great. But I'm really pleased with how you've started."

"I have more," Jensen said.

"More?"

"In my bag. I didn't know if you'd want this today or not." The girl reopened her knapsack and withdrew another bundle of pages, bound as before. "I might have more entries for Friday, too. Is that all right?"

"Sure," Vera said. "If you write the pages, I'll read the pages. However many you've got."

"Some teachers don't like to do that. They don't want to read extra."

"When the quality of the writing is as interesting as yours, I don't mind at all. There's just one thing I'd like to caution you about."

A look crossed Jensen's features, and Vera did not know how to translate it at first. Was it recognition—the look of one who had known that, sooner rather than later, the other shoe would drop?

"It's nothing bad," Vera said hurriedly. "I'd just like to ask you to be careful when writing about your classmates. And I'm not saying this for the reason you might think. It's not because I'm trying to *censor* your right to discuss your fellow classmates in your journals."

"But you'd rather I wrote nicer things about them."

"No, not even that. I'm just concerned that someone might get a hold of your journals and . . . use them against you. You see, this happened to me once, back when I was in high school and had a tendency to write down every little thing that I thought. A notebook got stolen out of my bag in homeroom. I got in a lot of trouble for some of the things I wrote. I'd hate for . . . I'd hate for such a thing to happen to you. That's all."

They sized each other up for a second or two. Vera searched for a way to shift the conversation to Jensen—perhaps something specific about the journals she'd read, something to demonstrably show Jensen that she'd read it and *gotten* it. She blurted out, "I liked that bit you wrote a couple of weeks ago about Holden's mother not making meat loaf."

Jensen grimaced. "That was kind of a throwaway. I had to end the journal entry somehow."

"Well, it amused me. And it certainly brings to mind the class issues in the novel. Holden is well-to-do, by most people's standards. I'll tell you a funny little personal story. One time when I was in a graduate school seminar, I made a passing reference to how much I'd enjoyed eating TV dinners when I was a kid—are they even called TV dinners anymore?—and my classmates, some of who were trust fund kids, were all agog. One girl said, 'Vera, *really*? You used to eat TV *dinners*?' They couldn't conceive of it."

Jensen's mouth moved a little—not a grimace this time but not exactly a smile, either. Vera had the distinct feeling that the girl thought she was being silly but was too polite to say so. "I think you'll like my new journal entry then. I actually wrote about . . . um, the haves and the have-nots, I guess you could say."

"Sounds promising," Vera said. "Very good, then. I'll see you tomorrow in class, yes?"

"You will," Jensen said. But now she seemed to have forgotten that she'd been on her way out the door. She shifted her weight from foot to foot and said, "I don't think you did anything wrong, by the way."

"I'm sorry?"

"With what you said in class. If anything, you might have even copped out a little. Don't worry about what Sufia thinks."

"I appreciate you backing me up on this," Vera said, "but I respect what all of my students think and feel. I know that I *try* to, anyway."

After Jensen was gone, Vera put her journal on top of the unread freewrites. As she was sorting the rest of them, trying to take her mind off all that had occurred after her last class, Sue MacMasters, the head of the English department, walked past her classroom, did a double take, and stuck her head in the door.

"Why, hello, stranger," she said, her words curling around Vera in a way that felt like an accusation. "How is everything going? I haven't heard much from you, so I assume you haven't had any questions."

"I think things are going well. We're already discussing *Catcher*. The students seem to tolerate me all right."

"I'm sure they tolerate you. They have ways of letting you know if they don't. I'm on my way to a conference with a parent, but please—don't hesitate to ask if you need anything. I know filling in for someone else can be rather overwhelming at first. I was just saying the other day that I've yet to see you come into the faculty lounge. You're a bit of a mystery among the teachers."

"Well," Vera said wryly, "it's good to know I have some mystique."

She was grateful that Sue couldn't linger. The brief attention from her boss had made her more self-conscious than ever. She knew she would have to buck up and start mingling with the other faculty at some point if she wanted any hope of having her contract renewed in the fall. But she was starting to feel, already, that forming close bonds with the faculty would somehow be traitorous to her students. Her first loyalty was to them. The side she was on would most likely always be theirs.

She returned her attention to the freewrites stacked before her. There was an hour-and-a-half gap between her first and second class—plenty of time to read and comment on some of these. One student, Chelsea Cutler—not the brightest bulb in the class, Vera had quickly ascertained—wrote about how the theme of *The Catcher in the Rye* is "the 1950s, where people talked different and thought different, which shows how no one can relate to them anymore." Another student, Katherine Arsenault—Vera noticed she had signed her name *Kitty*—had written, "Holden is someone who takes everything for granite. I think this book is about not taking things for granite." Applying a quasi-feminist analysis, Harmony Phelps wrote, "This is about how guys objectify women and tell lies and try to say they're something that they're not. Men cannot help it."

Enough, Vera thought. She would have to get to these later. She pulled out Jensen's journal entry. As with the girl's first submission, the title on the cover gave her a little jolt.

I Shoot People in This Hat:
Journal Entry #2, by Jensen Willard

Yesterday morning, before English class, we had an assembly in the auditorium. Were you there? I looked for you.

Vera stopped reading and pushed the paper away an inch, like someone who has resolved to not take another bite from her plate. This direct address took her off guard. But curiosity got the better of her; she pulled the paper closer to her again and continued reading.

I know our class talked about themes in The Catcher in the Rye. *One of the themes is artifice vs. reality—the real vs. the phony—and I mention this because school assemblies are exercises in artifice. I kind of wish one of Holden's cronies had been there to let out a colossal fart during the proceedings, just to keep things real.*

FACT: Getting a bunch of girls together in an auditorium is offensive to the senses. The whole room reeked of Coco Mademoiselle perfume—the fragrance most of the girls here wear. Same fragrance their mothers wear, come to think of it. Little miniatures of their parents these kids are. You can look at them now and see what they'll be like in ten years, in twenty years. They'll be exactly the same, except with more money and more bloat. They'll take positions in local government and build tennis courts in their backyards and complain about neighbors with unsightly, unmowed lawns.

It's the same way with the poor white kids on other side of the river, identifiable by their scruffy pseudo hip-hop clothes and baggy pants. Their futures are just as clearly mapped out, but unlike the rich kids, sometimes I think they know how depressing this is. They take Vocational and General and Remedial classes and, whether they make it out of high school or not, will soon crank out litters of sad, doomed, government-funded children—just what we need more of. I know of which I speak, because I'm a poor white kid, too. I live on that side of the river and used to go to their school up until last year. I'm a "scholarship kid" now. Aren't I the special one.

I'm not doing a very good job of setting the scene for the morning assembly, am I? I get distracted easily. I guess I could tell you how the dean of our school, Mr. Harold Finister, was up onstage doing his usual pointless shtick, handing out some leftover awards that he didn't get around to handing out earlier in the year. If it seems as though I have some bitterness toward Dean Finister, then you are reading this the right way. Earlier this year, thanks to Finister, I had to meet with this shrink and almost ended up in a hospital. This is not the kind of thing I can easily forgive.

Finister's big thing is keeping an eye out for girls who have alcoholic parents or are using substances themselves; he's always checking our eyes for signs of drug-induced pupil enlargement. He can't rag on me for substance abuse, so his thing with me is harping on depression. Every time he sees me he says, "You look sad today, Jensen." Every frigging time without fail. It's my own fault, though, because a couple of months ago he found me crying in the corridor, leaning against the wall because I thought I might collapse from crying so hard. I go on crying jags a lot, especially lately, and once I start I can't stop. He hauled me into his office because I guess it's bad if a girl sees another girl bawling unreservedly in the halls; it's either an eyesore or it's bad for morale, I'm not sure which. I sat there in the chair across from him and couldn't stop crying, and finally he handed me a Kleenex. "You're makeup's getting all smudged," he said. That was all he said at the time.

Later he called my parents and told them he was referring me to this shrink who charges on a sliding scale. I think this made my mother sad and worried, thinking I needed therapy, and I felt awful about that. I felt even worse when I met the shrink—a woman named Dr. Haskell who has some kind of weird mental defect that makes her incapable of saying anything other than "Uh-huh." I'm not kidding. No matter what you say, that's all she says back: "Uh-huh." You could say, "Dr. Haskell, the reception desk just got hijacked by Libyans," and she'll croak, "Uh-huh," and leave it at that. I suppose that's a therapeutic method, but I didn't think much of it. I think my parents were relieved when I told them I refused to go to therapy after the third week. Sliding scale or no sliding scale, forty dollars a week is a lot to pay for "Uh-huhs."

Poor Dean Finister. I ought to have more sympathy for him. It can't be easy having to spew that same silly pap about school spirit and class pride all the time, and then there's his home life. His daughter, Lyndsey, is the most matronly teenager known to man—only seventeen years old, and she already has a pigeon breast and a paunch. Looks just like her mother. It can't be easy having to go home to a wife and daughter who look like pigeon-shaped bookends. And then there's all that business with his dead niece. That can't be as fun as a barrel of monkeys, either.

The worst thing about school assemblies, aside from having to look at Finister, is that the right people never get awards. It's always the people like Cecily-Anne or Autumn who do—the ones whose parents give money to the school. Take somebody like Martha True from our class—she's actually not stupid, but she's not what Wallace likes to think of itself as promoting, so she's not going to get squat. I'm not even going to get into me. Which is not to say I deserve any awards, really. I don't go out of my way to get noticed. I don't like raising my hand or speaking up because this anxiety creeps in and I feel like I can't get any breath in my lungs as soon as I think about responding to a question or a point.

The phone is ringing for me—my Sunday night phone call. I will get back to this and write more later, if you don't mind too much.

LATER—*1 a.m.*

Ugh, I can't sleep.

I did sleep for a little while earlier, maybe an hour and a half, but I woke up and thought I saw someone in my window. My bedroom is on the second floor, so I'm pretty sure no one was there—no one could have been there—but for just one second I was sure a man was pressing his sunken face up against the glass. This used to be a regular thing with me, a trick of the eye in the dark. I used to sleep with my head completely covered so that if I woke up in the night, I wouldn't be tempted to look at the window because seeing a face in it was always my greatest fear. I've started doing that again, covering my head, ever since Angela Galvez was killed.

I don't think I should write about Angela Galvez, though. I need to try to calm myself down, not get myself worked up further. I guess this might be a good time to tell you a little bit about my boyfriend—the Sunday night phone caller.

But no, something even better: I want to tell you about my parents. I should start by telling you that earlier tonight, before I got started on this journal entry, the three of us—me, my mom, and my stepfather, Les—all watched Wheel of Fortune *and* Jeopardy! *together, like we do every night. "What?" you're probably asking. "A teenage girl who actually admits to doing something civil with her parents?" I'm all about defying expectations, but the truth is, I get along with them well enough.*

I know this is uncommon. Maybe other teenagers just don't know how to work their parents, don't know a good thing when they've got it. I saw that stupid old movie The Breakfast Club *on TV a couple of months ago, and I couldn't believe how the characters kept linking their unhappiness back to their parents. Worst of all was when this character, the supposedly weird girl who is really just a normal girl trying to play a weird girl, has that dumb line where she says: "When you grow up, your heart dies." When, I wondered, has my heart ever lived? I swear to God, if I do make it to adulthood, it'll only be for the satisfaction of not having to be a teenager anymore.*

My mother is this really funny mixture of earthy redneck, hippie, and prude; she swears like a sailor, but when you get her going on the subject of dating, all of a sudden she turns into a debutante from the 1950s. More about that later.

My stepdad is Les Cudahy. He's from San Fernando, California, originally, and he went to high school with some kids who later became movie stars. Not big names, but people you'd recognize if you saw them. His real first name is Leslie, but you'd have to call him that at your own peril. He is more than twenty-five years older than my mother; she's his second wife. He's older than most of my classmates' grandfathers, and in fact he does have grandchildren from his first marriage who are older than I am. But he's been my stepfather since I was two, after my biological dad, Mr. Stephen Willard, took off and became a champion deadbeat. (I don't even think I have any memories of him. No, that isn't true—I do have one memory, if you can call it that. I must have been about two years old, and I'd had a nightmare, so I'd gone to my parents' room and stood by their bedside in the dark, waiting for one of them to wake up. I was near my dad's side of the bed, and he was sleeping facedown in his pillow. Eventually he lifted his head a little—his hair was all matted, I remember that. "Jesus Christ!" he said when he saw me, and buried his face in the pillow again. In hindsight I wish I'd grabbed the back of his head and pushed his face in a little deeper. Thus ends my first, last, and only fond memory of champion deadbeat Stephen Willard.)

So those are my parents. Neither one of whom is exactly enthralled about my having a boyfriend, by the way. I can't say that I'm always one hundred percent enthralled *about it, either.*

I first met Bret Folger last summer when I was taking one of those courses in French at the community college. Bret was taking the same course, as some kind of precollege thing. He actually goes to Columbia University now. You might think that sounds bad, me dating a college freshman when I'm only a tenth grader, but he's a respectable sixteen years old—he did some kind of homeschooling thing where he got his high school degree two years early.

Bret and I never talked the whole time we were in French, but later that July I'd gone to this extremely pathetic student art exhibit at the library. The only reason I was there is because my semi-friend Scotty was supposed to have a painting on display. I refer to Scotty as a semi-friend because we used to be pretty close last year when we went to the same school; we were in the same gym class for a while, and we both had rage in common. Before gym would start, we'd have some downtime where we'd sit on the bleachers, both of us looking ridiculous in sweatpants and T-shirts, and he'd talk to me very enthusiastically about new kinds of homemade bombs he was working on. He's big on weaponry and explosives. We were always talking about blowing up the school, in a humorous way, of course, and that solidified our bond.

Also, Scotty and I were always comparing notes on how we wanted to kill ourselves if we were going to do it. (Do you think less of me now that you know this about me? Have you downgraded me to just some stupid punk kid? Or maybe placed me in the ranks of one of those wannabe school shooters who is really just looking for attention?) I said I would jump off a bridge, and he said he would slit his wrists. A couple times he tried, or said he did, but I'm not really sure how serious his intention was—he came to school one time with his wrists all bandaged, but when he showed me the cuts underneath, the cuts went across his wrists like bracelets instead of straight up and down, like you're supposed to do them.

The other main thing that Scotty and I both had in common was that we were both signed up for archery. In ninth grade you could choose between three different sports in gym, and I signed up for archery because it seemed a lesser evil than the alternatives—volleyball and basketball. I don't like things flying at me from overhead, and I don't like having to chase things around for no reason. So archery it is—me, Scotty, the fat girls who also don't like to run around and chase things, and the dorky guys who think they want to be Braveheart when they grow up.

Anyway, I was in the library looking for Scotty's painting and hoping to see Scotty there, too, I suppose. I hadn't seen him since school let out. Though we got pretty tight in gym, we were never close enough friends where I saw him after school or had his phone number or anything along those lines, so I guess he falls in the category of "lost" friends, right up there with Annabel. I didn't see Scotty, and I didn't see his painting there, either—just a bunch of other students' work, painful to behold. The product of my former high school's art classes reflected the preferences of the art teacher, Mrs. Plum, who thinks that drawings and paintings must celebrate Maine's Maine-ness and therefore be all about loons and lighthouses and lakes. I was standing there in front of a picture of a boat in the Penobscot River. It looked like someone had barfed up a bottle of Scope and superimposed a stick-figure boat over it. Then I got this uncanny sense that someone was standing far too close. I'm pretty good at telling when someone invades my personal space because my personal space takes up a little more room than most people's.

I turned around and saw all six foot five inches of Bret Folger hulking over me. I should say here that he is not a very attractive guy, physically. At least I didn't think so in the beginning. He's about a hundred and thirty pounds, tops, which gives him the appearance of a giant, slightly stooped tapeworm. He also has reddish-blondish hair that his mother cuts for him—it literally looks like one of those cuts where someone puts a bowl over your head and snips away to beat the band. I knew from French class that he was very smart, though, by scholarly standards.

"Hi," he said. "I know you. Jensen, right?"

I was surprised he knew my name. I was surprised, too, that he was bothering to speak to me. That's just not something that people ordinarily do. Even more surprising, he kept on talking.

"Do you like art?" he asked me.

"Some of it. Not this stuff."

"More modern?"

"No. Not too modern. Do you mean like crumpling up a Big Mac wrapper and throwing it on the floor and calling that art? I hate that kind of thing." I thought for a moment. Under his heavy lids, Bret's eyes—beetle eyes, practically all pupils—were looking at me like he wanted to gobble me up. It made me want to mess with him a little. "I like the Pre-Raphaelites. I know some people think they're tacky, but I like them. Anyone who exhumes the corpse of his dead wife like Rossetti did is probably a pretty interesting person."

Bret stared at me even more closely with those beetle eyes, trying to see if I was serious. This crazy-looking flush had started surging up behind his acne, and this made me think less of him—why would anyone blush on my *account?*

"You know," Bret said, "I'd always meant to talk to you in French class. You seemed pretty cool. I was wondering . . . do you like movies? Sometimes a group of us gets together on Thursday nights and rents stuff. Sometimes at my place, and sometimes at my friend Dave Epstein's, and sometimes at my friend Colin Mackay's. Last week we watched, um, Plan 9 from

Outer Space? *It was pretty cool. Anyway, tonight's Thursday, and we're meeting at my house."*

Let me interject here that I can't stand the word cool. *It just sounds so stupid, and Bret had gone ahead and used it twice. I wanted to walk away instantly. But something compelled me not to.*

"I could come," I said without even thinking about it. You might well ask, "Why would you go to Bret Folger's house when you find him repugnant and hadn't had a real social outing since the last time Annabel invited you to a pool party three years ago?" Maybe because the last social outing I'd had was when Annabel invited me to a pool party three years ago.

Bret gave me his address on this piece of wadded-up paper he'd had in his pocket—the paper felt warm, which was a little disgusting—and I put it in my knapsack. Funny, when I was on my way out the library about a half an hour later, I saw this kid Joey Fitts, who I knew a little from my old school; he used to skateboard down by the waterfront parking lot with Scotty sometimes. I asked him how Scotty was doing, and he told me Scotty hadn't been in school for a month or two, and that maybe he was either locked up somewhere or had dropped out. And yes, I felt a little jealous of my old friend, hearing that. I miss that kid sometimes.

Later that day, it took my parents some convincing that it would be okay for me to watch movies with a bunch of guys I'd never met, at the home of a boy I barely knew. "We don't even know this boy," my mother said, turning on her prim persona in a flash. "I'd feel better if we met him first."

"Why would you have to meet him? It isn't a date. My God, he repulses me."

"That sounds like a hell of a basis for a friendship. I guess you can go if Les is willing to drive you."

Poor Les is always driving me around everywhere, but he does it uncomplainingly for the most part. When it comes right down to it, my parents will do just about anything for me. There was no question that I'd be able to go.

So that's how I ended up lounging around in Bret Folger's living room, which turned out to be the sort of suburban space that looked as though it'd been lifted straight out of a catalog—leather couches that made squeaking, farting noises when you got on and off them, and those dumb little end tables that serve no real purpose stuck everywhere. Knickknack shelves with completely insignificant knickknacks on them; you could tell Mrs. Folger had just gone wild at a Pottery Barn sale rather than looking for interesting objects that would make a statement. The lights were turned down low, maybe to make the movie on the big-screen TV seem a little more cinematic. The cinematic masterpiece itself was Repo Man, *some movie from the '80s starring Emilio Estevez.*

The other people in the living room were Bret's aforementioned friends, Dave and Colin. Introductions were made all around. Dave has glasses and an eruption of frizzy hair, and he was sitting on an armchair with an afghan covering up his legs like an invalid. As for Colin, he was wearing eyeliner and mascara, which can look good on pretty, androgynous men, but not on Colin's big, blunt-featured face.

"We made a bet you wouldn't come," Colin had said as soon as I showed up.

"Sorry to disappoint."

I took a seat on a corner chair and tried to pretend I was paying attention to what was on TV. That it was perfectly ordinary for me to be someplace other than in my living room watching Jeopardy! *with my parents on a Thursday night. That I was used to sitting around with a small group of overly intense and slightly sweaty boys who had the lights turned down low.*

Colin and Dave, who go to the same high school, kept talking about something that had gone on earlier, involving Colin's car and a questionable driving tactic that Dave referred to as a "wicked burnout," when all of a sudden, right in the middle of the stunning dual dialogue of Repo Man *and Dave and Colin, Bret Folger asked me, "Do you like Poe? You look like somebody who would like Poe."*

"He's a little overrated, but he has his place."

"I agree with you. I mean, he has predecessors in the Gothic genre who were just as good but are barely remembered today. What are you reading right now . . . for nonassigned reading?"

"Madame Bovary."

"Madame Ovary," Colin said joyfully.

"Shut up, Mackay," Bret said. Then, to me: "What do you think of Kerouac?"

"Kerouac? Also overrated. It's the kind of writing that people with no real life think they can relate to. Also the kind of writing that all writers think they can imitate but shouldn't." I could feel myself turning very red at this point, saying all this.

"I kind of like him. Allen Ginsberg, too. Have you read 'Howl'?"

"I can't hear!" Dave Epstein whined. A bowl of potato chips had somehow migrated to his afghan-covered lap, and he was clutching it as though it would keep him afloat in times of crisis.

"Like you weren't talking over the movie yourself two seconds ago," Bret said. At me, he said, "Let's go into the bathroom and talk some more about books. This movie kind of sucks, anyway."

"The bathroom?"

"My little brother's doing homework in the den, and my mom might need the kitchen."

Either one of them might need the bathroom, too, I *thought, but I didn't argue. As we got up, Colin said something in a low voice that I couldn't make out, and Dave sniggered. I have never used the word* sniggered *in my life, with good reason—it's a stupid word. But I swear that's what Dave did.*

The Folgers' downstairs bathroom was perfect and pristine. Nothing like ours at home, with its stained, pink, ruffly curtains and the weird stuffed animals that my mother is so fond of—the ones that seem to leer at you when you're naked. Expensive toiletries were lined on a rack against the Folgers' bathroom wall, and a lot of pricey department store makeup caught my eye; I hoard makeup and toiletries, even though I don't use them much. I wondered if there might be something I could slip into my pocket, an eyeliner or whatever, but then I remembered that I didn't have pockets. Besides, nothing was in my color—just boring nude lipsticks and the dark beige foundation of someone who tans. His mother's stuff, probably. There was a wicker chair in the bathroom, too—what for, I'm not sure. In case someone needed to sit down and wait while someone else took a dump, I suppose. I sat down in it.

"So," I drawled, "literature. What about it?"

To my horror and—I hate to admit it—exhilaration, Bret reached out with one of his bony hands and swept away the hank of hair that always hangs in my eyes. "Your face is always covered," he said.

"Now you sound like my mom. She tells me I look better with my hair out of my face. But I think all mothers have some kind of contractual obligation to say that."

"I think it's better in your face. You look like a little rat peering out from under things. A pleasant rat."

"A pleasant rat?" I said doubtfully.

And then something sort of hideous happened—something I feel funny even writing about, but I've gone this far. Bret's face moved toward mine. He had to stoop way down to reach me sitting in the armchair. I could see the pores of his nose up close. They looked like little strawberry seeds. He's going to try to kiss me, *I thought in a panic. No one had ever tried to kiss me. Not even close. I imagined his mouth forcing my lips apart—a wormlike tongue, like you see sometimes inside parrots' beaks at the pet stores. I turned my face away.*

"Why are you turning away? Do you have bad breath or something?"

That made me laugh. "No. Well, maybe. Probably."

"Let me smell."

I breathed into his face.

"It's a little bit bad," he said, "but it could be worse."

I laughed some more. I couldn't help it.

"Are you going out with anyone?"

"Me? No. *I mean . . . definitely, no, I'm not."*

"Would you go out with me? I mean, just to try? I'm leaving for Columbia in about six weeks. But six weeks is kind of a long time away."

"Okay," I said. Just like that. I couldn't even begin to explain to myself or to you how this happened if you asked me. But I said okay. I really did. There was a part of me that thought: Well, maybe he'll come in handy somehow. *You just never know.*

It's almost nine months later, and Bret and I are still boyfriend and girlfriend. It's a funny kind of relationship, as you can imagine.

Even in those six weeks while Bret was still in Dorset, we mostly just talked on the phone, and when we saw each other in person, it was mostly in groups with his friends. Every once in a while, he'd sneak me over to his house when his parents were out and his brother was away. More often, we'd go to his Aunt Miriam's cottage when she wasn't there. But mostly it was phone calls for us.

Our phone conversations were epic. They still are, usually. I don't have a cell phone, so I have to talk on my parents' old corded phone in the kitchen—pacing around, sometimes going in circles and winding the cord around my body till I'm trapped in a web of cord and have to untangle my way out of it. And sometimes I lie on the carpet in the dining room and talk to Bret in the dark because conversations in the dark always feel a little more meaningful. In general, the subject of our conversations is predetermined by Bret; that is, we talk about things that he feels like talking about or is interested in. He is interested not only in fiction and poetry but also in the philosophical writings of Nietzsche, Hegel, and Kierkegaard. I'm having to do a little brushing up on this stuff to act as though I can keep up with him, to be honest.

We write letters, too—real old-fashioned letters, with a strict no-email rule. That's what I spend most of my time doing: writing him letters. I write him four or five a week, and I'm lucky if he sends me two a month. When he was here over Christmas break, we did this thing where we'd leave notes for each other inside books at the Dorset library, and it would be like this Easter egg hunt to find which book the other person had left the note in. Usually there were clues, though. Like if Bret said something about being assigned The Vicar of Wakefield *for class, I'd leave a note for him inside the cover of* The Vicar of Wakefield. *That was the most fun correspondence we ever had.*

I have let him kiss me, but we haven't gone further than that. Kissing isn't quite as bad as I imagined, but it isn't exactly what I would call good, either. His nose (which is sizeable) always knocks into mine (which is also sizeable), and his lips always feel chapped, and the whole thing feels kind of invasive. "You're a very tense kisser," he told me once, which is probably true. I wish people would kiss the way they did back in those old black-and-white 1940s movies, with their shoulders hunched up and their faces rigidly jammed together. It seems better than those probing, messy, exploratory kisses you see in movies today. But I guess I'm lucky that Bret doesn't show much interest in going further than that—from what I understand, from movies and books and such, that's pretty unusual.

I don't put a lot of faith in love and sex. I think it's kind of lame, if I'm being honest. I think people start having sex at about the age their parents stop hugging them because they still want that infantile closeness to someone that they used to have, except it's all muddied up in sexual desire. Maybe my views are tainted by my parents' weird combination of openness and close-mindedness; once, when I asked my mother to explain a passage about male-on-female oral sex that I'd found in one of her books, her reply was, "A man's face doesn't belong down there." I don't know. I haven't sorted this all out in my mind.

During the many phone conversations Bret and I have had since last July, I've found there are some things I can talk to him about and some things I can't. For instance, one time I was lying on the dining room carpet after having drunk most of a bottle of cough syrup, which had somehow made me feel more depressed instead of having the desired effect of making me feel mildly drunk. We had just got done talking about the mating habit of insects, specifically this mite that leaves its sperm behind in intricate patterns for the lady mite to sit on, if she approves of the artist's work. I said I thought that was romantic. Then Bret started telling me about this guy who lived in one of his dorms who'd gone to visit his family for the weekend and had shot himself. He said, "He was this brilliant musician. I can't believe he did it with a gun. I'm not even sure where he would've gotten one—not from his house, I know that. I met his mother once, and she had this huge peace sign tattooed on her leg and a 'Bread, Not Bombs' bumper sticker on her Prius."

Then, without even knowing I was going to say it, I said, "Sometimes I think it's a good thing I don't know how to use my stepdad's gun."

Bret paused so I could hear the full measure of his distaste. "Your stepdad has a gun?"

"Yes, the service pistol he got issued in the navy. I tried to pick it up once, but it's too big for my hand—about three pounds. Still, sometimes I think about what it'd be like to bring it to school and hold a classroom hostage. I could go up and down the rows of desks, pointing the gun at people, and decide right then and there who'd live and who'd die. Wouldn't that be interesting? I don't think I'd know what I'd do unless I was actually in that situation. Maybe I wouldn't even shoot anyone. Maybe I'd just make them think *I would."*

"I would call that extremely uninteresting*," Bret said, "and definitely not romantic."*

He didn't understand at all. He didn't understand that I was just blowing off steam when I thought about these things, like I'd done with Scotty. That was the last time I brought up anything serious or personal like that with him. Since then, we've stuck to safe subjects—subjects he likes. Whether or not dark matter exists. Whether homeless people are visionaries. Whether Andy Warhol was really an artist. The number of starving artists who are actually starving.

With Bret being away at Columbia, we don't even have phone conversations that much anymore because of the long-distance bill. So now it's just down to Sundays. And that's what got me started telling you about all this in the first place—because of that call I just got. That call where he seemed distant, though maybe I just imagined it.

This is part of the reason why my parents don't like Bret. They say he doesn't seem that invested in me. My mother always says, "An investment is something that you give to someone that you can't get back." Still, Bret's about as invested *in me as anyone else has ever been. And this, to me, has come to mean a whole hell of a lot—enough so that I don't know what I'd do without him.*

I'm going to try to go back to sleep now. I didn't mean to go on this long, but now I have, and I've worn myself out—and you, too, probably, if you actually read all this.

Vera laid the last page of Jensen's journal on her table. She wanted to write a comment on the girl's paper, an in-depth comment thanking her for the entries she'd written thus far—the sheer volume of them and the quality of thought therein. But somehow she could not think of how to respond to Jensen without revealing her own stories—stories, she thought, that were best kept to herself.

Instead, she took out a fresh piece of paper and began to write a response to affix to the end of Jensen's journal entries; she preferred the old-fashioned approach of handwritten feedback, though most teachers she worked with now relied on computers.

Jensen,

This is a general response to all the journals you've submitted thus far. I've made individual notes in the margins of each, responding to lines and phrases and sections that struck me particularly. What I want to say most of all, though, is that it is a pure pleasure to read your writing. I am honored by your candor, honored to know you have trusted me as an audience.

Your emotional honesty and flair for writing are very good for someone your age. I appreciate how the entries range from savagely funny (even a little bit Holdenesque at times, which I'm sure isn't accidental) to melancholy and derisive. You cover the whole spectrum of moods here. Though you make some statements that might alarm some readers, I want you to know that I don't disregard these comments, but I am not easily shocked by them, either. I am someone you can always come to with such thoughts and issues, and if coming to me with them helps, then so much the better. You mentioned something about a therapist in one of your entries—do you ever think about trying a different one? Do you think there would be any value in doing so?

Sometimes seeing the world too clearly can misfire and result in hurting oneself badly, but in my opinion, the clarity is still worth it in the end. In the best-case scenario, it can make you something quite special in this world. I know this may offer you little consolation now, but it is something to keep in mind for the future.

Sincerely,
Vera Lundy

She had considered signing it, "Yours, Vera Lundy," but decided at the last minute that that might be too much. She had said quite enough already, even while trying not to.

Chapter Four

The first morning of her fifth week of teaching, Vera sat reading an online journal article called "Criminology and the False Confession," written by a criminal psychologist named T. E. Rubin. It was still dark out—not yet 5:00 A.M.—and her overhead light burned over her as she stretched out catlike on her bed, listening to the starchy calls of the chickadees outside her window, vocal and vigorous after a long and subdued night. The article stated nothing she didn't already know, yet it struck her as especially resonant, the way a certain song heard at a certain time seems to hold all the answers to the world.

> **When the person making the false confession is delusional, the false confession becomes his reality. But in the case of the nondelusional confessor, the confession itself helps him to feel grounded in a reality that had heretofore rejected him. Taking credit for a crime often becomes a highly public action, one that the world responds to. The confession, then, becomes a misguided attempt at achieving intimacy between him and the rest of society.**

It was interesting, Vera thought, to compare Ivan Schlosser's ready confession (*Well, what do you want to know?*) to the initial false confession of Ritchie Ouelette. Had Ritchie, too, had a moment when he thought a confession might bring him closer to the world instead of further away from it, like a kid who seeks negative attention in a wrongheaded attempt to garner a mother's love?

Looking up from her reading and tapping her pen meditatively against the page, Vera smiled to herself. She knew what she and her girls would be discussing first thing tomorrow.

"Intimacy," Vera announced at the beginning of her first-period class. "Isn't that a pretty-sounding word? *Intimacy.* Some people name their daughters Chastity. Why not name them Intimacy? It has just as much of a ring, doesn't it?"

Clutching her library copy of *The Catcher in the Rye*, Vera paced the floor of the morning class, speaking of intimacy and how it related to Holden Caulfield's fleeting desires to connect with the opposite sex. "What do you make of that behavior?" she asked her students. "What do you think is the driving force behind it?"

"Desperation," Jamie said.

"Ah," Vera said, giving Jamie a congratulatory little rap on her desk as she walked past. "Good answer. But what does desperation *mean*? Have you ever felt it? Tell me what desperation feels like."

"It feels like . . . grasping at straws," said Katherine Arsenault, who seemed to have roused herself from the dead at that mention of intimacy.

"Good, Katherine," Vera said, and then remembered the way the girl had signed some of her recent journal entries. "Or do you prefer to be called Kitty?"

"I prefer Kitty."

"All right then, Kitty. Why is Holden Caulfield desperate and grasping at straws in *The Catcher in the Rye*? What would make a sixteen-year-old boy feel so desperate?"

"Hormones," Loo Garippa deadpanned.

"More than that."

"Loneliness?" Martha True said.

"To say the very least, yes. Here he is, wandering around New York City alone, and he has no idea what to do with himself. Lost in his own hometown, practically."

"New York City is a good place to be lost," Jensen Willard said. It was the first time she had ever actually contributed a comment during class, and Vera irrationally found herself wanting to hug the girl.

"Yes!" she exclaimed. "Have you ever visited there, Jensen?"

The girl nodded. But the invitation Vera had thrown her way, this small encouragement to say more, fell flat, for she fixed her eyes on the table before her and refused to look up again.

"Let's run with this idea of loneliness," Vera said, turning away from Jensen and trying to ignore the tug of rejection she felt. "It's such an important part of understanding Holden's character. And isn't it an important part of understanding the teenage experience, too? Isn't it a lonely process, sorting out who you are emotionally and intellectually?"

There were blank looks, a couple of shrugs. Vera was not completely unsurprised by this noncommittal reaction. After all, what teenage girl wanted to be the first among her peers to own up to this idea of sorting things out?

"Funny thing about admitting that you're lonely," Vera said. "It's like saying you're depressed. People think it's contagious. No one wants to be around you if you admit to loneliness or depression."

She was killing the discussion. As though illustrating her own principle, the mere mention of the words *loneliness* and *depression* cast a pall over the room, an almost palpable recoiling. She knew she had better shift gears.

"Let's talk about something else, then, that's not so unrelated if you think about it: Holden as a liar. He's always presenting himself as something he's not. How does his tendency to lie or embellish tie into his loneliness? What might be the reason behind embellishing stories like Holden does? Do you think he's trying to impress other people? Is it that he's not happy with the real stories or perhaps doesn't *know* the real stories yet? Either way, this goes back to what I said, about sorting things out intellectually and emotionally. And that kind of sorting-out process is the hallmark of adolescence itself, the key to coming of age."

"Coming of age to do what, though?" Aggie Hamada asked.

"Get secondary sex characteristics," Cecily-Anne St. Aubrey said primly.

"Be on the rag," someone else said in a stage whisper.

Vera cleared her throat. "Come on now, girls. What are the motivations behind a lie? Think about it."

After a few seconds, the answers began to come.

"To hide something?"

"To protect someone else."

"To make yourself look good."

"To fool yourself or others."

"Good answers, all of you." Vera was growing excited. She was scarcely aware that her pace around the classroom was quickening or that her low voice rose, rich and full-throated, in anticipation of the narrative she was about to tell.

"Let me tell you a quick story about a real-life adolescent who lived a lie for a little while. Any of you ever hear of Penny Bjorkland?"

Just as Vera had expected, no one had. She slowed her pace around the classroom, rubbing her hands together. She shot an almost defiant glance at Sufia Ahmed, who was sitting at her desk with her hand curled around a pen, ready to take notes.

"Penny Bjorkland was a seemingly ordinary teenager who lived in California in the late 1950s. One day she woke up and told herself, 'Today is the day I will kill someone.' That someone turned out to be a twenty-eight-year-old gardener named August Norry, who had the misfortune of offering her a ride that day. She fired eighteen bullets into his head, torso, and limbs. When the crime was later linked to her gun, she seemed unapologetic. She was described by the cops as a typical, gum-chewing, ordinary teenager with a tendency to giggle. When asked why she had done it, she said she had wanted to know what it would feel like to kill someone and not to have to worry about it afterward."

"Cree-*pee*, man," Loo Garippa said. "That's just weird."

"I daresay it's the *normalcy* with which she approached it that made it weird. This is a pretty extreme illustration of the adolescent's weakness in decision making, planning, and impulse control. On a much lesser scale, one can certainly see this in Holden Caulfield. Almost everything he *does* is based on impulse."

"But impulses aren't always bad," Cecily-Anne said, surprising Vera.

"No, of course not, Cecily-Anne. Can you think of a good impulse you've had recently?"

Cecily-Anne exchanged a glance with Autumn, and both of them giggled. Vera had the feeling they were laughing at her. "Well, I bought the Marc Jacobs bag I wanted," Cecily-Anne said, "but it was a really good buy."

Deciding to leave that one alone, Vera turned to the whiteboard and wrote down a word in large, slanting letters: EGO. She began to discuss what ego meant for the adolescent—how it represented the struggle of base, primitive urges against the expectations of society. The battle of what you *should* do versus what you *want* to do, deep down. There was a great, mushrooming silence that she interpreted as borderline hostile; she had probably used up the last of the students' goodwill for the day. They probably once again wished they were back with their regular teacher, Mrs. Belisle, woodenly reading lines from *Macbeth* out loud. Feeling almost perverse as she did so, knowing the students were not warming to this topic, she ended by assigning them a freewrite on the subject of ego.

"Are you going to collect these?" Chelsea Cutler asked.

"Yes, I am going to collect them. Your responses will be part of our discussion next time we meet."

Amid some noisy sighs and the sounds of loose-leaf paper being torn from notebooks, the girls began to write. Vera walked along the desks at the five-minute mark to check on the girls' progress. Some had written only a couple of sentences; others had filled nearly a page and showed no signs of stopping. Jensen Willard sat quietly in her chair, her head bent over her notebook but her pen held slack, the sheet of notebook paper blank before her.

"Thinking?" Vera asked her in a low voice.

"I have a hard time with freewrites," Jensen whispered. "I can't just think of things on the spot."

"It's okay," she whispered back to the girl. But perhaps it wasn't quite fair to the others, allowing Jensen to just sit there while they worked. Her conscience getting the better of her, she added in her regular tone, "Just have it ready to turn in to me on Monday. Class is almost over now."

A few minutes later, Vera told the girls to complete the sentence they were working on. "That's all the time we have for today, but please—don't leave without me collecting your journals. And please make sure you've noted the reading assignment I've put on the board. Thank you, and enjoy your weekend. Looks like I'll be spending most of mine elbow-deep in reading." Lest this sounded like a complaint, she added, "I can't wait to see what you've written for me this week."

As though by some mechanism, the students mentally shut off as soon as the words *That's all the time we have* were out of her mouth. More than half of them were already out of their chairs, waving their journals in front of them; some were already dropping them on her table before she'd finished speaking. Amid this upheaval, Vera pretended to be intent on putting some papers back in her suitcase, all the while crouched on the floor in an awkward way, given that she was wearing an above-the-knee skirt. When she glanced up, she saw Jensen still in her seat, reading something with what looked like absorption.

When she looked up a second time, Jensen was gone.

Between the journal submissions and the freewrites, Vera's first-period folder was now bulging with papers. She felt a mixture of anticipation and dread—dread because she knew that reading these works and composing her painstaking written feedback would be an exhausting undertaking. But what would she do, if denied that undertaking? She loved having too much to do. She no longer wanted to remember what it felt like to have empty weekend hours that left her feeling unmoored.

Watching the girls pass by in the hall, Vera opened the folder again and took out the first paper on top of the pile. It was Kitty Arsenault's. Her previous writing samples had yielded nothing of interest, so Vera had no real opinion formed of her yet; she looked at the freewrite exercise in front of her and slowly picked her way through the spiky, messy, smudged penmanship that filled up most of the loose-leaf page.

EGO, by Kitty Arsenault

In THE CATCHER IN THE RYE, Holden is egotistical. He lies to make himself sound better, and he talks about himself constantly. I don't think I am as egotistical as he is. Even when my teachers ask me to, I don't really like writing about myself because I am not sure that I am that interesting really. I should probably tell more lies so that my stories will sound more interesting, but I'm not sure how to do that. I think I only lie when I'm trying to spare someone's feelings. Like if someone gets a haircut and it looks awful and they ask me if it looks awful, should I tell them Yes or No? If they're really sensitive, it doesn't do any good to tell them "Yes, it looks awful," because then they'll just obsess over it and feel worse. And I don't see the point in making people feel worse when I could make them feel better. I am not sure if I have done this freewrite correctly?

Vera smiled to herself, took out her pen, and wrote a few notes at the bottom of Kitty Arsenault's journal. *Poor girl,* she thought—*nice and considerate of others, if a little dull. How lonely it must feel to be a nice, considerate, relatively ego-free teenager.*

Next in her pile was Loo Garippa's freewrite.

I think the idea of ego is pretty cool. Especially when you think about ego identity and how we add stuff to our personalities or take stuff away in order for us to figure out who we really are. Like Holden putting on that people-shooting hat and taking it off again. I guess my version of a people-shooting hat would be how I'm always trying to change up my appearance. My hair is purple right now, but I've had it blond, blue, black, and pink. I've had it buzz-cut, Mohawked, and dreadlocked. I'd like to get lavender streaks but first I have to wait till more of it grows back because I've fried it from dyeing it so many times. My dad always says: "How come you have to keep changing? What's the matter with the looks God gave you?" But life is all about changing, and now is the time to do it, right? I don't want to be an old lady of thirty still trying to figure out who I am or what looks good on me or what I enjoy doing. I'm glad this is a time for me to explore my ego identity.

Vera read the entry again, running her hand over her face. Not terrible—some of the connections Loo was making were decently observed—but it was not the sort of depth she had been hoping for. She decided to put this entry in the back of the pile until she could think of a suitable comment to write; she moved to the shorter entry on the next sheet of paper, only half covered in Sufia Ahmed's looping script.

I am not sure I understand concepts of Ego. In my culture you think of the community. You think what is best for everyone not just what is best for myself. Thinking "What is Best for Myself" is Western thinking. I think of my family, my parents, my brothers and sisters and how I can make them proud. I do not think Ego needs to exist. I think Ego only leads to bad and evil things like things you speak of in class.

"Miss Lundy?"

Vera looked up from her reading and saw a student from her later afternoon class standing there, looking sheepish. It was Kaitlyn Fiore, a girl who always had an anxious, scrunched face and had already started emailing Vera to ask her lots of unnecessary questions about the readings and the assignments. "Miss Lundy, I just wanted you to know I typed my journals, but I couldn't print them out for today. My ink cartridge ran out. I hope I don't get late points taken off for this because it really wasn't my fault."

Vera took a few moments to negotiate something that would ease the student's distress. She had finally sent her on her way and was about to return to the journals when another face appeared in the classroom doorway—that of Sue MacMasters. She looked blonder than Vera remembered. Was Vera supposed to acknowledge this? Compliment it? She had no sense of etiquette when it came to such matters.

"Vera! How are you?"

"I'm doing well, Sue, thank you. Reading the first major writing assignments. The first ones they've written for *me*, I should say. That's always an interesting experience."

"A bunch of us from the English department are going to get a bite in the cafeteria at twelve thirty. Why don't you meet us over in the teacher's lounge, and we'll all go over together? We'd love to have you sit with us."

Just like high school, Vera thought, though in high school no one would have professed to *love* to have her sit with them. She had, in reality, spent most of her high school lunch periods hiding in a bathroom stall. Sue's tone and phrasing didn't seem to suggest that Vera had a choice in the matter; the bathroom stall was not going to be an option this time around.

"I'll come by," Vera said weakly.

"It'll be a good opportunity for you to get to know some of the other teachers in the department better," Sue said, "and for them to get to know you. See you then."

Lunch period found Vera seated with nine other English teachers and Sue MacMasters. The women had all greeted her politely, but after a full round of introductions, Vera found that she could not tell her dining companions apart. She recognized Karen Provencher, the eleventh-grade English teacher whom she saw in the hall sometimes, but the others, despite their wide range of ages, all had a similar manner—bright, alert, cool, privileged. The woman sitting next to her, a ninth-grade teacher who looked as though she had just graduated from college, was wearing an earring-and-necklace set that probably cost more than Vera had earned at Dorset Community College in the past year. Vera picked at her salad, willing some of it to disappear. She hated eating in front of people she didn't know very well. She had grown so accustomed to having her meals at the little table in her studio, eating messy foods with barbaric abandon, licking her fingers while downloading TV programs on her laptop.

Sue's insistence that the English department would *love* to have her at lunch had been an overstatement, by Vera's estimation. Once the faculty had looked Vera up and down and asked what college she'd gone to and whom she'd studied with, they seemed utterly finished with her and even started asking Sue, "Have you heard anything about Melanie and the baby yet? Are they going to induce labor?" Melanie was Melanie Belisle, the pregnant teacher whom Vera had replaced.

"Do you have any children, Vera?" the woman sitting across from her said. Before she could curb the irrational response, she felt the same mild sense of affront that she always felt when asked that question. It wasn't that she was sensitive about not having children; rather, she always felt insulted when she was mistaken for someone who *did* have them. "No," she said, "I don't." And maybe some of her irritation had showed in her face because the woman turned to Sue MacMasters and changed the topic altogether.

As the conversation turned to summer vacation plans, the ninth-grade teacher sitting next to Vera said, "Melanie and I used to check in with each other sometimes. I always like to know how my ninth graders are doing as they move forward into tenth grade. You have a lot of my former students now. How do you like them?"

"Oh, I'm impressed with them. They're outspoken and seem to pick up things quickly."

"How is Cecily-Anne St. Aubrey doing? She was a favorite of mine. Melanie's, too. She and Autumn Fullerton are both really exceptional—so wonderfully driven and sensitive. Oh, and of course there's Jamie Friedman, too—she's quite special also. I know Melanie felt bad about having to just up and leave them."

Vera wanted to laugh. She could understand, at least intellectually, why Jamie Friedman would be held up as a model student; her conduct and work ethic were always impeccable. But she found herself hard-pressed to say something equally glowing about the other two girls. "Cecily-Anne and Autumn are a striking pair, aren't they?" she said diplomatically, spearing a sliver of carrot. She wondered if perhaps she had been unfair in her judgments of the two glamorous students, or perhaps Melanie Belisle had seen something she hadn't seen. Thinking for a moment, she asked the teacher next to her, "What about Jensen Willard? Did you have her as a student?"

The teacher wrinkled her brow. "Willard? Oh, no, I don't remember Melanie mentioning her specifically. I believe she transferred to Wallace just this year. On scholarship."

The way the woman said *on scholarship* made Vera decide to push it no further. She kept quiet for the rest of the lunch period, keeping a faint, interested-looking smile on her lips and trying to follow what the other women said to one another. When the women gathered up their plates to return them to the cafeteria line, Sue MacMasters brushed past her, poked her in the arm, and said, "Look at that plate! No wonder she's so skinny!" in a voice loud enough for all the other teachers to hear.

Vera's studio apartment seemed quieter than usual that night. Taking out Jensen Willard's latest journal entry, she glanced at the title—"You Don't Do One Damn Thing the Way You're Supposed To"—and at first thought it was meant as a direct hit, a pointed critique of her classroom methods. Then she remembered that Holden Caulfield's roommate had said those exact words to him. *Interesting title choice,* Vera thought, trying to suspend judgment until she had read more.

You Don't Do One Damn Thing the Way You're Supposed To: Journal Entry #3, by Jensen Willard

Hello again.

I know I'd said I'd make more of an effort to include literary analysis of The Catcher in the Rye *in these journal entries, but I'm having a really hard time focusing on that. Truthfully, I'm still kind of obsessing over the last phone conversation I had with Bret—I've got to make sense of all that first and foremost. But please, if it gets to be too much, just let me know, and I'm sure I won't have a hard time coughing up something else to write about. I can write about anything once you get me started.*

One other thing I've still been thinking a lot about lately is that girl who got murdered. Angela Galvez, the one they found in the Dumpster. She was strangled. Such an ugly word, strangled. *It sounds almost exactly like what it is. Like onomatopoeia. I remember the first day of class, someone brought up Angela, and you looked like someone pooped in your shoe. I guess I can't blame you for not wanting to talk about it. But I hope you can't blame me for not being able to stop thinking about it—for not being able to stop wondering.*

Specifically, I wonder what it's like to be eleven years old and to know someone is killing you. I wonder what an eleven-year-old's last thoughts are as she's dying.

I overheard Chelsea Cutler talking about something her aunt had told her—that Angela had claw marks on her neck, marks from her own nails where she had tried to remove Ritchie Ouelette's hands. And the nails were broken off. She tried to fight, but what chance did she have, being that small and young?

One of her purple shoelaces was missing when they found her. She'd had two laces, one on each shoe, when she left the house, her mother said. Purple laces, and the sneakers were silver. You have to wonder what happened to the other one or why anyone would think that was a good trophy to keep, out of all the trophies one could take.

Vera looked up from her reading. What was it about these lines that didn't sit well with her? It was the word *trophies*, she decided, looking at Jensen's last paragraph again. That was a police word—a word she didn't think Jensen would know to use in this context. Then again, how well did she really know Jensen? *Just because I didn't peg her as someone who watches* CSI *or reads crime novels doesn't mean that such things aren't known to her,* Vera told herself, and brought herself back to where she'd left off in the journal.

I knew Angela a little bit. That is, I babysat her and her little brother, Jared, once. Annabel used to do it on a regular basis, but one night she wanted to go to a roller-skating party and recommended me to the Galvezes instead. Big mistake. I'm an awful babysitter. It's not that I mean any harm, but I always end up being way too lenient because I figure, how is a few hours of leniency going to hurt anyone? And Angela was really too big for a babysitter anyway, but her parents were overprotective. Fat lot of good that overprotectiveness did for Angela in the end.

The Galvez kids were brats the day I sat with them. I know you're not supposed to say a dead little girl was a brat, but it's true, and that doesn't mean I'm not sorry about how she died. These kids wanted to play Truth or Dare out in the yard, and at one point Angela dared me to take off my bra and throw it up into the branches of this oak tree they have out back. So I did it. I didn't let them see my bare chest or anything—I turned around and maneuvered the bra out from under my shirt and pitched it in the air. You could tell they weren't expecting that I'd actually do it, which is why I did it. But then the bra was stuck hanging from a high tree branch, and the kids apparently told their parents about it later, because Mrs. Galvez called my mother that night and said, "Your daughter is the worst babysitter I've ever had, and I'm going to tell all my friends who have children." Which was kind of a relief, because I've never had a good babysitting experience yet.

Even though I wasn't sorry to lose a prospective babysitting job, I was sorry to lose the money. And I don't need Mrs. Galvez running around talking about me to half the town. For a little while, I really hated that kid.

Still, I thought about sending the Galvezes a card when Angela died. Just because they don't like me doesn't mean I shouldn't let them know I was sorry for what had happened to their daughter, but when I looked at the sympathy cards in the supermarket, they all seemed wrong. All these pictures of birds flying in clouds with gilded letters spelling out inspirational quotes about dying and the afterlife. Angela's death didn't seem to fit a card like that. Even my mother said, "Oh, we should send a card," but I don't think she ever sent one. Maybe she had the same problem I did picking one out.

This is making me sad. Sadder. Maybe it's time for me to talk about Bret now. But first, a snack. I feel like peanut butter crackers. Don't go anywhere.

Back again.

Here's the thing: I don't really have an outlet for talking about Bret outside of this journal. Sometimes I wish I still had Annabel to confide in, because she's pretty experienced with boyfriends and would probably have an opinion about what's going on. I'd talk to my mother, but she's so protective of me that she'd just wind up getting angry at Bret even if he hadn't really done *anything.*

So, journal it is. Journal and, by extension, you. I bet you feel really privileged.

I have one more Bret story, and after that I promise I'll shut up. I'm curious to know what you'll think about this one because it's about a teacher, sort of, and since you're one, too, it's possible that you might have a particular read on this. Then again, maybe not. Maybe you're not even reading this. I can't say I'd blame you if you weren't. I'm pretty sure the last English teacher I had, Mrs. Belisle, never read a damned word I wrote. One time I turned in a writing assignment that was nothing but word vomit and gibberish, and all she did was put one of her check marks on the top of it, like always.

I went to visit Bret at Columbia one time, this past October. I really liked it there. Here, I feel like people stare at me all the time. But there, on campus, no one would give me the time of day, and I kind of liked that anonymity.

It was a big deal to take a bus to New York all by myself, especially because I had to change buses in Boston—I'm surprised my parents even let me do it. I drank Bret's supply of vodka and orange juice and got violently ill the night I arrived, and all the girls in Jay Hall (that's his dorm) kept coming up and cooing about how cute it was that he had a girlfriend in high school. The next day, once I was sobered up, we went to go visit one of his professors at his apartment off campus, on Riverside Drive by the park. You might find it interesting to know—maybe you already do *know—that J. D. Salinger's family lived on Riverside Drive, too, just two buildings from where the professor lives now. I made it a point to walk past it and take a good look, but to tell you the truth, it just looks like any other building. That's one of the strangest things about New York, in my opinion; nothing ever looks all that special or distinguished. Even the supposedly special things blend in with everything else.*

This professor, whose name is Dr. Louis Rose, had taught a summer humanities program at Dartmouth two years before, the same one Bret had attended as part of a Gifted and Talented program; I guess Dr. Rose was part of the reason why Bret had wanted to go to Columbia. He'd kept in touch with him the whole time and wanted to follow him wherever he went. He's taken classes with him two terms in a row now. Kind of a man-crush, if you ask me. I'm not exactly sure what Dr. Rose was getting out of it in return, other than adulation.

"He's completely brilliant," Bret was telling me as we crossed Broadway on our way to the professor's apartment. "He's written two books about Edmund Spenser, who wrote The Faerie Queene. *He's a Spenserian scholar. It's pretty cool if you think about it."*

"You didn't have to put it that way."

"What way?"

"'Edmund Spenser, who wrote The Faerie Queene.*' I know what he wrote."*

"Have you read it?"

"Parts of it," I said, which isn't technically untrue. I have this big poetry anthology that I got at a yard sale once, and I'm pretty sure that an excerpt from it is in there. While I can't say I've exactly read it, it's possible that my eye has fallen on a phrase or two as I've flipped around in the book looking for other things.

I knew I was supposed to feel flattered that Bret had deemed me worthy of meeting the famed Spenserian scholar Dr. Rose. And I was flattered, I have to admit; I felt as though Bret wanted to show me off, for once. Once we got to the apartment—which seemed pretty small to me, for a professor's apartment—Dr. Rose turned out to be this wizened old man who had little boils on the back of his head popping out between tufts of thinning white hair. He was wearing an untucked shirt and cotton pants and loafers with no socks, which didn't make him look very scholarly to me. But I still felt ill at ease, meeting him. Like some country-mouse kid who had turned up uninvited at the door. He looked me up and down and then back and forth and sideways, then looked away and started talking to Bret about books.

He went to one of the shelves where his books were—his apartment had wall-to-wall shelves installed, which I admit made me jealous—and took down one book that looked even more ancient than the rest. "You would not believe what I paid for this," he said to Bret. "One of the oldest known copies left on earth, and now it's mine." He opened it lovingly, paused, and read aloud, 'Strange thing, me seemed, to see a beast so wild / So goodly won, with her own will beguiled.' That's from Amoretti, *as I'm sure you know."*

I was pretty sure Bret didn't *know, but he nodded with such vigor that I thought his head might snap off the end of his neck.*

Aside from books, Dr. Rose had a lot of plants in his apartment. I was sitting in a wooden rocking chair, sort of apart from Dr. Rose's armchair and Bret on the chair beside him, and all I could do was look at these plants. When people have too many plants in their home, it makes me think the plant owner's trying to hide something. I like the idea of camouflage, hidden things, mystery—even plain old distractions—but in this particular case I was waiting for a tiger or something to jump out from all that greenery.

"Bret, I still sometimes think about the students in the summer workshop we had together," Dr. Rose was saying. "Do you remember Charles, the boy with the long ponytail? The one who

always wrote poems about hitchhiking? I wonder whatever became of him. His work always had such interesting recklessness."

I thought the phrase "whatever became of him" was odd. I doubted that this Charles guy was old enough to have become *anything yet.*

"I heard he got early acceptance at Wesleyan," Bret said. "I don't know if he ended up going there."

"I always worry about boys like Charles going by the wayside. They so often do, when they're so clever and so scattered. That kind is easily led astray if they don't find some structure in college." And I swear Dr. Rose looked at me then. Had he decided, just from a glance, that I was scattered? That I was easily led astray? Or was he warning me of something?

Then—horrors—the famed Dr. Rose turned to me. "Bret tells me you're something of a writer yourself."

I wasn't expecting that. I'm not a fidgety person by nature, but I found myself wanting to fidget in the worst way. "I wouldn't say that. I do like to write sometimes."

"Who are your influences?"

"Influences? Oh, I don't write very well," I said, evading the question. "I guess I'm influenced by . . . anything dark. I just write, that's all." My voice sounded dumb even to my own ears. Schoolgirlish.

"You just write," Dr. Rose marveled, as though I had said something in a foreign language. Why can't I ever express myself properly?

But lucky me—Dr. Rose let me off the hook and started directing all of his comments at Bret again. He was going on about some poetry text he's translating from the French, from some poet I've never heard of and whose name I can't recall now. He took out some papers and started reading one of the translated poems aloud; Dr. Rose has one of those very theatrical "I'm reading capital-P Poetry" voices, and I was so busy hearing his meaningful pauses that I didn't really catch what the poem was all about. Something about a man seeing a woman whom he used to sleep with in Paris, only it was years later and he didn't find her attractive anymore.

"It speaks to the nature of lust and the waning of lust that comes with age or with settling," Dr. Rose said after he was finished. "I wouldn't call it complacency, but I do see it as settling for a more traditional, grown-up path. You, Bret, are still in the age of lust, are you not?"

Bret laughed. When he laughs, he always sounds as though he's dislodging something from his nose. "Believe me, if you aren't now," Dr. Rose went on, "just wait a little while. Someday you'll meet a real woman, and after that things will never be the same."

I felt as though I'd been slapped. As though I'd been written off as "not a real woman," just some dismissed kid, someone of no real gender and of no real consequence to anyone. After that comment of his, I didn't listen so much to what he was saying anymore. He said something about his photography hobby, and what he'd done with his garden the summer before, and how he was going to get his kitchen remodeled and take a trip to Reykjavik soon, and all I could think was, Who cares? Who cares about stuck-up people who have too much money to piss away on trips and kitchens? *When Bret and I were getting ready to leave, Dr. Rose surprised me by saying, "Jensen . . ." (He pronounced it Jen-*seen, *for some reason). "Jensen. May I take your picture before you go?"*

He didn't ask to take Bret's, or to take one of Bret and me together. This was just about the most catastrophic thing he could have asked of me. I don't even think I can begin to tell you how much I hate having my picture taken. The results are disastrous; I always end up looking like a squat little gnome with one wonky eye and a tense mouth. But I let him take my picture, because I felt like I'd screwed up enough already and wanted to be on good behavior in front of Bret. As he snapped the shutter, I could almost see myself through Dr. Rose's camera—a pasty, surly girl in oversized clothing and shoes that were falling apart. It was a really crappy thing to have to see.

As Bret and I started walking back to his dorm, passing by a guy sprawled out on one the park benches who looked like he might have been dead, he asked me, "What did you think of Dr. Rose?"

"He was a little pretentious."

"You're judgmental."

"A person can make judgments without being judgmental, you know."

"Well, you didn't come off as all that impressive yourself," Bret said. "You didn't present yourself as well as I'd hoped." And I didn't say anything to him for a long time after that, because I hadn't realized it was a test, even though I had already known, on some level, that I had failed.

A couple of weeks later, when I was back here in Maine, Bret called to tell me Dr. Rose had developed the photo he'd taken and given it to him: "It's not the most flattering photo, but it does look like you. I'll send it along with my next letter."

So. That leads me to this thought. And a pathetic thought it is, too—a pathetic note to end this journal on.

I don't think Bret realizes how much I've come to depend on the occasional kind word from him. How much I depend on praise or a compliment or a phone call or a letter. Nor can he understand how much it hurts when I don't get these things. If he knew, would he act differently? Would he give me more or give me nothing at all? I know it must seem beyond stupid, me starting off thinking he was repulsive and now needing his acknowledgment all the time and feeling like I'll die if I don't get it. Sometimes I feel like I almost hate Bret, and other times I think I want to have about twenty of his children, even though I really would rather hurl myself off a bridge than get knocked up even once. I realize none of this makes the least bit of sense. Does it make any sense to you?

Vera finished reading Jensen's entry. By the time she had reached the end of it, lying there on her mattress, she felt mixed emotions. The first was a sense of disappointment, knowing that Jensen had this weakness in her—the weakness of needing to be liked and cared for. *But it isn't fair to be disappointed,* Vera reproached herself. It wasn't fair for her to expect more from Jensen, a fifteen-year-old, than she felt for herself.

The second emotion, empathy, came from the nurturing part of her, which wished to counsel the girl—to tell her that yes, her feelings did make sense. Vera had been warned, when going through the multiple-interview process for her position at Wallace, that it was important to not act as a therapist to the students. "Many of them are bright, and with intelligence comes emotional problems sometimes," Sue MacMasters had said, wiggling around in her seat to lean in closer to Vera. Almost conspiratorially, she'd added: "Some of them are on medication. If you see any of the red flags we talked about, you must refer the student to one of the guidance counselors. Don't attempt to take on these problems yourself." Vera had nodded, privately irked by the way Sue's eyes had widened when she had uttered the phrase *on medication*. It was clear that this was something far outside the head of the English department's personal experience. Bizarre, Vera thought, that some of the faculty seemed more sheltered than the students.

She stood up and stretched, as though to shrug off Jensen's journal entry and this admonition of Sue MacMasters's. It was getting dark, and outside her studio window she could hear people in conversation as they walked by—people dressed up to go out for a Friday night. She found herself wanting to go out, too. She called her old friend Caroline on the off chance that she might be able to slip away for the evening. But Caroline was always so busy; she had recently launched her own literary magazine with the assistance of some local poets, and she'd had her first baby five months before. Vera had not actually been able to get her out of the house since then, and while common sense told her that it was hard for a busy mother to find child care, she suspected, rather childishly, that Caroline was so in love with her infant daughter that there was no love left for Vera. She got Caroline's answering machine, left what she hoped was a upbeat-sounding message, and looked out the window some more. *Another lost friend,* she thought, appropriating the phrase from something she had seen in Jensen Willard's writing.

More couples passed her window: young women in high heels that clattered precariously against Dorset's cobblestone streets and the shaggy young men who hovered at their sides. She decided to go to Pearl's by herself, have a drink or two, and head straight home.

***

A jazz ensemble played at the bar that night. The band was competent, if not exactly good, and Vera found herself singing a little to herself as she sat on her stool, humming and purring into her gin and tonic and then, changing it up, into her whiskey and Coke. When she had been a little girl, her father had liked listening to jazz and big band classics on one of the AM radio stations; whenever he drove her somewhere, this music played in the car, and though Vera went through a stage where she pretended she thought it was corny—some of the crooning harmonies, she'd said, sounded like people mooing—she loved those songs and had liked sharing them with her father.

"Singing and smiling," a voice next to her said. "Somebody's happy. Or is it the whiskey?"

Vera looked over to her left guardedly. A man had taken the bar stool beside hers. He seemed tall, judging by the way he hunched his shoulders and upper torso over the bar, and he had a long, not-unhandsome face. He reminded her of someone, but she could not think of whom. "You *look* like someone," she informed him, and when she put two and two together, she sucked in her breath a little. *Ritchie Ouelette.*

"I *look* like someone? Who might that be?"

"Jimmy Stewart," she said, recovering quickly.

"Jimmy Stewart, eh? That's a new one." The long-faced man stared at her openly for a while as she stirred the straw in the last of her drink. "You're very beautiful," he said. She ordered another drink.

She guessed the man to not be scandalously younger than she was—perhaps in his early thirties, which was not outside of the realm of decency. The man said he was up from Louisiana for the weekend, visiting a friend. They exchanged some banter above the sounds of the band and began to look at each other in a speculative way. They wove in and out of the bar to take cigarette breaks outside, though Vera had quit smoking a few years before; she borrowed his cigarettes and his matches. Wasn't there something in *The Catcher in the Rye* about Holden Caulfield lighting matches—some beautiful line? She couldn't remember. She leaned against the brick facade of the bar and closed her eyes as she drew the smoke into her lungs.

"You okay?" the bouncer doing door duty asked at one point.

"Yes," Vera said. She wasn't exactly sure if Jimmy Stewart was standing next to her anymore. She was aware only of cool air on her face and a humming in her ears from the music on the other side of the door.

What happened during the rest of the evening was something she had to piece together the next day. There had been more drinks, of course, and Vera had the faintest memory of being away from the bar, in a car heading to 7-Eleven for beer; she remembered the man who looked like Jimmy Stewart keeping his hand on her leg as he drove. She noticed a ring on his hand, and she heard the man's voice saying, "My wife and I have an understanding." She remembered, next, lying on a beach—whose idea had it been to go to a beach at the beginning of March?—and she could see the man putting his pants on, his mouth twisted up as though he wanted to laugh. "I'm cold," Vera remembered saying, sitting up in the sand with her arms wrapped around her legs—and then, when he didn't get the hint, she had whined, "Come hold me. I'm cold." Reluctantly, the man came and hunkered down next to her in the sand. He held her as if it were a duty, the way a young bachelor who doesn't want children might react when urged to hold a friend's infant. She was wearing her dress, but her tights were clutched in a ball in her hand. That was the last mental picture she had. The rest went blank, up to a point.

The next thing she remembered, she was walking home in the direction of her apartment. How she had ended up on foot was a puzzle; the beach was a twenty-minute drive from her place, so it was possible that Jimmy Stewart had either ditched her or, more likely, dropped her off somewhere at her behest. She always enjoyed a walk when she'd reached that level of intoxication. The wind on her flushed cheeks always felt good, and in such instances she liked to imagine her legs chugging along like forceful little pistons: *left-right-left.*

She remembered walking through Dorset Park, a shortcut. This was atypical and, she imagined, indicative of exactly how drunk she was; normally she avoided the park at night, preferring the safety of the well-lit sidewalk, but the drinks she'd consumed must have given her some bravura. Part of the reason why the park was to be avoided, she thought, was because she could sometimes hear a man in there, whistling from the deepest recesses of the trees—a whistle that was sometimes fluent and complex and sometimes staccato and repetitive. She took this to be a code—a drug deal in progress, maybe, or a male prostitute soliciting clients. Things to avoid, at any rate.

She did not remember hearing the whistler during this particular walk home in the dark. When asked about it later, she could recall seeing or hearing no one. No one, that is, until she came upon the figure under the tree.

At first she hadn't known it was a figure, hadn't seen it as such. It was fabric that she noticed first—fabric of skirts so voluminous that she thought she was seeing someone's tarp, bunched and abandoned on the ground. Then she realized she was seeing the traditional dress worn by Somali refugees. It was not unheard of to find a Somali sleeping on a park bench or even in the grass, though Vera could not ever recall seeing a woman in that condition; it was the men who passed out there, the wiry young men who'd had too much to drink.

She was inclined to hurry on past, not wanting to meddle and not wanting to be hounded for spare change if the woman under the tree happened to notice her pass by. Yet something about the way the woman was sitting made Vera take a second look.

Closer now, Vera could see that the woman was not *sitting* under the tree, as she had first thought. She was in a crouching position, with her back against the tree trunk; her skirts were hiked up to midthigh, creating the bulky silhouette of cloth Vera had seen from afar. The woman's knees were slightly parted, almost splayed, in the posture of childbirth; she thought about a student she'd had once, a boy from the Sudan, whose name, Tharjiath, spoke to a literal truth, translating roughly to "he who was born under a tree." And that was exactly how he had been born, as his mother stopped working in the fields long enough to push him out into the world—a story so cheerfully recounted in one of Tharjiath's compositions that Vera had never forgotten it.

But this woman, the woman in the crouching position, was not giving birth. Vera knew it even before she saw that the woman's head covering had been half pulled off and twisted around her neck and before she saw the improbable angle at which her neck lolled. *The woman was not giving birth.*

Nor was she even a woman. She was a girl. A girl Vera knew.

A passage from the Rainer Maria Rilke's *Sonnets to Orpheus* came to her: sonnet no. 2, which she had memorized and written an entire analysis of at Princeton:

She was almost a girl and forth she leaped
From this harmonious joy of song and lyre,
Shining through her springtime veils and clear,
She made herself a bed in my ear
And slept in me.

The girl, this almost-girl, was not asleep. This Vera knew. She had seen dead people only in photos before—her family believed in brisk, efficient cremations, no open caskets for any of them—but there was no mistaking death when she saw it in person.

Fully aware of her surroundings all at once, Vera reached into her purse for her cell phone and called 911.

Later, she would wonder why her self-preservation and survivor instincts hadn't kicked in. Surely it had crossed her mind that whoever had strangled her student Sufia Ahmed could be lurking somewhere nearby and that she herself might be in harm's way. Most women in her position, she supposed, would have run like hell and called for help once assured of her own safety; still, she didn't like to think she had been heroic for not running. Heroics had nothing to do with it. When the 911 dispatcher had asked her, "Is she breathing? Can you tell?" Vera had remembered saying, with a pleading note in her voice, "I don't think so. I don't want to get any closer to her. Is that okay?" A heroic person would never respond like that.

She would not get closer, but she would not leave her, either. She stayed with her because Sufia was her responsibility now, more so than ever, at least until the authorities took over. When she saw the flashing lights of cop cars entering the park and heard the ambulance not far behind them, she waved them down, herding them in like a traffic conductor.

"Hurry," she heard herself say, her own throat sounding constricted. "Hurry, hurry."

She stood off to the side only when the cops bent over the body and checked it, uselessly, for a pulse.

Vera stayed with Sufia even after the police cars and the EMTs had arrived. Sufia's eyes, no longer soft and liquid, seemed to bulge in Vera's direction, following her wherever she went, as though it were

Vera alone, and not these men and women who knelt beside her with cameras and evidence bags, who could make a difference. The officers pulled Vera off to the side, creating a wall with their bodies, trying to stand a little taller so that she could not see Sufia over their shoulders, but she still could *feel* the girl's eyes as she began to answer questions as best as she could. And the statement she kept coming back to—over and over and over—was not an answer, but a lamentation:

She's one of mine. She's one of mine. You have to do something; she's one of mine.

Chapter Five

Vera woke up in her own bed at about ten o'clock in the morning, desperately having to use the bathroom, and the soreness she felt brought some of the previous evening back to her. Intense self-loathing roiled in her stomach, followed closely by a need to vomit. She leaned over the toilet bowl and attempted to heave, and when that didn't work, she stuck her fingers down her throat until some of the leftover alcohol evacuated her stomach, watery and tart. Still wearing the clothes she had worn out to the bar, she now saw that her dress was inside out, and the bra she'd worn under it was missing. Her favorite bra. *What an impression I must have made on the cops,* Vera thought, and then, on the heels of that: *What a stupid thing to think.*

She felt ill, hungover, demoralized, and frightened—but her predominant feeling was one of numbness. The encounter with the man at the bar—the one who'd reminded her, at first, of Ritchie Ouelette—had been the cause of all the problems, she decided. Her irresponsible behavior, intended as no more than a sloughing off, a celebration of having survived a full workweek, had instead become a humiliating personal failure and a tragedy for another young woman's family. She saw the night's beginning and its ending as connected, a causal chain in which she was glaringly at fault.

She wondered if the story had hit the news yet. Vera felt that she needed to see it spelled out in order to believe it. Reading a news bulletin about Sufia might make things easier for her, might help her to remember her as a person, as her own quiet, responsible student and not just a dead body in the park. She wanted to see a photo of her—a photo of her from *before*, to cancel out the other image she had. Typing in search term after search term into her online browser window—*Sufia Ahmed, Maine homicide, Dorset Park body*—she found that there was no coverage about the dead girl. Was it too soon, or was the local media planning to sweep the story under the rug? *If it had been a pretty local white girl or well-connected kid like Angela Galvez,* Vera wondered, *would the story be all over the place by now?*

With her laptop still fired up, Vera ran a bath and settled into it to scour the beach sand out of her hair and eyes; she had a feeling she would be picking sand off herself and from the corners of her studio for a while. Even a change of her grit-covered sheets and a thorough sweep of her floor could not rid her of the last of it. This seemed nothing more than an added injury, a secondary source of despair. She lay back in the bath and remembered—quite out of nowhere—an earlier time that hadn't felt so long ago: a time when her life's ambition had been nothing more than to live with her parents through their dotage, haunting their upstairs rooms and acting as a hand servant to the end of their days, or to the end of hers if that came first. It had seemed such a quiet, focused, simple way to live. A better way, come to think of it.

Out of the tub and dressed in clean clothes, her hair still sopping down her back, Vera refreshed her Internet search—still nothing in the news. She logged out and, after some thought, went into her documents and pulled up the file called Manuscript.

I ought to retitle that, she thought, *so as not to confuse it with any future work*—but then, thinking some more, she realized that this thought was too optimistic, too suggestive of prolificacy. The Ivan Schlosser manuscript was the only manuscript she had even thought about since finishing graduate school. She had been stuck on it the way an old record needle sticks to a warp in a groove.

In her dark and self-punishing frame of mind, she thought last night's gruesome discovery might enable her to work on her book about Ivan Schlosser. A gift in disguise? No, Sufia's death wasn't a gift—her student's slack, dead face imprinted in her memory was anything *but* a gift—but at least she wrote better, she thought, from such dark places.

For Vera, the appeal of the Schlosser case was personal. Not only had Schlosser been a local legend for a time, but also his confession had diffused her connection to Heidi Duplessis. Following his confession, her fellow classmates forgot that they'd ever had Vera on their radar. But Vera didn't forget. In a strange way, she thought of Schlosser as her rescuer, as someone who had swooped in and saved her from further harm. If not for Schlosser, she might still be haunted by Heidi of the white teeth and tanned face, popular, easygoing Heidi.

Vera was sure Heidi had never known who she was, though they had gone to the same school. Heidi had been oblivious to the mousy freshman who'd positioned herself behind a speaker at a school dance, glowering at her as she danced with Peter Mercier. She'd had no idea how high Vera's hatred had risen as she watched her press closer to Peter; as they shuffled around the dance floor in that awkward, swaying slow dance, she could not fathom the depths with which Vera hated every inch of her, cataloging her hatred of the girl from head to toe, from the tips of Heidi's lightly teased bangs to the soles of her pink Reebok sneakers. She hated her even more as she watched Peter's hand rest on the small of her back and hover just above the curve of her behind. No, Heidi had had no idea that Vera Lundy, freshman, had summoned as much venom and ill will as she could and had even wished her dead. Wished her *gone*. She couldn't have guessed that Vera had written as much, in the notebook she carried around all through high school: "If I could find a way to get rid of Heidi Duplessis, I would. I think first I'd duct-tape her to her car, and then I'd shave off her hair with a pair of clippers. If I could kill her and get away with it, I don't think I'd hesitate."

Heidi's body had been recovered in the Androscoggin River six weeks after her disappearance. Dismembered parts of Schlosser's other victims—Rosemary Trang, the fourteen-year-old immigrant who lived near Durham, New Hampshire, and Margot Pooler, the twelve-year-old from Vermont—had been found earlier that year; at least he had kept Heidi intact, and he later said to the police, "It was because she was so pretty. I could tell from the way she looked at me she was a nice girl, and I felt kinda bad about having to go through with killing her." Not even serial killers could resist the charms of Heidi Duplessis.

Schlosser died in prison not long after being incarcerated; Vera wanted to understand his motives, to demystify the story that had dogged her through her teen years and had ultimately let her off the hook, albeit with unanswered questions. Thirty-two pages into her manuscript, she had achieved little in the way of demystification; she had, however, outlined a lovely narrative describing Durham, New Hampshire—the scene of the first crime—with the intent to have this bucolic scene disrupted by the description of the first murder itself.

Vera sat at her table with her laptop open and her disorganized jumble of notes in her lap for a long time, staring at her description of Durham. She could not think of another word to add to it. She kept seeing Sufia Ahmed in her mind, Sufia with her skirts bunched up and her head twisted back—the hijab used as a ligature to strangle her.

Ligature—*now there,* Vera thought, *is a good* CSI *word if ever there was one.* It had been a while since she'd seen that particular word, but Vera's mind attached it to a document she knew well. She got up, went into the milk crate in her closet, and dug out the manila envelope containing documents, notes, and photocopies that she'd thought might be useful in the creation of the Schlosser book. She took out the copy of Margot Pooler's autopsy that she'd acquired two years before—the Maine police had never let her have a copy of Heidi's—and her eye fell to a paragraph in the middle of the first page:

> *Removal of the underpants tied around the neck of the deceased (known throughout this report as Ligature A) showed that the victim had been nearly decapitated. Accompanying hemorrhage suggests premortem strangulation may have occurred beforehand. The victim's face was congested, and there was tongue bite. The upper one-third of the larynx was still attached to the head.*
>
> *Evidence Collected:*
>
> 1. *One white "Peanuts" comic strip T-shirt, child's size 10.*
> 2. *Green shorts with drawstring tie, size Small.*
> 3. *Velcro-style sneakers with pink and silver detail.*
> 4. *One pair white ankle socks with small pink pom-poms at the top.*
> 5. *Pink child's underpants with "Thursday" stitched on them.*
> 6. *One turquoise ring.*
> 7. *Samples of Blood (type B negative), Bile, and Tissue (heart, lung, kidney, liver, and spleen).*

8. *Seventeen (17) swabs from various body locations.*
9. *Fourteen (14) autopsy photographs.*
10. *One postmortem CT scan.*
11. *One postmortem MRI.*

The image of the days-of-the-week underpants that had served as a ligature hit her hard, but picturing the little girl's Velcro sneakers and pom-pom ankle socks was somehow worse. She thought of Sufia's feet and realized she had not noticed what she had worn for shoes. This bothered her. She should have paid attention. How could she not have noticed what the dead girl had on her feet?

She realized also that she didn't know if a ligature had been used in the Angela Galvez murder; she couldn't recall seeing any mention of it in the clippings she'd collected—but she recalled no mention of manual strangulation, either. If Angela had been strangled by one of her own items of clothing—an ad hoc ligature, created on the spot—then that might mean something. Whoever had killed the Galvez girl might have been the same disorganized type of killer who'd snuffed out the life of Sufia Ahmed, using what was available to him instead of coming prepared.

Only connect, Vera told herself. *Only connect. Because somewhere in those connections might lie the truth.*

The manuscript cast aside, Vera realized she needed to get out of her apartment. If she took a bus into Portland, she could visit the city's large public library with its extensive periodicals section, and there, with any luck, she might dig up more findings about Angela Galvez. Maybe, for that matter, there was something on one of today's papers that addressed Sufia's death as well. She unzipped the wheeled suitcase she used for school and took out three folders stuffed with student writings; she put these in her tote bag, stabbed her feet into a pair of black flats, and put on her coat and hat.

During her bus ride, surrounded by the usual mixture of elderly people strapped into wheelchairs, too-young mothers with squalling babies on their laps, and kids heading into town to the methadone clinic, Vera became industrious and took out her student papers, reading their contents and jotting notes so as not to have to look at anyone near her. She was glad she had thought to bring them along.

First in her pile was Martha True's journal entry, which began thusly:

> *Now that I've read the first few chapters of* The Catcher in the Rye, *what mostly comes to mind is that my mom and dad might kill me if they knew I was reading this. Up until last year, before I enrolled at Wallace, we were Pentecostals. This is a strict religion that has many rules about what's acceptable and what isn't. For example, I wasn't supposed to cut my hair or wear revealing clothing. My parents strayed from the church because my father had a personal grievance with the pastor. Since then, they have been a lot less strict about things and even decided to send me to a regular school. However, they still don't use profanity or drink alcohol, and I think they would flip if they knew I was reading a novel where the kid uses profanity, drinks in bars, and discusses sexual content. I am not really bothered by any of this myself, but sometimes I feel sorry for Holden. He might be better off if he had a little faith. Though I don't attend church now, I'm still involved in a youth group, and ultimately I believe God is good. I know He must be good if he can find it in His heart to love me and my imperfections.*

Vera moved the page to the back of the pile and gave a little start when she saw the name at the top of the next sheet. Sufia Ahmed, speaking to her from the dead:

> *I look up a little about Catcher in the Rye on the internets because sometimes the "slang" is hard to understand. My English is good if it is proper English, and I read it better than I speak or write. My best English area is grammar and punctuations. When I take the ESL I was told those are best, and I am still working on Vocabulary. I use a translation program on the internets sometimes which helps. To me this book is confusing sometimes because of its depiction of Americans. When I live in Somalia the teenage boys and girls do not act like Holden. There is wars in my country and terrible things and hunger and people then grow up very fast. We do not just get to be teenagers. Now in the States it is better, though it is hard for my parents. My father was a Doctor in Somalia and now he does not have the right training, but it is better for me because I will get trainings I need in the future.*

Close to tears, Vera read the entry again. She was touched by Sufia's comment "we do not just get to be teenagers." Quiet, lovely, pacifistic Sufia, who had thought Vera's comments about murderers had not been *right*. Sufia, who had written so lovingly of her parents' work ethic, how proud they were of her for being a daughter who carried on their values. She thought of the community Sufia had belonged to: the neighborhood Somalis who all thought of one another as family, congregating on sidewalks and calling down to friends on the street from their upper-story porches or their high apartment windows. They kept up their sense of family and community even after being relocated to alleged havens like the mostly white Dorset and Portland; only the children assimilated quickly, craving distance from their recent past.

You don't just get to be a teenager anymore, Vera thought, putting the sheaf of papers back in her tote bag. *I'm sorry, Sufia.*

Ejected from the bus near Monument Square, Vera dodged the slow-moving tourists who seemed to be present year-round and headed to the library to look at the newspaper collections. The reference area was quiet save for one elderly man who had fallen asleep in one of the chairs in the Reading Room; his breath came out as a soft grunt as she turned pages as quietly as she could, not wanting to disturb him across the room. Though the newspapers dated only a few months back, they already smelled musty. The word *strangled* in all of its permutations—*strangled*, *strangling*, and *strangulation*—kept jumping out at her from the articles:

> **. . . Galvez, 11, was found strangled to death behind the Dumpster that is located behind the Buck Street Laundromat.**
>
> **. . . first homicide in Dorset in 35 years, and the first strangulation death of a minor in Maine since the Ivan Schlosser killings of the 1970s and '80s.**
>
> **. . . the medical examiner estimates that the strangling took place between 7 and 8 p.m. She was last seen riding her bicycle up and down her street at 6:30, and she was due back indoors at 7. The bicycle was later recovered in Moyer Woods.**

Vera stopped to take a longer look at one of the articles near the end of the pile, an article with a title that caught her interest: SUSPECT ARRESTED IN GALVEZ SLAYING.

Vera knew as well as anyone that newspapers often got things wrong. Even the headline wasn't exactly right; the word *slaying* had a bloody connotation, and Angela Galvez had not bled—at least not outwardly. She examined Ritchie Ouelette's mug shot at length, and while Vera knew you couldn't judge a killer by his face—history had presented many baby-faced killers and would present many more—she did not think she was looking into the eyes of someone who would strangle an eleven-year-old girl to death.

Not for the first time, she wished she could talk to Ritchie Ouelette. If only the police would let her meet with him! But when she had called the state prison to ask if such a thing could be arranged—describing herself as a writer who was thinking of writing a profile of Ouelette—the person over the phone had said, "What, you want to touch his hand on the other side of the glass or something? That's only in Hollywood movies, ma'am."

She wished, for that matter, that she could see Ritchie's hands in the newspaper picture. One might be able to tell something about a strangler, Vera thought, by looking at his hands. She knew from seeing televised glimpses of Ouelette being led in and out of a courtroom that the suspect's hands were slim and almost girlish, hands befitting an accountant. Whoever had strangled Angela Galvez—especially if it had been a manual strangulation—would need hands strong enough to break the hyoid bone. Hands unafraid to get dirty. Vera looked down at her own hands, contemplatively furling and unfurling her short, stubby, ink-stained fingers, looking at her close-bitten fingernails and the little rims of dirt that somehow always besmirched them.

She put the newspapers back, since there was no one there to tell her not to, and took one last look at the copy of the local paper that someone had left spread-eagled on a table. Not one word of Sufia Ahmed's demise. She couldn't imagine why not, unless she had dreamt the whole episode in the park. To have believed a dream like that would mean that she'd lost her mind.

Was that possible? She dug her wallet out of her purse and took out the business card of Officer Gerard Babineau, one of the policemen whom she'd greeted at the scene—a stout, girthy man with sad, dark eyes. She remembered talking to him, remembered him asking her to call him if she thought of anything else to add to her statement of finding one of her girls under the tree. All real, every last bit of it, and the holes in her memory didn't make it any less so. *I'm not crazy,* she thought, looking down at the card, *and here is my proof. Here is the proof in my hand.*

The streets along Portland's fishing piers in the area known as the Old Port were populated with small, independent shops with wares that catered to out-of-staters and to residents who were willing to shell out a little extra money to jump on the "buy local" trend. Stopping to look in the windows of boutiques and import stores, Vera wondered if she looked as disoriented as she felt. As she lingered at the window of a new wine bar, a gray-haired gentleman in a fisherman's cap stopped and said, "It's a nice place. Have you been inside?" She hurried away as though she had nearly been caught shoplifting. She didn't slow down until she came upon the old discount shop where she sometimes liked to buy marked-down frozen dinners and frozen pizzas—the same food she'd been buying since she was a young college girl. She had to laugh when Facebook friends of hers—most of whom were people she knew only remotely—posted descriptions or even photos of what gourmet concoctions they were serving their families on a particular night. Was that part of being an adult—eating healthier, more expensive, more adventurous food and telling the world about it? Was this part of where Vera had gone wrong?

Her red handcart filled, she stood in line behind a woman paying with food stamps, a woman whom the middle-aged cashier seemed to know well; they were deep in conversation, ignoring Vera and the others who gradually fell in line behind her. Vera shifted her weight from foot to foot and tried to keep a pleasant expression on her face, one that wouldn't reveal the impatience she felt, when she heard the words ". . . another one got killed." She looked up sharply.

"Yeah," the woman with the food stamps was saying, "it's not just Portland that's getting bad. There was another one of 'em shot a few months ago right next to the apartment where my niece lives, near the old Italian sandwich shop that shut down. And it was drugs. It's always drugs, with them. Always drugging and raping and killing. They took a retarded girl off the street and brought her to a hotel room and just raped her and raped her until they were done with her. And this goes on *every day*. Don't think the police don't know what goes on."

"It's different over where they live," the cashier said, waving her hand as though Africa were somewhere on the other side of the street. "Back there they live like animals, and then they come over here and get help from the state. Get good jobs, too. I wouldn't mind a little help from the state myself, you know? But they say I make too much money. Huh! Minimum wage is too much, I guess!"

Another one of 'em. Vera knew they were talking about the Somali refugees; she had heard such things expressed before, quite vocally, from Maine residents of a certain mind-set. To such people each Somali was just *another one of them*, and the dead girl in the park was just *another one who got killed*. It was not surprising that news of the death had leaked before the news stories even appeared; that was the small-town grapevine at its finest and most functional. But Vera was nonetheless shaken, and not a little offended, to the point where she was tempted to abandon her frozen foods and leave the store.

Instead, she spoke up before she could stop herself.

"Few of them get good jobs," she said to the cashier. "They get the jobs most other people don't even want. The girl I think you're talking about—her father was a *doctor*, for crying out loud."

Both the cashier and the customer looked at her, and the cashier said something in an undertone. The customer laughed and collected her grocery bags: "Later, Cheryl! Call me!" she brayed. The clerk was curt as she rang up Vera's purchases, not replying even when she said "Thank you" in her meekest voice.

Coming out of the store, Vera took slow, deep breaths to calm herself down; she checked her cell phone, then compared that time to the folded bus schedule in her pocket. There was just enough time to get home for the six o'clock news.

Home again, a tall glass of vinegary wine in hand, she flipped compulsively between the three local news channels, waiting to see which one would first mention the dead girl in the park. By Dorset standards, this had to be front-burner news. And for once the news did not disappoint.

There it was, finally—the story she was looking for, and a name and a smiling face.

Sufia Ahmed. Fifteen years old.

She did not realize she was holding her breath until the end of the news report; she was holding her breath to see if her name would be mentioned in conjunction with the story, as she had asked the police to withhold this information from the media. They had honored her request, referring to her only as "a woman" who had come across the body in the park and had made the report to police. This, Vera thought, was a lucky break.

Relaxing a little, Vera took in the photo on the news, seeing Sufia's tentative-looking smile and wide eyes, the absolute youthfulness striking her anew: *fifteen.* She listened to the story of how Sufia's family had relocated to the United States when Sufia was just seven years old. Of how Sufia's mother was employed as custodial staff at the food court in the mall and that her father was a pesticide sprayer. The newscaster did not say that Sufia had been strangled—such an ugly word, *strangled*, as Jensen had said—but she did say her death was considered a homicide, and that the police had "several leads" in terms of a suspect. Coming to the last sentence of the news story, the newscaster said, "When asked if the homicide might have a racial motive, Officer Gerard Babineau said that the police were unable to comment on this at the present time."

A racial motive. What did that even mean? Vera wondered. Was it a reference to the black-on-black scenario that the bigoted grocery store clerk had assumed? Or was this innuendo, planting the seed of an idea that this had been a hate crime—directed against the Somali population, or perhaps at Muslims in general?

There was no mention of Angela Galvez. Two young females had been murdered in Dorset in the last six months—how could the news overlook what seemed to be a pattern in the making? Had the cops, too, chosen to overlook it because they wanted to close the books on the Galvez case now that Ritchie Ouelette was in custody? Or perhaps it wasn't even a choice; perhaps, Vera thought, the local police and media really were that obtuse.

No sooner was the news report over than Vera's phone started ringing. Not recognizing the local number of the incoming call, she stared the phone down and blanched a little when the phone buzzed with a voicemail notification. A half hour later, the phone rang again; two phone calls in one afternoon was never good news, and when Vera decided to brave her email a little later in the day, she divined the reason behind these earlier calls. Her email in-box, ordinarily so inactive, had begun to explode with activity.

There was an email from Jensen Willard, dated on Friday, with an attachment icon in the corner next to her name. Vera felt she didn't have the heart for one of Jensen's emails right now. She skipped ahead to one of the newer emails from Sue MacMasters.

To: velundy@thewallaceschool.edu
From: slmacmasters@thewallaceschool.edu

Dear Vera,

Are you okay? I just got a call from Harold Finister about the Ahmed girl. I know she was one of your students. I'll never forget what it was like the first time I lost a student. I could not have been more upset if it had been my own child. Just know that I'm here if you'd like to talk and that I will be reaching out to the student's other teachers as well. Harold will be sending out an email to all staff and faculty about how to move forward, so please stay on the lookout for updates.

Sue

There was a mass email from Lucy Grivois, the school counselor, discussing the effects of grief and loss on the adolescent girl and what teachers should expect to see over the next few weeks, given the "untimely passing" of one of the girls' own classmates. And there was a long email from Dean Finister, announcing that school would meet on Monday morning for a two-hour assembly. Grief counselors would be available, as would the services of Detective Helen Cutler, who was coming to speak to the girls about personal safety and area crime statistics in a manner that, Vera gathered, was planned to be reassuring. After the assembly, the school would be closed until Thursday, the day after Sufia's memorial service ("which all staff and faculty are encouraged to attend") on Wednesday.

At the closing of his email, Finister wrote, "As you can imagine, the loss of another young life in Dorset seems almost too much to bear, coming so close as it does to the loss of my niece Angela. I know how difficult the healing process can be, and how much harder it must be when that loss is of one's young peer." Vera tried to imagine Finister saying all this, in his pinched, nasally voice, and somehow couldn't.

Thinking, Vera got up from her computer and took a yellow legal pad off one of her kitchen shelves; with pen in hand, she began to write rapidly.

1. ***Angela Galvez: Eleven, female, Hispanic-American, strangulation. Body recovered behind local Laundromat. Death attributed to Ritchie Ouelette, twenty-five.***
2. ***Sufia Ahmed: Fifteen, female, African-American, strangulation. Body recovered in park. Killer unknown at present time.***

That was all she had to go on, but she studied the two short entries as though they might provide a more telling clue. She thought some more, paused long enough to print up the photograph of Sufia Ahmed, then downloaded a photo of Angela Galvez—a pretty child with her hair smoothed back in a headband—and printed that up, too. She cut off the white edges of both printouts with a pair of scissors, then taped each on the wall above her laptop, side by side, where she could look on them as she worked or typed. After some more thought, she went back to her milk crate in the closet and dug deeper into her papers, this time withdrawing an old folder filled with yellowing newspaper cuttings until she took out Heidi Duplessis's smiling school photo that had been reproduced in the *Bond Brook Gazette*. She taped Heidi up alongside the other girls, to keep them company. Together, the trio might whisper their secrets to her.

Chapter Six

Up onstage in the auditorium, the Wallace School Madrigal Singers were warbling through "Over the Rainbow." The girls' voices overlapped and wrapped around one another, the high notes soaring to the ceiling of the auditorium; the last of these notes clung like tremulous moths to the fluorescent lights.

Vera did not think this song—so evocative of Kansas, so inextricably tied to sweet, pigtailed Dorothy's innocent desire to venture away from home—was the right way to memorialize Sufia Ahmed. Nonetheless, she felt great annoyance with herself when a tear began to slide down the side of her nose. She wiped it away brusquely. Was it a good thing or a bad thing for her students to see her crying?

Following Dean Finister's orders, each Wallace School teacher was sitting with the girls in the grade she was responsible for, and Vera could pick out the faces of some of her own girls from Sufia's class. Jensen seemed to be absent, but Martha True sat just one seat away from Vera, with an empty seat in between them; Martha wept openly, her hunched, slim shoulders heaving up and down. Vera thought about reaching over to give the girl a one-armed hug, but the act would not have felt natural, and her arm didn't reach that far, anyway. Still, she felt that she ought to do *something*.

Aggie Hamada was seated one row in front of her, next to Jamie Friedman, and she could see the trace of a Kleenex appearing and disappearing from Jamie Friedman's purse; at one point she passed it to Aggie, who blew her nose audibly over the last plaintive strains of the song. *Why oh why can't I?*

And there was Harmony Phelps, sitting diagonally across from Vera. Harmony seemed to be bristling with an almost triumphant self-righteousness, as though her most negative suspicions about the world had just come true.

Throughout most of the assembly in honor of Sufia Ahmed's memory, Vera was in a daze. She saw people come and go from the stage in an aimless fashion, as though they were lost and had wandered up to the podium by mistake. Even Dean Finister fumbled, though he still spent a good fifteen minutes up there, overdoing it as usual and calling Sufia "a testament to the American dream." (*And what a testament,* Vera thought. *This is what the American dream gets you?*) On the movie screen that hung from the ceiling, Finister showed a collage of recent photos depicting Sufia at home and at school; Vera wondered how he had acquired them. The first slide showed Sufia, larger than life and dressed in a ski outfit, smiling her closed-lipped, tentative smile. In the next she was being embraced by her father, wearing a white dress for her eighth-grade graduation, and last of all was a moment of glory, photographed for all posterity: Sufia holding up a medal she'd received for delivering a winning speech. There was something terribly mawkish about this presentation—each posed photo selected for optimum emotional impact—but Vera cried again, furious with herself for being so easily manipulated.

But it wasn't about manipulation. It was about Sufia. It was about a girl who had died too soon, in a way that no girl should die. Sufia and she may not have been simpatico, but she did not deserve, Vera thought, what had come to her.

A Somali girl from one of the upper classes, presumably someone who'd known Sufia, got up and spoke of the dead girl's outstanding citizenship and industriousness and positive attitude. "May God make her presence touch all your lives forever," she said before bowing a little and stumbling off the stage.

The next speaker was different and seemed to break through the collective sense of paralysis. It was a female police detective—ruddy, rawboned, with a thinning shock of hair that was half gray, half carrot-colored—who introduced herself as Detective Helen Cutler. *Chelsea's aunt,* Vera thought, leaning forward in her seat a little as the woman announced that she was there to discuss issues of personal safety and self-defense. She moved through a PowerPoint presentation, startling in its lack of emotion after all that had come before, showing slides with graphs about local crime statistics, lists on how to deter a would-be assailant and how to practice safe habits so that one didn't end up a statistic like Sufia. Detective Cutler spoke with calm assurance, looking out into the darkened auditorium at the sea of blank, mostly white faces.

"This is not a time for terror," she said, "but it is a time for caution. You can never be too cautious. And you can never have too much common sense. So use common sense, girls. And by that I mean, don't go out after dark. Don't tempt fate. Traveling in pairs is always best. But *do* call us if you see or hear anything that you think might be helpful to finding who did this to your classmate. Even if you're not *sure* it's suspicious, give us a call on the number you see up here on the screen. In fact, take a second to put this number in your phones right now. Every single one of you should have it."

After Detective Cutler had finished her presentation, the school counselor, Lucy Grivois, got onstage to speak about grief counseling available to the students. Coming as she did after Cutler, her voice sounded thin and faded and uncertain. "Sometimes just indulging your grief is all you can do to move on to the next phase of healing," she said, "and sometimes you just need someone to hold you. Sometimes you just need a shoulder to cry on. If anyone would like to come up on the stage, right now, we have hugs for you. We have hugs for all of you." Two senior peer counselors flanked her, and upon mention of the "we," the three of them moved away from the podium and waited at the side of the stage while the Madrigal Singers, their red robes flapping, reentered from the opposite side. *This has got to be a joke,* Vera thought. *Hugs for everyone? There is no way any teenage girl in her right mind is going to go up onstage for a hug.* Then the Madrigals began the first notes of a dreadful song—one that Vera recognized from a commercial about abused and neglected shelter animals—and as the song ramped up and the three counselors waited expectantly, the impossible happened. First, one girl—a red-faced girl sitting near the front, visibly crying—climbed up the stairs to the stage and stiffly placed herself in Lucy Grivois's arms. Then another girl came up, and then another, until a few girls from every row had risen and formed a line at the foot of the stairs, waiting to hug out their grief.

It's like watching the Jim Jones cult get up one by one to drink the Kool-Aid—no, the Flavor Aid, Vera thought. *It was Flavor Aid that they actually drank.*

Seeing so many of the girls seeming to relish their grief, waiting for their benediction, was too much to process. And for Vera, part of the problem was that it was all too familiar.

It brought her immediately back to the memorial service for Heidi Duplessis, which had been attended by hundreds of students from her high school. Attendance had, in fact, been mandatory for all the students at her school. Oh, the crying and the carrying-on there had been! The people embracing outside the church and sobbing outright! And worst of all, the people who laid a claim on Heidi, scrabbling to make any connection they could find with the dead girl.

She was my friend, everyone said. Even those whom Heidi had never spoken to.

She said she liked my bracelet once.

She beat me in the eighth-grade Spelling Bee. I came in second. She deserved to win, though—I'm glad she beat me.

My brother used to play softball with her brother Kyle.

Anything for a connection. The students had milled about the reporters, hoping to be quoted for the paper or the evening news, while fourteen-year-old Vera had stood outside the church by herself and had found a reporter's microphone in her face. *You look awfully sad,* the reporter had said. *Was Heidi a good personal friend of yours?*

I didn't know her, Vera had replied. *And unlike everyone else, I'm not going to try to insert myself into the story and pretend that I did. People are acting like no one ever died before. But really, death is just a part of life.*

That was the line that had gotten her in the most trouble when it appeared in the *Bond Brook Gazette*. It had never occurred to Vera that they would even consider printing it. It was not long after that the notebook in which she kept her private thoughts was stolen by Stephanie Lord, a popular girl from her homeroom, and the items she had written about Heidi became well known throughout the school. Once the notebook had been widely distributed, the phone calls came, and the threatening notes stuck in the vents of Vera's locker. On one occasion she was even followed home in the dark. The resulting ambush, orchestrated by a particularly hard-bitten group of girls who had not been friends with Heidi but needed little encouragement to rough someone up, had been part of a night that Vera found hard to forget. Sometimes, when she was caught between a state of half sleeping and half waking, she could still hear their jeering, could still feel her face being pressed into the mud of her own front lawn, the sole of a sneaker braced against the back of her neck.

Did you kill Heidi? You wanted to, didn't you, you crazy bitch?

And she could hear their fists pounding against the windows as they circled her house, still calling after Vera even after she'd broken free and locked herself inside.

Vera was shaky by the time the assembly was over. The students, faculty, and staff were shuffling their way out of the auditorium now, clogging the exits, and Vera saw Sue MacMasters and one of the junior English teachers coming toward her as she rose from her own seat.

"It was a beautiful tribute, wasn't it, Vera? Oh, I can't get over how sad it all is. But I think this was a really great idea for the girls, don't you think? I *hope* it gave them some closure and some peace of mind."

"I think it did, Sue," Vera said. She wanted to be kind. Sue looked so beside herself, her eyes widened in what looked like genuine shock.

Vera had almost gotten out the side door when she felt a hand on her own shoulder, and she looked into the face of Detective Helen Cutler.

"How are you doing, Vera?"

"Doing?"

"You don't remember." The detective actually looked amused—an expression so out of place in this context that Vera felt the first prick-lings of alarm.

"I was on the scene last Saturday morning. In the park. We talked for a while."

Vera drew a quick intake of breath. "Oh. I remember you now."

"I doubt that. You were pretty intoxicated."

"No, I do remember." Vera rooted around in her memory for something to substantiate this lie. "It was you and—Officer Babineau."

"Gerry Babineau was one of the other ones who were there," Cutler acknowledged, still looking bemused. Vera tried to tell herself that maybe this was just the permanent set of the woman's lips. "You're looking better now than you did then, I'll say that much. Do you have some time to talk?"

"Right now?"

"Why not? Someplace quiet would be good."

"The classroom I normally teach in at this time would be empty." Vera looked around her to see if anyone was noticing the detective talking to her. Then she reprimanded herself for being so twitchy. "I can . . . I can show you the way."

As they walked down the hall, Detective Cutler a little too close at her side, she said, "This is really just a follow-up."

"Follow-up?

"Sure. It's been a little over twenty-four hours since we talked to you in the park. Who knows—maybe you remember more now than you did then. Something you saw. Something you observed."

"Oh," Vera said, entering her classroom and limply settling into the nearest chair. Detective Cutler shut the classroom door behind her and grabbed a chair for herself from one of the tables, scraping it across the floor and positioning it opposite Vera. "I wish I *could* tell you more," Vera said, "but honestly, I don't have much to tell. Are you going to tape-record this?"

Cutler, eyebrow raised, took a notepad out of her pocket and tapped it with her pen. "This'll do."

Vera, holding her hands in her lap so the detective could not see them trembling, went over what little she remembered of the evening.

She was embarrassed to tell her about the married man she had met in the bar—she could not even remember if she had shared this information previously—but she felt she should impart what few facts she could. "I was in the park, but I don't know exactly why I was there," she finished. "In fact, I don't have any consciousness of being there until the moment I saw Sufia and realized who she was. Then I took out my phone and called you."

"How many drinks did you have that night, Vera?"

"How many *drinks*? I don't know. I don't think it was all that many. Five? Maybe five mixed drinks?"

"Well, that's progress," the detective said, scribbling in her pad. "On Saturday morning you told us two. Do you get blackouts often when you drink five drinks?"

"Sometimes."

"Take any medication? Prescription or otherwise?"

"I take a very low dose of an antidepressant. Fluoxetine—that's generic Prozac."

"A recent prescription?"

"Oh, no. I've been on it for years."

"Probably shouldn't be drinking at all then."

"No," Vera admitted miserably. "I probably shouldn't."

"Do you have any sense, looking back, on how much time passed between the moment you found Sufia under the tree and the time you called us?"

"Just seconds," Vera said. "It was almost instantaneous. And then . . . well, they got there—you got there—very quickly."

"Do you remember anything else you saw in the park, besides Sufia and the tree? Anything that looked out of place? Any sign that someone else was around?"

"No, nothing like that."

"What about touching anything at the scene? Touching Sufia or any part of her clothing?"

"I'm positive I didn't," Vera said. "I was afraid. I kept some distance once I knew what I was looking at."

"Do you know anyone who disliked Sufia Ahmed? Took some issue with her or her family?"

Vera shook her head.

"We're asking that question of everyone. You don't need to look so petrified."

"Sorry."

The detective stood up, brushing her red hair back with a large hand. *She could probably palm a basketball with one of those hands,* Vera thought. "I think that'll be all for now, then," she said.

"Detective Cutler? May I ask one thing?"

"Ask away."

"I haven't mentioned to other staff or faculty that I was the one who found Sufia."

"And why is that?"

"I don't know. I guess I don't want people asking me about it. It isn't a nice thing to have to talk about over and over."

"Talking about it with people might make it easier to process. Might even be good for you."

"I'd prefer they not know," Vera said, "so if there is any way you can keep them from knowing when you speak to them, that would mean a lot to me personally."

"I'll do what I can, Vera. That's the best I can promise. Just so you know, we'll probably be checking in with you again. Maybe just a phone call next time. Memory's a funny thing. A couple more days, and maybe there'll be something different you remember."

After the detective had left, Vera could not shed her sense of unease. She did not think she wanted the burden of remembering any more than she knew now, much less being prodded to remember.

Wednesday was the day of Sufia's funeral. Vera had been surprised to see that it would be held at St. Sebastian's Church; she had assumed that the Ahmeds were Muslim, not Catholic, and she wondered if they had converted somewhere along the line. Had they been Muslim, perhaps they would have preferred a quieter service and burial. But Vera knew from the scuttlebutt around the school that the funeral would be spectacular, that half the town was planning to attend and pay their respects to the promising young immigrant as she was laid to rest.

Vera decided not to go. Part of her wanted to, but she had only ever been to two funerals in her life—Heidi's and her father's—and felt that that had been enough.

She stayed home, thinking she might do some writing, perhaps catch up on some old emails, but instead she slept most of the day and then found herself riveted by the six o'clock news, with its coverage of Sufia Ahmed's funeral.

The scene was very much as she had expected it to be. Media from all three local TV stations were there, positioned outside the cemetery gates and collecting sound bites from teenagers who were all too eager to appear on TV for an instant. She recognized a girl from her afternoon class as one of those who spoke to the reporter from WCTL. "Sufia was *really* popular," she said. "She is going to be missed." People streamed past her as she leaned into the microphone, and Vera thought she caught Jensen Willard in the background, walking by quickly, her hair almost obscuring her face. *But it can't be* her, Vera thought; since when did Jensen ever walk with any spring in her step? The news story also showed the outside of Sufia's parents' house, whose crooked front gates were now festooned with flowers, balloons, and stuffed toys left by well-meaning kids who had wanted to leave a tribute of some kind. Seeing this, Vera had an almost visceral reaction, and she thought: *I should have left something, too. I should have at least sent some flowers for Sufia. Violets, perhaps, for such a quiet and unassuming girl. Sometimes she wore a violet-covered hijab, which framed her face so beautifully . . .*

For the first time, Vera wondered if the Ahmeds even knew who she was. Had the police revealed her identity to them—told them about the drunk woman, Sufia's own teacher, who had surprisingly had the wherewithal to call for help but had been of so little use to the authorities after that? Would they see a gift from her as unwelcome, as taboo—see Vera herself as a bringer of bad luck? She hoped not.

Thinking about this, Vera looked up the Ahmeds in the phone directory and found that their house was located on Preble Lane, in a working-class neighborhood not far from where Vera lived. She could walk there. It was still not quite dark, and the town had not rolled up its sidewalks yet; she would have time to pick up a modest floral arrangement at a store along the way. She could leave that for Sufia. This small gesture was the least she could do to pay tribute to the dead girl toward whom she felt a deeper, more personal connection than she had ever felt in life.

Vera had no trouble finding the Ahmeds' house. It was a small, old duplex with a sagging porch, a home badly in need of a paint job, but its front gates suggested an eerily party-like atmosphere, bedecked as they were with heaps of flowers, hand-lettered notes, and lumpy, dull-eyed teddy bears. Vera stood outside these gates with the small potted violet she had bought and bent down to place it in an unobtrusive spot. Straightening up, she read one of the signs that had been taped to the Ahmeds' wooden fence:

REST IN PEACE SOPHIA, YOUR ONE OF GODS ANGELS NOW.

Vera stood there a while; she wasn't sure exactly how long. She knew she was beginning to feel cold, even in her winter coat and hat, and she was just about to turn away and head back home when she saw the wooden gate open up and a familiar face peering through it with a high-beamed flashlight. Squinting against the light, Vera stepped back and shielded her eyes.

"Hello, Vera. Looking for something?"

It took Vera a moment to identify the speaker—this uniformed man at the gate. It was only when she looked into his eyes—those sad, dark eyes, downturned at their outer corners—that she remembered him.

It was Officer Gerard Babineau. The officer who had taken her report at the crime scene. The one whose card she still carried in her wallet.

"No," Vera said. "I was just . . . I was just leaving some flowers. A plant, really."

"I heard Helen Cutler talked to you at the school the other day. We didn't see you at the service, though."

Were the police keeping tabs on such things? Keeping tabs on *her*? "No, I . . . I didn't go. I thought about it, but it didn't feel right to me."

The officer nodded. "Understandable. But what brings you here now? The Ahmeds don't wish to be disturbed this evening. I'm sure you can see why they'd like to have a little privacy and quiet after such a difficult day."

"Oh, of course. I wasn't planning to disturb them, Officer."

"If you'd like me to get those flowers to them, I can take them inside."

"That isn't necessary," Vera said. "But thank you."

Babineau just kept looking at her with those sorrowful eyes that made her feel as though she needed to apologize for something. Vera mumbled something else, something that *was* half apologetic, and made haste on her way back to her apartment. She felt as though Officer Babineau were watching her all the way down Preble Street, and she didn't care for that feeling at all. What had he been doing at the house? Had the Ahmeds requested a constant police presence there, in the wake of their daughter's murder?

It's because the perpetrator often likes to go to the victim's grave or to where the victim lived or to the scene of the crime, Vera thought, turning blindly around the corner. *Their ego prevents them from staying away. I should have known that. I should have known that someone would be there, monitoring the entrance of the house, waiting for someone who doesn't belong to show up. Someone just like me.*

Later that evening, the three murdered girls—Heidi, Angela, and Sufia—looked benevolently at Vera from their spots on the wall as she sat in front of her laptop and stared at the in-box of her Wallace School email account.

There in her queue of unread messages was the old one from Jensen Willard—the message from days before, which she had ignored last Saturday night. She could no longer remember why she had avoided it. In the grand scheme of things—in days darkened by death and shame and worry—a message from Jensen Willard seemed like nothing to be afraid of.

To: velundy@thewallaceschool.edu
From: jawillard@thewallaceschool.edu
Subject: journals

Hello,

I am writing this on Friday afternoon from the school computer. I'm feeling bad now about the journal I turned in—if you've read it already, you know it isn't very good. I know it's stupid to go on and on about a boyfriend—so typical teenager-y—but I have one more entry I want to send to you. I'm sorry to have to make you read all this; I'll have something better to turn in next time, I hope. Things are a little difficult in my head right now, but writing usually helps.

Sincerely,
Jensen Willard

Vera remembered precious little about Jensen's last journal entry, much less understood why it warranted an apology. Hadn't she written about Bret again? What else would a young girl write about, if not her boyfriend? It seemed a long time ago—ages ago—since Vera had given it any thought.

The attachment at the bottom of Jensen's email read only "Gore." Vera bit her lip, looked at it, and squinted closer at the screen as it filled with Jensen's boldface heading:

You Never Saw Such Gore in Your Life: Journal Entry #4, by Jensen Willard

I ought to warn you that I'm a little angry right now. And when I get angry, I don't see red, like you're always hearing about in books. I see white. *Everything turns to snow in front of my eyes. Eventually this page will fill up with black ink but even then I will still see nothing but a white page.*

I mentioned to you in the last journal that Bret hadn't called me in a while. Well, he did call me, a little earlier than our usual scheduled talk, and things are as bad as I suspected.

Worse.

What makes it worse is that he started off being all normal about everything. He started talking about how he was teaching himself to read Gaelic. He talked about a reading he'd been assigned in his ethics class. He went on and on about this for so long that after a while, I just couldn't stand it anymore, so I broke in and said the dumbest thing imaginable to him.

I said, "I miss you."

There was this long silence and this crackle at the other end of the line (the connection wasn't very good—it never is). I heard a background noise like someone talking, or maybe a voice from the TV—I couldn't tell. "Your parents are ultimately paying for this call," I said after a while. "Don't you want to talk to me?"

"Jensen, listen. There's something I should probably tell you about. Do you remember Tova, the girl in my calculus class I mentioned?"

I vaguely remembered him saying something about having a study partner and how she had burned him a "really cool CD" of techno music. The whiteness was already starting to creep in, and with it a coldness.

"Don't tell me anymore," I said. "Don't say another word."

But he kept on going, the bastard.

"We fooled around a little. I didn't exactly intend for that to happen."

"What does 'a little' mean?"

"Um . . . almost to the point of penetration?"

I should have hung up the phone. Bret's voice sounded so stupid. Who says "almost to the point of penetration"? He made it sound like a laboratory experiment or something.

"There's something else I should tell you, too," he said. "You know my roommate? Max?"

I couldn't even speak. I just waited for him to go on.

"Max and I have experimented a little," he said. "I don't think it really means anything. But I just thought, since I was telling you about Tova, I should tell you about Max, too."

"I hate you," I said at last.

"What?"

"No, I don't. I don't hate you. I'm sorry. I didn't mean it that way." (What was I apologizing for? Why do I apologize when it's other people who should do the apologizing?)

"I'm the one who's sorry." Bret sounded almost contrite, with an emphasis on "almost." He needs to work on his sincerity. "It's meaningless, really. I mean, I find Tova very attractive, but she isn't as well read as she could be. All she reads besides assigned readings are those Douglas Adams hitchhiker books. I find Max attractive, too. But I don't really see that going anywhere."

The sentences "I find her very attractive . . . I find him at-

tractive, too" oozed through my head. I wanted to kill Bret. I wanted to go down to Columbia and find him and Tova and Max and smother the three of them with one pillow. I simmered and boiled as the air grew colder around me. I felt like one of those people with hypothermia who experience a great heat just before they go mad and freeze to death.

I still do.

"Jensen? Are you there?"

I didn't feel as though I was. I felt as though I were already gone. But, for the sake of formality, I said, "I think I have to go now."

"I know we haven't had sex or anything," Bret said. "You and I, I mean. But intellectually, I feel much closer to you than anyone. I don't want to lose you. I've never told you this, but I'm in love with your mind."

I replaced my parents' old phone on its cradle.

I kept replaying what he had said about being in love with my mind. It seemed like just about the meanest thing a guy could say to a girl.

Would it kill him to just say he found me attractive and just leave it at that? Even if it weren't true?

The unspoken part of being told you have a beautiful mind is that it means the rest of you leaves a lot to be desired. I know it's considered shallow to worry about being pretty, but I don't have much to worry about in that department—even my own mother refuses to give me that affirmation. Once, when I was about twelve, I asked her, "Mom, do you think I'm pretty?" and her response was that looks aren't important. Translation: Either I'm too ugly for words or her staunch New England upbringing makes her incapable of handing out compliments for fear that

I might get ideas about myself and start trying to shit above my ass. I kid you not.

The thing is—the really sad thing is—that Bret has been getting better-looking to me all the time, in my mind. I wish you could see a picture so you could judge for yourself; I'm not sure what you find attractive or unattractive. After first meeting him, my mom took me aside and exclaimed, "What do you even see in him? He looks like a baby egret—like he's not done yet." (So much for looks not being important.)

I've tried to explain what I see in him.

I try to explain to her that Bret and I have read some of the same books. That together, with our collective brain wattage, we could be a formidable force against the universe if we so chose. I don't bother trying to explain to her that to me, he has started to look less like a baby egret or a sleepy-eyed tapeworm. His grotesquely scrawny limbs now look exotic and exquisite to me, like he's the androgynous singer in a glam-rock band. (You probably think this is funny. It is funny, or it should be, but I can't laugh about anything right now.) I guess I have grown to love him a little bit.

Who am I kidding?

I know I have grown to love him a lot. I should never have let this happen. Me, of all people.

I wish I mattered more to Bret. I wish I was the most important person in the world to him, the most beautiful. I wish I was this to someone. But I don't want to be hurt by him anymore.

I didn't tell my mom or Les about what Bret had told me, even though I talk to them about almost everything. I know what they'd say, if I did tell them. My mom would say, "Why would you get yourself worked up over a boy who's not even done yet and is about as useless as tits on a boar-hog?" And Les would jump in with, "He's an asshole! In my day, if I had a girl, I would call her every day, and if I couldn't call, I'd mail a goddamn letter!"

I don't think I could make my parents understand that I'm not crying over a boy. Not exactly. I am crying because of all this wasted time. My whole life so far, all fifteen years of it—just wasted time.

Vera blinked at that last paragraph. The phrase *wasted time* made her think of Sufia Ahmed—*the waste of a young life*, as the cliché would have it—and she wiped this out of her mind as fast as she could, like someone swatting at a fly, looking up at her former student's smiling picture for forgiveness.

It was funny, Vera mused; Jensen Willard had complained in a journal entry that her peers were oblivious to tragedy and heartache, but Jensen was not so different—her tragedy seemed exasperatingly small compared to what Vera had seen in the earliest hours of Saturday morning. Still, her heart went out to her student, who presumably had written this entry before she had known of Sufia's death. Her pain was still real, no matter what its cause, and deserved to be dignified with a response. She read the journal entry a second time, then a third time, and then she remembered more of how she had felt after she'd read Jensen's last journal entry—the annoyance she'd felt at Bret Folger and at thickheaded boys of his ilk. And then she knew exactly why it bothered her—the reasons she had not wanted to consider, the stories she had deliberately refrained from telling Jensen before.

In a split-second decision, Vera hit the reply button and felt her fingers flying over the keyboard, hammering at the keys until they shook:

Dear Jensen,

I found your last journal entry far from stupid, so please do not worry about what I thought of it. My only objection to reading that entry is that your boyfriend, Bret, does not seem as sensitive to your needs as I would wish for you. Hearing about your relationship reminds me a little of how things were with my own first boyfriend. It may or may not be helpful for me to tell you something about this. I can tell you that I was seventeen at the time and that my first boyfriend's name was Peter. Many years later, he became my fiancé. A few years after that, he became my ex. Before he was mine, he was the boyfriend of a girl named Heidi Duplessis. But that is a separate story, perhaps one for a different time.

Peter and I went to the same high school in Bond Brook, but had never spoken—kind of like you and Bret in the French class. I was shy, so painfully shy in those days that other students made fun of me, asked me if I was deaf and dumb, made goading comments in study halls while the teachers looked the other way. But Peter was someone I had noticed. I liked his pale, bleached white-blond hair that fell in a swoop over his forehead—its natural color was a medium brown—his short, compact body, and his black trench coat that flapped theatrically around his ankles when he walked. I liked the way he bounced on his the balls of his feet and the way his voice cut through the din of the halls. He was often smiling, but his eyes seldom smiled; they were an almost silvery blue, a color so seldom seen in nature that it was impossible to detect any warmth in them. In a diary I'd kept at the time—I'm embarrassed to even think about this diary—I included Peter in a list of "10 Boys I Would Like to Date," with an explanation of why next to each person's name. Next to Peter's name I wrote, "He seems like a very unique kind of boy."

But as I said, Peter never noticed me in high school. He went to Temple University after graduation, and we didn't start dating until we ran into each other during his Thanksgiving break. By that time he'd heard some things about me, things that weren't so nice, but still somehow we clicked.

On our first date, we went to a nightclub in Portland that had chem-free dance nights twice a week; the nightclub was like nothing I'd seen in Bond Brook, and I instantly fell in love with it.

Jensen, I wish such a club was still around for you. Zuzu's was the name of it, and it was the place to go if you were a disaffected boy who wore makeup or a disaffected girl with a shaved head. This was the place to go if you were a pale, scrawny girl with Cleopatra eyes and a short dress and a pair of boots with four-inch soles; it was also the place to go if you were a great big girl spilling out of your corset, a crucifix nestled in your cleavage. Girls like this came from small schools all over Maine and had names like Scheherazade and Cymbeline. On the dance floor you could view hunchbacked kids, praying mantis kids, midget kids who moved like Tasmanian devils; some did leaps that raised them several feet in the air—you'd think they were figure skaters doing triple axels, but with flailing gestures added for dramatic effect. You should have seen them! There was one girl who always wore a white latex bodysuit and danced like she was fighting off a swarm of bees! I didn't dance at all, and I half hated, half admired these kids' wanton exhibitionism; I'd just sit with Peter at the back of the club, sometimes even sitting on the floor with our backs up against the wall, with the thump of the speakers catching my heart up and tossing it cruelly around. The DJ spun songs by the Cure ("Boys Don't Cry"), the Smiths ("Heaven Knows I'm Miserable Now"), and Siouxsie and the Banshees ("Cities in Dust"). During a lull, a slow song that just about cleared the dance floor,

I felt a cool hand over mine. Peter's. I looked at him sideways and saw a sheen in his silvery eyes that might have been emotion.

After that, Zuzu's was always *our* place.

I am sure you are wondering at this point why I am telling you this. I am telling you this because I think perhaps you will have some understanding of what I experienced.

Over the remaining weeks of Peter's break, we saw each other every day. I went from being a girl who couldn't even speak to a boy to a girl who could have endless conversations with a boy while in bed with him, arms wrapped fiercely around him. I remember rolling around on the floor of his house while the hot air blew in through vents on the floor, tickling us. I remember him being so thin that his pelvic bones hurt me when we had sex—that was what Peter called it, "having sex," though I secretly thought that "making love" sounded nicer. Maybe it's just as well that you and Bret aren't doing all that. The word *love* was never used between us, but on those nights at Peter's house when we lay together—his mother was somehow *never* home—he would say, "I need you." And I believed that he did. I had never felt needed before, except maybe as my parents' daughter. I'd never felt anything other than laughable or expendable to someone close to my own age.

Vera stopped typing, aghast. What was she doing? She did not need to disclose all this to Jensen. She doubted the girl would even want to hear about her teacher in this context; what student would? Yet there was part of her that wished to go on, to tell her about how, when Peter had gone back to college halfway across the country, something inside Vera broke. She wanted to tell her how she had written feverishly to him every day—topping Jensen's four or five letters a week to Bret—and how Peter wrote her letters in return, packets filled with clippings and comic strips and things he thought might amuse her. She wanted to describe how she had torn into these envelopes, tossing aside all the clippings to find what she really wanted—the letters, the words, some scrap of affection in writing. A simple "I need you, Vera" or "I miss you" had made her weep with relief.

After a hot, full, indolent summer together, when Peter was preparing to return to school for his sophomore year, he told Vera he thought she was too intense. That it might be best if they started seeing other people—and then, she presumed, he had gone on to do exactly that, for they didn't speak again for another fourteen years.

In the interim, her life had not ended, as she had once guessed it might. She *had* gone on to do other things—things she was sometimes even proud of, which she supposed could be said of almost anyone's life. Her life so far had been a series of peaks and valleys, steps forward and steps backward, with her graduate school experience and time in New York City being the highlight. She had had other relationships of a sort, but nothing that took. Ending up back in Bond Brook because of Peter just seemed like a hiccup in retrospect, an interruption of the good path she'd been on. She would never make such a mistake again. When she thought of Peter and his new fiancée, Betsy, all she could think was: *Betsy will never know the skinny, white-haired, silver-eyed boy with the trench coat flapping like bat wings around his heels.* She would know someone quite different. She was lucky, Vera thought, to know something quite different—to not be lured back by the false promise of having teenage love softened and made right.

Vera realized she was crying a little, the cursor still blinking near the text of her unfinished email. The blinking seemed disapproving, impatient; it made her wipe her eyes and delete the email she'd started, word by word. When the screen was empty, she started anew, her mouth set in a resolute line.

Hi Jensen—

It's fine that you didn't turn in more entries, as you have already gone above and beyond the call of duty by turning in so many pages early and writing them in such a thoughtful, original way. I'm looking forward to seeing more from you. And I agree—writing does help with difficult times. Try to enjoy the rest of your time off, and I will see you in class soon.

Sincerely,
Vera Lundy

School resumed on Thursday morning, the day after Sufia Ahmed's memorial service. Vera had already put some thought into how she would address her girls when they came into her morning class; she had not spoken to them directly since before the tragedy. They would be expecting something from her, she knew. They would be looking to her and all the other adults at Wallace for cues of how to behave, how to carry on.

To Vera's utter lack of surprise, most of the girls looked red-eyed, weary, and beaten down as they took their seats. She found that the comments she had rehearsed in her mind—the boilerplate script about loss and coping that Lucy Grivois had suggested all faculty deliver to their students—simply would not do.

"Tough times," Vera said quietly when it seemed that the last of the girls had come in. "Tough times indeed."

Jamie Friedman nodded at Vera, meeting her gaze in such an adult way that Vera felt an understanding pass between them. *We're the grown-ups here,* the gaze seemed to say, and Vera did not object to this idea at all. She was not sure she was up to the task of being the only grown-up in the room.

"Do you guys want to talk about things?" Vera asked, looking from girl to girl. "Or are you all talked out?"

"All talked out," Autumn Fullerton said wearily, fiddling with her hair.

Loo Garippa nodded in agreement. "No one's telling us anything anyway," she said.

Vera stole a glance at Chelsea Cutler, whose eyes, though focused on Vera, gave away nothing. Had anyone told *her* anything? "I don't think there's much to be told at this point," Vera said to the girls. "There's some . . . there's some really sick people out there in society. That's the only absolute fact we have to work on. And it will be hard—it will be hard to grasp that Sufia won't be with us anymore."

It was then that Jensen Willard came in, dragging her army knapsack by its strap. There was a grayish pallor to her skin, and she carried herself more stiffly than usual, as though her joints pained her. She took her place at the long table near the back. Normally, she sat one seat away from Sufia Ahmed, with one empty chair in between them. Now two empty chairs stood between her and her closest classmate, Aggie. In the small classroom, these two empty seats seemed a wide gulf separating Jensen from the rest of the girls. Vera found her eyes resting on the seat that had been Sufia's.

Suddenly the dead girl's face appeared before her again—wide-eyed, doleful, accusatory. Vera looked out at the eleven students sitting at the tables and felt something awful beginning to happen within her body, a hideous and rapid metamorphosis. A great, swollen, bloated thing—*panic*, she thought—was bobbing up from her chest to her throat like some gaseous old body in a swamp. Vera carefully sat down on the edge of the table at the front of the room, not trusting her legs to hold her steady, and at that exact moment Jamie Friedman cleared her throat. "I would like to say something, Miss Lundy."

"Please do, Jamie."

"I just wanted to share a memory I had of Sufia. I think sometimes the best way to deal with sadness is to remember something good."

"Oh, I think that's a beautiful thought. I think that's very wise." And Vera really did think it was, although beauty seemed far away from her right now; her voice, she realized, sounded as though she were being strangled. Just thinking that made her breath come more shallowly, and she held her elbows closer at her side so that her arms would not twitch. There was something comforting about this; she felt as though her arms were holding her rib cage in place, keeping its contents from spilling out.

"I'll always remember Sufia's lunches," Jamie said. "They always smelled good, and if you asked her what she was eating, she was always willing to share some of it. It was because of her that I first tried *sambuusas*."

Vera thought of sambuca, the liqueur. But then Cecily-Anne said, "Ohhhh, are those like samosas?"

"Yes, but *better.* The spices are different."

Aggie Hamada raised her hand. "I think it would be nice if we all shared a memory of Sufia. I have one I'd like to share."

The twitch had begun to settle into Vera's lips and into the muscles of her cheeks. She listened as Jamie told a story of how Sufia had been a valuable member of the debate team. "Mrs. Fortunato—the debate coach—used to call her our secret weapon," she said, "because she stuck by her beliefs and always let her argument unfold in a . . . patient way."

The other girls began to add to the stories. Soon, almost everyone had something they remembered: the extra pens Sufia always carried, in many colored inks, which she willingly lent to girls who'd lost or forgotten their own; Sufia's laugh, which was rare but delightful, making her whole body shake from head to toe.

"These are such lovely memories," Vera said when the stories began to dwindle. She was sure at this point that her students could see her tremors, and she thought that a couple of them were even looking at her with a mixture of revulsion and concern. Jensen Willard in particular was looking at her with what Vera thought might be sympathy, in her pale, gray, watchful way. Vera realized that Jensen was the only girl who had not shared a story about Sufia. "Anyone else?" she said, fixing her gaze on the girl. "Anyone else who has a memory to speak of?"

Just as she could have predicted, Jensen Willard pressed her lips together and shook her head.

Vera looked at the clock. There were still forty-five minutes left of class time. She had planned to allocate some of the day's class time to a discussion of *The Catcher in the Rye*, but Vera knew that talking about Holden Caulfield's slow disintegration and denial of the same were not the right topics to take on just now. "Let's do something a little different today," she said, her lips still twitching. "Poetry. I don't think you'll mind taking a little break from *Catcher* for a day or two, will you? Take out your literature anthologies and turn to page 646. Richard Wilbur, 'The Beautiful Changes.'"

Not budging from her perch on the table, Vera let students monopolize the discussion of the poem, interjecting very little herself; she even let Martha True read it aloud, in her girlish, quavery voice. In the remaining class time, she asked students to start drafting poems of their own. "You can write about loss if you'd like," Vera said, "or about sorrow. Or, if you don't want to, you don't have to write about those things."

As was often the case, she was rather amazed when they obeyed her. She still had not gotten used to the fact that she could say something like "Everyone start writing a poem," and everyone would actually do so. But her girls were essentially still children, and children were obedient creatures. As the girls frowned and scribbled and frowned some more, Vera thought they even *looked* childlike; the tip of Kelsey Smith's tongue protruded from her lips, making her look like an earnest toddler crafting a painting, while Jensen Willard's tousled cap of hair fell in her face as she started working out her first lines. Vera took this opportunity to sit quietly and feel the panic ebb out of her. When the last of the tremors had ebbed away, she felt weakened all over, as though she'd been run over by a truck.

Once the exercise was finished, Harmony Phelps said, "Are we going to get our journals back today?"

"Oh," Vera said, jumping up off the table, "I do have them. Thank you for reminding me."

She reserved a minute at the end of class to hand back students' journals, fully expecting that the girls would head for the door as soon as they received them. Instead, each girl sat with her journal just as Jensen had a few days prior, taking time to read Vera's handwritten feedback. For a moment she felt simultaneously flustered, pleased, and self-conscious, adding to the mental confusion she already felt; then she realized they were probably just subdued, rather than entranced by her comments.

The girls finally started to leave. Aggie Hamada said "Have a nice day" as she passed. Katherine "Kitty" Arsenault, one of Vera's most reticent students, called out "See you tomorrow!" on her way out. It proved to Vera what she had seen play out time and again in other classes she'd taught: You could stand before a class all day long and exchange ideas till you were blue in the face, but there was no greater bond to be formed than when grief and vulnerability were shared. That's where she liked to think their sudden kindness came from, anyway; she didn't like to think that they just felt sorry for her.

Her strength regained, Vera stood up and called out, "Jensen? Could I speak to you for a second?" just as the girl was lifting herself arthritically out of her seat.

Jensen did as she was asked, and Vera could see that the whites around her amber eyes had a yellowish look that she'd never noticed before. It occurred to her that the girl might not be getting enough sleep. And no wonder, given all that was going on lately. "Are you doing okay?" she asked.

"I'm doing all right. Why?"

"I know from your journal entry that you're going through a little bit of a rough time, that's all. And then, well . . . there's Sufia."

The girl shrugged. "Are *you* okay?" she asked Vera.

Vera took this as a jab at her visible nervousness in the classroom. Even if the question was well-meaning, coming from a place of genuine concern, she had no intention of answering it. "I'm fine. Listen, while I've got you up here, there's something else I want to ask of you. Could you please make an effort to be on time from now on? Class begins promptly at eight o'clock. Everyone else is on time, so it's only fair that you are, too. I know maybe this is a funny time to bring that up, but I've been meaning to mention it for a while."

"Okay. I can make an effort."

"I'd appreciate that."

"I'm sorry I'm a little late sometimes. I have to motivate a little bit before I get from class to class. But did you know this is my favorite class?"

"Is it? Thank you." Vera hadn't been expecting that. She felt herself blushing at the compliment and feeling ludicrous for doing so.

"You're welcome. It's nice of you to put up with me and read all my writing."

"I worry a bit, that's all. It's not a question of *putting up* with you."

Then Jensen said something that nearly floored Vera. "It must have been awful for whoever found Sufia in the park like that."

"Yes," Vera said. "I'm sure it was."

"I wonder what she looked like. I mean, being dead and all."

Her chest tightening again, Vera said, "I don't feel quite comfortable with this line of discussion."

"You know what else? I heard that her boyfriend did it."

"Where did you hear that from? Chelsea Cutler, maybe?"

"Just around." Jensen's lips moved in something as close to a smile as Vera had ever seen from her. "I have to go to French now," the girl said. "Bye." She turned on her heels, dragging her knapsack behind her in a clatter of buckles.

Uneasily, Vera watched her go, until the clattering grew fainter and fainter down the corridor outside her classroom door.

The rest of Vera's classes were better. Though she now felt foolish for moving into a poetry unit, she repeated the morning's discussion with her last two sections, not wanting one group to get ahead of the other in their *Catcher* readings. When classes were over, Sue MacMasters stopped her outside the door of the faculty lounge with another invitation to meet up with the English teachers for tomorrow's lunch. The underlying purpose of this, Vera knew, was for the group to commiserate about Sufia Ahmed. Vera was tempted to say she was so bogged down in paperwork she couldn't possibly join them, but she knew the solemnity of recent events required her presence. Besides, these faculty lunches, though still strained, were getting a little easier for her. She had now met informally with the English faculty three times, and each lunch period had been a little less painful than the one before. They weren't a bad group of women on the whole, Vera had to remind herself during those seemingly protracted forty-five-minute lunches. They were well-meaning, and they seemed as though they accepted her, or were at least getting used to her quiet, standoffish ways.

Once Sue was gone, Vera went inside the lounge to check her mailbox. She sorted through a few memos, threw out a postcard one shamelessly self-promoting faculty member had distributed to advertise her pottery exhibit, and retrieved one short, typed document that looked like a student essay, though it had no name or title at the top. She looked at it, flinched, and looked at it again, first checking around the room to make sure no one else was with her.

I'm still thinking about Sufia. I can't help it. And I can't help wondering about you. It seems this is really getting to you.

One has to wonder about someone who just goes waltzing through the park at two or three in the morning and why she would be there to begin with. What did this person think when she first saw Sufia? I've read accounts from other people who've stumbled across dead bodies and how they thought they were seeing a department store mannequin or a doll. Is that what this person thought?

I've been reading all the articles about Sufia I can find—

mostly the same one, reprinted over and over in different papers. It feels like Angela Galvez all over again, doesn't it?

If I'm being completely honest, I'm jealous of both of them—both these dead girls. Not because of the attention, but because they got away. I wish it was that easy for me to escape. Sometimes I like to think of death as an adventure, a retreat. It would be the nicest vacation I'd ever have, and the best part would be that it wouldn't have to end.

Think of it: No more worrying about being disappointed. No more worrying about disappointing other people. No more trying to impress people who I can't even impress. And I suppose this is the very definition of egotistical, but I can't help wondering what people would say about me once I was gone—would anyone miss me? Would Bret? Or would I just continue to be that whispered-about weird girl doing another weird thing, the weird thing to end all weird things?

How nice it would be to just die for a little while and come back when the coast is clear. But I don't think it happens that way. Even if I believed in life after death, which I'm not sure I do, there would be no guarantee that we could come back when we felt ready; we would have to come back at somebody else's whim. I wonder if Angela and Sufia are going to come back. Maybe they already have. Maybe they're already here—right here beside you, in the room you're standing in now, just waiting for you to notice them.

Vera, having read the last line, whirled around as though expecting someone to have crept up behind her. There was no one there. Her hands had begun to tremble again, causing the typed pages to rattle, and she sought out the cubicle in which the school secretary, Eileen, worked.

"Eileen?" she said. "Did a student drop off a paper for you to put in my box? A short, dark-haired girl?"

"No," said Eileen, a salty young woman who seemed years older than her actual age—a woman who always looked at Vera with a hint of mockery, as though thinking she could take her in a bar fight. Which she probably could.

"I have a paper in my box from a student," Vera said. "I'm just wondering how it got in there since students don't have access to the lounge."

"Beats me," Eileen said.

School had ended only fifteen minutes before. Many students were still in the halls. Vera took off from the lounge and sped through the corridors, garnering looks from the students she passed; panting, she ran up and down the rows of lockers on all three flights of the school, searching for Jensen Willard. She was nowhere to be found.

Chapter Seven

On Friday, Jensen Willard was absent from Vera's class. She was absent again on the following Monday, and by the time Wednesday rolled around, she was still a no-show. This was cause for concern. Per the Wallace School's policy, any student who missed four consecutive school days was the recipient of a check-in from the attendance office—a phone call asking when she planned to return. Vera had been contemplating an informal check-in of her own, but she could not bring herself to email the girl. Her drafts folder was already full of unfinished queries she could not and would not send—drafts that ranged from accusatory ("Why did you put that journal in my mailbox? What do you know about me?") to appropriately concerned ("Your comments worry me. Do you need someone to talk to?").

She knew it was fear that prohibited her from sending them. Not fear of Jensen Willard specifically—she didn't like to think she was becoming *afraid* of the girl—but fear of the girl's mental state, which she saw as something quite separate.

Her quandary was solved when Sue MacMasters came by on Wednesday afternoon and said, "I need you to send me the last few days' homework assignments for one of your students." She paused to look at the name written down on her clipboard. "Jensen Willard. Her mother called the school office and requested that all her teachers send the work."

"Is Jensen all right?"

"Sick," Sue said briskly. "Though her mother did say she's on the mend. Specifically, she's started sitting up again and drinking tea."

"Sounds like a bad flu, maybe?" Vera kept her tone mild. She did not want Sue to see that the mere mention of Jensen Willard rattled her. Vera took out her notebook and started writing down the past few days' readings and written assignments. "I'll make a list of the missing assignments and see that Jensen gets them. If you do happen to speak to her mother again, send my wishes for a speedy recovery."

"Oh, *I* don't take phone calls like that. Are you kidding? That's Eileen's job."

Vera's classes, minus Jensen, resumed their discussions of *The Catcher in the Rye*, which was finally winding down to its last chapters. The girls seemed confused by Holden's low spirits and compromised physical health, unsure of what to make of the novel's penultimate chapter when Holden is nearly in tears while watching his little sister, Phoebe, go round and round on the Central Park carousel.

"I don't see why he'd get all worked up about that," Kelsey Smith said. "Little kids ride on carousels all the time."

"They do," Vera said. "That's just it. Haven't you ever had a moment where something ordinary strikes you as extraordinary? Where something ordinary seems wonderfully beautiful or wonderfully sad?"

When Kelsey shook her head, Vera had to stop and process that for a moment. How was it possible to not be struck by such things? "Maybe in time you will" was all she could say to the girl, moving past her seat.

"It says in the last chapter that he ended up getting sick," Jamie

Friedman said. "But he's talking to a psychoanalyst . . . Is he in like a mental hospital or a regular hospital?"

"It isn't made explicitly clear. Most readers assume he is in a psychiatric facility, but one might argue that he could be in a sanitarium of some kind for his physical health. Whatever the case, he is receiving psychiatric treatment."

"But he was happy right before the last chapter," Aggie Hamada said worriedly, as though happiness and sadness could not coexist or follow each other in close succession.

"Maybe it's because he'd just promised Phoebe he wouldn't leave," Jamie said. "He was going to leave, and then he changed his mind and decided to go home. Maybe that made him happy in a way, to have finally *decided* on something."

"Speaking of deciding," Vera said, "this coming weekend will be time for you to decide on your big essay topics for *The Catcher in the Rye*. Remind me to set aside a few minutes at the end of class to discuss what might make a good topic versus what might make a weak topic."

On Friday afternoon, Vera's mother called to ask if she'd heard about the woman who'd been strangled in the park ("So close to where you live!" she'd lamented). Vera had known it was only a matter of time before her mother got wind of the news story and took it as further proof that Vera was in grave danger living all by herself.

Exasperated, she said, "Mom, this happened the week before *last*. What did you do, read a week-old paper that was kicking around at the doctor's office or something?"

"Yes. And I can't believe you didn't call me, when somebody got killed practically in your own backyard, where you walk all the time!"

"It wasn't practically in my yard, Mom, and I don't walk through the park at night. I'm alert to my surroundings. I lived in New York City, remember?"

"You sound stressed. I'd feel better if I could see you. Why don't you come down? You could call in sick on Monday, and you could have a nice, long, quiet weekend. I think you'd find it good to get out of there."

Vera was almost persuaded. Perhaps a relaxing weekend *would* be just the thing right now. But reason won out. "I have a lot of work to do this weekend, Mom," she said, not without regret. "And this would be a really bad time to call in sick. My girls need me." As soon as she said it out loud, she sensed the inherent foolishness of this comment. She doubted that they *needed* her for anything.

The following Monday, Jensen Willard returned to class. She was not late this time—in fact, she arrived before several of the other girls did—but she did not make eye contact with Vera as she came in and settled into her seat. She bent over her notebook, underlining the page's blue rulings with a black pen.

"Feeling better?" Vera said.

"A little." Jensen still didn't look up. She had a spot of high color on each usually pale cheek, like a child who had been playing hard outside in the snow. *Maybe she really* does *have the flu,* Vera thought.

"Do you want my make-up homework now? I still haven't done my final essay for *Catcher*."

"Those aren't due till next week. Let's talk *after* class is over." Vera noticed that some of the other girls were beginning to shift in their seats. What was it about a simple utterance from Jensen Willard that seemed to make the other girls physically uncomfortable? Vera recalled the accounts people had given of interacting with known psychopaths, Ivan Schlosser among them: *There was just something about him that made the little hairs on the back of my neck stand up.* But was Jensen really a psychopath? And why hadn't she noticed before that the girls reacted this way to her? *Perhaps,* Vera thought, *I am simply projecting.*

When class was over, Jensen remained at her seat until the last girl had gone. Then she got up and spoke, her gaze now redirected to the top of Vera's table. "Sorry I missed so many classes. I wanted to talk to you about some topic ideas I had for my *Catcher* final."

"There's something else I'd like to discuss first." Vera reached into her first-period folder and took out the two typed sheets she had found in her faculty mailbox days before. "I've been wanting to ask you for several days how you got this journal entry into the faculty lounge."

"What journal entry?"

Vera rustled the two sheets together. "This one right here."

"That isn't a journal. It's a freewrite that I assigned to myself."

"Your freewrite, then, if that's what you want to call it. I call it very strange. Why did you put it in my box anonymously, as it were? Why not just give it to me in class?"

"I don't know," Jensen said.

"You don't *know*?"

"Seriously. I wrote it, but I didn't mean to pass it in. I don't know how it got in your box. I'm sorry if it bothered you."

This was a stalemate. Jensen looked Vera in the eye, a rarity, but Vera found her affect so flat that she could not tell if the girl was lying or not. The red spots in her cheeks seemed to darken, and Vera could not tell if this was an angry flush, or a defensive one, or one of pure embarrassment.

"I really I hope you aren't toying with me, Jensen. I don't find it cute or funny. You know that I . . . you know I think highly of you. But please don't toy with me."

"I'm not. I don't know why you would think that. I did turn a new journal entry in today, though, when everyone else passed their stuff in. It's really short. I'm sorry about that, too—it being so short, I mean."

Vera put the two typed pages back into her folder, looking up at

Jensen. "Well," she said almost gruffly, "you've been so prolific with your other entries. I don't think a shorter one is something you need to be sorry for. It's not *length* I'm worried about. It's more a question of the content. Some of the things you write . . ."

"Can we talk about my essay ideas now? I have Advanced French coming up in ten minutes."

There were many things she wanted to say to the girl. She wanted to ask her to explain her comments about Sufia Ahmed and how she envied her for being dead. She knew, as an educator, she should try some outreach to the girl if she was having such thoughts—but there was something about the girl, her funny dignity and privacy, the need for personal space that was bigger than most people's, that made her unable to ask.

And then, of course, there was that fear. That inexplicable *fear* that seemed to be getting worse and worse.

They reviewed Vera's expectations for the final essay on *The Catcher in the Rye*. When they were finished, Jensen had made it as far as the door before she turned around slowly, teetering a little from the weight of her knapsack. "Miss Lundy?"

She had never called her that before. She had never addressed her in any way at all, Vera realized.

"Miss Lundy? When do you think you'll be able to read the new journal entry I turned in today?"

It struck Vera as a loaded question. "When? I can't tell you exactly. I may not get to it right away because I'm still catching up on so much other work. But by this weekend, I'm sure I'll be able to look at yours and everyone else's. Why?"

Someone was coming into the classroom—Kaitlyn Fiore again, with her forehead puckered and her mouth already open, as though she were about to launch into a tale of woe. She didn't hang back seeing that Vera was talking to someone but instead sidled up to her and waited expectantly. Jensen turned around again and was just out the door when Vera called after her, "Jensen? Was there anything else?"

The girl's mumbled reply was almost inaudible, but Vera thought she could make it out well enough. "No," she said. "Nothing else."

Her school day finished, Vera found an envelope containing a two-hundred-dollar check for her in her mailbox at home, wrapped in a note: "Spend this on something nice for yourself. Don't give it to those nasty student loan people. Love, Mom."

She wasted no time cashing it, purchasing a sixty-minute phone card on her way home and calling her mother from a coffee shop to thank her, resulting in forty-five minutes used on her card. With the remainder of the money she would buy a new bottle of not-bottom-shelf conditioner for her hair and bank whatever was left. *Lean times indeed,* she thought, *when drugstore conditioner is a splurge.* After picking up the conditioner, she stopped in at the library to return her books and pick out a few more. The same humorless librarian she always saw, the one in the turtleneck-and-jumper set, gave her the evil eye as she brought three new crime books to the circulation desk.

The rest of the school week passed without event. The empty chair where Sufia Ahmed had sat still seemed to occupy its own large space in the classroom, but every day it became a little easier to look the other way. The news articles about Sufia still appeared in the *Dorset Journal* on a daily basis, but the front-page story eventually found its way deeper and deeper into the pages of each issue until it ended up occupying a quiet space in the Lifestyles section one Sunday morning, under the heading A MOTHER'S GRIEF.

Another Friday came and went, and Jensen Willard had made no further ripples in class. In fact, she kept her head down through Vera's class discussions, drawing more and more lines in her notebook until they were so heavily inked that Vera, nearsighted as she was, could see the black ink slashes from several tables away. The vehemence of these suggested, to Vera, a chaotic state of mind. But for once she did not feel tempted to try to draw the girl in. She was content, for now, to leave her alone in her solitary bubble, where she could pose no threat to her or the other girls whom she'd begun, to her own surprise, to feel protective toward.

Later that Friday evening at home, trying to talk herself out of going to Pearl's—she had not been since *that night* and instead had made do with drinking at home—Vera drummed up the motivation to start looking through her students' journals. Though she at first thought of leaving Jensen Willard's self-professed "short" journal entry for Sunday, she made herself look at it first. Perhaps it would give her some insight into the girl's reason for sending that worrisome previous journal—or the *freewrite*, as she'd called it.

It didn't take long for Vera to locate Jensen's entry within the pile. It was handwritten, for one thing, in neat, rounded letters. All the other girls typed their entries, and Vera wondered what had kept Jensen from doing so this time. Also, unlike her previous journal entries—but much like the writing she had put in Vera's faculty mailbox—there was no title at the top, not even a name. But its authorship was clear enough, Vera saw as soon as she started reading.

It's a funny thing about knowing you have a limited time to live and that you can literally take your own life in your hands, as the saying goes. My life is a small life. I guess it would fit in my hands all right. But the thing I'd always thought—always counted on—was that I would know to the day and hour when I was going. I would have those last few days to know I was saying good-bye, and though no one else would know it, and I'd have some closure for myself before I left. Now it isn't going to be like that, exactly.

I have figured some things out.

Vera, who had been reading this with a mounting sense of dread, turned the page and saw that more was written on the back, but Jensen's handwriting became drastically smaller here, its pen strokes fainter, like those of a feeble old woman. Seeing this transition made her hold her breath.

Earlier this evening (it is Tuesday night right now—actually, Wednesday morning at 1:30 A.M.), I went downstairs with an idea of what I might do. My mother was snoring away on the couch while The Late Show *played on TV in the background. I stood by the side of the couch for a while, looking down at my mother. I wondered if she might wake up. But she didn't. It seemed particularly significant that she was not awake for me. It seemed to reinforce that I was meant to go through with my idea.*

After I had stood beside her a long time, I went into the kitchen and looked around in the cupboards, where we keep our over-the-counter medicines. There wasn't much in there. A big bottle of Tylenol. The remainder of some cough syrup that I hadn't drunk yet. Les had had a sleeping pill prescription once that he'd gone on when he had to quit smoking—I thought those pills were still in there. I rattled around in the cupboard, looking. From the living room, my mother called out in a sleepy croak, "Honey? What're you looking for?"

"Nothing," I said. I shut the cupboard door.

"You were looking for SOMETHING*."*

"A Tylenol."

I can't do it here at my parents' house anyway. I realized this when she came into the kitchen, her two-piece pajamas rumpled and her hair in curlers, to see if she could help me find the Tylenol that I had already found. I do know my parents love me. I can't die in the house because I can't have them be the ones to find my body. I don't think my mother would ever recover from that.

Plan B came to mind then, and this is the plan I'm sticking to. In an indirect way, I got the idea from Holden Caulfield; I was thinking about his time spent in hotels, going down to the piano bar and drunk-dialing women and having a prostitute sent to his room. Not that I'm planning to do any of that, mind you. I could check in to that new hotel on the Wheaton Road and do what I have to do. Some poor hotel worker will have to find my body looking all putrid, but that's a job hazard for them, I'm guessing. They probably have to take a "What to Do When You Find a Putrid Body" class when they major in hotel management and hospitality.

I've gotten my stepfather's old service pistol out of my parents' closet. I'm not sure if I know how to use it, but I'm watching some YouTube tutorials. It can't be that hard. I don't think I'll use it on myself. I think I will pick a different option there. But if my parents or the police get wind of this, I won't hesitate to use it on myself just to get the business over with quickly.

Friday night is when I'm going to check myself in.
It is also the night I am going to check out for good.

A suicide threat, Vera thought. *Or maybe a promise. And she wanted to be sure I heard it.*

Numbness was one of her first reactions. Was this a real threat or just schoolgirl melodrama? Given what she had begun to think about her student, Vera felt it was real. Jensen had now moved beyond being a mere squeaky wheel—one who sought attention in passive-aggressive ways—and into the most serious sort of problem. And Vera knew she had a responsibility, as an adult and as her teacher, to respond to it.

The second clear thought Vera had was, *This is a hell of a time to have only fifteen minutes on my phone.* But fifteen minutes would perhaps be enough, if she handled everything just so.

No police, Jensen had said. No parents. But the parents *would* have to be contacted. She had no choice but to reach out to them if she wanted to get any sense of their daughter's whereabouts.

Her hands shaking, she took the phone book off the top of her refrigerator. Checking the listings, Vera couldn't help but think of Jensen's parents, envisioning them as Jensen herself had described them: She pictured Mrs. Cudahy looking like an older Jensen, slim-hipped and with salt-and-pepper hair, and imagined the husband who was twenty-five years her senior. Two people who, if Vera had read between the lines correctly, loved their daughter beyond measure.

She was in luck; a Leslie Cudahy was listed with a Pine Street address—no more than a ten-minute walk from her studio and only a few streets away from the Ahmeds' duplex. She punched the numbers into her phone, and as she waited for the ring, she felt her paralysis and terror replaced by an almost preternatural sense of calm. *I've got this,* she told herself. *I've got this under control.*

A drowsy-voiced woman answered on the third ring.

"Hello," Vera said. "Would this be Mrs. Willard?"

"*Used* to be."

"Oh, I'm so sorry! I meant Mrs. *Cudahy*. I don't know why I said Willard."

"Who is this?" The woman—Mrs. Cudahy—sounded patient, as though she were used to being roused from sleep to answer such calls.

"My name is Vera Lundy. I'm Jensen's English teacher, her substitute English teacher for the rest of the school year."

"Oh, right, I've heard about you."

How odd, Vera thought, that Jensen had spoken of both of them to each other—Mrs. Cudahy to Vera, and Vera to Mrs. Cudahy—weaving a familiarity between two women who hadn't met. "I was just hoping to find Jensen at home. I wanted to speak to her about something."

"I'm afraid she *isn't*. She's doing a sleepover at a friend's house."

Vera's stomach lurched. She realized she had been half expecting that Jensen would be home watching *Wheel of Fortune* with her parents and that the threat presented in the journal entry would be a false alarm. "A sleepover with a friend?" *But she has no friends,* Vera wanted to say. Not unless you counted Bret, or her former friend Annabel, or her semi-friend Scotty—none of whom seemed a viable candidate for a sleepover.

"Yup. Her new friend Phoebe, from English class. You must know her."

Vera had an urge to laugh—the sort of anguished, ill-timed laugh that can easily end in tears. There weren't many girls named Phoebe nowadays, and the only Phoebe Vera had recently heard mention of was in a book. "Phoebe? She didn't say her friend's name was Phoebe *Caulfield*, did she?"

"Yes, Phoebe Coffle. About an hour ago she got dropped off. You want the number there, or you just want me to give her a message? There isn't anything *wrong*, is there?"

Vera wanted to tell her that quite possibly something was wrong, very wrong indeed, but she could not say this to the sleepy but good-natured voice on the phone. Instead she took the number down, wanting to stall for time, keep Mrs. Cudahy on the phone longer in hopes that she might disclose something else that could be of use. She was thinking hard, trying to improvise, but deception did not always come so easily to her; she could only thank her politely for the information she'd received and apologize once again for being a bother. "No bother," Mrs. Cudahy said. "I probably owe you a thanks. You woke me up just in time for my show."

Eleven minutes left on her phone.

She dialed the number Mrs. Cudahy had given her and found that it was not a working number. She went on the Internet, cursing her connection for its slowness, and performed a Google search for hotels in the Dorset area until she found what she was seeking: A newly erected Roundview Hotel was in business on the Wheaton Road, all the way on the other end of town. Things were adding up, painting a clear and ominous picture in Vera's mind.

Ten minutes left on her phone.

Twelve dollars in cash in her wallet: Vera took the time to count them. Twelve dollars, and no time to waste finding an ATM. She hoped this would be enough as she dialed the number of a taxi company and asked to be picked up. The dispatcher on the phone said, "We'll send someone right over," so Vera sat on the stoop of her building and waited, shivering in her coat and hat. The air was pregnant and still, as though a light, spring snow were coming. She was already mentally calculating what she would cut from her monthly budget in order to afford the cab fare; about four morning coffees, she figured—but no, she couldn't go without her coffee. Perhaps she could write a smaller check for the cable TV bill and pay the difference later. *Why,* she berated herself, *are you even thinking of this now? Another girl could be dead. Your very own student could be dead in a hotel room, and you're thinking about twelve dollars.*

The cab, when it finally came, had an interior that smelled sharply of underarm sweat, forcing Vera to mouth-breathe as she tried to respond to the driver's perfunctory questions about how long she'd lived in the area and whether she'd heard anything about the snow that had been forecast for later in the evening. She wished herself back in New York City, where the cabbies never bothered with politesse, never felt compelled to fill silences with small talk.

It was critical that she be able to think. Riding alone in the backseat, she thought about Jensen Willard being alone in a hotel room for an hour—about what could have been accomplished in an hour. The calm self that had taken over was starting to recede, and nervousness kicked in as the cab nudged its way through the dark.

Another ten minutes passed before she reached the hotel. Entering the lobby, she saw an indifferent-looking young man shambling behind the reception desk—a tall desk designed, it seemed, to make its patrons feel diminutive. With as much poise as she could muster, Vera leaned against the desk, lifted her face to the young man, and said, "I wonder if you can help me. I'm looking for someone who I think is staying here tonight."

The desk clerk gave her a once-over through hooded eyes. As he leaned in closer, Vera got a distinct whiff of strong, skunk-like pot emanating from either his hair or his clothes. "What's the name?"

Vera told him, and spelled it upon his request.

"Hold on a sec," the desk clerk said, and he scrolled through the computer records with maddening leisure. "Nope," he said at last, "Don't have anyone registered with that name."

"Oh." She should have expected that this might be a possibility, yet she refused to accept it. Had the girl gone somewhere else and planned to check in later? Should she do a stakeout in the lobby?

"I do have a *Phoebe* Willard, though."

"That's it! That's got to be it. Could you call her and see if she'll meet me in the lobby? Please tell her that her teacher Miss Lundy would like to see her."

Vera held her breath as she waited for the young man to call the room number. *Please,* she thought, *let it be her number. Let it be her and let her answer. And let her not do anything drastic as a result of me coming. She said that her parents and the police shouldn't interfere, but she didn't say anything about* me, *did she?* She allowed herself to exhale, not a moment too soon, when she heard the desk clerk saying, "Someone's down in the lobby to see you. Some woman who says she's your teacher." He hung up the phone, looked over at Vera, and said, "She'll come down to meet you. Have a seat if you want. There's free coffee."

Vera took a seat in one of the stiff-backed chairs in the lobby. Her chair faced a cement fishpond, the sort one sees in Chinese restaurants of a certain type; three dark fish swam lethargically, their long fins wilting in the water. A few pennies were scattered at the bottom of the pond—what did tossing the pennies signify? Some kind of luck? A wish granted? She felt around in her coat pockets, but her pennies were kept up at home, stored in a canister intended for flour—emergency money for hard times.

She realized she was scared again, now that she knew Jensen was all right. Relieved, of course, but what would she say to her now? She had planned to convince the girl to go back home, to forget her melodramatic idea of killing herself. She had no idea what to expect from

Jensen. If she was becoming as unhinged as she'd sounded in her recent communiqués, convincing her might not be easy. She might even lash out. *What if she brings that pistol downstairs?* Vera thought.

The elevator made a humming sound; its up arrow lit green, then its down arrow. Someone was heading to the lobby. When the little bell declared itself and the elevator car reached its stop, Vera watched its doors open and saw Jensen Willard emerge. The girl was dressed in a baggy, dark-gray T-shirt and military pants that were much too long; she kept treading on their hems but somehow didn't stumble over them. This boyish ensemble made her look younger and more delicate, almost gamine, as she inched her way over to the lobby.

Her hands were empty, and Vera could see no sign of a bulky weapon in her pants pockets. She didn't appear to be carrying anything other than her own dark mood and the weight of her own slight body.

"Well, hello, *Phoebe*." Vera got out of her chair, and the quick motion made her feel light-headed for an instant. The girl was very much alive. *Now what?* she thought. "I'm glad I found you."

"Why?" Jensen's voice was solemn, and her breath was fragrant with alcohol—vodka and orange juice, unless Vera missed her guess.

"I read your last journal. I only guessed that this might be where you were."

"Oh," Jensen said. "*That's* why you're here. By the way, were you looking for a penny? I have one." Jensen reached into one of her deep pants pockets, leaned forward, and let a single coin drop into the pond. The fish swam for the far ends of the fountain and quivered there, waiting for this disturbance to pass. "Since you've come, maybe you'd like to come up and see my room? There's wall art with lighthouses on it."

"Goodness," Vera said. She wavered for an instant, wondering if this was an invitation she wanted to accept. Her instincts told her that she did not want to be alone with Jensen Willard. She thought of her saying, *It must have been awful for whoever found the body,* with a little smile that, in her recollection, had taken on a ghoulish sort of pleasure. "Why don't we just talk down here? It's quiet, and we have this whole space to ourselves."

"I'd rather not."

"You'd rather not talk? Or you just don't want to talk down here?"

"The last one."

Vera thought for a moment. She had come for a reason, and that was to help; she could be of no assistance to her student if she backed out now and let her walk away.

"I guess I could come up for just a few minutes," she said.

She followed her into the elevator and sighed as the door slid shut; after the door had closed and the elevator shaft jerked its way upward, Jensen murmured, "So how did you guess 'Phoebe'?"

Vera was relieved that Jensen had broken the silence and that her question was benign enough. "I didn't, exactly. I did call your house and get the name of your sleepover buddy. I take it your parents aren't big readers."

Jensen did not crack a smile as Vera had hoped she might. The girl might be playing it cool, but her nonresponse conveyed that this was still not a time for jokes. *What's wrong with you?* Vera reprimanded herself. *Nerves? You can't botch this. You can't say stupid things.* The elevator stopped at the fourth floor, and Jensen led Vera down the length of carpeting, stopping at the last door and opening it with her keycard.

Behind the door was a perfectly usual, perfectly drab hotel room. Two double beds with cheap, scratchy-looking floral comforters faced a TV tucked in a cabinet; the TV was on, but the volume was at its lowest setting, its voices reduced to staticky whispers. On a table near the large double windows, Vera saw a nearly full bottle of vodka and a carton of orange juice, plus an ashtray with a mostly unsmoked cigarette stubbed out in it. Next to the chair were Jensen's combat boots and beside that, her army knapsack, unbuckled and crumpled on the floor.

"I didn't know you smoked," Vera asked, then wondered why she had said *that*, of all the possible opening gambits she could have used. *So much for not saying stupid things.*

"I don't. But my parents do. I thought tonight might be a good night to start."

"I see you have two beds here. Why didn't you get a single room?"

"I think they made a mistake." Jensen sat down on the bed closest to the window in a ladylike fashion that was very much at odds with her clothes; she crossed her legs and sat up straight, looking like a conscientious girl preparing to get the most out of a class.

"I'm surprised you even came down to meet me," Vera said, gingerly seating herself on the bed across from Jensen's. "I mean, I'm *glad* you did. Did you want me to be here, Jensen? Is that why you were so specific about your plans in your journal? You wanted to make sure I read the journal before tonight. You wanted to make sure I prevented you from doing anything."

"Not necessarily."

"Then why? Why tell me such things? I have to tell you, I don't know what to make of any of this. It's all so . . . *irregular.*"

Jensen shrugged, stifled a yawn behind her hand, and directed her attention to the TV; Vera had a feeling this was an affectation, for her posture was still ramrod-straight. Vera's eyes followed the girl's and saw that an old *Twilight Zone* episode was on, featuring a young but already-balding Robert Duvall as a man who was in love with a doll—a beautiful, grown-up lady doll who lived in a museum dollhouse. She remembered the episode. It had been one of her favorites when she was a kid.

"Perhaps we can turn the TV off?" she suggested.

"I like *The Twilight Zone*. Hey, do you want a drink?" Jensen asked, springing up off the bed. "If you do, you could put it in the extra mouthwash cup."

"I don't think that's a good idea." She wanted to tell the girl that *she* probably shouldn't be drinking, either, but to do so seemed almost trivial under the circumstances.

"I don't even like alcohol all that much," the girl said, dumping vodka into her cup and topping it off with a splash of orange juice. "But I thought it might help me tonight. I have a fake ID my friend Scotty made me once, but I never had a chance to use it for anything." Then, without looking at Vera: "What'd my mom say to you on the phone?"

"Very little. But since you mention it, I should tell you that I didn't say much, either. I didn't give anything away. I didn't mention anything about what you'd hinted you would do here tonight—you know, the whole 'checking out' thing. When I called, I had every intention of saying something about it. But I changed my mind."

"Why?"

"That's a complicated question, Jensen."

"*Why* is not complicated. It's the answer that might be complicated."

"You're right about that," Vera admitted. "I don't know if I can answer that right this second."

"You know what? You look different outside a classroom. Younger."

"I was just thinking that you look older, not sitting behind a desk."

It was a white lie of sorts; Jensen, having resumed her position on her bed, looked younger than Vera had ever seen her look. But she could tell the comment pleased her student. Vera remained on the opposite bed and looked from her hands to the moving TV shapes to Jensen, trying to think of what else to say. She realized she was perspiring, pressured as she was to make every word count . . . and also because she was deathly afraid. The girl seemed calm, harmless, and small enough in person, but that didn't mean she wasn't a loose cannon. That didn't mean it wasn't of utmost importance that Vera choose her words very carefully. "I suppose I didn't mention anything to your mother because I thought I could spare you some . . . awkwardness at home. Maybe you'd find it easier to talk to me instead, just like you talk to me in your journals."

Jensen gave her a sidelong look. "I hope you aren't about to tell me this is all 'just a phase.'"

"Rest assured I'm not going to."

Jensen continued to stare at the nearly muted TV, but Vera could tell she was listening.

"This is awful of me to say because you'll probably recoil from this idea. It's not something a girl your age would want to hear from . . . someone older like me. But when I first started teaching in February, when I first met you, you reminded me of myself when I was your age. Maybe you sense that, too. Maybe that's why you've written the journals for me to see. I don't really know, Jensen; this is all just me guessing. I don't know what you're looking for from me exactly, but I want to provide whatever it is you need."

"*How* do I remind you of yourself?" Jensen asked. She didn't sound irritated. More bemused than irritated.

"Well, my own teenage years were . . . quite tortured, emotionally. I tried to off myself several times."

"*Off myself*—that's a nice phrase," Jensen said amiably. She was looking at Vera now with interest. "You know, the British say *top myself*. It sounds so jovial."

"It does."

"*Why* did you want to kill yourself?"

"Much of the same reasons you do, I assume," Vera said. "My emotions were outsized, as was my intellect. It wasn't a good combination. Those four years of high school were like . . ." She hesitated, thinking of how to characterize it without saying too much. "They occurred in slow motion, as though protracted. They still live in me as a raw period of time that I can't completely shake off. I'm still that fifteen-year-old in a lot of ways. I am not sure that this is the norm. I would guess that most people my age would say they feel far removed from the fifteen-year-old they once were."

"I can't even picture you as a fifteen-year-old."

"I don't think I ever was one. I was always a miniature adult when I was young. It was only later in life that my immaturity cemented itself." Vera thought of saying more. She thought of telling Jensen how she had thought in high school that she'd like to be a teacher someday, in hopes of making young men's and women's lives a little different from how hers had been. She thought of telling her that she had been so shy that she had flunked her undergraduate teaching practicum and been kicked out of the secondary education program, which left her with a creative writing degree and a library aide job before she moved on to graduate school and all that came afterward. She wanted to explain that it took her a lot of guts to finally pursue a teaching track—that it still took a lot of guts—and that it was only remembering the frightened girl she had been that enabled her to get up every day and face her students.

Focus on Jensen, she told herself. *Don't let her sidetrack you.* "Jensen," Vera asked bluntly, "did you have a plan for how you were going to kill yourself tonight? Were you going to use that gun?"

"Only if the police showed up. That wouldn't be my first choice, though."

"You once wrote about jumping off a bridge as a means of killing yourself. Why jumping?"

"Because you can't really go back on that decision once you've made it. You can't stop midjump. I suppose shooting yourself could also be foolproof, but then I'd prefer not to have my head splattered all over these walls. Too messy."

"You know, when you jump from a great height, your organs get ripped up in your own body. As you land, your rib cage essentially shatters and impales all your organs. And the death isn't always instantaneous. It isn't a pretty way to go, Jensen."

"I don't think there *is* a pretty way."

"There isn't," Vera agreed. "But some are uglier than others."

"I have an older cousin who worked in a hotel in Providence. A woman killed herself there once. She drank bleach. No one heard from her for a few days, and then her room started to smell. They sent my cousin to go unlock her door, and she saw her lying naked on the bed. She was so discolored that at first she couldn't tell if she was a black woman or a white woman."

"This couldn't have been pleasant for your cousin."

"It wasn't. She quit the next day."

"I doubt it was pleasant for the woman, either," Vera said, "drinking bleach."

The TV had distracted Jensen again. Vera looked, too, and saw that Robert Duvall had somehow found his way into the dollhouse and was sitting next to his ladylove on the dollhouse-size sofa. "Oh my God, how did he get inside?" Jensen asked.

"Jensen," Vera said, trying to keep the wheedling note out of her voice. "Jensen, let me ask you this. You aren't really thinking of killing yourself because of *Bret Folger*, are you? Because, really. He's just a *boy*. Not even a particularly special one, by the sounds of it."

Jensen cocked her head to the side as though processing this. Then she nodded a slight, acquiescent little nod.

Taking a deeper breath, Vera asked, "Is it because of the girls who died? The ones who got murdered? I know you said you envied them. I hope you aren't trying to follow in their footsteps."

Jensen smiled in a cagey sort of way as though Vera had said something that secretly pleased her. "You know what's funny about Sufia Ahmed? I used to see her walking around my neighborhood all the time. She'd go to the halal market, and sometimes I'd see her in the regular corner market, translating things for her mother. Her mother didn't speak much English. Outside of school Sufia spoke—what language do you call that? African? She was so American in some ways, though, with that phone she was always carrying around. And sometimes I saw her wearing jeans under that drapey stuff she always wore to school."

"I imagine what you were hearing them speak was Somali. Possibly Arabic. But you didn't answer my question."

"Somali, right. What was the question? Am I trying to follow in her footsteps? No. Do you think I'd want all those people coming to my funeral? That was all so *disgusting*."

"What about Bret? Does he—or your recent conversation with him—have anything to do with you coming here tonight?"

Jensen shrugged.

"I'm just checking," Vera added. "If Bret has something to do with this, I don't think you should find fault with yourself. Believe me, I know what it's like to want to be cared for by someone who doesn't deserve your affections."

Jensen turned toward Vera, holding out her cup. "Ugh, I can't finish this. Do you want it?"

"No," Vera said. Then: "Yes." She was thinking of police interrogation techniques and wondering if she could use what little she knew of them for her own purposes. Detective Vachon had spoken to Schlosser on his own level to get him to relax, making jokes about how women were bitches and how teenage girls were the worst cock-teases of all; it was all a ruse, of course, but Schlosser had bought into it. If she shared a drink with her student, would that foster trust? Vera accepted the cup before she knew she was going to. She took a small sip; it was nearly undrinkable, but not entirely. She took a larger swig and swished it around in her mouth.

"Didn't you say you used to live in New York City?" Jensen asked.

"I did," Vera said, "for almost ten years. Then I came back here. Maine is where I was raised. People always told me that everyone who leaves Maine comes back to it eventually. I swore I wouldn't be one of those people. What makes you bring that up?"

"Sometimes I thought I'd go down to New York to live with Bret. I was thinking that especially when we were reading the book. You know, *Catcher*. I printed up this map once of all the places Holden visits in New York, thinking I might go there sometime. Maybe I still will. But I guess a lot of those places aren't around anymore. When I went to visit Bret that one time, I only got to see Morningside Heights."

"Some of the places are still there. Most of the hotels aren't operating as hotels anymore. But all the big places . . . Central Park, the Metropolitan Museum of Art, the Radio City ice rink . . . they're right where they've always been, naturally." Vera noted, but did not mention, that the girl had used the future tense—*maybe I still will.* A slip of the tongue on Jensen's part, or a small victory on Vera's? She finished her drink in one concentrated gulp.

"I really did feel embarrassed writing all that stuff about Bret," Jensen said. "I don't want to be thought of as the kind of girl who goes all crazy over a guy. It's not Bret. It's *people* who make me crazy."

Vera got up and stood by the window, refilling her empty cup with a small amount of vodka and a large amount of orange juice. She could be fired if the school knew she was drinking with a student—a fifteen-year-old student at that. "Can I borrow one of your cigarettes?"

"Take the whole pack."

Vera lit the cigarette with one of the matches left out on the table, pushing the window out so she could direct her smoke into the night air. She was deep in thought, trying to frame what she wanted to say to Jensen.

"I mentioned I could tell you some stories," she said. "There's one little story about a boy I want to tell you, if you don't mind listening." Her back to the girl, she spoke in the direction of the air, watching her smoke ribbon out and disappear.

"In high school I had a boyfriend named Peter. This was the late 1980s, and in Maine you didn't see as many punk or alternative-type kids as you do today. It wasn't normal to see kids with blue hair or T-shirts with skulls on them. Well, there were those Grateful Dead pothead kids, but that was different. That was dime a dozen. What I'm talking about was something quite unique and off-putting to most, and if someone looked like that, it actually *meant* something." Vera went on, in her soft but full voice, to give Jensen a brief account of her relationship with Peter—about how he had gone to college halfway across the country. Of how she had found him online years later and begun a correspondence again.

"He had moved back to Maine years before, and he had a successful business. Maybe moving back to Maine wasn't such a terrible idea,

I thought. I wanted to redo my painful high school years, make them right and good. That, as it turned out, was an ill-conceived plan. He wasn't the person I remembered. His rebellious streak was gone. He was a straight-arrow businessman, concerned about public image. He wanted someone to be a perfect little wife who could cook and clean and look poised at his little functions. That wasn't me at all."

"You don't seem so rebellious to me," Jensen said. "I mean, you're a teacher."

"You're right," Vera said. "I'm really pretty square. I'm not expressing myself very well. I guess what I'm really trying to say is that things don't turn out the way you might expect. But even when things turn out differently from how we expect, we can still be okay."

She stubbed out her cigarette and turned to face Jensen, who was watching her carefully. "Believe it or not, I didn't come here to talk about me, even though somehow I keep doing so. I came here to talk about you."

"Are you leading up to the 'life is worth living' speech? The 'things will get better' speech? People always promise that."

"Not exactly what I'm getting at. Though that would be the expected song and dance."

"What, then?"

"Jensen, have you ever read Mark Twain's essay 'Two Ways of Seeing a River'?"

"Not a fan of Twain."

"He's not all Tom Sawyer and Huck Finn and boys being boys," Vera said. "But anyway, listen, it's a very short essay. You should read it. He talks about how he sees the river as this beautiful thing, this majestic thing, but the more familiar he becomes with the river, the less beautiful it becomes to him. He doesn't see the beauty anymore, only the dangers and the pragmatic aspects of it."

"So you're saying I shouldn't lose sight of beauty."

"I realize it's easier said than done. But perhaps focusing less on the morbid and more on the beautiful would do you good."

On the TV a new episode of *The Twilight Zone* was beginning. Vera couldn't yet identify which one it was. A distressed-looking gentleman in a bow tie ran chaotically around empty, suburban streets.

"Do you know what I think is beautiful?" Jensen asked.

"What?"

"That part in *Catcher* when Holden talks about how he likes to light matches and hold them until he can't hold them anymore. Then he lets them drop. That's one of my favorite parts. And do you know what else I like? That part where he says he feels like he's disappearing every time he crosses the street."

"The matches," Vera said, remembering. "And the street. Yes. Those are two beautiful moments. Small ones, but beautiful ones."

"And then there's the ducks in Central Park. How he wants to know where they go in the winter."

The drinks Vera had consumed made her feel as though she were in a small boat, floating farther and farther away from the crisis that had brought her here. "Everyone remembers that part," she said dismissively. She was stuck on the idea of disappearing—in particular, on the last chapter of *The Catcher in the Rye*, when Holden is walking around Fifth Avenue and starting to worry every time he crosses the street. She thought of him thanking his dead brother every time he made it across the street to safety, still present, still visible, still *real*.

"I'm still having a hard time coming up with my essay topic," Jensen said.

"Next week," Vera said, "we can talk about it some more if you're still stuck." She drained her second drink and decided against pouring another. The calm person who had handled things earlier had come back, steering her gently where she needed to go.

"You asked me earlier why I didn't tell your mom my concerns about you," she said. "The reason I gave you is true, but beyond that there's another reason why I've kept what you've written to myself. The reason is because I feel for you, Jensen, and I don't want to betray you. I know what it's like to want to look cool and competent and not like an emotional wreck. I do get concerned when you start talking about these girls who've been killed recently and how you want to be like them. But I know some of it is just blowing off steam, to use a phrase from one of your earlier journals."

She thought, but didn't say, that she felt Jensen had been mishandled on previous occasions when she'd tried to show a vulnerable side. Getting fobbed off on a psychiatrist who clearly hadn't done any good—that couldn't have been a picnic for the girl. And being rejected by Bret Folger, on one of the few times she expressed need—the girl needed an ally, someone unequivocally in her corner.

"For my discretion," she went on, "and in exchange for the consideration I'm showing for you—I'd like to ask one thing. I'd like to ask that you please not do anything to harm yourself tonight. Can you assure me that you won't?"

"I can," Jensen said, "but tomorrow is another day."

"I'd like to ask that you please not do anything tomorrow, either, but at the moment I'm most concerned about getting you through tonight. Do you think we could check you out of this hotel and get you home? We will have to walk. I'm afraid I don't have any cash for a cab ride."

"Oh, I have cash," Jensen said. "But I can't go home. I said I was doing a *sleepover* at someone's house. No one leaves a sleepover in the middle of the night."

Vera felt uncomfortable with the idea of leaving her there. She was tired—more tired than she had been to start with, drained from both her interchange with Jensen and what she saw as a degree of success in getting through to the girl. She could sleep there in the second bed, get up in the morning, and see her home in the daylight. What harm would it do? But somehow spending the whole night with her student seemed too aberrant—more questionable still than covering for her, than turning a blind eye while she drank alcohol, than drinking alcohol with her.

As though reading Vera's thoughts, Jensen said, "I guess I could go back home. I can always make up some excuse to my mom. But could we stay a little longer and watch some more of this marathon? Please? At least the end of this episode."

Vera agreed. The girl grabbed the remote control from the table between the two beds and turned up the volume. "No talking," she said sternly, putting a finger to her lips.

They watched another episode and a half of *The Twilight Zone* without a word between them. When it was nearly eleven o'clock, Jensen got off her bed, put on her boots and her long black trench coat without prompting.

"You know, it's misting out," Vera said. "Kind of a half rain, half snow."

"I don't mind walking. I'd rather."

Vera got up, too. She had never taken off her coat or hat the entire time; it had never occurred to her to do so.

She waited in the lobby while the girl checked out. They said little on the longish walk back to Jensen's house. Vera fell into her usual habit of counting steps when she walked and trying to keep her breathing even; sometimes she counted in a whisper, aware that her moving mouth might look strange to passersby on the road, but she couldn't help herself. The cold precipitation—somewhere between rain and snow and light hail—prickled her through her hat. She wondered what Jensen was thinking. The girl's expression looked as serene as she had ever seen it.

Vera and Jensen walked through Dorset's east end, up and down steep, sloping hills, past old houses whose charm was, to Vera's thinking, enhanced by their need for some fixing up, past the tall embankments where Vera knew that wildflowers grew in the spring—the Queen Anne's lace and the black-eyed Susans that she'd picked in her youth, growing up in Bond Brook. This end of town was quiet on a Friday night; only one truck passed them, then another, the second driver honking at the sight of two females. What did he make of them, Vera wondered, these two brunettes in their winter coats? Mother and daughter? Sister and sister? Two friends separated only by age? As they descended down Pine Street, Jensen said, "If it's okay, I'd like you to just drop me off on Middle Street. My house is only six doors down. You can even see the roof from here—see the one with the chimney that's missing a brick?"

Vera knew this to be true, for she had been keeping her eye on house numbers as best as she could in the dark. "Are you sure? I'd like to see you to your door."

"Positive," Jensen said. "You live close by, don't you?"

"Maybe another ten to fifteen minutes' walk."

Vera decided to let the girl have her way. She imagined that she didn't want to risk being seen approaching her house with her teacher, if Mrs. Cudahy happened to be awake and peering out a window; it would be easier to explain walking home alone than walking home with Vera.

Jensen, having come to a standstill, fished around in her coat pockets until she found a roll of peppermints. "Want one?" she said. "It hides the alcohol smell."

"I'm okay, thank you. I've no one to hide from."

Jensen stood in place for a few seconds, looking at nothing particular, her hands thrust back in her coat pockets. The wind blew her hair half over her face. Vera thought of what Bret Folger had said about how she looked like a little rat peering out from under things. It didn't do the girl justice at all.

"Thanks," Jensen said. "For talking to me and . . . everything."

"I didn't do much. I don't think I did much at all."

"I really do feel a little better, though. I have a feeling that the next thing I write for you is going to be a lot less gloomy."

"Then that makes me glad."

Jensen turned around and continued heading down the street. Vera stood still and watched the girl's straight back, saw the lightness in her step. From a few feet away, her coat began to blend into the darkness. Soon all she could see of her were her white hands and the whiteness of her exposed neck where her hair was scraped up in a rubber band. She watched until the girl crossed the street, until she couldn't see the whiteness anymore, and then Vera turned to make her own way home.

Chapter Eight

Vera spent the remainder of the weekend in an unusual frame of mind. She kept seeing Jensen Willard as she'd left her: relieved and almost restored, as though she'd made peace with something. A different girl, practically. She kept seeing the lightness in Jensen's step as she retreated down the hill to her house, the back of her neck pale and straight in the moonlight. She almost felt she could trust what she'd seen—that she could have full faith in the girl for the first time since she'd first read her journals.

Vera, too, felt lighter—freed from the heavy sadness that usually clouded her mood. She attributed this to a sense of fulfilled purpose. She had had a hand in circumventing disaster, had reached the girl in some meaningful way; it was not often that she felt her actions had any meaning or import. It did not counteract the irrational sense of responsibility and guilt she had felt ever since finding Sufia's body, but it made her at least feel she had done something good and right by somebody for a change.

Returning to school on Monday morning, she had planned an introduction of the girls' next required reading: Sylvia Plath's *The Bell Jar*. Her original plan had been to teach Conrad's *Heart of Dark-*

ness, but she had changed her mind over the weekend, remembering how Jensen had said she'd liked Plath's novel. She was prepared to begin class by telling the girls a little bit about Sylvia Plath, the all-American, overachieving college girl, and how her one novel thinly fictionalized her nervous breakdown and subsequent stay at the famous McLean Hospital in Belmont, Massachusetts, years before her suicide.

Her intended focus was usurped, however, when Loo Garippa, of all people, came to class champing at the bit, wanting to share something that couldn't wait. As soon as attendance was taken, she asked Vera, "Did you grade our *Catcher in the Rye* essays yet?"

"I haven't. I've fallen a bit behind on the grading, but I'll be catching up in the next day or two." Vera gave Harmony Phelps a preemptive look—Harmony, who always gave Vera the stink-eye when work wasn't returned fast enough for her liking.

"Well, you ought to read mine first. I think you'll like my topic." Looking exceedingly proud of herself, Loo said, "I came up with a really good theory of why serial killers like *The Catcher in the Rye*."

Vera decided not to correct her once again on her misuse of the term *serial killer*. She glanced anxiously at the classroom door, hoping to see Jensen Willard making a late arrival. Her seat stood empty.

Stop looking at the door, Vera told herself. Aloud, she said: "All right, Loo. What've you got?"

Harmony Phelps raised her hand and began speaking before Vera called on her. "Is it okay if we don't talk about this? I don't think it's right after what happened to Sufia."

"This has nothing to do with Sufia," Loo shot back.

"It's in *poor taste* to talk about stuff like that now."

Almost merrily, Loo said, "But check this out—it comes right from the book's title. Holden mentions how he wants to be the catcher in the rye after he hears this poem that goes, 'If a body catch a body coming through the rye.' Get it? Catch a *body*?"

Before Vera could stop her, Harmony, lips pressed together and shaking her head in disgust, scraped away from her table and exited the classroom, slamming the door behind her to underscore her point.

"I'll go get her," Cecily-Anne said, already starting to rise from her seat.

"Would you, Cecily-Anne? Thank you," Vera said. She knew she had to regain control of the classroom somehow before things got worse. Turning to the rest of the girls, she said, "Let me clarify something that might make you all feel a little bit better. The poem Holden refers to is by the Scottish poet Robert Burns, and Holden misunderstands its meaning. It's about a man coming through the rye—you could think of it as wheat—and stealing a kiss from a girl he knows, who's presumably wet from walking near the river." She turned to the computer to find the poem on the Internet, turned on the overhead projector, and read it aloud to the class from the movie screen, ruing her lack of a Scottish brogue:

O Jenny's a' weet, poor body,
Jenny's seldom dry:
She draigl't a' her petticoatie,
Comin' thro' the rye!

Gin a body meet a body
Comin' thro' the glen,
Gin a body kiss a body
Need the warld ken? . . .

The poem's last syllable was still ringing when Loo said, "Yeah, but even so, Holden *thought* it was a body, and he wants to stand there at the end of a cliff catching kids' bodies. That's what he wants to *do* with his life. It's like he wants to be a child killer. Or maybe a future child molester. Or maybe *both*."

"Can we *please* just change the subject?" Autumn Fullerton said. "*Seriously*."

Vera saw that Autumn and Harmony weren't the only ones bothered by this turn in the discussion; almost all the other girls looked worried. Only Loo Garippa remained unperturbed. *Under different circumstances, Loo Garippa and I might have been friends,* Vera thought. *She may be a poser and an undercover pill-popper, but she's got spirit.* "I agree about changing the subject," she said, "but let me just make a few more points for your consideration before we put a lid on this."

Vera spent the next ten minutes trying to disabuse the class of this distressing notion Loo had put forth, citing instead Holden's own childish nature and his unrealistic desire for heroism—a would-be savior to children rather than a destroyer of them. But at least half the girls seemed stuck on the other interpretation, as though *catcher in the rye* might be a synonym for *bogeyman*. Frustrated by her failure to contain the discussion and increasingly worried when it became evident neither Harmony nor Cecily-Anne was coming back and that Jensen Willard was not going to show up at all, Vera let the class out ten minutes early.

She was nearly an hour into correcting papers when someone rapped on the door frame of her open classroom. The force of the rap caused her to look up with a start. Without waiting to be invited in, a man had already advanced halfway to Vera's table.

He wore a spotless white collared shirt and dark-colored pants and carried a clipboard and some folders under his arm; for a minute Vera entertained the idea that a Mormon missionary might be making the rounds, intending to convert the Wallace School teachers one by one. Did that actually happen? She had heard stories of incensed Christians showing up at the school in the past, protesting the inclusion of an elective class called the History of Paganism.

The man had reached her table before she had decided if she should stand up or not. There was something about the way he walked toward her, something purposeful in his stride, that suddenly gave her a sense of real trouble.

"Vera Lundy?"

"Yes?"

He reached into his pocket, took out what looked like a leather wallet, and opened it matter-of-factly, flashing a police badge and replacing it before she could feel anything other than stunned. "I'm Detective Ray Ferreira with the Dorset Police Department. I understand you have some time between classes right now."

Another figure appeared uninvited into the classroom then—a woman. Vera had just registered the newcomer's impressive height and her faded red hair, which pointed wildly in all directions, when Ferreira said to this newcomer, "There you are. What took you so long?"

"I got waylaid talking to the department chair," Detective Helen Cutler said. "Chatty little thing, isn't she, Vera? Hope I didn't miss anything good here. I take it you've met Detective Ferreira."

"Yes," Vera said. "Is this about Sufia again? I still don't remember anything other than what I've told you. But please . . . please have a seat, Detective. Sit down, both of you."

Cutler shut the classroom door while Ferreira pulled up a chair across from Vera's table, then a second chair for his partner. Sitting there, Ferreira looked like an aging, oversized student with an adult man's face; Vera wondered how she could ever have mistaken him for a clean-scrubbed missionary. His features were far too angular and knowing for that. As for Cutler, her complexion looked like she exfoliated with sandpaper. The bemused twitch of her lips that had been present during the school assembly was nowhere in sight.

Clearing his throat, Ferreira said, "Jensen Willard is a student in one of your English classes, is that right? I understand you've only been subbing a short time."

"That's right. I just started." Stricken, Vera realized that somehow, deep down, she had known as soon as he'd flashed his badge that this would not be about Sufia but about Jensen Willard.

"When was the last time you saw Jensen in class?"

"Last Friday."

"That squares with what's on the attendance records. Any chance you saw her after that? Outside of class?"

Vera fell silent. "No," she said. The word escaped from her before she premeditated the lie. All she could think was *Jensen's run away. She's found her own way to escape somehow, and she wouldn't want me to let on that I know.* She looked from one detective to the other, wondering why Cutler was so quiet, why she was just taking notes while Ferreira did the talking. "Detective, please. What *is* this all about?"

"Jensen Willard hasn't been seen since Friday night. Her parents have filed a missing persons report."

"Does your niece know this?" Vera asked Cutler.

The female detective raised an eyebrow in response, still jotting something down in her notepad. "She doesn't yet, although I don't see what that has to do with anything. Chelsea will be told later today."

"But . . ."

"But?" It was Ferreira's turn to cock an eyebrow, wreathing his forehead in deep lines. His eyes held hers with an alertness that made her feel quite exposed. He wasn't stupid, this detective—that much she could tell. She couldn't assume that Cutler was stupid, either. Vera thought as fast as she could, sorting out fiction and fact and erring on the side of the latter.

"I called Jensen's house on Friday night. Her mother said she was at a sleepover."

Ferreira nodded. "Jensen's mother indicated that you had called Friday night. I wanted to check in with you about that. What were you calling about on a Friday? Did it have anything to do with those journals she was writing for you?"

"No," Vera said. "I mean, sort of. I did want to talk about her writing." *He already knows about the journals,* Vera thought. *Maybe he's even read them.*

"And this couldn't wait till Monday?"

Vera frowned. "I guess it could have," she said. The stunned feeling was beginning to wash away, replaced by an engulfing sense of shame. She was thinking so many competing thoughts that no single, clear idea could emerge. All she could see was an image in her mind of Jensen waving good-bye as she crossed the street, her hands looking like small, white mittens in the dark. What could possibly have happened to her between there and her house, just a few yards away from where Jensen had left her? "Wow," she said, beginning to realize the implications of it at last, "this is terrible. Is that why you're talking to *me*? Because I spoke to her mother on the phone? Or is it . . . is it because of Sufia? Of me finding Sufia?"

"We're asking some routine questions of some of her teachers, Vera, and we plan to speak to some of the students, too. You just happen to be first on our list."

"I see," Vera said. She didn't buy it. "The other teachers—well, I don't know that they'd have much insight to offer. Maybe you could try talking to Melanie Belisle? She was her teacher from September to February, and she might know more than I do."

"She's already on our list."

"Oh, good. What about talking to Jensen's friends? I know she doesn't have very many. She used to be friends with a girl named Annabel Francoeur, who lives in her neighborhood. She had a friend named Scotty from her previous school. I don't know his last name. Oh, and she had a boyfriend who goes to Columbia now."

"Boy, you're right on top of things, aren't you, Vera?" Cutler said, looking up from her notes. "But you're not ahead of us. You can be sure of that."

Feeling herself blush, Vera said, "I'm sorry. I don't mean to imply that you aren't on top of things yourself. I guess I'm just trying to be helpful. Can I ask you something? Do you think—You can't possibly think Jensen's *dead*, do you?" Her shoulders jumped as the word *dead* came out of her mouth.

Both Ferreira and Cutler seemed to give this some thought, as though deliberating whether the question was worth answering. "Can't really speak to anything at the moment," Ferreira said at last. "We've taken the hard drive from her computer. Kid didn't use the Internet much—no social networking stuff, which is rare for kids these days—but it turns out she wrote a lot. School files, poetry, stuff that might be fiction. Hard telling what's what. Then there's that journal. That's the other thing we wanted to ask you about."

Ferreira took out one of the folders he was carrying and, with a knowing glance at Cutler, tossed it in front of Vera. The gesture was intended for full dramatic import, she knew; he could have simply placed it in front of her instead of chucking it like that. She also knew what it was without opening the cover. She made no move to open it.

"Here's the hard copy of something we found in her room. School assignment. I assume you've read it since it's got your comments on it."

"Yes," Vera said. She made herself look at the folder, turning some of its pages. "Those are my comments. I wrote those."

"Interesting little writing exercise. Fifteen-year-old kid writing about bombs . . . guns . . . suicidal thoughts. Any of that strike you as cause for concern when you were reading it?"

Detective Cutler wasn't writing anything in her notepad now. She was staring Vera down. "The things you talk about in class might also be considered cause for concern. One has to wonder what place they have in an English class."

Vera shook her head, the sort of head shake tourists give when asked for directions in a language they don't understand.

Ferreira took the folder from Vera and turned to a page that was flagged with a Post-it note. "You say in your written comment, 'You make some statements that might alarm some readers. I want you to know that I don't disregard these comments, but I am not easily shocked by them, either.' You don't think it's shocking, a kid writing something like that? You don't think you maybe should have reported this to someone in the school?"

She found her voice. "As I say later on in that written comment, I was aware that Jensen had had some therapy in the past and apparently had been referred by the dean. I felt she was covered and cared for."

"You also say, 'I am someone you can always come to with such thoughts and issues, and if coming to me with them helps, then so much the better.' Did she come to you with any issues outside of what she wrote here, Miss Lundy?"

"Nothing beyond what she wrote here."

"You seem a little nervous."

"I *am* nervous. This is extremely upsetting. Jensen Willard is a good student. A very bright young woman." Vera was finding it hard to keep up with both the detectives' unrelenting eye contact. "I'm sorry about the nerves. I don't know why I'm like this."

"With all that you've experienced lately, I think you've got a pretty good excuse."

"You aren't suggesting anything, are you, Detective? You're not suggesting . . ."

"Look, ma'am . . ." (Vera closed her eyes for a fraction of a second, annoyed that Ferreira had called her that). "We aren't *suggesting* anything. Nine times out of ten, these missing teenagers turn out to be runaways, and there's plenty reason to believe that the Willard kid falls in the same category. But with some of the things this kid has written, we've got to look into this seriously. Not to mention the recent death of one of her classmates—of which you are fully aware." He got up without ceremony from the chair, not bothering to put it back where he'd dragged it from.

"We good here, Hel?" he asked his partner.

"We're good," she said.

Ferreira gathered up his clipboard and folders. "Some advice for you," he said, looking down at Vera, who was still seated. "Trying to be the 'cool teacher' really does your students a disservice. Don't be surprised if I come back to speak to you again. Here's my card if you think of anything you want to add in the meantime." And with that he was done with her, but on the two detectives' way out the door, Cutler gave Vera a parting look that she could not interpret—was it pitying? Contemptuous?

Vera studied the card with the detective's name on it. She felt as though she'd been taken to task; worse than that, she felt hurt. *Nine times out of ten, these missing teenagers turn out to be runaways,* Ferreira had said. On the surface it seemed more believable than any other explanation Vera could think of—but the more she thought about it, the less it made sense. Where would the girl have run to in the middle of the night? What else could have kept her from making it six houses down to her own front door, then, if not for running away? *Don't be surprised if I come back to speak to you again,* the detective had said, and as Vera tapped the detective's business card against the palm of her opposite hand, she heard his voice in her head, thick with insinuation.

She wondered if she would have been better off owning up to seeing Jensen on Friday night—better off admitting she'd met her in a hotel and walked her home afterward. It seemed as if she was in enough trouble just for not having reported the journals to a higher authority in the school. *If he read the journals,* Vera thought, *he already at least knows about the hotel.* Then she remembered that the last two pages Jensen had submitted were handwritten—the pages stating her intentions for that Friday night. The version the officer had in his possession was likely incomplete, stopping where the typescript ended. She looked at the card in her hand again. She should call him, she thought—for this was something he probably needed to know. The suicide threat—all of it.

She was so numb that she felt nothing at all when Sue MacMasters came into her classroom just minutes later. Sue had the same incredulous look she'd had when speaking to Vera about students with emotional difficulties who took medication.

"Oh, Vera, what a mess," she said, and for a second Vera thought she was referring to her role in it specifically—the mess *she* had made. "What an awful time for a student to go missing, right after we've lost Sufia. I'm sure this girl is a runaway, but what are the students going to think? I'd like to have Jensen Willard's teachers meet with me in my office today at lunch. We need to discuss this problem amongst ourselves, I think. I'll send out for sandwiches and things so that no one has to go hungry."

The idea of going hungry was the last thing on Vera's mind. "I'll be there," she said.

"I must say I've never had a conversation with the girl personally. But when that detective showed me her picture, I did recognize her. Small, mousy girl. Always wearing dark-colored clothing. Easy not to notice in the halls. Now, of course, I wish I'd paid more attention."

Vera hadn't been in Sue's office since her final interview before being hired. Today, at the lunch hour, her boss's rather nondescript space—Georgia O'Keeffe print on the wall, tear-off calendar propped on the desk next to pictures of her grown children—had been converted into what looked like the most joyless party imaginable, with a tray of cut-up submarine sandwiches on the center of Sue's cleared-off desk alongside bottled water and lemonade and a plate of cookies. There were four other teachers in the room when Vera got there, all buzzing around the food and loading up paper plates before squeezing into their chairs; she had seen them around, seen them eyeing her archly whenever she hogged the photocopier, though the blond and bearded teacher—Tim Zabriskie, one of the few men who taught at Wallace—was the only one she could name.

"Thank you all so much for coming in here on short notice," Sue MacMasters said. "I know we don't have a lot of time, but since you all share Jensen Willard as a student, I thought perhaps we could benefit from talking about what's happened."

You all share Jensen Willard as a student struck Vera as a funny way to put it. She looked around at the other teachers—Tim Zabriskie, and then the weary-looking woman with the frizzy salt-and-pepper hair and the tapestry skirt, and two younger teachers with immaculately pressed clothing and what looked like expensive shoes. "Before we get started, I should quickly introduce Vera Lundy, who, as I'm sure you all know by now, is our long-term sub for Melanie," she said. Vera gave a stiff, robotic nod. "Do any of you have any questions about what went on this morning? And since you all know Jensen Willard better than I do, is there anything in her behavior or class conduct or anything else that might suggest why the girl is missing?"

None of the other faculty seemed to want to take Sue's questions head-on. They had other things they wanted to address first. The woman in the tapestry skirt, who turned out to be Jensen's social studies teacher, complained that she felt her civil rights and morale were compromised by having a member of the police force invade the "safe haven" of Wallace. Jensen's math teacher—Tim Zabriskie—said, "When I taught in public school in Lewiston, I had this happen once, where two students went missing. Turns out they went off to see a concert. That's usually the way it goes with these kids." The two younger teachers, who seemed to be friends, practically spoke in unison. One said that she had been trying to get Jensen to participate more in class by teaming her up with partners or small groups, but that the girl insisted on working alone and defying the structure of the group activities. The other said that Jensen had scored poorly on a recent French quiz, filling in the blanks with "nonsense words" instead of straightforward answers about shopping along the Champs-Élysées.

"She's not a math person, I can tell you that much," Tim Zabriskie said. "I've made her come in for extra help after school, and it's clear she doesn't understand a word I'm saying. She's one of those ones who you really can't *teach* if it's something she doesn't already know. How did she end up on scholarship again?"

"She won a national essay award during her freshman year in public school," Sue MacMasters said. "Vera, even though you've only just joined us, I'm assuming you've had an opportunity to see some of her writing for yourself?"

The detectives hadn't said anything to Sue about Jensen's journals, then. Why would they not have mentioned it? Vera stammered that yes, she had read the girl's writing, and added that she thought she wrote well. The insipid, inadequate words filled her with self-loathing as soon as they came out.

The experience of hearing other teachers talk about Jensen Willard left her feeling more displaced than ever. There were times when Vera had considered the possibility—knowing, of course, that it couldn't be true—that she had conjured the girl into being. At times the girl had almost seemed like a backward projection of her younger self—especially in those first two weeks of teaching, when she had been smitten with the girl's writing ability and sardonic wit. Now, at last, was proof that she existed outside of Vera's mind—that others had seen her. They had not *really* seen her, but they had seen her in the limited way that most people actually see one another.

"Does she have a boyfriend? Maybe a girlfriend?" asked the social studies teacher. "She could have run off with someone. I assume the police will be looking into that."

"I hope no one thinks it's a *crime*," one of the well-dressed teachers said. "Not *another* one. Though with all that's happened here lately, I can see where someone might jump to that conclusion. With that poor little Galvez girl, and then the Somali girl."

"Sufia," Vera mumbled.

"Pardon? I'm sorry, I didn't catch that, Vera," Sue MacMasters said.

"I just said her name: Sufia. Sufia Ahmed."

Some of the other teachers were talking over her—some with their mouths full. The second of the young teachers made a great production out of lifting her finger in the air, as though she wanted to have the floor, before chewing and swallowing her food. "Don't you think we should have some kind of speech prepared for Jensen Willard's classmates? It doesn't seem right to have police coming in and out of the school and not have everyone clued in on what's going on. I'm sure the rumor mill has already started. Especially if they start thinking this might have something to do with those other two murders."

Sue MacMasters said that this was partly what she wanted to talk to them about. "The full story's probably going to break in the *Journal* tomorrow. In view of that, I think an assembly tomorrow afternoon to address any concerns students might have wouldn't be inappropriate. I would advise not saying anything to your students before that time. If somebody asks beforehand, best to say you have no information. We'll let Dean Finister handle it."

"Such a shame this kind of publicity is being attached to our school," the teacher who had claimed the floor said.

"Regardless of recent events," Sue said, "the school itself holds no responsibility. Of this we can be certain."

Later that night, Vera walked all the way across town to the hotel where she'd met with Jensen on Friday. She went into the parking lot but didn't go past the hotel doors; counting under her breath, her mouth moving as though feeling around for something, she turned around and slowly retraced her steps back to Pine Street, where Jensen lived. Not wanting to repeat her earlier mistake at the Ahmeds' house by getting too close, she stood at the corner of Middle Street for a long time, staring down at the approximate spot where she'd last seen Jensen Willard; from there she could just make out the roof of the Cudahys' house.

Feeling bolder, she crept six houses down the street, careful to situate herself behind a large pine tree across the street as she squinted at the Cudahys' white Cape Cod with the blue Dodge parked in the driveway. She tried to think where a teenage girl might go if she were trying to disappear between this house and Middle Street. Perhaps she had cut through someone's lawn as soon as she'd crossed the street and was out of Vera's sight.

Or what about the bushes and hedges that flanked so many of the neighboring houses—were these places where an attacker might have hidden, waiting until just the right moment when he could grab Jensen unseen? Might he have hidden behind the exact tree Vera stood behind, across the street from the girl's house, watching both females come closer in the dark? For all she knew, he had watched them for some time. Maybe he'd had it all planned out. That was what Ivan Schlosser had done with his three victims—watched them until he knew just the right time to pluck one off the street, another from her school yard, and the third from the house where she was babysitting an infant boy.

In the early days, before anyone knew what had happened to Schlosser's victims, those who knew them remarked that it was as if the earth had opened up and swallowed them whole. In the weeks following Heidi Duplessis's disappearance, Vera had often lain in her bed at night and imagined Heidi Duplessis being swallowed by a crack in the earth, sucked gently into its center until the earth closed over her again. It was more comforting to think of her this way, nestled in the center of the world and curled up in permanent sleep—though the reality of such disappearances, Vera had known even then, was never that gentle or peaceful.

Rilke's sonnet, the one that had come to mind when she'd found Sufia's body, returned to her again, as intimate as a hushed voice in the dark:

She made herself a bed in my ear
And slept in me.
Her sleep was everything . . .

Vera rested her forehead against the trunk of the tree. She felt dizzy. Tomorrow, she thought, she would call Detective Ferreira and apologize for not having told them everything sooner.

The next day was afflicted with a heavy, grayish, pelting rain. Vera went into the bodega on her morning walk to school to pick up some coffee, struggling with closing her umbrella and getting her big, wheeled suitcase through the door. She was waiting in line behind someone buying scratch-off tickets, selecting which ones he wanted with the indecision and anticipation of a kid picking out penny candy, when she saw the newspaper headline.

Pulling the paper off the rack, she saw Jensen Willard's face looking up at her, one eye half shut against the camera flash and wall-to-wall bookshelves behind her. Vera recognized this as the photo Jensen had written about, the one taken in Dr. Rose's apartment on Riverside Drive; the girl would be mortified, Vera thought, to know *that* was the photo the newspaper chose to run.

Feeling that peculiar sense of calm that sometimes overtook her at the least likely times, she added the paper to her purchase, being careful to zip it in her suitcase so that it wouldn't get wet. She had just enough time to read it before her first-period class started. It was the first thing she did when she arrived in her classroom; she didn't even remove her coat or turn on the classroom lights or stop in the ladies' room to fix her running mascara.

15-Year-Old Scholarship Girl Missing

Authorities in Dorset have begun a search for a scholarship student enrolled at the Wallace School who disappeared Friday evening and hasn't been heard from since.

Jensen Willard, 15, was last seen on Friday at about 7 P.M., when she was dropped off at a Wheaton Road address by her stepfather. Willard had told her parents she was attending a sleepover at this address, but the elderly couple who resides there do not know Willard and did not receive a visit from a teenage girl that night. According to Dorset Police Officer Gerard Babineau, none of the neighbors spotted her, either.

"It is uncertain at this time whether she vanished voluntarily," Babineau said.

Willard is described as a white female with dark-brown hair and brown eyes. She is 5 feet 2 inches tall and weighs approximately 98 pounds. She is believed to be wearing olive-colored pants, a black T-shirt, combat boots, and a long black coat. She was also carrying an army knapsack. Her mother, Linda Willard Cudahy, and her stepfather, Les Cudahy, are hopeful that making her photo public may help her to be found.

Anyone with information regarding the girl's location is urged to contact the Dorset Police Department.

Vera was reading through the brief article a third time when Chelsea Cutler and Kelsey Smith came in. "Why is it dark in here?" Chelsea asked.

Vera wiped at her mascara-smudged eyes, ran a hand over her dampened hair, and got up to turn on the lights. "Is that today's paper?" Chelsea asked, looking on Vera's table. "Did you see that story about Jensen Willard being missing?"

"I did," Vera said. She took the newspaper and folded it back into her suitcase, as though doing so might curb any further discussion on the issue. She removed the file of handouts she would need for the day.

"My aunt says they're going to talk to all the registered sex offenders."

"Oh my God, that's so creepy," Kelsey Smith said. "Are we having another assembly today? I heard we were going to."

Other girls were starting to come in. Some had heard about the morning news, and some had not. Those in the know were happy to fill in those who weren't.

"As far as I know, yes, there *will* be an assembly today," Vera said, raising her voice above the hullabaloo the girls were creating. "I don't really know what it's going to entail."

"It's really weird to think about missing persons," Loo Garippa said. "To think somebody can just be there one day, and the next day they're just gone. And sometimes they're never found at all. It's like they never even existed."

Vera tsked a little. "I am *sure* Jensen will be found."

"Yeah," Loo said. "She might be found like Sufia!"

"Now, listen . . ." Vera began.

"My aunt says it's suspicious," Chelsea said. "She says they know a lot of things that they can't say in the newspaper yet."

"I heard Jensen had a boyfriend somewhere," Jamie Friedman said. "But he's older. He's, like, in his thirties or something. Maybe he had something to do with it."

"Please," Vera said. "Stop it. It's bad enough that you're speaking about the girl when she isn't here. Worse still that you're referring to her in the past tense. Everyone take out your copies of *Literary Hori-*

zons. In addition to our regular assigned reading from *The Bell Jar*, there will be an essay test on the poems of Edgar Allan Poe tomorrow."

She had never spoken so severely to her class before. Some of them looked as though they'd been stung, while others—Loo Garippa, Harmony Phelps, and the two modelesque girls especially—put on sullen expressions so quickly that Vera suspected they'd been keeping them in reserve.

Vera directed the girls to "Annabel Lee." She realized, as she began reading it aloud, that this poem that focused on the loss of Poe's very young ladylove was perhaps going to be more difficult to discuss than she'd anticipated.

"It's so singsongy," Loo objected when Vera had finished the reading the poem out loud.

"I think it's beautiful." Jamie, the class conscience, seemed to be trying to make amends for her comment about Jensen and a boyfriend. "It sounds like a rhyme a child would say, and maybe that's because he was in so much pain that he was reduced to childlike state."

Vera let the class take the discussion with little interference. She feared she would not have been able to say much even if she'd wanted to, for a large lump had lodged itself into her throat and stayed there. She reserved a few minutes at the end of class to review some of the literary terms she wanted the students to be aware of for the next test. When class was over, an announcement came on the intercom—Dean Finister's voice—summoning them all to the auditorium for another assembly at 10:00 A.M.

The mood in the auditorium was different from the mood during the assembly memorializing Sufia Ahmed. Instead of appearing wounded and disoriented, the students and faculty presenters seemed tense, as though Jensen Willard's disappearance were just one other thing that was meant to test their endurance.

"Jensen Willard," Dean Finister was saying from the stage, "our newest sophomore and already one of our finest students, has now been missing for several days." Next to Dean Finister, a photo of Jensen Willard filled the old movie screen—that unfortunate photo from Dr. Rose's apartment again. As Dean Finister talked, all Vera could think about was Jensen's account of how he'd buttonholed her in the halls to tell her, *You look sad today.* Would he mention that sadness, Vera wondered? Did he even make the connection between the girl whose blown-up image stood next to him and the girl who'd wept in his office till her makeup bled? If he did, he gave no sign of it. The dean spoke of Jensen's close relationship with her parents, of her past writing award, and of the "independent nature" that several of her teachers had described her as having. Vera compared this to what she had heard from the girl's teachers in Sue MacMasters's office and, with supreme effort, kept a derisive sound from coming out of her closed-up throat. She leaned against the wall, arms wrapped around her stomach, away from the rows of chairs where the students sat.

The students were unusually quiet and attentive during this assembly. They became even quieter when Dean Finister introduced police officer Gerard "Gerry" Babineau. As Babineau got up from his metal seat onstage and approached the podium, Vera found herself shrinking back against the wall, hoping he wouldn't notice she was there. "We want you to continue your classes as normal," the officer said, "and go about your daily lives just as normal, too. But at the same time, we ask you to keep your eyes and ears open. One bit of information that may be helpful: Jensen said she was going to visit a friend named Phoebe when she was last seen. Her parents don't recall the exact last name

Jensen gave them. Their best guess is Collins or Crawford. We do know that the address and phone number she gave for Phoebe was false, but we have not been able to identify who Phoebe is, if she is in fact a real person. If any of you know someone with a name like Phoebe Collins or Phoebe Crawford, this could be of great help to the police."

Vera could have sworn she felt a stirring as some faces in the seats turned toward her. She picked out Martha True's face, pale and troubled. Officer Babineau was still talking, reviewing statistics of missing persons and missing teenagers in particular, but Vera heard only his closing lines: "Let's do what we need to do to get Jensen home right away."

Some of the students started to clap. The smattering of applause grew until it seemed to rise in the air and warm the whole auditorium, creating a dense, bright heat.

Vera realized that she was having a difficult time balancing the weight of her own body. She stumbled down the aisle of the auditorium, past other standing teachers, and toward the exit, where she saw Sue MacMasters standing there, blocking her way.

"Are you all right?" Sue exclaimed over the applause.

"No," she said. "I mean—it's my stomach. I feel very faint."

"Go home," Sue said without hesitation. "I can get someone to cover your other two classes."

"Oh, Sue, I'm so sorry."

"Don't even worry about it. You look awful. You've probably already pushed yourself too hard today."

Vera mumbled a thank you and fled, stopping only to retrieve her things from the teachers' lounge. Tim Zabriskie was in there, tucked into one of the small round tables. "Bailing out on the assembly?" he said. "I figured I'd hide in here and get caught up on some work. Don't tell anyone." He was correcting a set of math exams, writing *X*'s next to errors with the zeal of one solving a puzzle.

Vera nodded, avoiding his eyes as she put on her coat and hat and grabbed her suitcase by the handle. How could he not notice something was wrong with her? Why was it that so few people ever noticed anything? *And how could he not know just from looking at me,* Vera thought, *that I would be the last person to ever tell anyone anything?*

Home in her studio apartment, Vera logged into the Center for Missing and Exploited Children website and typed *Jensen Willard* into the search window. Sure enough, Jensen's picture—a different one from what the newspaper had printed—appeared on the screen along with a list of basic information: case number, case type, sex, race, date of birth, height, weight, hair color, eye color. The photograph looked like a Wallace School ID picture; it had the same unforgiving, muddy-gray backdrop as Vera's own faculty ID, which had been snapped in the admissions office.

What was it about seeing a stark photo of a missing person that inspired such terror? Was it the not knowing—the possibility that the person had slipped away into someplace more terrifying than life, more terrifying than death?

Vera remembered being a very young child and having her first exposure to the idea that children could go missing—that unimaginable things could happen to them: things even worse than being adopted into a cult, worse than being sold on the black market to the underground sex trade. As a precocious eight-year-old, she had been leafing through one of her mother's *Reader's Digests* and read a story about Dee Scofield, the ponytailed girl with the slightly overlapping teeth who had gone missing from a Florida shopping center in 1976. Dee had never been found. Vera had looked her up on this very same website once and had seen the age-advanced, computer-generated photo of what Dee might look like if she were alive today: The image of the smiling, bespectacled woman could well have been a friendly children's librarian or a church organist. But in all likelihood, this version of Dee Scofield had never existed—had been denied the chance to exist.

Was it quick, Dee? Did you call for your mother right in those very last moments? I hope it was quick.

But it was foolish to think that way, to even make this comparison. Jensen was surely not in harm's way. Surely this disappearance was of her own design.

In Jensen's school photo, her wary eyes looked a little more sunken than they looked in real life. She looked as though she could be any number of ages—anywhere along the spectrum of late childhood to the middle years of womanhood. Below Jensen's photo were a few brief lines of text.

Circumstances: Jensen was last seen on March 30 of this year. She was wearing olive-green pants, a black T-shirt, a long black trench coat, and black combat boots. She was carrying an army knapsack. Jensen has one small chicken pox scar above her left eyebrow and a small brown mole on her upper right arm. She has never had any dental work.

Vera let that last thought sit for a while. She guessed "has never had any dental work" meant that Jensen had never been to a dentist, which was not so unusual among Mainers; that meant no dental records, if she should ever be recovered. *Recovered*—the word specifically used when a dead body was brought home. She shivered. *Found,* she corrected herself; *use the word* found.

Closing out the window, Vera typed the words *Jensen Willard* into a Google keyword search. The search term turned up the article in the *Journal*, and something else. On a homespun website called BRING JENSEN HOME, Vera saw the older, more familiar picture of her student; above it, a curving green font seemed to swim across the screen.

Are you a whiz at computers? Handy at making flyers? Able to give some of your time to answer phones and help our busy police? Are you caring, dependable, and passionate?

BRING JENSEN HOME is a volunteer group working with Our Missing Kids, a nonprofit group out of Concord, New Hampshire, that assists law enforcement in finding missing loved ones. We are accepting applications for our search and rescue committee, which is spearheaded by Jensen's parents, Les and Linda Cudahy, and the supervising Dorset Police Department.

Below that was an email contact for those who wanted to request an application. There was a boldfaced note near the bottom of the home page inviting anyone who had information about the case and wished to remain anonymous to click on the link below. Vera's cursor hovered over it for a few seconds. Then she moved it away.

Elsewhere on the home page was a basic overview of the case and, in that same swimming font, a section titled "A Word from Jensen Willard's Mother."

If you have come to this website, thank you, first of all, for your interest in our missing daughter and her safe return.

On the evening of March 30th, our daughter and the light of our life, Jensen Alice Willard, packed up her army knapsack and headed for a sleepover at her friend Phoebe's house. The last time

we saw her was when we dropped her off at the address she gave. Since then, we have learned that no girl named Phoebe is enrolled at Jensen's school. The address where she was dropped off was not the house she said it was.

Jensen is fifteen years old. She stands five foot two inches tall and weighs about one hundred pounds. She has dark-brown hair cut a little below chin length, often worn in a short ponytail. She has light-brown eyes and light skin with a few freckles. When she chooses to share it, she has a beautiful smile.

Being a teenager has not always been easy for Jensen, but she is a strong girl. I always say that she might seem meek, but if you back her into a corner, boy, will she come out fighting! Because of that, I believe that wherever she is, she must be okay. But there is a huge feeling of emptiness in these last few days since our daughter has been gone. If somebody knows her whereabouts, please let us know. If you have her, please return her—no questions asked.

There has been too much loss in Dorset lately, and too much within the course of our own lives. We cannot have Jensen be another tragedy.

The site had enabled a feature for public comments, which Vera presumed were screened before they were made visible to the public. There were words of encouragement and sympathy, of support and condolences. There were stories from other people whose loved ones were also missing—parents' accounts of children who'd been found living and dead, as well as the continued, wistful hopes of those whose children had never been found. This outpouring of pain made Vera feel voyeuristic, as though she didn't have the right to be privy to this particular brand of sadness. Still, she wanted to read every post. She wanted to see what people on both ends of the equation had to say—

those with losses and those with reclamations. But that, she thought, was best saved for another time.

She did, however, take the time to save Jensen's picture in her documents and print it up. She taped it on the wall above her laptop, taking care so that the edges of the paper aligned with the faces of Heidi Duplessis, Angela Galvez, and Sufia Ahmed. The row of missing and dead was growing, occupying a greater stretch above her laptop. She wondered when and where it would stop.

Chapter Nine

Wednesday morning on her way to school, Vera stopped at the bodega and pumped herself a cup of coffee out of the self-serve coffee urn. But then a strange thing happened. Staring at the arrangement of creamers, sugar, artificial sweetener packets, and stirrers, her mind went blank. She could no longer remember what she liked in her coffee or even how to prepare it. She stood motionless at the counter, willing the memory to come back, the ease of this morning ritual, until she slowly lifted the spoon for the nondairy creamer and tore open several sweeteners. The next several minutes were spent looking for the lids to the cups, which were stacked right in front of her.

She didn't see how she could be expected to make it through her classes in this fugue state, even though she would be only administering a test—an easy day for her. She started to make her way over to the counter with her coffee, the cup sloshing over a little—she hadn't affixed the lid tightly enough—as she dragged her bumping, rattling suitcase behind her. Next to the counter, the latest *Dorset Journal* headline caught her eye.

Missing Girl Possible Runaway

She seized the top newspaper from the stack and tossed it onto the counter as though it were smoldering.

"You read newspaper now, eh?" the clerk said, whistling through his teeth as he rang her up. "Before, you just get coffee. Now you like newspaper, too."

Outside again, Vera propped her suitcase against the bodega and stood under its canopy, hurriedly reading the article in the *Journal*. She had not expected another article to appear so soon, and this one was worse than she could have prepared herself for.

Jensen Willard, 15, who disappeared last Friday, may have taken some inspiration from a novel she was reading for her sophomore English class.

When last seen, Willard was dropped off at 113 Wheaton Road, which she gave as the address for a friend of hers named Phoebe Caulfield. Police have since verified that no one bearing that name lives there and that Phoebe Caulfield is a character from *The Catcher in the Rye*, a novel that is required reading for tenth graders at Willard's school. This was brought to the police department's attention through multiple tips after Officer Gerard Babineau made a presentation at the Wallace School.

According to Willard's English teacher, Melanie Belisle, who is currently on maternity leave, *The Catcher in the Rye* is a story about a 16-year-old boy who hides from his family after being expelled from school. "Jensen Willard is not a student I got to know as well as some," Belisle told the *Journal*. "She was very private. But it isn't hard to imagine that she might have run away to look for some excitement."

Willard's parents disagree. "If Jensen had a problem, she always came to me," said her mother, Linda Willard Cudahy, 55.

"She has had some trouble with depression and got help for it. Since then she has been fine. It's hard to believe she'd just up and run away."

On March 30, the day before she disappeared, Willard withdrew several hundred dollars from her bank account, leaving only a small sum in savings.

Recent national statistics on missing teenagers show that the vast majority of children between the ages of 12 and 17 who go missing each year are runaways. However, Babineau says that the police force is "looking at all options and possibilities." The law enforcement response to date has included interviewing neighbors and relatives, contacting registered sex offenders, and questioning drivers who travel the Wheaton Road in case they might have seen something unusual. Yesterday a sheriff's team covered a 12-square-mile area extending from Willard's home to the point on the Wheaton Road where she was last seen, and farther past that into Portland.

People have called in with tips about sighting a girl matching Willard's description, but none have panned out.

Vera read the article again. She was still holding her leaking coffee cup in her free hand, and she set it down on the ground by her suitcase. She thought of the desk clerk at the Roundview Hotel; why wasn't he coming forth with what he knew about a young girl named Phoebe Willard? Recalling the clerk's enlarged pupils, the pungent and unmistakable smell of weed that had wafted up as he leaned over the counter, Vera thought that maybe he didn't have the brainpower to put two and two together after the fact. But this was not something to be counted on with any sense of security.

Digging around in her purse for her phone, she called the number of the Wallace School and got Sue MacMasters's voicemail. Her impulse had been to call in sick, but the sound of Sue's voice made her lose her resolve; she hung up without leaving a message. Still, she felt soul-sick and a little doomed, like someone whose days of grace are numbered, as she dragged her suitcase in the direction of the school.

Vera arrived in her empty classroom almost an hour early and set about arranging her handouts for her three English classes. While she was reviewing her day planner, a woman came into her classroom with a clicking of high, stiletto-heeled boots. *Please,* Vera thought, *please don't be another cop.* Dressed in an exquisitely tailored jacket, her hair slicked back into a chignon, this woman looked at least as old as Vera was—possibly older. As she came closer, Vera saw her smooth, taut skin, marred only by one poorly camouflaged pimple on her forehead; she then recognized one of the young teachers she'd met in Sue MacMasters's office.

"Hi," the teacher said as though she and Vera were old friends. "How are you doing?"

"Not too bad." Vera tried her hardest to remember the woman's name and to keep this particular ignorance off her own face. Amanda? Amber? Something that bore no resemblance to either?

"I hope you don't mind if I bug you for just a minute. It's about Jensen Willard. Have you seen this?"

Vera was expecting to see that copy of the morning paper again, but instead the woman handed her a printout from the home page of the BRING JENSEN HOME website.

Are you a whiz at computers? Handy at making flyers?

"Oh, the website? Yes, I *have* seen it."

"Well," the woman said, "my husband, Paul, is one of the organizers. He's known the Cudahys for years. And I've signed on to help him as much as I can. I know teachers are busy—I'm definitely busy myself—but those of us with *any* time to spare owe it to one of our students and her family to offer some small bit of help, don't we? Even if it's just an hour out of our day."

Vera gave this quietly impassioned young woman a long, appraising look. "I'm so embarrassed to say this, but I've drawn a blank on your name."

"Amy Nimitz."

"Oh. I knew that, I think."

"I'm Jensen's psychology teacher."

Vera hadn't heard that Jensen had been studying psychology. She felt a twinge of envy. How fascinating it must be to teach psychology to such a psychologically unusual specimen as Jensen Willard. "You teach in an interesting field," she said, looking at Amy Nimitz with new respect. "I took quite a few psych courses as an undergrad myself."

"My background is in sociology, but I'm credentialed to teach psych, at least at the high school level. Anyway, can I interest you in taking another look at BRING JENSEN HOME? You know, we've set up temporary headquarters at the print shop on Chamberlain Street, so we have some actual manpower. There's a downloadable volunteer application on the website—only two pages, nothing too complicated. Karen Provencher has already been approved to work with us. And Lacey Tondreau—she's Jensen's French teacher."

Vera remembered the young teacher, who had sat next to Amy in Sue's office. "I'll certainly give it some thought. What is this organization doing, exactly—are you doing organized foot searches?"

"Oh, no, nothing like that. Don't worry—you won't have to get dirty! This is more like clerical stuff—working with photocopies, emails, phone calls."

"Ah," Vera said, a little disappointed. She wouldn't have minded getting dirty. "I'm sure it sounds like a worthy venture, and I'd like to be a part of it if I could. May I ask you one other question? Sort of a . . . personal question, just between you and me?"

"Of course."

"As Jensen's psychology teacher . . . what was your impression of her? I mean, was there anything about her overall emotional well-being that struck you, either positively or negatively?"

"Well, as you know, I'm not a therapist. But there was nothing about her that struck me as all that unusual for a girl that age. Maybe a little rebellion, but that's normal enough, don't you think? I said more or less the same thing to the police when they asked that same question."

"I see," Vera said, as though that explained it all. "I do thank you for dropping in, Amy, really. I'm sure we'll be in touch."

After Amy Nimitz left, Vera thought: *There is no way this is ever going to happen. No way in hell can I apply as a spontaneous volunteer.* She knew that such nonprofit agencies worked closely with the police, and any applicant would need to be screened. And while her criminal record was as clean as a whistle, she was well aware that the local police did not hold her in high regard at this moment. They might question her motives, her desire to draw herself closer to the case. Perhaps they would even think the worst. Perpetrators often return to the scene of their crimes or offer to help in search parties; Ivan Schlosser, for instance, had later admitted that helping volunteers comb the woods in search of one of his victims had given him a great thrill.

Vera, alone in her classroom again, seated herself at the school-issued computer and typed in the URL of the BRING JENSEN

HOME website, looking at the home page whose features she had already committed to memory. She looked again at the icon where one could fill out an online application to volunteer for the committee. *I had better be careful,* she thought. *I'd be better off avoiding this like the plague.*

On the other hand, wouldn't her role in looking for Jensen help vindicate her somewhat? Wouldn't it show her goodwill? Wouldn't it demonstrate that she *cared*? And better still, wouldn't serving on the volunteer committee give her access to information she might not otherwise have—information that might even allow her to locate Jensen all on her own? The more she flirted with this thought, the more her muted excitement grew—for she could not deny that this was an *exciting* prospect, filled with possibilities.

Vera kept thinking of Jensen's mother and stepfather, wondering how they were coping with it all. Her own mother had called her the night before to ask about the missing girl she'd heard about on TV. "This really scares me," she had said, after Vera had recounted for her a much-abridged version of Jensen's case. "Two girls dead, and now another one missing? You have to promise me you won't walk around in the dark."

"Nobody thinks there's any connection between the three girls," Vera had said.

"Well, that doesn't make it any better. Dead girls are dead girls."

"Only two are dead."

"That you know of!" her mother had said. "Just be careful. Promise me."

"Me? I'll be fine, Mom. Even if there *is* someone who snatches people off the streets, he prefers young girls. I'm too old now."

Vera sat in deliberation for a few minutes. There was no way her mother could know exactly how enmeshed she'd become in the disappearance of Jensen Willard. The worry might kill her, Vera thought. But providing Jensen's parents with what little information she had just might save them. They deserved to know about their daughter's hotel stay and what Vera had observed on that last Friday night.

She clicked on the icon asking for anonymous information. In all lowercase letters, which she hoped would help her masquerade as someone whose English skills were subpar, she rapidly typed:

> i have reason to believe jensen willard checked in and checked out of the roundview hotel on the night of march 30.
>
> after that she probably walked in the direction of home.
>
> police might want to focus on that area. thank you.

She paused, and then, almost reluctantly, highlighted and deleted all the text she had just written. IP addresses could be traced, she knew. She moved the cursor elsewhere on the page—back to the icon linking to the application for the BRING JENSEN HOME volunteers. She skimmed the requirements of the document—contact info, available hours, specialized skills, criminal history, and three personal references—and began to type.

Vera had walked to the copy center on Chamberlain Street on a Thursday afternoon. She had been greeted by an older woman who sat knitting at a front desk, an L.L.Bean tote bag of yarn tucked between her enormous, parted knees. "Paul's in the back room" was all she said when Vera handed over her ID, and the large woman pointed to a doorway past the computers and photocopying machines.

The copy center had been set up in an old split-level house, which was often the way with small local businesses. The back room, Vera found, was only one of many back rooms on the ground floor. It was dominated by a massive, unused fireplace and a long conference table. At one end of this table sat a well-muscled woman with a short buzz cut; she hardly bothered to look up from her assiduous envelope stuffing as she noted Vera's arrival. At the other end, pacing back and forth as he spoke into his cell phone, was a short, intensely energetic-looking man whom Vera guessed was Paul Nimitz. "Vera!" he said, covering the mouthpiece of the phone with his hand. "How nice to meet you."

Vera had hoped that Amy might be at the center, too, or even Karen Provencher or Lacey Tondreau; any familiar face was better than none. Not that Paul was unwelcoming by any means. After terminating his call and introducing her to the woman with the buzz cut—Robin was her name—he gestured for Vera to follow him and led her into yet another room—an employee kitchen, by the looks of it, outfitted with one small table that took up most of its floor space.

Paul Nimitz sat down, and Vera followed suit, noticing that Paul was the sort who looked unnatural sitting still; his legs immediately began to jiggle under the table as he smiled at her and said, "Helen Cutler speaks very highly of you."

"Does she?" Vera had to prevent herself from quipping, *That's a surprise.* It had been Cutler who had called her to tell her that her volunteer application had been approved; she'd even said, in her laconic way, "Maybe this'll be a good experience for you. We've got police checking in there every day, so you and I will be seeing a little more of each other." It had almost been enough to put Vera off the idea of volunteering.

"Does the detective come by here a lot?" she asked Paul Nimitz.

"There's a few from the police department who take turns. We're lucky that we have the police working so closely with us. Once in a while, the Cudahys—Jensen's parents—even come by. But they stay home as much as they can. They're afraid they might miss a phone call from Jensen, or even miss her return. That would be the best-case scenario, of course—her just walking through the door one day."

"That *would* be ideal," Vera said. She cleared her throat and pressed her hands together as if in prayer, resting her fingertips under her chin. "In terms of what I can actually offer you for time—I was thinking maybe evenings from four to six? And I was thinking maybe I could help you edit the website. I'm a good editor. I'm not so tech savvy, but I'm constantly learning, so if you show me around the website, maybe I could help put updates on it, or even edit the comments feature or the tips."

"Oh, the tips go directly to the police, and thank God for that. I wouldn't want to have to make sense of all the bullshit that comes in. So far we've had four people reporting that they've seen Jensen dead, and eleven people reporting that they saw her alive. I guess one person even claimed he'd locked Jensen in the basement of the Franco-American Social Club, but that turned out to be a joke. You've got to wonder what makes people want to take ownership of stuff like this. It's pretty sick."

"Well," Vera said, "over two hundred people confessed to the Lindbergh baby kidnapping, back in the day."

"You don't say." In a lower voice—even though no one else was around to hear—Paul said, "We've had some doozies, and that's not even including the phone calls. We've heard everything from Jensen practices witchcraft, to she's working as a prostitute in Romania, to she's a raging drug addict who crossed the Mexican border. None of which seems to have any basis in reality. And then there's the snail mail. I'm not even going to get started on what's come in the mail."

"Good heavens. Those *are* doozies."

"It's such a strange case overall. It doesn't help that some of the most unreliable information comes from Jensen herself. That journal she kept—she mentions friends who don't even exist. The police looked into them and found nothing but dead ends."

"People who don't *exist*? Like who?" Vera ran through a mental checklist of non–Wallace School people whom Jensen had mentioned in her journals. Was the neighborhood girl, Annabel Francoeur, a fictive construct? Scotty, who was big on weaponry and explosives? Bret Folger—was it possible that even Bret Folger wasn't a real person?

"It's all neither here nor there, really." Paul Nimitz looked behind his shoulder at no one, seemingly embarrassed, as though he had been caught gossiping. "Getting back to the question of how you might be of service . . . we've got the edits covered. That's my area, actually. And we've got Robin handling most of the phone stuff here at headquarters. Frankly, the flyer distribution is where we have the greatest need. Let me show you what we've got for our flyer prototype right now. Amy designed it herself, and the idea is to get these made up and good to go within a couple of days."

Trying to squash her feelings of disappointment at the idea of being relegated to flyer distribution instead of something more hands-on, Vera looked at the countertop where Paul was gesturing; a flyer with Jensen's squinting face and the words HAVE YOU SEEN ME? printed across the top in large letters—as though Jensen were somebody's missing pup, Vera thought.

Over the next couple of workdays, Vera became familiar with the ways of the BRING JENSEN HOME committee. While she waited for the flyers to be ready, she stuffed envelopes and smoothed return labels on their upper corners and dabbed liquid sealant on their flaps. Once she got into the groove of these mundane tasks, she found them less than hateful; she even began to look forward to this transition from her long, tiring, interactive days teaching to this steady, self-contained, almost Zen-like work. Still, she sometimes brought student papers along with her to correct during the slow times. No harm doing busywork, she reasoned, when there was no actual work to do.

Jeannette Blais, the woman who owned the copy shop and always sat at the front desk with her bag of yarn, was a regular fixture at headquarters—the person who always greeted her comings and goings with a characteristic grunt. Secretly, Vera considered Jeannette her favorite person among the volunteers. She seemed the type who spoke only when she had something important to say, and when she did, her voice betrayed a thick, halting French-Canadian accent.

She might not have had such affinity for Jeannette had not Paul, who was turning out to be the most delicious sort of gossip, mentioned that the woman had donated more than one thousand dollars of her own money to the BRING JENSEN HOME effort. "It's because she had a grandson who disappeared in 1985," he had whispered to Vera during her second day at headquarters. "He would've been Amy's cousin, but she wasn't born yet."

Once, when it was only she and Jeannette in the office, with Robin working in the back, Vera had sat close to the older woman, after asking if it would be all right if she worked near the sunny window in the front office.

"I don't care," the woman had said. So Vera took her stack of student papers and curled up in the window seat by Jeannette's desk, enjoying the rhythmic clack of knitting needles. The big woman's silence and steady, unflinching presence was somehow comforting to her. Occasionally, when she dropped a stitch, she cursed in French and sucked on her upper denture.

"You spend a lot of time here," Vera stated when the woman had taken a break from the knitting to clean her eyeglasses with a tissue.

The woman nodded, not looking up from her task. "Oh, yes," she said with a knowing roll of her eyes, which looked small and puffy without her glasses. "It's my shop."

"But you stay here even beyond business hours."

"What else am I going to do?" The woman shrugged. "I like it here. Nothing better to do. Nothing better for you to do either, eh?"

"Maybe not," Vera said. She itched to ask Jeannette Blais if the grandson who had disappeared in 1985 had ever been found alive. She had a feeling, however, that she already knew the answer, and she did not think it was right to try to chip away at the woman's stoicism.

She closed her eyes and listened to the sound of knitting needles flying again as she waited for Robin to finish her work and give her the next assignment. She was glad that Jeannette Blais allowed her to sit there in companionable silence without asking her to leave. In a strange way, her volunteer efforts gave her a sense of something she didn't ordinarily have: a quiet sense of belonging.

The new flyers were ready a few days later, still warm and gleaming when Vera showed up at four o'clock; their stacks covered the length of the conference table, and more boxes of them were stuffed underneath it. Paul showed these proudly to Vera. "I was thinking you could start distributing some of these on the east end today? I have a map with all the businesses that have approved them."

"I could," Vera said, not wanting to say no. She had not considered the logistical angle of flyer distribution up until now. Then, hesitating: "I don't actually have a car. It might be hard for me to get to the east end carrying a really heavy stack."

"You don't have a car? You mean you walk over here every day?"

"Yes," Vera said firmly, seeing his pitying look. Why couldn't the locals adjust to the idea of someone who couldn't drive? "I *like* walking."

"We'll switch your route with Amy's, then. She'll do the east end and you can do the neighborhood right around here."

Vera, her tote bag filled with flyers, rolls of Scotch tape, and packets of thumbtacks, set off down the street. She tacked the signs onto the bulletin boards of coffee shops, hair salons, and small grocery stores around Dorset. Sometimes passersby stopped in their tracks and ogled her, wanting to see what she was hanging up; most walked away, seeing nothing that interested them, but others felt compelled to comment.

"Oh, I've heard about that girl," one woman in a flowered, tent-like dress said. "So heartbreaking for the parents."

Another woman, her words suspiciously slurred, asked: "Is that your daughter?"

"What?" Vera said, horrified. "Oh, no. She's one of my students."

Vera stopped on one quiet residential street in a neighborhood where all the house facades had been designed to look alike: *The village of the damned,* Vera thought, expecting malevolent towheaded youngsters to start drifting onto their doorsteps. Down the street a ways was a bus terminal whose glassed-in walls seemed a good place to tape another flyer. Several discarded bottles of vanilla extract littered the ground below the terminal bench; Vera noticed these and hypothesized that some of the local teenagers had bought these in order to get drunk. *Maybe not such a quiet neighborhood, after all.*

A boy of no more than thirteen or fourteen—*one of the imbibers?* Vera wondered—was riding a skateboard up and down the outer edge of the sidewalk. He wore army pants cut off at the knees and Chuck

Taylors like Vera had worn in the '80s, though his looked cleaner and newer than hers had ever been. The sight of these new, clean sneakers touched a nerve in Vera; she did not know why, but her intuition told her to be mindful of this young boy.

Out of the corner of her eye she watched him slow down, and he and his board came to a stop a few feet away from Vera, one foot resting on his skateboard and the other on the pavement. She could feel him watching her as she stood on her tiptoes, assessing the height of the glassed-in walls and trying to place the flyer at what would be eye level for most people.

The boy laughed softly. His laughter had a strange, adult quality, and Vera could not have been more startled if he had reached out to her and touched her on the cheek.

"What?" said Vera, whipping around so fast that she dropped her roll of tape to the pavement. The flyer with Jensen's picture on it fluttered to the ground. "What's so funny?"

Pointing at the fallen flyer, the boy said: "That bitch is *evil*. She scarfs down crazy-berries for breakfast, lunch, and dinner."

Vera cocked her head and looked at him, giving his comment the same grave consideration she might give to one of her own students. "I'm sorry? How do you know that?"

"Oh, trust me, I *know*. A lot of us do." He laughed again, as though Vera were too stupid to understand, and mounted his skateboard and took off down the street in a squeaking of wheels. He wore a long-sleeved T-shirt with something printed on the back; straining to read what it said, Vera first saw the word FETISH, and then the letters settled down and arranged themselves into what she could only assume was a surname: FITTS. She wondered fleetingly: *Do I know that name from somewhere?* She didn't think so. The boy wore a second shirt tied around his waist, a black button-down, and it flapped in the wind as Vera kept her eyes on him, hoping he might turn his skateboard around; it was only when the boy was well out of sight that Vera bent down to pick up the dropped flyer. A partial footprint from Vera's own shoe now covered Jensen Willard's half-closed eye, leaving an impression like a bruise.

Though it was still April, the cruelest month—a time when freezing winds and snowfall weren't uncommon in Maine—the weather outside was warming, almost humid. The restlessness of spring had already infiltrated Vera's classroom; her girls were now about a third of the way through *The Bell Jar*, and they were not responding to it as Vera had thought they might. They did not like the young protagonist, Esther Greenwood. They found her dated and laughable, with all her mentions of finger bowls and hats and gloves and dances, and they zeroed in on the inconsistencies of her voice and her mood.

"One minute she's cracking jokes, and the next minute she's thinking about killing herself," Cecily-Anne St. Aubrey said. "Who does that? I really think she just likes being unhappy. Happiness is a *choice*. And what does she have to be so unhappy about, anyway? She has a mother who loves her. She's going to a good college. She gets to do all these cool things in New York City."

The girls seemed to have even more derision for Esther than they had had for Holden Caulfield. They cut her no slack at all. *Typical female self-loathing,* Vera thought sadly. *Or am I really this out of touch with what today's girls might respond to?* How she wished Jensen had been there—if not to defend the book publicly, then to write her journal responses with their own inconsistencies of mood and voice that proved the other girls wrong.

"Before I let you go today, I do want to share with you a memo that

I received earlier this morning," Vera said to her girls. "It seems that Katherine Arsenault's parents have withdrawn her from Wallace. They plan to enroll her at Andover. This is a decision that was made rather suddenly, so far as I can tell." She waited a beat, stopped dramatically between the rows of tables, and intoned: "And then there were nine."

She meant it to be funny, but as soon as the words were out there, she knew they were not.

"I hope we don't lose any more people," Jamie said.

"I hope that, too. Are we going to hold strong at nine, girls? Is anyone else thinking of transferring elsewhere? I certainly *hope* no one else is of a mind to disappear."

"My parents are talking about moving," Autumn said, sounding bored. "They think it isn't safe in Dorset anymore."

"Anyplace can be unsafe, Autumn, but far be it for me to question your parents' wisdom. I would hate to see any one of you go—just know that much."

The girls' flat expressions told Vera that this feeling of attachment was not mutual. She told herself that this was all right—they didn't *have* to like her in order to respect her. Whether or not they respected her was another story, but that, Vera thought, was something best left unexamined for now.

It was only two weeks before Vera's Wallace School girls were to have their weeklong spring break. Vera had begun to think that the hiatus from classes might do them all some good.

With the days ticking by, bringing her closer and closer to her school vacation, Vera had distributed all the BRING JENSEN HOME flyers she could possibly carry and had even carpooled with Lacey Tondreau and Karen Provencher to circulate the flyers as far south in Maine as

York and Kittery, near the New Hampshire border. Now that the supply of flyers was temporarily exhausted, she had been assigned the duty of making phone calls to local businesses to thank them for their donations and slyly gouge them for more. Vera, who hated that sort of thing—both the assertiveness required for it and the possibility of rejection—took as much time as possible to go through the names on her list, sometimes going for a head-clearing walk around the block before proceeding to the next phone call. The other volunteers noticed her behavior and saw it as a source of humor: "There she goes, revving up for the cause again!" Paul said, and Vera did not have the heart to tell him it wasn't a question of revving up but of avoidance.

One afternoon at headquarters she sensed the excitement among her fellow volunteers that was always palpable right before law enforcement stopped in. She had seen Detective Helen Cutler at the copy center only once, but at that time, the detective had made a special point to stop by Vera's semiprivate workstation near the kitchen.

"Good to see you getting even more involved," Cutler had said.

Stifling the urge to say something wry, Vera had said, "Thank you for approving it. I do want to help my student and her family if I can."

On this day Cutler came in and spoke quietly to Paul for a while, then to Robin, who handed her a series of notes that the detective looked through with care. What was on those notes? Why was Robin given all the *interesting* things to do? When Cutler had finished checking in with the other volunteers, she came by Vera's station and informed her that the Cudahys were planning to stop in soon and would probably want to meet with her. This news hit Vera from out of left field.

"Jensen's parents want to meet *me*?"

"Well, yes. You were Jensen's favorite teacher. I plan to sit in for the conversation, if you don't mind."

This seemed like a setup. Vera didn't like it one bit. However, she didn't feel as if she was in any position to say that she *did* mind Cutler sitting in, and she had to admit that she was keen to meet Jensen's parents—to meet the people she felt she already knew through Jensen's journals. She went into the bathroom and tried to spruce herself up so that she would look more refreshed. Dabbing water over the crown of her head, where cowlicks were always appearing, and wiping away some of the makeup that always seemed to smudge around her eyes, she decided she looked presentable enough.

When the Cudahys came in a half hour later, Vera was taken aback. She had seen in the paper that Jensen's mother was fifty-five years old—that made her forty when she had had Jensen, not what most people would think of as a young mother—but she looked a good ten to fifteen years older than her actual age. A stooped, gaunt man was at her side, holding a basset hound at the end of a leash. Both the man and the basset hound seemed to be sniffing the air in the same discontented way, with the same glum expression. Had the basset hound been given clearance to come in? She guessed so.

"Are you the teacher?" Jensen's mother said. "The English sub?"

Vera felt a hitch in her stomach as the woman's watery eyes sought out hers. Detective Cutler remained passive in the background, but Vera was deeply aware of her, and she thought: *If you're going to watch me, damn you, I'm going to kill the whole lot of you with kindness.*

She stood up and extended her hand. "Vera Lundy. And you must be the Cudahys." Both Jensen's parents' hands felt slight and tremulous as they gripped hers in turn. Seeing Jensen's parents, the frailty of them, made her think of her own parents—her lonely mother, her late father—and a feeling of protectiveness swelled inside her.

"Would you like some coffee? I hope you don't mind instant," Vera went on, her naturally low voice rising by half an octave—higher and sweeter. "One of the girls here—Amy, maybe you've met her—she usually bakes something. She brought in some homemade hot cross buns today. Would you like some? I haven't tried them myself, but I hear they're quite good."

Without waiting for an answer, Vera headed toward the kitchen in the back. She filled the coffeepot, turned on the stove burner, and loaded a plastic tray with Amy's hot cross buns, paper plates, and napkins.

"Oh, boy," Les Cudahy said when the tray appeared. Up until this moment, he had looked like a sulky kid who hadn't been invited to the party; the appearance of baked goods seemed to cheer him, to make him feel included. Inspecting the hot cross buns, he said, "You know, I bet these'd be real good if you put raisins in them. I never heard of hot cross buns without raisins in them."

"How can you think of a thing like that right now?" Linda Cudahy said. "These people have more important things to do than bake to order."

Vera, trying not to laugh, said, "Actually, it's a quiet afternoon. But I don't think we have any raisins here." She went back to get the coffee, making sure to bring a third cup for Cutler, who was chatting with the Cudahys as though they were old chums—which, she supposed, they practically were at this point. Cutler had that infuriating, elliptical smile on her face again, the cat-that-ate-the-canary smile.

The basset hound, freed from its leash, plodded around the adults' ankles, looking morose. Vera was trying her hardest to picture Jensen as part of this family—mother, stepfather, dog. She couldn't, quite.

"Les, you remember me telling you about the teacher who called on the phone that Friday night," Linda Cudahy said, accepting the mug of coffee from Vera. "She was already gone by then."

She. She meant Jensen, of course. Looking from Les, who was still admiring the cross-shaped icing on his hot cross bun, to Mrs. Cudahy, Vera said, "Yes, I did call that night. I'm so sorry about everything you've been through."

"It's nice of you to want to help out here. We've had so many offers of help already. It's overwhelming sometimes, but it's very kind. Do you have any children, Miss Lundy?"

"No, I don't."

"Well then." Jensen's mother settled back in her seat, looking almost smug. "You can't really imagine what it's like for us. But in a way I think that makes it more admirable that you want to help. I'm sure those flyers are helping. Police are telling us to get Jensen's name and face out there as much as we can. We can only do so much on our own, you know . . . and Les, with his bad heart and all, can't do much at all."

"Jensen is a pretty unusual student," Vera said, "and she's worth whatever assistance I can offer. She's . . . she's one of the more talented student writers I've ever seen."

"She's always been such a writer. Practically from birth. You can't *teach* talent," Mrs. Cudahy said.

"Oh," Vera said. "I forgot to ask if you wanted cream and sugar in your coffee!"

"Just a drop or two of cream would be good, dear."

Vera went back to the refrigerator and came back with a carton of half-and-half. She was impressed with the comment about not being able to teach talent; she was tempted to expand on this idea, but she knew this was not the time to wax pedantic. She poured the milk into their coffees while Mrs. Cudahy broke apart one of the hot cross buns with her bare hands. "Are you planning to eat that," she said, nodding at her husband, "or do you just want to sit there drooling over it?"

"Well, Jesus Christ," Jensen's stepfather grumped. "I wasn't going to just *dig in* before you ladies got any." He balanced the paper plate on his lap and resettled in his chair near Vera's, surveying the back room with a certain dignified imperiousness. Vera found herself touched by this display of pride in the elderly man.

Jensen's mother took a big bite into her pastry. Then, without warning, she swallowed hard and began to weep. A dollop of piped white frosting hung from her lower lip.

"God, I'm sorry," she said to Vera, covering her mouth with her hand.

Vera felt she should be close to crying, too, but her eyes were dry. She saw that Cutler had put a hand on the woman's back and was patting it absently.

"I can't help it," Linda Cudahy said. "It's the stress, you know? One minute I'll think I'm okay. I think I'm so big and strong and tough, but I'm not."

"Our house feels bleak without Jensen," Les said from the corner, and Vera saw that his eyes were watering, too. There was nothing worse, to her thinking, than seeing an old man weep. He put a wad of bread in his mouth and uttered the word again, as though it satisfied him somehow: "*Bleak.*"

Tentatively, Vera said: "I saw the new article this morning about your daughter."

"Us, too. We get the paper."

"I'm guessing you already know that it was my class that was reading *The Catcher in the Rye.*" She looked over at Cutler in a manner that she hoped looked confident and conspiratorial: *We're in on this together, you and me.*

Mrs. Cudahy had controlled her tears but was still swiping at her eyes with a paper napkin. "She loved your class," she said. "I feel so stupid. I read *The Catcher in the Rye* when I was a kid myself, but that was forty years ago. It must not have made much of an impression. Do you know what I did, though? I found Jensen's copy in her room and started rereading it. But then the police came by and took it so they could look at it themselves. That Detective Ferrari—he thinks he's so smart."

Cutler coughed good-naturedly.

"No offense, I know you work with him, Helen. He thought our daughter might have written in it, with underlines or highlights or something." The woman looked at Cutler, whose smile only broadened with a sympathetic cast, then back at Vera as though waiting for her to say something. "I think that woman is full of it—the teacher who had the baby. I think her comments in the paper today are insulting, and I'm half of a mind to call her up and tell her so. I don't see any connection between Jensen and this book at all, do you?"

"Not really. Only in a loose sort of way. But you know, Mrs. Cudahy—"

"Call me Linda."

"—Linda. You know that Jensen was writing a journal for my class. The journal requirement was to make connections between the novel and the student's own lives. Were you aware of this journal?" She turned to Helen Cutler. "Did you—I mean, is this something you've discussed with them before?"

Cutler nodded, but the look she gave Vera seemed to contain a warning that Vera couldn't read.

"Oh, sure, we've been asked all kinds of questions about it," Jensen's mother said. "But like I've said to Helen, Jensen's always writing something, you know. Always carrying a notebook around with her. When she was younger I used to tell her, 'Don't ever write down anything that you wouldn't want the world to read.' And a couple years ago she started arguing with me about this and saying that a writer *has* to write everything down, even if it hurts some people. I've been trying to understand it."

"Mrs. Cudahy. *Linda*," Vera began again. She steeled herself, for she knew that the next thing she needed to tell her must be phrased in the most prudent way. "The police also may have mentioned this to you, but in some of Jensen's journal entries, she sounded . . . upset. Especially in the final pages. She wrote them as though she was thinking about . . . hurting herself. I feel like I should have told you this much sooner. I feel remiss, not having told you."

Vera wished she could say the next part—the part about how her phone call had been originally meant to warn them of Jensen's intentions on Friday night. But in so doing, she knew she would also have to own up to her own role in how Jensen had vanished. If only Cutler had not been sitting there, she was sure she would have said something; instead, she found herself wishing the Cudahys were sharp enough to read between the lines of what she was saying—sharp enough to read her mind.

"Something you need to understand about my daughter," Mrs. Cudahy said. "This is the same thing I keep telling the police over and over: She likes to write things for shock value. She's always thinking about how to get reactions to the things she writes. Even when she was little, she would write stories and add in these touching details that would make me cry because my tears would make her feel . . . I can't think of what the word is . . ."

"Affirmed?"

"Not what I was thinking, but I guess that works, too. I was thinking more like *powerful*. I brought some of Jensen's early writings for you to look at. As her English teacher, I thought you might get a kick out of seeing them. Would you?"

Vera said that she would. She had not expected Jensen's mother to be this receptive to her, a stranger. She guessed that Mrs. Cudahy missed her daughter so much that any opportunity to talk about her, to share thoughts with anyone willing to listen to her, was welcome.

There was no other explanation for her warmth—unless, of course, this was all part of the setup that Cutler had puppeteered. She could not lose sight of that possibility.

"Shit," Mrs. Cudahy said. "I left the papers in the car. Give me a second and I'll go get them."

While his wife was away in the parking lot, Mr. Cudahy said, "My heart can't take all this. It's too much, isn't it, Tessie?" Vera inferred that Tessie was the basset hound. The dog had settled into a fat puddle at her master's feet and had begun licking at her red, raw-looking belly. As the old man leaned toward her, scratching her neck under the collar, the dog's grunts filled the room.

"Your stepdaughter will come home soon, Mr. Cudahy," Vera said. "You can't lose hope."

"She was two years old when I married her mother. I always think of her as mine, you know . . . my own little girl. And she's a good girl, mostly. A good girl. I never thought she'd run off like this. She knows how much it would upset her mother and I."

Her mother and me, Vera almost corrected him, but stopped herself just in time.

Cutler was saying something consoling to him, something Vera could not hear, when Mrs. Cudahy returned with Jensen's writings. Vera looked through some of the pages, written in the large, generic printing that most children have before they develop the idiosyncrasies of their own penmanship. There was a story by Jensen about a little boy who rode on a magic feather bed that floated through the air. There was another story of a girl who sat on the moon, looking down at all the things on Earth below her. Vera thought that the recurring theme might not be insignificant—the idea of solitary children separated from others, looking down at others from on high. What she said out loud was, "They're very sweet. You can definitely tell that she had writing ability even then."

"All my kids were talented, and all of them were good people," Linda Cudahy said.

"All talented," Les echoed from the corner. "Every last one of 'em."

"I have two older sons," Mrs. Cudahy explained to Vera. "I know I should say *had*, but when anyone asks how many children I have, I say I am the mother of three. Ross was eleven years older than Jensen, and Nicholas was eight years older. The boys died together in a car accident when Jensen was only four. My daughter didn't write anything about that?"

The surprise must have shown on Vera's face. She managed to say, "She didn't. I'm so sorry to hear this." She glanced at Cutler, whose expression was placid; clearly this was not news to her.

"Les, show her that picture from your wallet," Mrs. Cudahy said, and the elderly man took his sweet time getting it out, even pulling the photo out of its cellophane sheath to place it in Vera's hand—this small, black-and-white portrait of two chubby little boys seated close to each other on a bench. The bigger of the two was dark-haired, looking rather like Jensen and, Vera supposed, like Linda Cudahy. "There's Ross and Nicholas. All three of my babies were built like little Sherman tanks. Even my daughter, though you'd never know it now. Both boys were very much their own people, just like Jensen is. Ross was going to be a filmmaker—he was only fifteen, but he'd made these short films that would knock your socks off. And Ross was a writer, too, like Jensen—you could already tell. I always told my kids, 'Be whatever you want to be when you grow up, just as long as you grow up to be a good person.' And all my kids would have grown up to be good people—no one can ever take that from them."

"Or from you," Vera said.

Without asking, Vera got up and refilled the Cudahys' coffee mugs.

Detective Cutler had not touched her own coffee. "She likes you, you know," Mrs. Cudahy said.

"I'm sorry?"

"Our daughter likes you. That's why she wrote all that stuff in her journal. If she likes you, she'll go on and on and on and on. Lots of words. Lots of thoughts. All written down. She said you seemed different from the other teachers."

The corners of the woman's mouth were starting to jerk tearfully downward again; her effort to fight against this and force a smile verged on grotesque, and Vera had to look elsewhere. "It just makes me sick to think what might have happened to her. I just can't see her running away. A runaway is a *bad kid*, a kid who doesn't worry about hurting her parents. At first, though, I hoped she might have gone to see her boyfriend, who's going to school in New York City."

"Bret Folger," Vera said. Recalling what Paul Nimitz had said about some of Jensen's friends being fictitious, she couldn't help but feel a jolt of relief to know that Bret, at least, was the real deal.

"Oh, so you know Bret?"

"Only from Jensen's journals. And even then, it's a pretty limited portrayal, I think."

Ignoring that last comment, Mrs. Cudahy said, "She went to New York to see him one time—with permission, of course. So I got this idea that maybe she'd gone down there again to be with him. Now bear in mind, my girl *doted* on him, hung around near the phone every Sunday night waiting for his phone call. But the police have spoken to him several times. There's no reason to think she's there with him, so they say. Still, I wonder." The woman shot a defensive, almost apologetic look at Cutler. "I know there's no reason to think that anymore. But I'd rather think that's where she is than think—something else."

"Wow." Vera mulled over this for a while. The dog had lifted itself up from Les's feet and now whined at her side. She thought of petting it, but the dog smelled sour and sharp—*like somebody's behind,* Vera thought. "Judging by what Jensen wrote about Bret in her journals, he doesn't sound like a very sensitive boy."

"He is number than a pounded thumb. And spineless? Let me tell you about spineless! I wouldn't trust him to tell the truth if she's with him."

Vera thought about New York City. She thought about Jensen saying, with a dreamy look on her face, *Sometimes I thought I'd go down to New York to live with Bret. I printed up this map once of all the places Holden goes in New York, thinking I might go there sometime.* It seemed a long shot; how could she have gotten there? By bus? There were coaches to Boston that ran every hour, twenty-four hours a day. Unlikely though it seemed, a blind hope began to rise in her.

"I lived there for a few years," she told Mrs. Cudahy. "New York City, I mean—not far from Columbia University. I daresay I know Bret's neck of the woods pretty well."

"Hell of a place," Les said ambiguously.

"Yes," Vera agreed. "Hell of a place indeed."

The conversation seemed to fizzle out. Jensen's mother smiled at Vera—whether sincerely or insincerely, she could not tell—and Vera looked from her to her husband to the mute detective, who gave no indication whether she was paying attention to any of this, though Vera knew that she had to be. After a cumbersome silence, Jensen's mother said she needed to excuse herself to go to the lavatory.

"It's to the left," Vera said, charmed by the old-fashioned word *lavatory*—a word straight out of her own mother's vocabulary.

"I know where it is. Do you want to join me?"

Vera did not know how to respond to this invitation. She had never been the type of woman who liked an entourage when she took a restroom break, and she didn't particularly wish to join the woman in the bathroom. Absurdly, she thought of Bret Folger inviting Jensen into his bathroom so he could kiss her. But then she told herself: *Don't be a dummy. This is your one chance to talk to her without Cutler horning in.*

"If you'd like," she said. She got up and followed Jensen's mother down the hall. *Take that, Cutler,* she couldn't help thinking.

"I wasn't sure about Jensen going to the Wallace School, to be honest," Linda Cudahy said as soon as she'd shut the bathroom door. The bathroom had a tub in it—sometimes the volunteer committee used this tub as storage space for flyers—and Vera perched on its porcelain rim, discreetly turned away from Jensen's mother as the woman unzipped her pants. She tried not to reflect too much on the ridiculousness of this situation; the woman's voice rose over the resounding stream of her urine. "All those snotty people, and the teachers are the worst of them. But you really are different. I want to thank you for that. Thank you for becoming a friend to my daughter in such a short time. Thank you for what you've done, and for what you're doing."

"You shouldn't thank me," Vera said. She felt humbled—a sensation she was not used to feeling. She was not used to feeling humbled by the basic goodness of people. The basset hound, loose still, was scratching outside the bathroom door to get in. Vera thought about how she used to follow her own mother into the bathroom, chatting at her while she bathed, chatting at her while she peed, barely taking note of the fact that she was using the toilet and might prefer some privacy. For some reason the thought made her sad. That kind of closeness to anyone had all been such a long time ago.

Jensen's mother, having finished her bathroom business, gave

Vera a hug, flustering her even more. Back in the workroom, Vera shook hands with Les Cudahy and even gave the dog a farewell tap on the head as she bade the Cudahys good-bye and wished them well. Cutler stayed behind, writing something down in her notepad, and Vera waited until Jensen's parents were gone before she spoke to her.

"How do you think that went?" she asked.

"Went? I think it went fine. What did you think of them?"

Now why had Cutler asked her that? Did she think the Cudahys were suspects in their own daughter's disappearance? Flattered that Cutler wanted to know her opinion, Vera said, "I guess they seem on the up-and-up to me."

"Good people."

Vera couldn't tell if the detective was agreeing with her or simply trying to clarify what Vera had meant. "Good people," she seconded. "So far as I can tell, anyway. What do *you* think?"

Cutler looked less now like the cat that ate the canary than like the cat who has pocketed the canary in its cheek for safekeeping. "Classified information," she said.

On the Monday of her school break, the lethal boredom of Saturday and Sunday had already done its work on Vera, and she could no longer stand to stay sequestered in her studio or wander pointlessly around Dorset looking for something to do. She headed to the BRING JENSEN HOME headquarters early in the afternoon, her thoughts full of last Friday's morning class and their further attempt to discuss *The Bell Jar.*

"Can I ask something?" Harmony had said, raising her hand near the end of class—something that she rarely bothered to do. Usually she just spoke outright, a habit that Vera had never discouraged.

"Yes?"

"When we finish up with this book, can we read something more *upbeat* afterward? All these people going off to mental hospitals is getting a little depressing."

"I'll see what I can come up with," Vera had said.

"And not something about death, either."

"I'll make note of this," Vera said. "No death. No psychiatric hospitals. Perhaps there's a good story about puppies or kittens that was left out of our anthology."

Harmony smiled an almost blissful smile—another rarity. "I *love* puppies and kittens."

"You girls," Vera had said, feeling a wash of affection for all of them—even Harmony, whose face was rather transformed by that smile. "Don't forget to give me your journals before you go. And I'll say so long but not good-bye, because we'll be meeting again in just nine short days."

Seven days now, Vera thought. *And they can't come soon enough.*

At headquarters she found Amy Nimitz and Lacey Tondreau in the kitchen, stuffing themselves with homemade oatmeal cookies that Amy had brought in.

"Did you know the police have a good lead?" Amy said to her as soon as they had exchanged greetings.

"On Jensen?"

"Yup. Robin hinted as much yesterday, but I don't know exactly what it is. Only that it's good."

The other two women talked so much—their subjects shifting from speculation to gossip to the latest clearance sale at J.Crew—that

Vera was not able to accomplish much over the next couple of hours. When she decided to leave and take her unfinished paperwork home with her, Amy pushed a bag of leftover cookies into her hands, insisting she take them with her, and told her she would see her tomorrow.

Vera was already out the door and halfway down the front walk when the door of the copy center burst open and Amy came running out. "I forgot to tell you, you got some mail!" she said, holding an envelope out at arm's length.

"I did?" Vera said. The envelope she took from Amy was oversized, with the stiffness and thickness of a greeting card, and bore a New York postmark. "There's no return address. Who would write to me here, from New York City?"

"Maybe it's something from a donor you reached out to. A thank-you for a thank-you, or something like that."

"That's probably it," Vera said, tucking the envelope into her bag, She lifted her hand in a half wave and continued down the walkway, rounding the corner and crossing the street; as she neared the first set of traffic lights, a car door slammed shut, and she turned to see what she had been too preoccupied to notice before: the unmarked police cruiser slowing down beside her.

Out of the passenger seat came Detective Ferreira wearing another one of his pristine white shirts under a light jacket; Vera could just make out Cutler in the driver's seat.

"Vera Lundy," Ferreira said. "Just the person we're looking for."

She felt herself submit—a process so easy, so effortless, that she wondered why she hadn't done it sooner. Submission, when one agreed to it, was the easiest thing in the world.

"What can I do for you?" she asked.

"I'd like to bring you down to the precinct to ask you a few questions."

She got into the back seat of the car without a word. "Am I under arrest?"

"Now why would you ask that?"

"I don't know."

"If you were under arrest, I'd be reading you your rights and telling you you were under arrest."

The submission came with a huge sense of relief that she hadn't expected, and there was an undercurrent of something else, too—a sense of déjà vu that she couldn't place at first. On what other occasion had she been feeling this same glad surrender, in such a similar way? Then she remembered.

It was the end of her first semester at college, the beginning of Christmas break. Her weight had fallen to seventy pounds. She could barely walk from class to class. She had told the college that she wouldn't be back for the spring semester, and when her parents drove up to get her, loading all her things in their trunk, she could feel only as though she'd been rescued. Riding away in her parents' car, she had settled against the back seat cushions and seen her bony chin reflected in the passenger window. She had been grateful to know she was going home. She had just enough strength left for gratitude. The feeling was much the same now, riding in the back of Detective Ferreira's car on the way to the station.

Chapter Ten

Vera had never been to a police station before, and despite her penchant for true-crime cases, she had never been a fan of TV shows about cops. She didn't know what to expect as Ferreira and Cutler brought her past the front desk manned by a boyish-looking officer and down a hallway broken up by cramped, pedestrian-looking workstations that hummed with energy and tension. She didn't know if she would be searched or fingerprinted—was that only for people who had been booked? And what did it mean to be "booked," exactly? Cutler opened the door to a small, plain room, mostly empty except for a round table; the plastic chairs tucked into it were the same as those in Vera's own classroom. "Have a seat," she said.

"Am I being recorded?"

"Do you have an objection if you are?"

"No. I was just asking. Would you like some cookies?" Vera was still holding Amy's bag of leftovers, which the detective had glanced inside when she'd gotten into his car—looking for weapons or drugs, probably, and finding wholesome baked goods instead.

"You're kidding, right?" Ferreira said.

"No," she said. "I'm sorry. I just thought . . . I don't know what I was thinking." She put the bag down on the table.

"Let's get right down to it," Ferreira said. "We're here to follow up about your student Jensen Willard. I'm going to ask you one more time: Did you see Jensen at any point after that?"

"No, sir," Vera said. She moistened the outer corner of her lips with her tongue and thought: *It's pointless. They know something.* Hesitating, the words catching in her throat before they broke free, Vera looked the detective right in the eye and corrected herself: "Yes, sir. Yes, I actually did. And I do know that you're expecting me to say something. I'm just not sure where to start."

"My suggestion? Start by changing the story you told before, and make it factual this time. Otherwise this isn't looking so good for you."

Vera tried to tell him. "On that Friday . . ." she began, but her throat again clenched around the rest of her words. Propping her elbows against the circular table, she covered her face in her hands. "I'm so sorry. I don't think I can explain."

"All right. If that's how it's going to be, I have a little something I'd like to show you."

Lifting her face, Vera belatedly noticed the TV set and the video equipment on a wheeled stand in the corner. Detective Ferreira turned on the TV and slid a tape into the player. From the picture quality, Vera knew she was looking at a surveillance tape. The still, grainy image on the TV was that of a glass door—a door with no one behind it. It reminded Vera of the cheap scares prevalent in horror movies, when a quiet interlude is followed by a killer blasting in. A shadow appeared in the frame, advancing toward the door until the shadow was a person: no killer but Vera herself, recognizable in her distinctive coat and hat. Before disappearing from the frame, the grainy onscreen version of Vera looked up, almost as though acknowledging the surveillance camera above.

"Notice the time and date in the corner," the detective said. "Eight thirty at night on Friday, March thirtieth. This was at the Roundview Hotel, as I'm sure you're aware. Let's fast-forward to ten fifty-eight p.m. on that same evening and see what we see."

While he advanced the tape, she knew already what she would see: the glass door again, a view of two females exiting. Herself, and a slightly smaller girl in a long black coat who was carrying an army knapsack. As the sliding door opened for them, the girl turned as though she was saying something to Vera; even in the grainy footage, the lines of her profile were sharp.

"That look like anybody you know?" Detective Ferreira asked.

Vera nodded. "It's Jensen Willard."

"See, the kid who was working the night shift at the Roundview has been in Vegas for a nice little vacation," Cutler spoke up. "He wasn't around to see the local news stories. But he got back last night and happened to see a paper. He recognized Jensen Willard's picture as being a girl he'd checked in a few days before. He remembered something else, too: a woman coming to meet her in the lobby, then leaving with her a little later."

Cutler paused, clearly leaving an inroad for Vera to say something. She kept her mouth shut.

"And one more thing," Ferreira said. "We've got a truck driver who said he saw two females heading toward Pine Street on the night of the thirtieth, sometime before midnight. He said that one had a long, dark coat and the other had a paler coat with a fur collar. Just like the one in the surveillance tape. Just like the one you're wearing right now, as a matter of fact."

Vera almost said, *It's* fake *fur*—a reflexive response, meaning nothing—but caught herself just in time. She did not want the detective to think she was being either flippant or combative.

"You have nothing to say for yourself?" the detective prodded.

In a weary but resolute voice, Vera said, "I do, actually. I do have something to say."

It took some time as she attempted to fill in the gaps of the narrative told by the video: how she had gone to the hotel because she was concerned that Jensen had checked into a room to kill herself that night. She told him of how she had convinced her to check out and walked the girl home as far as Middle Street.

"How did you know she was going to be at this hotel?" Cutler asked.

"She wrote it in her journal. She more or less said where she was going to be, almost like she wanted me to find her there. I have two handwritten pages that you didn't see. They're at home now if you want them."

"Didn't you think this information could be valuable? Why didn't you mention any of this when I spoke to you before?"

"I thought I might be in trouble with my boss and . . . I don't know, maybe legally. My first instinct was to protect Jensen, which is why I didn't tell about what she wrote in the journals. My second instinct was to protect myself, for not having spoken up right away. But I really have been thinking every single day that tomorrow would be the day I'd tell you. I really did."

"Funny how tomorrow never came along. You've made a poor decision, as you've doubtless figured out," Ferreira said.

"I know."

That pause again, and that penetrating look. It took all of Vera's self-control not to squirm around in her chair. "You're known to have some weird hobbies. What's that all about?"

"Hobbies?"

"All these books about serial killers you're always checking out from the library."

Vera wondered how he had known. She wanted to ask the detective if he found serial killers interesting, too; she imagined that he did, or he wouldn't be in his profession. But again, such a comment might be misconstrued. Best to keep her answers clipped and straightforward. "I just find serial killers interesting," she said.

Detective Ferreira settled back in his chair. He looked as if he was holding back a smile; it was the same smile Vera sometimes held back when her students stumbled upon a truth more profound than even they realized. "Do you know what *I* find interesting? Getting answers. And seeing justice done."

"As do I, Detective."

"I see that Ivan Schlosser's another one of your hobbies. My father worked on that case, just so you know."

Vera furrowed her brow, thinking. "Your father worked on the Schlosser case? Was his name Ferreira, too?"

"No. Vachon. I was adopted by my stepfather."

"Oh, right . . . Vachon. I remember reading about a Vachon who worked on the case." Vera looked up at the detective, abashed. "I'm sorry . . . it's just that I know a lot about the Schlosser investigation."

"I doubt that very much. I know things you'll never know, even if you read all the articles ever printed on the subject. Maybe you're thinking you're going to write a little something about it. Maybe a book to titillate the masses. But you know what's not titillating? Finding a twelve-year-old girl with her head cut off and having to tell her parents what you've found."

Vera could not argue with this. She could only nod, unsettled by where this line of conversation might be going.

"That could be Jensen Willard now. She could be in that same condition. But we don't know, do we? We don't know because you left her there on Middle Street after dark."

"And I hate myself for it, Detective." The unplanned words came out in a rush, and once they began Vera was afraid she might not be able to stop them. "I look back at that night and wish I could redo it. I think: What if I had insisted on walking her all the way to her door and making sure she got inside? Or what if I'd stayed overnight in the hotel room with her, in the next bed, which was what she suggested at first? Then I'd never have to wonder if my actions caused all this."

The detective was tapping a pen back and forth between thumb and forefinger, looking at Vera more intently than anyone had looked at her before. Cutler, too, looked highly engrossed in what she was saying.

"Vera," Ferreira said, "you're a smart enough woman. You're a smart woman who does stupid things. I'll be honest with you—I don't think for a minute that you have much of a role in the Willard kid's disappearance other than what you've told me. In terms of being *directly* responsible for that girl going missing . . . I just don't think it's likely, even though we have some unanswered questions still."

"So I'm not a suspect," Vera said. "But I'm a person of interest. Do Jensen's parents know this?"

"They'll be brought up to speed soon enough. And in case you were wondering, you can expect your employer will be notified, too. I have a feeling they're not going to risk the well-being of another one of their students in the future."

Hearing this, something inside Vera snapped loose. She lowered her head, scrunched up her face into its least attractive expression, and let the tears come down, trickling along her chin and onto her dress front.

The detective pushed a box of tissues toward her, and she scrabbled for a handful.

Cutler spoke up then. "You do understand, I hope, that all this has to be looked into. Especially since you haven't been straight with us. We have a warrant to search your apartment. We're expecting your cooperation."

"Of course," Vera said, laughing hollowly behind her tissue at the thought of police detectives searching her tiny place. "There isn't much to search there. But please search all you want."

The detective made a phone call, short and cryptic on his end, and into the room came a third face Vera had seen before—sad-eyed Officer Babineau, who reintroduced himself to Vera in a manner that struck her as being close to apologetic. She allowed the three of them to lead her out of the room and then out of the building, not daring to ask where they were going; with two detectives on one side of her and a police officer on the other, she sensed that some of the employees at their workstations were looking at her as they passed. She wondered if they already knew who she was, knew the story that the rest of Dorset was about to know.

She said nothing as they drove back to her apartment. She took them up the three flights and unlocked her door for the detectives and the officer—a model of graciousness for one whose residence was about to be searched. For the first time she was conscious of how truly small her studio looked, with the big mattress and box spring filling up most of the space. There really wasn't room enough for all of them. Ferreira and Babineau both stopped in the kitchen, and Vera followed the line of their gaze to the four printouts of the four girls taped above her laptop.

"Take these down, Gerry," Detective Ferreira said with something like disgust, and as the officer peeled back the tape and put the pages in a clear folder, Vera said, "It helps me to look at the pictures. I've been trying to figure out if there's a connection between these last three girls. Don't you think it's striking, two girls dying by strangulation in the same town? And now a third is missing. One can't help but wonder."

The detective grunted. "I need those journal pages you said you were going to hand over," he said.

Going over to her worktable, she felt around under some ungraded papers and handed him Jensen's last entry. "The last two pages are the handwritten ones I told you about," she said. "Have you guys . . . I mean, have the police looked into any possible links between Angela and Sufia? I know you have one man in prison now. I just hope you have the right one. If there's *any* doubt . . ."

"Ma'am?"

"Yes?"

"I'd like you to step aside and be quiet."

She nodded shamefacedly. She didn't know whether she was supposed to stay in the studio or excuse herself, perhaps go sit on the stoop so they could search in peace—not that her presence seemed to inhibit them. Watching Ferreira, Babineau, and Cutler mauling her belongings was not something she wished to oversee. She pressed herself up against the window in her room as the detectives worked around her, looking out and trying to pretend that nothing unusual was happening. She observed the normalcy on the sidewalk below, hoping it might somehow rub off on her: a woman struggling with a baby carriage as she talked into her cell phone. A rangy kid wobbling along on a skateboard—not the same boy she had seen on the street while hanging flyers, Vera determined. Cars stopping to refill their tanks at the gas station across the street, and a blind man with a white cane a few yards away, waiting for the streetlights to change. Behind her she heard the sound of milk crates being dumped on the floor, milk crates holding various lesson plans from all her past semesters of teaching, and a rustling as they leafed through an envelope of photographs taken of herself and her few friends at Princeton.

"You were right," Detective Ferreira said a short while later. "You don't have much to search." Vera saw that he was holding her laptop under his arm.

"When will I get the laptop back, Detective?"

"When we're done with it, that's when. I don't expect it'll be a long time. We can see that you get a search warrant inventory."

"Thank you," she said, as though the detective were a handyman who had come in to repair something.

"My advice? Stay in town for the next few weeks. Just to be on the safe side."

"I can do that."

"And no more volunteering. We know what we need to know now."

She remained in the window as the detectives and the officer left her apartment, and she saw them reappear on the sidewalk and get into their car. They didn't look as though they were saying anything to one another, and they didn't look back up toward her window as they drove away.

Vera stepped from the window to survey the mess they had left behind. They had made a good show of putting things back, which was more consideration than she felt she deserved, but nothing was organized exactly as she liked it. She began to replace things, to repack her milk crates till the files were in the order she wanted them in, to pick up the silky dresses that had slipped off their hangers as the detectives had rifled through her closet. She neatened the piles of papers that sat next to where her laptop always sat; now the space was empty, just like the space above the wall where the four girls' pictures had been displayed. The blank white wall taunted her. There was one piece of tape still stuck to the plaster—the one on the far end, the spot where Jensen Willard had squinted down at her only minutes before.

Vera thought for a long time, staring at that single piece of tape. She had several different ideas at once, each larger and more overpowering than the next.

When her studio was once again in order, she took her phone out of her purse and called Sue MacMasters's number. "Sue?" she said to the answering machine. "This is Vera Lundy again. I think you're going to get a phone call about me later. Or maybe the dean will. Either way, I'm just letting you know now that I'm not coming back to Wallace after the break. I'm just establishing that now so that you won't have to bother with calling me yourself. I can fax you the grades I've recorded since February."

She hung up the phone and remained seated on her bed for some time, unsure of what she felt about this. She knew she should feel sad. She knew she should feel ashamed. She knew she should, on a purely mercenary level, feel worried about where her next paycheck was coming from. But all she could think was: *It is strange how things can change so quickly.*

No more job, she thought again. *No more afternoons at the copy center.* She remembered the envelope in her tote bag then, the one with the New York postmark that she'd picked up at headquarters. She had forgotten all about it.

Vera felt around in her bag until her fingers latched on to the stiff envelope. Pulling it out, she held it in her hands for a moment, then scraped one bitten-off fingernail against the seal until the envelope was open.

Inside was a greeting card with an image she had seen before. And as soon as Vera saw it, looking straight into the rolling eye of a carousel horse, she knew that this card had not been sent to her by a donor.

The face of the card was a reproduction of the original cover of *The Catcher in the Rye* on it—the scarlet cover with its loose, fluid drawing of the Central Park carousel. The horse's body was contorted as though in agony, its one visible eye telegraphing something to Vera—violence, she thought, or terror.

She did not want to open the card, but she made herself do it. At first she thought the inside was blank. Then, at the very bottom, in the tiniest, faintest hand lettering she had ever seen—a handwriting she was sure she had seen before—was this message:

Bret would like to meet you. He knows more than he's saying.

Vera turned the card over, half expecting to see something else written on the back, but there was nothing but the bar code and the copyright. *Bret would like to meet me; he would like to speak to me,* she thought, and her mind flashed back to Sufia Ahmed, so self-possessed as she'd stood before her in the classroom: *Miss Lundy, I would like to speak to you.*

Not long after that, the girl was dead.

It is strange how things can change so quickly, Vera thought again. *But what can be done can also be undone.*

She was sure that the handwritten note had been sent by Jensen, just as she was sure that she was the recipient of this message for a very particular reason. *I'm the elect one,* Vera thought; *I'm the one she's reaching out to. But why? What is she trying to tell me about Bret?*

Chapter Eleven

It was early in the morning, so early that most people were still in their beds, but the Dorset bus station already had a hard-luck assortment of people waiting to board—people so derelict and defeated that they were nodding off in their metal seats before their buses even arrived. Vera moved past them all to get to the ticket counter, and when it was her turn to be waited on, she took out her credit card and placed it in front of the seller. "I'd like a round trip to New York City," she said.

"When will you be returning?"

"I don't know exactly. Maybe I'd better make it a one-way."

"There's a transfer in Boston."

Vera nodded, studying the ticket seller for a minute, and then reached for the newspaper she had stashed in her tote bag. The paper was folded so that the most recent article about Jensen Willard stood out. "By any chance," she said, holding it up for her to see, "does this girl look familiar to you? Do you remember selling this person a bus ticket within the last week? She might have used a different name."

"No. I know who that is, though. That's the girl who's gone missing." She handed Vera her ticket. "Bus leaves at eight thirty."

Almost everyone in Dorset recognized Jensen's face by now, Vera surmised. It wasn't often that its young residents went missing. She wondered how the girl would feel, knowing she was becoming a local celebrity of sorts, that the BRING JENSEN HOME committee and the Dorset police forces were so actively looking for her. Probably, in typical Jensen fashion, she would shy away from the scrutiny just as much as she craved it.

Vera felt both hopeful and afraid—an anticipatory feeling that she always felt at the onset of traveling anywhere, though this time it was weighted with the uncertainty of what was to come. She had brought a book with her, a mammoth volume called *The Comprehensive Book of True Crime*, which she'd been wading through for months; she had thought it might be a relaxing diversion for her bus trip, but she now regretted her choice of reading material. Burying herself in such a sordid book among the slumped figures that were also waiting for the bus seemed an inauspicious way to start her journey.

With a half hour to kill before her departure, she crossed the street and went into the variety store, glancing at the newspaper rack; she didn't see Jensen Willard's picture today—that seemed a good sign—but then the headline under the fold made her do an almost comical double take. She picked up the newspaper and read the article where she stood.

Missing Girl Last Seen with Teacher

A new development in the case of Jensen Willard, the 15-year-old Dorset girl who has been missing since March 30, came to light when an employee of the Roundview Hotel returned from a trip out of state and recognized Willard's picture in the *Journal*. According to the employee, Willard checked into a room at the hotel on the evening she disappeared. The Roundview Hotel is located

on Wheaton Road, right next to the address where Willard was dropped off by her stepfather.

Detective Ray Ferreira and Detective Helen Cutler, who have been working together on the case, found surveillance records indicating that Willard later left the hotel with a woman. This woman has been identified as Vera Lundy, 39, who was Willard's substitute teacher at the Wallace School.

Sue MacMasters, head of the English department at the Wallace School, responded to a query by email: "Given recent occurrences, Vera Lundy is no longer under our employ as of today."

Lundy, who was questioned by police, claims to have visited Willard because she was worried about her mental state. Willard is known to have been treated for depression within the past year. Lundy reportedly walked the girl a few houses away from her Pine Street address. This was the point at which she was last seen.

Ferreira says that Lundy's involvement is not considered suspicious. But librarian Lillian Platt, who refers to Lundy as a "regular" at the Dorset branch of the Southern Maine Community Library, says, "She comes here every week to check out books about murderers. Sometimes more than once a week. I find that very peculiar."

Vera's first reaction was to find this depiction of herself preposterous; in a different circumstance she would have found it funny. The librarian, of all people, with her unfounded dislike for Vera—what did she know? And didn't librarians owe their patrons a little privacy? Then she thought of all the people she knew in town who would read this article—her former students, the Cudahys, even Paul and Amy Nimitz—and became more circumspect. She purchased the newspaper along with a copy of *Vogue* and a cup of coffee, trying not to seem furtive in her body language as she completed her transaction; though her photo was not included, she would not have been surprised if the clerk had pointed at her and said, "Hey, aren't you that teacher? The one in that article right there?" She hid the newspaper in her bag with the older issue before anyone could see it and draw that parallel.

Back at the bus station, the line for those waiting to board was growing, and some had trickled outside; a few of these people, she could tell, were native New Yorkers who had found themselves in Maine and were anxious to get out. She wondered if she looked more like one of them or like one of the slumped, defeated people inside the terminal. She hoped for the former as she waited outside with all of them, feeling the morning sun on her face.

She wondered who Sue MacMasters had found to take her English classes and what her students would be doing that day—other than talking about *her*, of course, and wrapping up the final discussion of *The Bell Jar*. It didn't seem right to Vera that someone else was finishing what she'd started. She wondered, too, if any of the students would miss her. She was certain that she would miss some of them, if only a little bit; such a strange feeling, Vera thought, to be missing other people when they aren't missing you. It was the closest thing she could imagine to being a ghost—the phantom in the room that is unseen, unsensed, unwanted.

Four hours later, Vera had completed the first leg of her trip and had boarded the Boston bus bound for New York City. Almost five hours of riding remained, but her knees were already stiff from sitting still for so long—an unwelcome reminder that her joints were not as resilient as they'd been when she was a Princeton graduate student commuting on holiday visits.

She shared her seat with a gentleman whose face was cut deeply with wrinkles, a man who sat with his legs spread so far apart that she had tried to make herself smaller to prevent his bony knee from touching hers. Shortly after the bus had left Boston, the man took notice of her and started pulling mysteriously stained religious tracts out of his pockets, thrusting them under her nose and asking, "Have you been saved?" When that didn't get a desired reaction, he leaned in so close that she could feel his dry lips brushing her earlobe, and he whispered, "Ever been with an *older* man?" She had the window seat and felt pinned in place; all the other seats on the bus were taken, and she didn't dare ask to switch with anyone. She remembered reading a news item a while back about a woman who got stabbed to death on the back of a bus, and no one noticed till they reached their stop, hours after the fact.

Eventually the man fell asleep, his mouth hanging agape. Vera reached into the tote she kept at her feet and reread the copy of *Vogue* she had already flipped through. She felt around in her bag a little more, trying her hardest not to wake the man, and took out a yellow legal pad and pen she'd brought. Turning to a blank page, she wrote a heading at the top: "Possibilities: What Bret Might Know." After underlining this heading several times, she began to compile a list:

Possibilities: What Bret Might Know.

1. *Jensen killed herself, and Bret knows all about it. Possibly even knows where the body is.*
2. *Jensen has run away someplace (New York City?), and Bret knows where she is.*

3. *Jensen has been abducted but is alive. Bret knows something about who took her.*
4. *Jensen was abducted and is dead. Bret had a hand in it somehow.*

Vera wrote down the number five, but then her fingers wrapped more tightly around her pen, as though to restrain it from what it wanted to write. She wondered if it was the word *dead* that had stopped her cold. Or perhaps it was because the word *abducted* itself struck her as sinister and strange, like an operation requiring the removal of a vital organ: *I had an abduction that needed twenty-seven stitches.*

Possibility no. 2, on the other hand, was inviting—a possibility filled with other, greater possibilities and part of what had brought her to this point. If Jensen was actually in New York City, despite what the cops thought, then Vera stood a chance of finding the girl herself. And what a coup that would be—how redemptive in the eyes of the Cudahys and the police, if the person indirectly responsible for their daughter's disappearance was the one to bring her home.

Folding her notebook page over, Vera started a secondary list:

Possibilities, Part 2: Jensen is in New York. (Places?)

1. *Columbia University area (Jay Hall—where Bret is?)*
2. *Holden tour: Central Park (Lake where the ducks are? Or by the carousel??)*
3. *Grand Central Station*
4. *Rink at Rockefeller Center (would it be open??)*
5. *Metropolitan Museum, Museum of Natural History?*
6. *Near Salinger's apartment???*

Columbia University seemed the best prospect, but Vera felt she could not rule out some of the others; Grand Central Station was an excellent place to hide if one was feeling especially daring. She couldn't really picture Jensen Willard at the ice rink (too sporty) or at the Museum of Natural History (too nerdy), but the Metropolitan Museum was a possibility; she saw Jensen as the sort of burrowing creature who would like small, dark corners and cubbyholes to hide in, just as Vera herself would.

Where, she wondered, *was the best dark cubbyhole of all? And what had driven her to into its recesses?* She closed her notebook and allowed herself to doze, waking up only periodically from the jolts of the bus.

When the bus passed through Stamford, Connecticut, she called her old friend Elliott on her phone; she got his voicemail and spoke in a low voice so as not to disturb the other passengers, especially the man sleeping next to her. "I'm leaving Stamford now," she said. "It shouldn't be too much longer. I'll be seeing you soon."

She had first called Elliott on the previous afternoon, not long after her apartment had been searched—email was no longer an option, with her laptop confiscated—and when he heard of her plans, Elliott's response had been typical for him: "You're a nutter, Vera. I see nothing has changed."

"I'm looking forward to seeing you, too, you old coot," Vera had replied.

Elliott Kinkel had been a fellow student in Vera's graduate nonfiction workshop at Princeton. Twelve years older than Vera and known to be cantankerous, he had not been well liked in the writing workshop; when commenting on others' pieces, his suggestions were sound, but his delivery lacked finesse. Vera, who did not make friends easily but enjoyed the challenge of winning over difficult people, had liked him instantly. After graduation, when both he and she had moved to

New York City apartments in Morningside Heights, they often rented movies together and critiqued the screenplays, for Elliott considered himself a budding screenwriter. Most of his half-written efforts were crime dramas, which Vera had edited with enthusiasm; his writing, she thought, was actually pretty good, exhibiting a flair for hard-boiled dialogue.

Though she hadn't seen him in three years, she knew he would not hesitate to help her out in her unique situation. Years before, when the lease on her New York apartment had run out and she had yet to find a new place, he had let her sleep on his sofa bed for three weeks and had even cooked all her meals, not asking for a penny in return. She didn't like to take advantage of anyone's kindness, but Elliott enjoyed showing a magnanimous side under all his crotchety layers. When better times came, she had repaid him, in her fashion, by buying him an expensive, framed Pop Art print that he'd had his eye on—Richard Hamilton's *Just what is it that makes today's homes so different, so appealing?*—and as far as Vera knew, that print still hung in his living room.

In Port Authority now, the signs at last brought Vera to the train she wanted—the number 1, 2, and 3 train—and she scuttled to the very end of the subway platform, where she knew she stood better odds of getting a seat. When her train arrived, however, the front car was packed; she squeezed her way in and ended up with her face pushed into a tall man's armpit as he clung to the overhead grip. Another man behind her had his crotch pressed against the cleft of her bottom. Despite the fact that all these passengers were too close for comfort—or maybe because of it—no one made eye contact or said a word, but continued to hang on for dear life as the train bumped and swayed its way uptown.

Sweating a little, she climbed out of the station and into the daylight of West 116th Street and Broadway. And there was Elliott, waiting for her as promised, sitting at one of the little round outdoor tables outside a coffee shop Vera used to frequent—though the coffee shop was now a pizza place.

He stood up, seeing her, and enfolded her in a hug before she could protest.

"You look like death warmed over," he said, holding her out at arm's length. "Maine has not been good to you."

"Oh, shut up. You've looked better yourself."

It wasn't true. Elliott had more gray hair than he had the last time she'd seen him, but his face was still unlined, and his eyes, behind his thick glasses, shone with good humor. Elliott still wore the facial expression he'd always had—that of a wide-eyed adolescent boy who has accidentally peeped at an attractive, semiclad woman through a window and is unsure whether to find this a wonderful development or a scandalous one.

"Terrible greeting I gave you. Can I redo it? Welcome back to the city, Vee, and let's pretend you're looking well. What do you want to do first? Get a drink? Some food?"

"I've kind of gone off drinking. I suppose I could eat."

"Dine in, takeout, or some of Elliott's home cooking?"

Elliott was one of the few people she knew who could get away with referring to himself in the first person. "I think eating at home would be good. I'm pretty wiped out from the trip."

He reached out and gave her arm a squeeze. "You're all soft and bony. No muscle tone at all. You don't work out, do you? I remember when you used to have a derriere."

"That was a while ago, wasn't it?" Vera said. "Gosh, all the way back in the days when I was a nubile grad student."

Elliott had the same apartment he'd had for eleven years—at the corner of La Salle Street and Claremont Avenue, which was technically in Harlem, though not in Harlem proper. Vera had lived next door for four of those years. She felt a great deal of nostalgia as they walked the city blocks toward Claremont. She intuited that Elliott had asked her to meet him at the 116th Street station instead of the nearer 125th Street so that they might enjoy this brief walk together, this literal stroll down memory lane.

Inside Elliott's apartment, she saw that the lumpy, misshapen sofa bed was still there. Vera immediately went to his bookshelves to look at his books—many of which were how-to guides for aspiring screenwriters—and to ogle his DVD collection. "You have a lot of new movies," she observed, "and some of the old ones are gone."

"Sold 'em," Elliott said. "Out with the old, in with the new. Quit pawing at my books and tell me what's going on with you. You sounded pretty nonsensical on the phone yesterday. Missing students, dead girls in parks, and something about Holden Caulfield? All I can gather from that is that you've been on some kind of murderous rampage. Bumping off your students one at a time because they can't use commas correctly. Am I getting warm?"

"Don't even joke," Vera said, dropping down so heavily onto the sofa bed that a puff of dust shot up from its cushion. "I'll explain everything. Just give me some time to decompress first."

While Elliott went into the kitchen to start frying up hamburgers, she began to tell him about all that had happened over the past few weeks—half speaking, half shouting over the sound of sizzling meat and clattering pans.

"See, this is what happens when you leave civilized New York for the wilds of Maine. I tried to warn you." Elliott's voice carried over his labors in the kitchen. "And look where you are now—jobless, with a prize pupil who's probably in the mountains reading scripture with her adopted cult leader parents as we speak." Hearing her pointed silence, he poked his head in the living room doorway and said in his normal tone of voice, "Aw, you know I'm kidding, Vee. You want two hamburgers or one?"

"Two," Vera said. "Tomorrow, first thing in the morning, I'm going to the Columbia campus and looking around there for Jensen."

"You think maybe she's staying with that boyfriend?"

"I don't know. It seems worth a shot. I know I've got to track Bret down, at the very least, to see if he really *does* know anything."

"But why would this Jensen kid send you that message? Have you thought about *that*? Doesn't it kind of make you wonder if you're being played in some way? I think you should have just given that card to the police if you really do think it amounts to anything."

"I've already been played, Elliott. The police have had their eye on me for quite some time. This is my attempt to get myself *un*-played."

"Ah," Elliott said, approaching with a plate of hamburgers. "Pride goeth before a fall, and all that." He tossed an open bag of potato chips on the coffee table in front of her and set up condiments—ketchup, mustard, and pickle relish—all in a row. "What I want to know," he said, "is why are you so determined to find her yourself? Isn't this kind of out of your reach? It's definitely beyond the confines of your job description."

"Mm," Vera said noncommittally. She cracked open one of Elliott's Diet Cokes and took a haul straight from the can.

"You think this Jensen kid is in trouble," Elliott said, plunking himself down on the ottoman in front of her. "You think she's running away from something. And I think you have a pretty good idea of what that is."

Vera took a big bite of her first burger and took her time chewing it; Elliott was one of the few people whom she could eat comfortably in front of. "I have no idea what you're talking about," she said once she'd swallowed.

"Oh, come on. This girl sounds like she's been dropping hints since day one. Kids kill other kids all the time nowadays, haven't you heard? Whole different world from when you and I were young."

"Don't be absurd," Vera said, trying to laugh; all that came out was a choking sound, and she placed a hand to her throat as though to blame the food. "If you could *see* this girl, you'd know how impossible what you're suggesting is. She's tiny. She's not imposing."

"Manson was tiny, too. So was Charles Starkweather. So was *Mussolini*."

"Let's drop it. But before we do, let me explain one thing, okay? And I'm only going to say this once, so you'd better listen. I'm the one who's potentially in trouble for Jensen Willard being lost. So I'm the one who's going to find her and bring her back. It has nothing to do with my reputation—that's already shot. It has to do with what I think is *right*."

"Oh, Vee," Elliott said. "You're a nutter, but you've got a good heart."

"What, this leathery old thing?" she said, tapping at her breastbone.

After Vera had eaten a second burger and followed it up with a large wedge of store-bought chocolate silk pie when it was offered, Elliott asked, "How much money do you think you'll need to get around tomorrow?"

"As little as possible. Maybe some subway fare and a few extra bucks. I *will* pay you back."

"You can pay me back by fattening yourself up," he said, "though at this rate, old Elliott'll do that for you in no time."

***

Vera felt refreshed the next morning, having slept surprisingly well on the old sofa bed. Elliott, who operated under a schedule of his own making, could still be heard snoring through his closed bedroom door as she got up, dressed quietly, and slipped out of the apartment.

She walked down Broadway until she reached the gates of College Walk, the main entrance to Columbia University's central campus. She passed by students who were draped all over the steps of the Low Library, taking in a little sun near the *Alma Mater* statue; elsewhere students were seated on benches outside or on tables, studying or just idling between classes. The more she looked around, the more she felt justified in her earlier thought that the Columbia campus might be a good place to disappear. She tried not to think about Esther Greenwood's line from *The Bell Jar*—the one asserting that New York City is also a great place to kill yourself.

Bret Folger's dormitory, Jay Hall, was easy to spot; it was one of the taller, newer, and uglier buildings on campus, not far from the Butler Library. She found an unoccupied stone bench within view of Jay's entrance and took a seat there, carefully smoothing her skirt over her knees. She had brought her *Comprehensive Book of True Crime* with her so she could sit and look as though she were studying while keeping one eye on those who were coming and going. Two copies of the *Dorset Journal* also remained in her tote bag—the one where Vera was mentioned and the one with Jensen's picture on the front page.

An Asian girl with a small backpack sat on the far end of Vera's bench, lighting up a cigarette. Vera watched her out of the corner of her eye for a bit, debated whether to speak to her, and then reached into her tote bag and pulled out the older of the two newspapers. "Have you seen the girl in this picture around on campus?" she asked, showing it to her.

The girl looked over. "I don't think so," she said.

"What about Bret Folger? Do you know Bret Folger? He lives in Jay."

"I live off campus," the girl said. She leaned again toward the picture and looked at it for more than a second this time. "Maybe she does look familiar. I can't really tell. It's not a good picture." She stood up and ground out her cigarette and left, clearly annoyed at having her would-be reverie broken by an intrusive woman with a newspaper. Vera couldn't blame her.

She kept watch outside Jay for nearly an hour. Even though the students seemed to be soaking up the warming April weather, there was just enough of a chill to drive Vera indoors; she made a mental note to borrow a sweatshirt from Elliott the next time she made such an outing. She went into Butler Library and signed up for a guest pass before climbing the familiar winding staircase with the wrought-iron railing. She walked all around the circulation area, looking at the students typing away at computer terminals; the look she gave some of them was too obvious, too searching, for some stared back at her, frowning.

There was a tired-looking girl at the circulation desk, probably a student worker, and Vera considered showing her the newspaper but decided against it; she looked so unreceptive. Instead she walked past the desk to the elevator leading to the book stacks, and on her way there she passed what appeared to be a custodian. His face seemed friendly and relaxed as he wheeled his mop and bucket along. Vera flagged him down, and when he stopped, she showed him the picture of Jensen Willard, speaking to him in a combination of English, pidgin Spanish, and pantomime.

The custodian nodded his head, pointing to the photograph. "In stacks," he said.

"In stacks? Really?"

"In stacks," he said, sounding surer of himself.

"What floor of the stacks? *Dónde?* Do you remember?"

But now he was shaking his head. "*No se,*" he said, leading his mop and bucket away.

Vera tried not to let her hopes get ahead of her. Before getting into the elevator, she reviewed the map showing what collections were housed on each floor. She selected the one where the literature collections were kept—her old favorite haunt, and a good bet for where Jensen might retreat.

The library stacks were dark and forbidding; each row of bookshelves had timed lights that went on and off, so one could be standing in a lit area looking at a book and abruptly find oneself in pitch darkness. A few students worked at small tables, squinting at the work in front of them and looking tortured. She walked up and down each row, glancing down the rows of shelves on either side of her. In the collection of Restoration literature, she saw a small-boned girl with a cap of dark hair sitting cross-legged on the floor, her head bowed over a book; as Vera came closer, the girl looked up. She was an Indian girl wearing heavy cat-eye makeup. Not Jensen Willard.

Vera continued her way past the literature stacks. The somber lighting and the acrid smell of old books made her feel reverent—a kind of piety most people feel when they enter a temple in a moment of conversion or tread lightly on cemetery grounds. Then a potent reminder of present-day reality hit her, for she saw that she was nearing the end of the Modern American Literature section of the stacks. The marker at the end of the stacks indicated that the books on this shelf included authors whose surnames began with letters *RE* through *SA*.

Salinger, Vera thought, looking down at the bottom shelf closest to her feet. *It seems I can't get rid of you.* And there, just as if she had summoned it into being, was the serial killer copy of *The Catcher in the Rye,* perched on the bottom shelf atop the other books, with a second book jammed underneath it, spine out. Seeing the title of the book on the bottom, Vera stooped to close her fingers around it: the paperback edition of *The Bell Jar,* by Sylvia Plath. Shelved out of order.

Not so unusual to see these two books together, Vera rationalized. *Probably a lot of English majors read those books back-to-back, since Esther Greenwood was touted as a female Holden Caulfield when* The Bell Jar *first came out.*

Vera was about to place the book under her arm, intending to shelve it in its proper location among the *P*'s, when she saw what looked like something wedged between its pages. Slipping it out, she found a glossy black-and-white photo of young J. D. Salinger dressed in a herringbone tweed jacket, his hair smoothed back with pomade and his generous mouth twisted into a cynical half smile. It was the front of the sort of postcard one finds in university bookstores, alongside ironic T-shirts with original covers of *The Fountainhead* and *To Kill a Mockingbird* printed on their fronts. The sort of postcard students taped to their dormitory walls, calling it art.

Vera turned the postcard over, expecting it to be blank. But near the bottom of its clean, white surface was a familiar, faint, black-inked handwriting—the same handwriting she'd seen on the card that brought her to New York.

Looks like we just missed each other
Guess I don't feel like talking yet
Oh well, back to ME I suppose

Vera was sure that this message was meant for her. It wasn't hard to imagine Jensen Willard standing in this exact spot, pairing *The Bell*

Jar and *The Catcher in the Rye* as she slipped this postcard inside the cover of the former. The odds of Vera finding the books were slim, but for Jensen, it was no longer about the odds, Vera was beginning to realize; it was about the game itself.

Vera wished she hadn't touched the books and the postcard—wouldn't this be considered contaminating evidence?—but now it was too late. She needed to take these items home with her regardless, for any and all might contain Jensen's prints. She turned each book's pages until she found the hidden tattle tape meant to set off the library alarms; removing these, she slipped the two books into her bag, intending to offer them to Detective Ferreira later. He could excuse her thievery, she hoped, in this instance.

She felt a clarity of mind that she had not felt in a while—the clarity of knowing one is on the right track. There was no doubt that Jensen was continuing to reach out to her for reasons yet unknown, patiently teasing her out like a snake charmer wooing a cobra out of a basket. But if Vera had just missed her, as the note said, then what chance did she have of finding the girl? And what did "back to ME" mean? It sounded like the title of a bad 1970s song about female empowerment.

Or was it an abbreviation? *ME is the abbreviation for Maine,* Vera thought. *Back to Maine, maybe?* But that had to be a red herring. Jensen was probably still around somewhere, and wherever she was, Bret could not be far behind—Bret, who knew more than he was saying.

Leaving the library before she could be caught with stolen goods, she stopped by Jay Hall again and eyed the students going in and out of its doors. She imagined that Bret Folger would be easy to spot—an emaciated, six-foot-five, reddish-haired white boy would be noticeable on campus. She remembered Jensen writing that Bret had taken two consecutive classes with Dr. Rose, the famed Spenserian scholar; she wished she knew of a way to find out which of Dr. Rose's classes he was enrolled in now and when it met.

She fished out her phone and gave Elliott a quick call; there was no answer, and she left a message on his voicemail. "I need you to look up something on the Internet for me," she said. "Can you look up Dr. Louis Rose at Columbia? You should be able to find an office phone number for him. I'm not going to be home till later, but I'd like to have this number as soon as possible."

Crossing Broadway, she walked down Riverside Drive, slowing down in front of the Salinger family's old apartment—the building where J. D. Salinger himself had been born, just two doors away from Dr. Rose's place. She guessed Dr. Rose lived two doors south, as that was building was nicer and grander-looking than the one to the north. Standing before its door buzzers, she saw that ROSE, L. was taped next to the fourth buzzer from the bottom. Vera traced the shape of the upraised button but did not press it.

She went back to the Salinger apartment building and stood there for a while, looking up at all the windows, trying to imagine which unit the Salinger family had lived in—mother, Miriam; father, Sol; older sister, Doris; and the new baby, Jerome David—and then tried to picture the people who lived there now. New York apartments had such high turnover that history mattered little. History didn't stick. Jensen had written as much in her journal: *Even the special things in New York seem to blend in with everything else.* Yet that lack of specialness, Vera supposed, was just what made the city special, in its own paradoxical way. There was room for everyone—for the ambitious, for the hopeful, for the defeated—even, she supposed, for the depraved.

***

"Did you call old Lou Rose?" Elliott asked Vera later.

They were sitting at his round table in the corner of the living room, eating what Elliott called the "school cafeteria version" of shepherd's pie—he had had a lot of leftover hamburger from the night before, as it turned out. To Vera, the heavily salted slop tasted like heaven. Around her mouthful of potatoes and corn, she said, "No. I chickened out because I didn't want to bother him."

"This is not what I would call impressive detective work," Elliott said.

"But I haven't told you everything yet. Not only did I feel like Jensen was in the Butler Library, but I could *sense* her there. And just when I was sure I was going to find her, I found *this* instead." She pushed back from the table and returned to show him her purloined library copy of *The Bell Jar*.

"What does that prove?"

"I found it stuffed right underneath *The Catcher in the Rye* on the library shelf. And Jensen Willard specifically mentioned in a journal entry that she liked *The Bell Jar* better than *The Catcher in the Rye*. Circumstantial, sure, but now look at the back of the card I found inside it. She mentioned in another journal that she used to leave notes in library books all the time."

"That's a pretty generic message," Elliott said, pushing his glasses up on his nose to look at the Salinger postcard more closely. "It isn't addressed to anyone, and it could be *for* anyone. 'Looks like we just missed each other' could be a message between a couple of libidinous kids who'd planned a sexy assignation in the stacks."

"But it isn't—that's the thing. You just don't understand," Vera said, "and I'm afraid it's all too complicated for me to explain right now."

Vera's phone buzzed from inside her purse. She checked the number of the incoming call and saw that it was her mother—her third attempt to call since Vera had left for New York. She had no doubt that her mother had gotten wind of some of the most recent stories appearing in the *Dorset Journal* and was in a panic trying to reach her, but she couldn't bear to talk to her just yet—not until she had better news to report. She waited until her phone trilled, letting her know that yet another message had been recorded, before sighing and saying, "I suppose I've got to bite the bullet and find out what my mother has to say for herself."

"While you check your messages," Elliott said, getting up with his plate scraped clean, "maybe I'll give you some privacy and mosey onto the Internet and see what else they're saying about Big Vee Lundy in the Dorset newspapers. Maybe they're going with the idea that you've kidnapped Jensen Willard and made her your personal sex slave."

"You're extremely unfunny. And don't you dare call me Big Vee Lundy." Vera pushed the phone buttons to retrieve her voicemail while Elliott got on his computer; his line about "giving her some privacy" had been facetious, for his computer was only a few feet from where she was sitting. She listened to the first of her mother's messages, which started off shrilly: "Marvita came over today to show me the paper, and your name's in it, honey. What is that about? It says you walked that missing girl home before she disappeared? Call your mother right away." The second message started off with an exhortation, the pitch of her mother's voice even higher this time. "Vera! Call your mother! This is an order. I'm worried sick. Where are you? Marvita says that . . ."

Vera deleted the message before finishing it and decided to leave the remaining one unlistened to, for now. She knew it wasn't fair to prolong her mother's anxiety, but if she told her she was in New York City, she would become apoplectic.

"No interesting news on the Internet," Elliott said. "How is your mother?"

"In hysterics," Vera said. "Tomorrow I think I'm going to go back to Columbia again. I was really hoping to run into Bret without having to reach out to one of his professors. I think the poetry classes mostly meet in Philosophy Hall, so I'm hoping maybe Louis Rose will have his class there. I might go to the Metropolitan Museum and to Central Park, too, if I have time for all that."

"Sounds like you've got your work cut out for you. Damn it, I just got emailed some work myself. New blog entry for a junk food site . . . a comparative look at cheese puffs this time. Considering the amount of concentration and intellectual prowess this is going to require, I'm going to have to ask you to amuse yourself for a while. Here's a thought: Did Ivan Schlosser break out of a jail to start killing a fresh crop of prepubescent girls, the most recent being Jensen Willard? Maybe that's a new chapter you could look into."

"Ivan Schlosser is dead," Vera said.

"That's too bad," Elliott said, already starting to type. "Imagine the scads of money you could make if you could pin it to him somehow."

In Columbia's Philosophy Hall the next day, Vera walked into the lounge on the first floor of the building and found that students were serving high tea, a precious Ivy League custom she had sometimes seen at Princeton; she backed out of the large room with the alacrity of someone who had accidentally walked into a stranger's house. She went up and down the steep, winding, Gothic stairwell in Philosophy Hall and tiptoed past the classrooms on each level, but the classes in progress were all taught behind closed doors.

Columbia University has tens of thousands of students, she told herself. *Admit it. You aren't going to just run into Bret unless you somehow make it happen.* This was a discouraging thought, but not an insurmountable one.

After spending another hour in the Avery Library, where the school's collections of art books were kept, Vera began the long, south-easterly walk to the Metropolitan Museum. She ignored the suggested admission price and gave the woman at the front desk two rumpled dollar bills, receiving a withering look in return, and went off to look at some of the exhibits.

What would Jensen Willard want to see if she were here? The Old Masters? The modern works—excluding those that were *too* modern? Charlotte Corday's revenge in *The Death of Marat*, maybe? No, that wasn't at the Met. That painting was somewhere in Belgium, if Vera remembered correctly.

Just as she always had on previous visits, Vera walked aimlessly from exhibit to exhibit until she grew tired. She found a cushioned bench in a quiet room of Japanese art, next to a rock outfitted with an unseen mechanical device that gurgled as though water were bubbling inside it. The rock relaxed her in a way nothing else had over the past few days. She sat and listened to it until a security guard approached her and asked her if she was all right, which she took as her cue to leave. She had been in the museum for close to two hours and had seen nothing that had made her think of Jensen Willard particularly.

Descending the stairs of the Met, Vera's phone buzzed from inside her purse. Expecting to see her mother's number, she saw instead that the incoming call was from Elliott. And Elliott, she knew, despised phones—using them only when necessary, and even then with obvious displeasure.

"Vee?" his voice said. "Where are you right now?"

"The Met. Why?"

"What? I can't hear you. Oh, for Chrissakes."

The line went dead, and Vera zipped the phone back in its compartment, rolling her eyes. Brusqueness was part of Elliott's nature, but hanging up on her, she thought, was taking things to the extreme.

It was three o'clock in the afternoon, and she was too close to Central Park to have a good excuse for avoiding it. She remembered that Holden Caulfield, too, had not had a very charitable view of the park: "It made you depressed, and every once in a while, for no reason, you got goose flesh while you walked," he'd said of it.

Where might Jensen go in Central Park? There was the carousel near the zoo, of course—the carousel Phoebe Caulfield had ridden near the very end of *The Catcher in the Rye*, though Vera knew that Phoebe's particular carousel was no more; it had been destroyed in 1950 and was later replaced. Walking through the park, she noticed a sign saying that the carousel was closed for renovation. *Typical,* she thought. So much for Phoebe going around and around, nearly moving her brother to tears because she looked so nice.

The lagoon near Central Park South was an area Vera didn't mind. Growing up in Maine around so much water made her partial to lagoons. Besides, she had always felt a secret happiness, watching ducks' antics; ducks in New York were not so different from ducks in Maine, she thought as she settled down on a rock near the water, not minding if her skirt got a little dirty. Same sleek heads, same bumbling walks. Sometimes the ducks commingled with Canada geese, gliding along the water or hunching along the shore. As she watched one duck, presumably male, waddling intently after another duck, she remembered reading somewhere that during mating season, female ducks sometimes hid in the tall grass to avoid being chased by amorous males. But it wasn't mating season, was it?

"Stupid ducks," Vera murmured, not without affection, and she wondered if Holden Caulfield felt the same way about them—forgetting, just for a second, that Holden Caulfield was not a real boy.

The phone in her purse buzzed again, making Vera jump. She checked her phone and saw that Elliott was having another go of it. "Why did you cut me off last time?" she asked sharply.

"I didn't cut you off. My battery was dying. Vera, where are you—the Met still?"

"No, Central Park. I'm over by the lake."

"Watching the ducks à la Holden Caulfield?"

"You got it."

"Those damned ducks. You know what's funny about that? Holden Caulfield wonders where the ducks go in the winter. But the ducks never go anywhere, have you noticed? Even in the winter they're always right there."

"Interesting observation. This is what you called to tell me?"

"No, sorry, I wanted to check in with you about something. I've got to go out tonight, but I've got to figure out a way to leave you my extra set of keys."

"Can't you leave them under the doormat or something?"

"My dear old sausage, you must be joking. You've been living out of the city too long."

"If you aren't leaving for a while, I'll just come back to your neck of the woods then."

"Any interesting finds?"

"Not a one."

"Well, when you get back to the apartment, you ought to have a gander at the online edition of your local Maine paper. Seems like there's some intrigue back in Dorset that you're missing out on."

"Is it—is it another body?" Vera asked, her heart dropping.

"Nothing quite *that* intriguing, but I'll let you find out for yourself."

Replacing her phone, Vera shook her head ruefully. Knowing Elliott's perverse sense of humor, she would not have been at all surprised to find the "intrigue" he'd spoken of in Dorset was a headline about a rash of henhouse break-ins, or the Sportsman's Club hosting a youth fishing derby. But perhaps there really was something to it, after all. Standing up and brushing the loose grasses off her rump, she thought, *What if it's Jensen? If it isn't a body, then what if it's Jensen they've found, alive and well?* All at once she felt it imperative to get back to Elliott's quickly.

When Vera arrived at the apartment, Elliott was there pacing in the living room. "That didn't take long. What did you do, *fly*?" he asked, pressing the keys in her hand.

"I ran part of the way. Are you leaving already?"

"My friend Juliet wants to eat at this little Vietnamese place downtown before we go to the movies. Three train transfers to get there."

"Aw," Vera said. "A movie date, with popcorn and holding hands? That's adorable."

"Juliet is an out-and-proud lesbian, thank you very much. Speaking of adorable, don't forget to look at the latest news back in your hometown. It's about your young swain, Ritchie Ouelette—he of the soul patch, the two teeth, and the 'Born to Lose' tattoo."

"He doesn't have a—" Vera began, and then stopped, seeing that Elliott was teasing her. "I'll be sure to check it out," she said. "Enjoy your night on the town."

When Elliott was gone, Vera made sure to watch him from the apartment window until he had disappeared down the street; if he came back having forgotten something, she did not want him to find her at his computer, overeager to see whatever news report it was that he'd alluded to.

As the day's edition of the *Dorset Journal* loaded on the screen, Vera scooted the wheeled desk chair closer to the monitor, her features bunched together in concentration as she began to read. The story was no joke, she quickly saw—no joke at all.

New Suspect in Galvez Killing

Bombshell evidence recently presented in the Angela Galvez murder has exonerated current suspect Ritchie Ouelette and implicated another party. This surprise discovery turns the investigation upside down. "Because the new suspect is a minor, we are not revealing any names at this time," Officer Gerard Babineau told the *Journal*. When asked if this recent development will lead police to refocus their investigation of the death of Sufia Ahmed, Babineau said that the Dorset Police Department cannot comment.

Vera kept reading, her eyes darting between the text and the accompanying photograph of Ritchie Ouelette being escorted down the steps outside the county jail, looking as unsteady and bewildered as though he'd just been hatched to the outside world.

New information provided by Ritchie Ouelette, who has been in police custody for more than five months, plus the cooperation of a second party, has led to a second confession in the case. "We have every reason to believe this new confession is credible, and that it cancels out the first one," Babineau said.

The suspect is a minor, Vera thought. Was the suspect also the second party, the bringer of the credible new confession?

The suspect is a minor. Bret Folger is a minor. Jensen *is a minor,* Vera thought. Her palms were clammy with excitement, but she knew there was no point getting ahead of herself. Much as she wanted to hop a bus back to Maine straight away, much as she wished she could call Paul or Amy Nimitz at the center to find out more about what was going on, she was persona non grata in Dorset now, and her work in New York, despite what she had told Elliott earlier, was far from finished.

If the suspect was Bret himself, then he was no longer in New York City. She could no longer waste any time waiting to ascertain his exact whereabouts. These whereabouts needed to be determined, and fast. Taking a deep breath, she found the number for Dr. Louis Rose that she had saved in her phone's address book.

Chapter Twelve

As she was preparing to punch in Dr. Rose's phone number, Vera sat on the edge of the lumpy sofa bed and rehearsed what she might say into the Spenserian scholar's answering machine—something about needing urgently to reach his pupil Bret Folger—and was thrown for a loop when an actual human voice answered the phone, a voice that sounded vaguely English and vaguely perturbed.

"Dr. Rose? I'm sorry to bother you. My name is Vera Lundy. I'm Jensen Willard's teacher—Jensen is your student Bret Folger's girlfriend, and I believe you may have met her once. I need to get in touch with Bret about something concerning her."

"Bret Folger's girlfriend?" The old professor sounded more puzzled now than annoyed. "I don't remember a girlfriend."

"She came to your apartment, and you took a photograph? Sometime this past fall, I think?"

"Oh, Jen-*seen*. You mean Grendel."

"*Grendel*?"

"That's the name I gave her when I met her," he said—loftily but not unkindly. "'An unhappy being who has long lived in the land of monsters.' Is she all right?"

"I don't know," Vera said. She hadn't expected the professor to speak to her this way, to say these kinds of things.

"Does this have something to do with Bret not being in my last two class meetings, I wonder? It's unlike him to miss a class. It never occurred to me that it might be girl trouble. While it would be unorthodox for me to give you Bret's number, I do have it. I suppose if you really think it's urgent . . ."

Vera got the number and repeated it inwardly to herself after she'd hung up the phone; when she was sure she had it committed to memory, she dialed it and was directed, this time, straight to voicemail via an automated message. After the beep, she struggled to raise her voice over the sound of the train coming over the 125th Street platform outside. "Is this Bret? This is Vera Lundy, Jensen's English teacher. I'm in New York City now, not far from you, and I would really like to speak to you right away, if that's possible. Meet me on the stone bench right outside Jay at six o'clock. If you have a class or a prior commitment, please cancel it, because I'll be waiting."

The message finished, she checked the time. It was five o'clock. She had no way of knowing if Bret would receive the message before six, but she could be patient if she needed to; if she needed to call again, she would call again. She would wait outside Jay all night if she had to. She felt motivated, fueled from within, as she went to the sink in Elliott's bathroom and splashed water on her face. Gently patting her skin dry with a towel, she told herself that there was nothing foolish at all about applying fresh makeup and fixing her hair for her confrontation with a sixteen-year-old boy who may or may not come to meet her.

***

Vera sat on the bench outside Jay Hall at the appointed time, still as a statue. She did not move or flinch when her phone vibrated, recording another message from her mother and a text message from Elliott, which included a photo of a plate of food and the following message: "Conversation's lousy, but the banh mi is damned good. How's old Ritchie Ouelette treating you?" She felt people moving and parting around her without actually seeing her. For once this phantomlike invisibility made her feel that she had an advantage: *I may be cleverer than all of you,* she thought. *I may be on the verge of knowing far more than I knew before.*

Then she saw Bret coming. As she had envisioned, he was hard to miss and could be mistaken for no one else. He was weedy and pale, with bangs cut straight across his forehead, framing a pair of worried-looking eyes. The worry had not been a part of Vera's mental schema. She did not know what to make of his concern. Upon spotting Vera, he stopped in front of her bench and said, "Are you the teacher?"

His voice, a slightly hoarse tenor that suggested shyness, was lovely.

"I am," she said. "And you must be Bret. Won't you sit down?"

He did not sit at the farther end of the bench, leaving a gap as most strangers would, but sat right in the area she'd patted beside her. She could feel warmth coming from him, the hazy, humid warmth of a young boy. She willed herself not to inch away, to assert more space for herself.

"This must be about Jensen," he said.

"It is." Vera resisted the urge to break eye contact with him. His gaze was so direct, and so infused with genuine solicitude, that Vera felt he could see clear through her, the way some children see clear through the facades of adults. She wasn't sure that she liked this feeling. There was no time for discomfort, however. "Bret," she said, his name sounding harsher than she meant it to as it came out of her mouth, "I have a question for you—one that I'm sure you've already been asked by police. Have you heard anything from Jensen at *all* since March thirtieth?"

Vera, expecting a ready *no*, nearly fell off her bench when Bret said, "I don't think so."

"You don't *think* so? You either know or you don't."

"Well, I got a postcard. It wasn't signed." The creeping flush that Jensen had written about was starting to appear on Bret's face, bright finger marks on each cheek that made him look as though he'd been slapped.

"Tell me more about this postcard."

"The front of it was a picture of Edgar Allan Poe. That famous portrait where his face looks kind of lopsided? The back of it was blank. I mean, there was nothing written on it but my address, and there was a Maine postmark. I thought maybe it was from Jensen because we talked about Poe the first time she ever came to my house."

"She told you that Poe was a little overrated, but he had his place," Vera remembered.

"How do you know that?"

"Not so important how I know. Did you tell the police about this postcard?"

"No."

"Why not?"

"I was afraid."

"I understand, I think," Vera said. "I understand that fear. I know a lot about Jensen, but I don't know everything, Bret. I need you to *tell* me everything—everything you know about her. Okay, maybe not *everything*, but anything you can think of that might be worth knowing about. But before you do that, I want you to take a look at this. Does this look like Jensen's handwriting to you?"

Bret, looking a little frightened of Vera's intensity, peered at the Salinger postcard that Vera held out. "It looks like it, but she likes to change it sometimes. Are you working with the police?"

"Not exactly," Vera said. "It's more like a parallel investigation. Same destination, different tracks. This isn't the first message I've received from Jensen, you see." She told him about her time volunteering at the BRING JENSEN HOME headquarters and the unsigned greeting card with its promise that Bret Folger knew more than he was saying.

"I don't know why she'd write that," he said. "I don't know any more than anybody else does. And aside from the postcard, I haven't had any contact with her since we broke up."

"What precipitated the breakup?"

"Huh?"

"Did your breakup have anything to do with your romantic interest in your classmate Tova, or your intimate involvement with your roommate, Max? Sorry if these questions are a little personal."

"What?" Bret's eyes widened, his blush now verging on purple. "My *mother's* name is Tova, but that's the only Tova I know. And Max . . . Max is my little brother. My roommate's name is Sudip. He's from Bangladesh."

"And you haven't had any such involvement with *him*, presumably."

"No. Oh, no, I'm not like that. Jensen is the first and only person I've ever even kissed. Did she tell you something different? She must have." He shook his head in disbelief. "I said I didn't think we should see each other anymore because I was getting weirded out by her contradictions and lies."

"I think I'm sort of getting the picture here. Can you elaborate a little more on some of these . . . contradictions?"

"Well," Bret said, chewing his lip, "I can give you some examples,

I guess. She was always talking about killing herself. That's something I had a really hard time with, but I knew she'd never actually go through with it. I think she thinks too highly of herself to do a thing like that, even though she likes people to think she has low self-esteem. Is that bad of me to say? I'm not trying to make it sound like I *wanted* her to kill herself, because of course I would never want that." Bret was staring straight ahead now, his hands folded on his lap, his brow furrowed in thought. Vera found herself feeling pity and warmth toward him; he was, after all, just a boy—a befuddled sixteen-year-old boy—and more than the shallow, pretentious person that Jensen's journals had prepared her for. He was, on the contrary, someone she herself might have liked, if she'd been closer to Jensen's age. And he was blameless—that much was clear. More blameless than she was.

"She's clever and naive at the same time," Bret went on. "She thinks she can get away with anything, and half the time she does. She's honest, and she's not honest at all. She's passive, but she likes to manipulate."

"Any examples of this?"

"Of the manipulation? Sure. She was trying to do to me what she did to Scotty."

Vera sat up alertly. "I thought there *was* no Scotty."

"What do you mean?"

"Considering she mentioned a false Tova and a false Max in one of her school journal entries, wouldn't it make sense to assume that Scotty isn't real, either? The Dorset police said most of the friends in Jensen's journal are fictitious."

"Well, Scotty wasn't. I saw him once in Portland when we were walking along Monument Square. Jensen and I had stopped at the square to watch some street performers doing a show . . . they were spinning fire and stuff like that. This kid Scotty was standing off to the side near us, and Jensen pointed him out to me. He saw us, but he didn't come over to talk. I got the feeling it might have been because I was there. I'm not really sure."

"Do you know Scotty's last name, or if he's from Dorset?"

"I hardly know anything about him. But I think he and Jensen might have had something going on. She hinted it. I didn't want to believe it was true. I'd heard her talk about him plenty—her bragging about how he'd been this cheerful kid whom she'd converted. That was her word, *converted*. She bragged about how she changed him from a normal kid to someone who had these homicidal and suicidal thoughts. She liked thinking she had that power over people, to change their whole outlook on things."

The boy turned to Vera then, holding her gaze once more, his eyes large and imploring. "I know it sounds weird that I could ever have feelings for someone like her."

"It's not that weird to me, Bret."

"She's so dark. I liked that, at first, but she's darker than she lets on. Now I wonder if I ever really loved her or if I just thought I did. How do you *know* when you really love someone? I've never been able to figure that one out."

"I guess that's a good question," Vera said. "I guess that's as good a question as any. I wish I had an answer for you."

Vera was not sure how long the two of them sat next to each other in silence, thinking their separate, brooding thoughts. At last she said, "I suppose the police already asked you if you had any ideas about where Jensen might have gone."

"I didn't tell them about Aunt Miriam's house."

"Sorry?"

"My aunt Miriam has this cottage she doesn't use much. She lives in Boston, but sometimes she's in Dorset on weekends. She has a cat that she brings back and forth, and sometimes I cat-sit, so I have a key to the place. I took Jensen there a couple of times because she's not allowed to come over to my house anymore—my parents don't like her." His eyes flickered toward Vera as though this last disclosure embarrassed him. "Anyway, the key disappeared. I always kind of figured Jensen stole it, but I didn't want to rat on her, so I just told Aunt Miriam I lost it. She never bothered to change the locks."

"So you think Jensen could be in this cottage, am I understanding that correctly? But you didn't tell the police this theory at all?"

"No. If I told them, she'd know I was the one who said something. And I wouldn't want that. I don't even like to think about how she'd react. Like I said, she scares me." Again, that flickering, discomposed look.

"You can tell *me*, though, can't you? Tell me where this cottage is. Your aunt's place."

"It's the last house at the end of Bleachery Road. The blue one on the hill."

"Would you go there with me? If I found a way to buy you a bus ticket back to Maine?"

"Me? I can't," Bret said. Something changed in his face. "I have exams. I don't think my professors would let me make them up. But if you're planning to go yourself . . ."

"Yes?"

"Nothing," he said. "I guess nothing. I was going to say *be careful*, but I guess that would be stupid to say. You're a grown-up, right? I really have to go now. I'm supposed to be tutoring someone . . . I'm already a little late, to tell you the truth. Are you going to be here long? In the city, I mean?"

Vera shook her head. "I don't think so."

"Have I told you enough, then?"

"You've given me something to work with. I thank you for that, Bret. Really I do."

"Good luck with your investigation," he said. "I'll be glad when you guys find her."

"Me, too," Vera said. She tried to smile at the boy in parting, but she had a feeling her smile was a sad one.

She continued to sit there after Bret Folger got up and left, and even after it had begun to grow dark and the lights of Butler Library came on, illuminating its facade from between its Italianate pillars, she did not relinquish her spot. *How could I have forgotten how beautiful the library looks at night?* she wondered. She felt tears stinging her eyes and was not sure why they were choosing to come just then. She knew only that she wouldn't mind sitting on this stone bench for the rest of her life, perpetually warmed by the steady glow of these lights. *What a shame it is sometimes,* she thought, *to have to be a grown-up, and to have to try to understand why anyone ever does anything.*

Back at Elliott's empty apartment, Vera checked the Internet for updates about Ritchie Ouelette and, finding none, decided to draw herself a bath. The bathroom smelled strongly of cologne—a scent so optimistic that it only heightened Vera's feelings of melancholy. She lay in the bath for a long time, the steam rising around her, occasionally sitting up to look at her distorted, pink face reflected in the steel faucets. She wondered what she would do next. Perhaps another day or two in New York was in order before she called it quits and tried to find out more of what was breaking in the Galvez case. Perhaps she could even arrange another brief meeting with Bret; there were other things that she wished, in hindsight, she had asked him.

Out of the tub and dressed in the loose-fitting yoga pants and slightly sour-smelling T-shirt she'd been sleeping in for the past few days, Vera noticed a missed message on her phone. *Ferreira* was the name that flashed in the screen, and before she could talk herself out of it, she hit the CALL button, nervously smoothing her wet, stringy hair off her forehead as though the detective could see her.

"Vera," he said instead of a regular salutation. "Where are you?"

"Where am I? I'm out of town right now, Detective."

"Out of town *where*?"

"Actually, I've been out of *state* for the past couple of days," Vera said, winding a wet strand of hair around her finger. "I'm in New York."

"I thought I told you to stay close to home."

"I apologize. Am I in trouble?"

There was a heavy sigh on Detective Ferreira's end, which did little for Vera's peace of mind. "When's the soonest you can get yourself back to Dorset? We have some things we'd like to go over with you. You might even be of assistance to us."

"Um, I'd have to look at the bus schedule. Maybe there's a bus I could hop tonight?"

"Do that. And call me when you get in."

"Does this have anything to do with the break in the Galvez case?" Vera asked.

"Jesus Christ," the detective said. "Just call us when your bus gets in, like I said. We'll pick you up at the depot."

Vera hung up the phone, trying to process the significance of this call. The possibility of being *of assistance to* the police was an effective bait, too good to refuse. She checked the bus schedule on the Internet and found that a late-night bus would make its slow passage back to Maine.

Back to ME, she thought.

She did not have a lot of time to waste. She put on her coat and shoes and began to pack what few things she had—her pajamas, her toothbrush, *The Comprehensive Book of True Crime*—into her tote bag. She wondered whether to interrupt Elliott's evening with a phone call to inform him of her sudden departure or to leave a note, if that wouldn't be too gauche; she decided on the note and scrawled it quickly, taping it to the bathroom mirror, where he would be sure to see it when he got home.

Elliott, you old dog,

Heading back to Maine on a late bus tonight. Sorry for the lack of forewarning, but I've been ordered by higher-ups to get back there. This may or may not have to do with recent developments in Dorset, so details will follow. Thank you for the use of the couch, and for all the food and hospitality and insults. I promise it won't be too long before I come back to see you again and repay my debts.

Love,
V.

Vera placed Elliott's extra keys on the sink below the mirror and took one last look around the apartment before she left. Unlike the last time she had departed from New York City, she did not feel as though this had to be good-bye. The city would always be there for her if she wanted it. There were no rules dictating how many times a life could be revisited or even started anew. After all, it seemed that things in Maine were taking on a new life, a new beginning that she could never have prepared for—and she was eager, if a little uneasy, to see what it entailed.

Chapter Thirteen

The Dorset-bound bus pulled into the station just after 7:00 A.M., but Vera did not call Detective Ferreira first thing upon arrival. The long ride had given her plenty of time to reflect, and she had come to the solid conclusion that there was one thing left that remained undone. She called the cab company and asked for a driver to take her to a remote spot on Bleachery Road.

She had not slept during the bus ride back to Maine and was beginning to feel the scrambled, disordered thinking and the near-tearfulness that always hit her when she was sleep-deprived. When she'd had fits of moodiness or sadness in her childhood, her mother had always clucked, *Somebody's tired!*, and this reductive assessment had always made her fighting mad; there is a big difference between tiredness and sadness, as any child knows. But Vera, in her current state, had to admit that there had been a germ of truth in her mother's words. She *was* tired. Though she could sense the fine line between her exhaustion and her sadness and even her burgeoning hysteria, she could not afford to nurse any of these just now. She sat at the edge of her seat in the back of the cab, ready to spring out at a moment's notice.

Deposited at the mouth of the long dirt road, Vera began to make her way toward her destination. She was glad that the dark was lifting. The darkness of quiet, isolated areas was always more terrifying to her than city darkness, and Miriam Folger's cottage at the end of the road was the most isolated house of all.

Aunt Miriam's cottage sat at the top of a small hill. Instead of grass, the hill was blanketed with pebbles, so Vera walked up this path feeling glad for her sensible shoes. The cottage was a compact ranch house, the sort of space that probably offered very few hiding spots within; she pictured Jensen Willard inside it with Bret—their heads bowed together, speaking of concepts too big for them—and tried to visualize Jensen inside it now: asleep, alone, clutching her coat close to her body to keep warm. She could already see that the blinds in the windows were closed and that no lights were on, but that didn't mean there wasn't an occupant in there somewhere. As she approached the front door, she played out the scenario in her head, a scenario that, to her thinking, unfolded most naturally:

The door opens to my knock, and Jensen Willard stands there in the exact outfit she'd worn at point last seen: the dark-gray T-shirt, the oversized pants—both of which look as though they've been slept in for consecutive nights. Her hair covers most of her face, but her eyes light up with curiosity, seeing who her visitor is; she tucks a hank of hair behind one ear, and then her expression resumes its flat neutrality.

—Hi, *she says, opening the door a little wider to let me in.* I'm glad it's just you.

—Just me indeed.

—This place belongs to Bret's aunt. I guess you found it because I mentioned it in one of my journal entries?

—Not exactly.

—Well, Bret and I used to come here all the time. I thought it would be a good place to stay when I just feel like being by myself. Do you remember what I wrote to you, about how I wanted an adventure or a retreat? This is it.

—You've worried a lot of people, Jensen.

—Really? People are talking about me?

—To say the least.

—I don't mean to worry people, but I've figured some things out. That last Friday, after I got back from the hotel, I didn't go in the house right away. Instead I lay in the grass in the backyard and looked up at the stars for a long time. I hadn't done that since I was a kid—not since I'd done it with Annabel. Annabel is *real*, didn't you know? Just like Scotty is real. Just like everything is real, in its own way.

After I'd been lying there for a while, it became clear to me that I didn't have to die. Not yet. But I also knew I couldn't go on living the way I was living. I couldn't do *anything* until I felt like doing it. So what I decided to do was nothing. Nothing except disappear . . .

Vera interrupted her internal script to knock on the front door. There was no answer, no pale face appearing behind the glass window. She knocked again, bowing her head, as though someone were more likely to appear if she averted her eyes. Still no response. She moved away from the doorway and pressed her face to the nearest window, hoping to see something through the blinds, but saw only a muddied hint of yellow that seemed to bathe the entire room. *Yellow curtains,* Vera thought. She pounded on one of the windows, then tried to open it, but as she had expected, it was locked up tight.

She went around to the other side of the house. The hill sloped downward on this side of the hill, making the windows seem higher—just an inch or two out of her reach—and she noticed right away that something else was different here. One of these windows was open a crack. She felt victorious. Not many people would leave a window open overnight in April, in a currently vacant property—unless, that is, someone was inside.

She wished there were something for her to stand on, to give herself some added height and leverage. A ladder was too much to hope for, but an upturned trash can, a stray bucket, a sturdy plant pot all might make enough of a difference in helping her reach the screen. Lacking any of these, she could only stand on her toes and pound on the window some more, feeling her fatigue give way to mounting hysteria as she did so. *I need to stop this,* she thought; *I need to stop carrying on like this*—but that voice in her head seemed faint and far away.

Behind the window, something shifted—an advancing shape that was clearly human. But the shape was wrong, the silhouette too big.

The shades jerked up, and Vera found herself eye to eye with a startled-looking man, his face pockmarked and haggard.

She screamed—a muffled scream, but one that frightened her almost as much as it frightened the man on the other side of the glass. "Jesus, lady!" she heard him say, and as he fumbled for the window, she pivoted on her heels and broke into a run.

She was still running down the hill when she heard the window wrench the rest of the way open and the man weakly yelling after her, "Christ, lady, I just needed a warm place to sleep. Hey, you calling the cops? Don't do that, okay? I wasn't bothering nobody!"

Vera wasn't sure how long she ran for—five minutes, maybe as many as ten—but she had never had a runner's strength and stamina. She dropped down on the ground on the outskirts of some woods, clutching her tote bag to her and gasping for air. She put her head between her knees and tried to slow her breathing, tried to recollect herself. *A homeless man,* she thought, *that's all.* She should have known. She remembered overhearing a story from one of her former

Dorset Community College colleagues about being shown an empty apartment and having a terrified homeless man spring out of the walk-in closet when the landlord opened it.

She got up in search of a road sign to determine her whereabouts. She was on the Old Roland Road, a good forty-minute walk back to her apartment. Best to head back in that direction, she knew, but she was not ready to concede defeat just yet.

She walked about twenty minutes before stopping for a rest in downtown Dorset near the small waterfront parking lot where skateboarders often practiced their flips, grinds, and jumps. But it was too early for skateboarders. She looked out over the river, spotting the distant heads of ducks gliding along the water's surface; they were her only company.

"You're right, Elliott," she said out loud. Now that she thought of it, she couldn't remember ever *not* seeing ducks year-round. She remembered something else—sitting in the Roundview Hotel room across from Jensen as she mentioned the line about Holden at the lake in Central Park.

Do you know what I think is beautiful? That part where Holden says he feels like he's disappearing every time he crosses the street. And then there's the ducks in Central Park. How he wants to know where they go in the winter.

She could still visualize how Jensen had looked as she'd said these words, one leg crossed over the other as she perched on the edge of the hotel bed, her face contemplative and a little childlike.

Elliott's voice in her head again: *The ducks never go anywhere, have you noticed?*

She thought of Jensen's parents. She thought of Les Cudahy saying, *She's a good girl, mostly. A good girl.* And of Jensen saying her parents would do anything for her.

Where had Jensen redirected herself, if she had left New York City?

Back to ME.

Back to ME I suppose.

What if Jensen had gone back to Maine and had sought refuge in her own parents' house? What if they were hiding her? She pictured herself in the Cudahys' driveway, seeing the light from the TV reflected in one of the windows; she imagined knocking on the back door, which would be closest to the light, and hearing the basset hound bark lustily in response. She imagined a long wait before she heard an inner door open and saw Mrs. Cudahy standing behind the screen door dressed in a nightgown, her gray hair in pink foam curlers. She even pictured herself from Mrs. Cudahy's perspective: worn and disheveled from traveling, her overstuffed bag in one hand.

But then what? If Vera were to ask if Jensen was hidden somewhere in her home, she could not imagine that this inquiry would be well received. *I can't believe you, of all people, would come here and suggest a thing like that to me,* Mrs. Cudahy might say. *Don't you think the house has already been searched? That was the first thing those cops did. Parents are always the suspects first, even when there isn't a crime.*

And what would Vera say in response? *Look, Mrs. Cudahy, I know you've lost two children already. And I know Jensen wanted to disappear. Perhaps she's returned but has asked you to pretend she's still lost out there somewhere so that she wouldn't have to go to school, wouldn't have to go out among people. Maybe there's another reason, too—a bigger reason that she'd want to stay hidden. These things aren't unheard of. These things happen. And I imagine that someone who's lost her first two children would do just about anything for her daughter, if she asked.*

No. She couldn't say any of that. It was something only a madwoman could cook up, and the only net result would be Mrs. Cudahy calling the cops on Vera and having them remove her from their home. *If anyone's going to call the police on me,* Vera thought, *it's going to be myself. They're expecting my call, anyway.*

She realized that she was too tired to walk back to the Greyhound depot and pretend she had called Detective Ferreira as soon as the bus came in, as she had promised she would. Like a sheepish teenager asking to be picked up at a party that had gotten out of hand, she called the detective's number and told him where he could find her. She remained seated on the low brick wall that formed a border on one end of the parking lot, dully half watching a flock of crows' raucous fight over a bag of fast-food leftovers that they'd found in a nearby trash can.

The detective's sedan pulled up in less than ten minutes. Vera lowered herself off the wall and walked toward the vehicle as the detective rolled down his window. "Whatever happened to calling when you got to the bus station?" Ferreira asked.

The detective looked almost as fatigued as Vera felt. The furrows between his eyebrows ran deep, and his thick, gently graying hair was ruffled up like rooster feathers at the back of his head.

"Sorry, Detective. I had a little nervous energy I needed to blow off first."

"Seems a little early for nervous energy. Hop in the back, why don't you."

Vera did so. "I was in New York checking in on a few things," she said candidly as she fussed with her seat belt, sensing that Ferreira was planning to ask her about the reason for her out-of-state trip. "I don't know that I accomplished anything, really."

"Checking in on a few things, eh? Sounds like trouble to me."

"I talked to Bret Folger. Jensen Willard's boyfriend."

"No wonder you didn't accomplish anything. Kid's got nothing to contribute." Detective Ferreira turned around in the front seat, slowly and deliberately, and glared at Vera as he put the car in drive. "These little exploits have got to stop. I'm telling you, if you were anyone else, I'd have charged you with obstructing justice by now."

"But you haven't," Vera said.

"Want to press your luck?"

"Oh, no, I don't want to press my luck," Vera said, sitting up straighter like a child who is being upbraided. "But you did say I might be of assistance to you here."

In the rearview mirror she could see the detective purse his lips as though weighing this comment in the balance. "You know," he said, still staring ahead at the road, "when someone puts themselves into an investigation as much as you do, usually I assume one of two things. One, that the person is involved in the crime somehow. Or two, that the person is simply a megalomaniac who gets a charge out of being overinvolved."

"*Megalomaniac*. That's a good word."

"Some bored little schoolteacher trying to scare up some excitement for herself," Ferreira went on, ignoring her interruption. "And that doesn't usually get rewarded, believe me. Don't think you're special just because we'd like your input on something."

"I don't think I'm special, Detective. I promise you I don't. I'll behave."

Vera caught the detective's face in the rearview mirror. He was trying not to smile.

"Music?" he asked, reaching for the radio dial.

"I don't mind it."

The detective settled on a station playing classic rock—a song that had been popular among the big-haired metalhead girls when Vera had been in high school. For some reason—perhaps because she was so tired and dreams seemed so close—she felt as though she'd been transported back to a high school dance in her old gymnasium, and as she closed her eyes and reclined against the back seat, she thought she could almost see, toward the very back of the crowd, the swaying, bouncing, undulating form of her onetime classmate Heidi Duplessis.

Back at the police station once again, Vera was led into the same claustrophobic interrogation room she'd been in previously. In true Ferreira style, he cut to the heart of the issue and broke through the glaze of her dissociation—that tired, disembodied, almost drunken feeling that had begun to overtake her again. "What have you heard about Ritchie Ouelette and the Angela Galvez murder?" he fired at her as soon as she'd sat down.

"Only what little they printed in the newspaper," Vera said, and she recapitulated what she remembered from the brief article.

"So you know we have a different suspect in custody now. A minor."

Vera nodded.

"I've brought you here this morning because there's something I'd like you to hear. This is not something we've shared with anyone else outside the department except for Jensen's parents hearing a little. I want you to listen, and there's no need to comment until you're spoken to, got it?"

"Got it."

"Here's the context so far as we know it. Short and sweet. This seventeen-year-old punk kid shows up at the station the other day, copping to all kinds of stuff, including the murder of Angela Galvez. After we cracked down on him for a day and a half, we got him to confess to the Ahmed killing, too. What you're about to hear is only a small part of that confession."

Him, Vera thought, exhaling with a sense of relief. So the voice on the tape, the underage confessor, was not Jensen Willard. Why, then, would the police want to share it with her? She leaned toward the tape player, which the detective had placed between them, resting the weight of her upper body on her elbows and propping her fists under her chin, her eyes shut tight so as to listen without distraction.

The detective hit the PLAY button, and the room welled up with the husky voice of a very young boy. His words sounded a little muffled, and Vera could not tell if this was due to the poor quality of the recording or if the speaker was in the throes of a head cold.

"When Angela Galvez died, it was just something that happened. I was kind of made to do it on the spot. I didn't have anything against that kid personally. For months before that I'd been getting pressured to see what I was made of. To see if I could take a life, just to prove that I could, and to prove that something like life and death really doesn't matter."

Vera heard Ferreira's voice on the tape then: "And who was pressuring you, to see what you were made of?"

"The girl I was with."

"And the girl was Jensen Willard, wasn't it?"

"I'd rather not say."

"You killed Jensen, too, didn't you, Frank? You know there's no logical way your brother can take the heat for this one."

"No, I didn't kill her. I don't know where she is now. She just took off."

"Took off where?"

"She just took off, like I said. We got as far as New York City together, and then she was just gone."

"But she didn't make it to New York City, Frank. She didn't get there because you killed her before you ever left Dorset. We found her combat boots by the riverside."

A feeling began to uncoil in Vera's stomach—the sick feeling of some hibernating creature, like an ancient slumbering eel stirring within her guts. She looked at Detective Ferreira, her lips starting to form a question, but the detective gave her a look that warned her to hold off.

"If I killed her, why would I leave her boots behind? That doesn't even make any sense. Drain the river, I guarantee you won't find her. She left those boots there herself to make it look like she was dead. I lent her a pair of my Chucks, and I gave her my hat to hide her hair under so people wouldn't recognize her right off."

"So you say. We can get back to that a little later. Let's review what you said about Sufia Ahmed. Or are you going to tell us Jensen Willard pressured you to do that, too?"

"I got nothing to say about that."

"But you already have, Frank. You admitted in your statement earlier that you killed Sufia."

Vera heard a sigh and a long, staticky pause.

"She had a plan for it, that's all. Jensen wanted to do three killings, and she was thinking maybe with the second one we could make it look like this teacher of hers had something to do with it—this dumb substitute teacher who was all into murder and stuff. We didn't get very far with that, though."

The detective turned off the tape. "No prize for guessing who the dumb teacher is," he said.

"Me?" Vera, who had not breathed for the last thirty seconds, shuddered at how her voice came out sounding: thick, husky—not unlike the boy's on the tape.

"Bingo. Do you recognize the speaker at all, Vera?"

"No. My God, should I?"

"Not necessarily. I just wonder where Jensen Willard and this kid would get the idea to try to implicate you. If you give me a sec, I'd like to show you something we received shortly after the Willard girl went missing."

The detective took out his phone and tapped the screen a few times until he found what he wanted. He held it out for Vera to examine, and she squinted at an image of blurred text that looked like it might have been photographed from a microfilm screen. "I can't read that," she said. "Is there any way to enlarge it?" She was glad the detective did not invite her to hold the phone herself, for her hands were trembling so badly that she was sure she would have dropped it.

Ferreira adjusted the image until the text popped into Vera's view. HUNDREDS MOURN HEIDI, the old newspaper headline read, and Vera remembered the photo that had accompanied it: two students from her high school, hugging each other, their faces exaggerated caricatures of grief. The rest of the old article was there, too—the coverage of Heidi Duplessis's funeral, and Vera's infamous quote toward the end of the article: *People are acting like no one ever died before. But really, death is just a part of life.*

"Oh my *God*," Vera said again. "Why would someone send you this awful old thing?"

"Beats me. We already knew about what you said. I know you don't believe it, but we do our homework. The question is why someone else would want to bring our attention to it. Among other reasons, it was just one more mandate to keep a close eye on you. We couldn't trace where the text came from because the sender had a disposable phone, but guess who didn't throw away his disposable phone? We found this same image in the kid's stored photos when we took him into custody."

"Who *is* this kid, though? Can you at least tell me who he is?"

"His name is Frank Ouelette Jr." The detective waited a beat, and then, before Vera could ask, supplied the rest. "Ritchie's little brother."

Vera sank back in her chair. "Wow" was all she could say.

Ferreira took in Vera's reaction with what she thought was grim relish. "Quite the heartwarming family story this is. Ever since Ritchie's been trying to raise his brother on his own, the kid's been a mess. Dropped out of school, spent some time in a psych ward for a half-assed suicide attempt, disappears for weeks at a time. One day this kid comes into the police station of his own volition, confessing that he'd let his brother take the heat for Angela Galvez."

Vera shook her head. "I'm not seeing where I fit in here."

"Ouelette and your student Willard were schoolmates for a very brief period. Where you 'fit in,' as you put it, is not entirely clear, but if you don't know this Ouelette kid, chances are he learned about you from the girl."

"But do you really think . . . do you really think Jensen isn't alive? You really think this Frank might have killed her? I find that almost impossible to believe." Vera dug clumsily around in her tote bag, feeling under layers of cosmetics and pajamas and bus ticket stubs until she found the two stolen library books and the J. D. Salinger postcard she'd found within one of them. Handing the postcard over to Ferreira, she said, "I'm pretty sure this is Jensen's handwriting. I found this in New York City just a couple of days ago. And it wasn't the first message I got from her." She relayed the earlier message she had received back at headquarters. "I couldn't prove she wrote the first one, but once I saw this one, I knew the author had to be one and the same."

"So this is what you were doing in New York," the detective said, looking at the postcard from every angle, then turning it back to its front and giving Salinger a second appraisal. Taking in the herringbone tweed coat and narrow tie, he snorted. "We'll check it out. For now, though, just so we're clear, I'm putting it on the record that you don't recognize this kid's voice. And I take it you've never heard Jensen Willard say anything about being friends with a Frank Ouelette Jr."

"Definitely not. Not in her journals or elsewhere."

"There's just one more thing, then. The kid has asked if he can speak to you personally."

"To *me*? What for?"

"Says he won't be right with his *conscience* if he doesn't." The detective uttered the word *conscience* with an inflection that told Vera he doubted that Frank Ouelette Jr. even had one. "He'd have his lawyer present, and I'd be there with you, too. But this is only going to happen if you're willing to do a little jail trip later this afternoon. Today's the last day we can hold him, and after he goes home for a while, there's no telling if he'll change his mind about wanting to talk. Ever visited a jail before, Vera?"

When Vera stammered that no, she never had, the detective handed her a brochure and told her she might find it handy: WHAT TO EXPECT DURING YOUR FIRST PRISON VISIT, read the boldfaced heading on its cover. "To sum it up," Ferreira said, "no sharps, no weapons, nothing that's going to give you a hard time going through a metal detector. Leave your purse at home unless you want to pay to have it put in a locker. No phones, no cameras. No low-cut blouses or short skirts."

"No low-cut blouses or short skirts?" Even in her state of relative shock, Vera could not keep the irony out of her voice.

"That's what I said, isn't it? Come to think of it, whatever you wear, bring a sweater. A big, baggy, frumpy one—just in case."

As Vera waited in her studio for Ferreira to pick her up later that afternoon, she changed into her longest black skirt and a drab, oversized crew-neck sweater, but she could not refrain from fussing with her hair and dabbing on some dark lipstick. She had tried to rest, per the detective's suggestion ("Get a couple hours of sleep—you look like shit" had been his piquant way of putting it), but had found that as tired as she was, she could not rest. Her mind kept crackling with agitation and confusion as it reviewed the morning's new information, which seemed to cast its particular, cruel new light on everything that Vera had assumed about her student Jensen Willard.

Her mind wanted to reject it all. The girl may be dark, even darker than Bret Folger knew her to be, but she could not imagine her coercing anyone into murder. She thought of the girl's journal entries—so often funny, self-effacing, filled with adolescent pathos and precocious intelligence. True, she had given Vera occasion for fear and doubt more than once, but the accusations leveled by Frank Ouelette Jr. had to be false. *Had* to be. She wanted nothing more than to look the boy right in the eye and see this lie for herself.

The county jail had the musty smell of a basement or a high school locker room—a smell that hit Vera's nostrils as soon as she passed through its doors. After being checked by the security guard, she followed Ferreira down the hall and into an elevator, willing herself into feeling more *present* as Ferreira, having spoken to another guard and exchanged some paperwork, escorted her into a private room. "You want some coffee?" the short, stocky female guard who had led them down the hall asked. "They should be along in a couple of minutes."

"Coffee would be nice," Vera said mechanically.

A moment later, Vera sipped from the Styrofoam cup she'd been given—black, rotgut stuff, but she did not dare ask if there was any creamer to be had—while Ferreira talked on his phone with someone in a lackadaisical way as though she were not there. He answered his phone two more times and made one call of his own before Frank Ouelette Jr. and his entourage came into the room.

Vera saw the two adults who accompanied Frank before she saw the boy himself. One was a corrections officer in full uniform, and the other was a woman in a misshapen suit with shoulder pads; Vera guessed she must be the attorney. Frank Ouelette Jr., standing between these two people, looked very small.

He was lithe and slightly built, not much taller than Vera, with none of his brother Ritchie's impressive height. He had a rounded, elvish face and sandy brown hair that sprang around his face in curls. His clear blue eyes were the one feature that bore a trace of his older brother; they were the sort of eyes one thinks of as honest, with a thick, arching sweep of eyebrows above them. He was, in Vera's opinion, a rather handsome boy—or would have been if he had not looked so abjectly uncomfortable.

"Frank, this is Vera Lundy. Vera, Frank Ouelette Jr.," Detective Ferreira said. To Vera's surprise, the boy extended a hand to her—cool, pale, and fine-boned. She had thought he would be handcuffed; she had imagined him with his arms behind his back like a boy about to offer her a secret bouquet of freshly picked wildflowers, though common sense told her that his hands would be handcuffed in the front, if he had any restraints at all. She took his hand in hers and was unsure later if she had actually grasped it back when he shook it; nor could she remember letting go. Was this the hand that had strangled Angela Galvez? Sufia Ahmed?

"Thanks for coming," the boy said. His voice was the voice she had heard on the tape—young-sounding, with a throat that sounded full of tears but wasn't.

The attorney, whose name Vera quickly forgot as soon as it was shared with her, seemed as uncomfortable as a mother whose son has been called into the principal's office. She leaned toward her client and blinked with mistrust at Ferreira and Vera from behind her large-framed eyeglasses. Vera guessed her to be fairly green in her profession.

"Nice day out today, isn't it?" the attorney said to Ferreira, as though offering him an olive branch. "Seems like spring is really here."

"Honey of a day," the detective agreed.

Were they really talking about the weather? And were they really doing so in front of a young man who had been in lockup for three days? Embarrassed for them, Vera lowered her face and sipped the dreadful coffee. She was trying her hardest not to stare at Frank Ouelette, who was seated directly across from her.

Presently Ferreira said, "I think we can get started here. I need to be back at the station in half an hour, give or take. You ready to say your piece, Frank?"

"I am," the boy said.

"And Miss Lundy is just hear to listen," Ferreira said. "Right, Miss Lundy?"

"Right," she said in a whisper, then wetted her dry lips with the tip of her tongue.

Locking eyes with Vera as though he and she were the only two people in the room, the boy began to speak.

"The first thing I wanted to tell you is that I didn't kill your student. I mean, not Jensen. I guess Sufia was your student, too, but that wasn't my fault—not completely. It was all Jensen Willard's idea, just like Angela before that.

"Jensen was starting to get curious about what it would be like to kill someone. For weeks before the thing with Angela happened, Jensen kept saying: 'In order to be a writer, you have to experience *everything*. How can we know what it's like to kill somebody unless we actually do it? Maybe it'd be easy. Maybe no one would ever even connect it to us. Wouldn't it be interesting to find out?' But I was sure that was just talk, like all the other stupid talks we had. And besides, I don't even want to be a writer. I hate writing. That was pure, one-hundred-percent Jensen—not me.

"My car was broke down at the time, so I was borrowing my brother Ritchie's shitbox Ford—sorry, I don't mean to cuss—and one night we were riding around with nothing to do and saw Angela Galvez along the bike path. I didn't know who she was, but Jensen said, 'There's that brat whose mother is talking crap about me around town. We should take her and mess with her, just to teach her a lesson.'

"So we stopped and got out and talked to her for a while. I remember Angela saying to Jensen, 'Your bra is still in our tree!' She was a funny kid. Cute. I didn't want to do anything to her, or even get her into Ritchie's car, but Jensen told her to get in and we would get her an ice cream over at the Dairy Queen. The kid got right into the front seat next to me. Jensen took a seat in the back, right behind her.

"This Angela kid was pretty smart, because she figured out right away that we were driving in the wrong direction to go to Dairy Queen. I wasn't sure where I was driving, but I was trying to get to someplace off the main roads. And after a few minutes she started whining, like, and saying, 'I want to get out now. My mom is expecting me. I want to go home. I don't feel like getting ice cream anymore.'"

The lawyer, who had been keeping a hand on Frank Ouelette's shoulder as though to restrain him from his own torrent of words, interjected then: "You don't have to go into all this, Frank. It's already on the record."

"But I want to explain it to her," the boy said, jerking his chin toward Vera. "I want to explain because I know what she must be thinking. I want to do what's *right*."

Vera could hear herself in the boy—could hear her own desire, however poorly executed and belated, to do what was right also. This was a similarity she did not want. As for what she was thinking, she had no idea how Frank Ouelette could be so sure what was on her mind; she was too horrified to formulate any thought other than the vague, sinking idea that everything the boy had said so far smacked of the truth.

"Angela was saying stuff, but Jensen wasn't having any of it. She said, 'We're not getting ice cream, you little bitch. You're going to get a lesson that's a long time coming, and you'd better stop whining about it.' That just set Angela off even more. She was trying to get the passenger door open. She was pounding on the window and screaming, and I thought she was going to break the window, and I got nervous, and I yelled something, and the next thing I knew Jensen had reached around from the back seat and had both hands wrapped real tight around this kid's nose and mouth. Angela tried to bite her, I think, because then *Jensen* screamed and she was screaming at *me* to do something, and at this point the kid was thrashing around like a fish on the end of the line, and I was freaked out by the screaming, afraid someone would hear it, so I pulled over on the side of the road and put my hands around her neck, and these weird noises were coming out of the kid, kind of like she'd got a dog's squeak toy stuck in her throat, and then she went quiet and the passenger side of the seat underneath her was all wet. She'd, uh . . . she'd emptied her bladder."

Frank Ouelette Jr. did sound, now, as though he were going to cry. He took a few big swallows and a few extra seconds to compose himself again before he continued.

"So you see, it really wasn't planned. I think *Jensen* might have planned it, but I sure didn't. I'd never even seen a dead person before except for the pictures I sometimes looked at on these gore sites where you can, you know, look at photos of people with their heads blown off and stuff. But this was nothing like looking at a photo. It was more real. And we couldn't just keep this girl in the front seat, with . . . the way she was.

"We ended up driving the shi—the Ford into the woods, and we got a tarp out of Ritchie's trunk and wrapped Angela in it real fast before stuffing her into the trunk. I think we were both in shock by then, and even Jensen was crying a little now, saying, 'It's ugly, it's ugly,' and I didn't know if she was talking about the body or about what we had just done. We just sat in the woods for a while, a few feet away from the Ford, because neither of us knew what to do next or where to take the body. When it got darker, Jensen said, 'We should put her behind the Laundromat because that's where all the crack dealers go. They'll think one of them did it.' So that's why we left her where we did."

Vera hadn't known that Angela had been wrapped in a tarp. That detail had been omitted from the news reports. She thought of Sufia Ahmed, in her traditional dress, which she had first thought was a tarp when she'd seen her body under the tree in Dorset Park. She thought of the fiber evidence found on Angela Galvez—the fiber evidence that had come from Ritchie Ouelette's car—and the DNA evidence in the front seat, which she now knew was the dead little girl's urine. These concrete details felt more burdensome than illuminating. Now that answers were coming, she did not want them anymore. She wanted to turn her back on them, to run from them. But where was there to run?

Vera wanted to ask: *If this was so terrible, then why did you go on to kill Sufia?* But she knew she was not supposed to ask questions. And she was not sure she wanted to hear this detailed response, anyway. She leaned toward Detective Ferreira, feeling self-conscious about the proximity of her mouth to his ear, and whispered, "Can you ask him what this has to do with me?" What she really meant was, *Can we cut to the chase, please, because I really can't take much more.* So much for amateur detective skills, she thought; in the face of the truth, her heart and her stomach were deplorably weak.

The detective voiced the question on her behalf, and Frank Ouelette, looking straight at Vera again, said, "Well, I'm up to the part where you come in, kind of."

He went on to tell her how Jensen had described her new English teacher as being, as he put it, "really into true crime and murder and stuff." "Jensen had Googled you, and she found out that there'd been a murder in your hometown back when you were in high school. She also found out there were some people back then who'd thought, for a little while, that you'd done it. She was real excited about that. She had this, like, fascination with you or something. Not a crush or anything, but this *interest* because she felt like you and her had something in common. She told me you'd said in class that anyone could kill someone. It got her all worked up, knowing a teacher thought the same way she did."

"I didn't say—" Vera began, but she stopped herself. Because she *had*. She *had* said it, but when she had said it, she hadn't really meant *anyone*. She had only been referring to a certain type of anyone.

"She saw you talking to Sufia Ahmed after class one time and said you seemed mad, that you guys were having some kind of a fight, so she got this idea that maybe we could get rid of Sufia and have everyone think you'd done it. That might give the police someone to look at other than Ritchie—someone who wasn't me. I didn't feel right about Ritchie taking the rap. So we thought . . . well, maybe point the finger somewhere else. It was like I'd become a robot. I could do anything anyone told me to at that point, and I wouldn't feel a thing. Jensen said, 'All you need to do is grab her by that thing she wears over her head and pull it really tightly around her neck. You can do it from behind, and you won't even have to look at her.' So that's what I did. It was easy to get Sufia to come out with us because she wanted to learn how to skateboard. It was supposed to be me, Jensen, my friend Joey Fitts, and this other kid who goes to Bonny Eagle all teaching her some moves, but when we met up in the park, it was just me and Jensen. Jensen actually didn't watch. She waited over by the little pond and told me to come get her when I was done. Once I was, we figured we'd leave Sufia in the park because we knew that was right across the street from where you lived."

Fitts, Vera thought. *So that's how I know the name.* "I wasn't mad at Sufia," Vera said, starting to tear up.

"Well, Jensen said you had a fight."

"It wasn't a fight."

Ferreira shot Vera another warning look. "I'm sorry," she whispered, looking down at her hands folded on top of the table.

She could not drink her coffee anymore. She could not do anything but stare through brimming eyes at Frank Ouelette, who no longer seemed on the verge of tears himself but had become calm and conversational, the second death obviously bothering him less than the first.

"Jensen had one last idea before we left town. She thought maybe we could get rid of you, too. Make it look like you killed yourself. Write a suicide note for you and everything. Maybe one with a confession in it. She was going to invite you to this hotel and do it there all by herself, but I think she chickened out, because nothing came of it."

"Was she going to use a gun?" Vera asked, remembering the service pistol Jensen had alluded to having with her. *But that wouldn't have worked,* she thought. *They would have traced it to Les Cudahy so easily. Or maybe,* she thought . . . *maybe a little poison slipped in some vodka and orange juice?*

"I don't know what all she was thinking of doing. I just know we took off later that night—I was waiting for her behind her house, outside the dog fence, and my car was parked down the street. I'd gotten it back from the shop by then. We spent that night on a campground in New Hampshire, and from there we went to Vermont for a while, but that got boring pretty fast, so we ended up in New York City on the Lower East Side with this guy everyone calls Bob the Punk. He's seriously old-school, like in his forties or something. He's an allright guy, though.

"One morning I woke up and Jensen was just gone. She wasn't in Bob's squat anymore, and we spent two days looking around for her before we figured she didn't want to be found."

Seeing that the monologue had moved away from details of the killings, Vera felt she could almost breathe again. She wanted to go backward, to ask him how he and Jensen had met, how he had come to know this girl—this terrible, monstrous, unfathomable girl whom Vera would never have associated with the Jensen Willard she knew and her journals.

She leaned toward the detective again and murmured, "Can you ask him where he knows Jensen from?"

Frank overheard her and, to her dismay, held her gaze again, his blue eyes guileless and confiding. "She was at my school, but I only talked to her a couple of times before I stopped going. After I dropped out, we still met up in the woods sometimes and kept talking about the same kind of stuff we'd started talking about in phys ed. Crazy stuff—setting fires, putting pipe bombs in the local schools, taking hostages. I never thought anything would come of it."

Vera thought for a while. Something had begun to occur to her. Forgetting once again that she had been coached not to ask questions to the young boy without a go-between, she found her voice, and clearly said, "You say you met her in phys ed. Was there any reason why she would have ever called you by the name Scotty?"

"Yeah, once in a while. I thought it was dumb. It was after some author she liked—F. Scott Fitzpatrick. Because my real first name is Francis, just like that guy's, I guess."

Fitzgerald, Vera almost said aloud. She thought of the Fitzgerald bookmark that she had used for her copy of *The Catcher in the Rye* and of how one of Jensen's first-ever comments to her pertained to it—her approval of the ill-fated Scott and Zelda. Had Jensen already done some research on Vera at that point in time? Was it then, or sometime even earlier, that she had pinpointed Vera as someone to be taken advantage of? She remembered how Jensen had emailed her before they had ever even met: *I look forward to meeting you,* her first-ever message had read. Had she already done her research by then and put her in her sights?

Vera could tell Ferreira was annoyed with her for speaking up, but at the same time she could also tell that this was his first time hearing that Scotty and Frank Ouelette Jr. were one and the same. He looked a little chagrined. Perhaps in an effort to take the bull by the horns again, reclaim his position as the one in charge, he turned toward Frank Ouelette's attorney. "Miss Lundy found a note in New York City that she thinks Willard might have written," he said. "This is all off the record for now, but I'm sure Miss Lundy would like to know why your client's friend would have left her such a note, or written a note giving her the idea to come to New York City in the first place."

"I don't know anything about that," Frank Ouelette spoke up, again directing his response at Vera. "That's weird that she would write to you. She told me she didn't want to hurt you because you didn't seem so bad, after all, but she might have changed her mind.

"Anyway, that's kind of why I wanted to talk to you in person. To tell you that I didn't kill Jensen, and that I wish I'd never laid a finger on those other two girls or even thought for a minute about putting you in a bad spot. We both got duped by the same girl, I guess. Funny, right? You seem like a nice-enough lady. I don't think Jensen's dead, and she thought of doing something to you once, so who knows? She might get that idea again. You'd better be careful."

"I think we're done here," Ferreira said. With a nod to the corrections officer, he said, "You can take him back now, Wade. Thanks, Frank, for being willing to talk again. We'll talk again soon, I'm sure."

When Frank Ouelette and the entourage were gone, Vera looked up at Ferreira helplessly. "I don't think he killed Jensen Willard," she said to him. "Let me be the first to admit that I'm a much worse judge of character than I ever thought. But when he says she's still out there, I believe him. I could be wrong. She could be in the river, like you think, and he could be lying through his teeth."

"That's what we're trying to sort out."

"Are you planning to try him as an adult?"

"Not for me to decide. Do I look like the courts to you? Nice work with the Scotty connection, by the way. We hadn't gotten him to pin down exactly where he met Willard. Can't use this as evidence, of course, but it's a useful thing for us to know."

Vera suddenly felt her entire body sag. She put her head between her knees and moaned softly.

"You going to be okay?" Ferreira said.

"I think I'm going to be sick."

The detective pulled the garbage can from the corner and planted it in front of her just as she leaned forward and retched. Coffee-colored saliva and bile hit the edge of the trash can liner, and Vera wiped her chin with the back of her hand, embarrassed. "My God," she said.

"You've been through a lot," Ferreira said. "You're looking a little worse for the wear. I wonder if there might be a close friend or relative you might stay with for the day."

Vera tried to heave again, this time bringing up a pasty gruel that she took for the package of crackers she had eaten shortly before Ferreira picked her up.

"I'll be all right by myself," she said, but she was not sure that she would be. She realized she was too spooked to go home alone. She thought of Frank Ouelette—Scotty—telling her to be careful, and of Bret Folger nearly saying the same thing before that. She wanted to be careful.

"I'd feel better if I knew you had someone to keep an eye on you," Ferreira insisted.

It was nice to know someone cared. And the more she thought about it, the more she decided what she wanted to do and whom she wanted to call. She found herself pumping quarters into the pay phone at headquarters and dialing her mother's number while Ferreira looked on. She barely got out a hello before her mother let out a relieved squawk and launched into a series of recriminations for not having answered her voicemails, for not having called her much sooner.

"Mom," she said, "Mom. I can't really talk right now. But I need a favor. Things have gotten bad. I need to come home, Mom."

No place was home, Vera thought, but sometimes a substitute had to do. She wondered if Jensen Willard's substitute home was now the river—if she was cradled on the riverbed, the water lapping gently over her, the bottom-feeding sea creatures feasting on what remained. She doubted it. She replaced the receiver in its cradle and then closed her eyes because it hurt to keep them open, and the more she looked at the empty chair where Scotty had just been sitting, the more she felt the urge to throw up again.

It was an hour's wait before her mother could reach Dorset. She wondered if she could nap there in the police waiting area. She thought once again about the young girl who might or might not be in the river, and for the first time she felt a great divide between herself and this girl—a divide of decades and experience and maturity and mortality and even conscience. She remembered what she had said to Jensen in the hotel room: *I'm still that fifteen-year-old girl in a lot of ways.* In some ways, perhaps that still held true. She might always be the awkward, self-doubting girl she once was. But in other, more significant ways, a door had closed on that fifteen-year-old girl forever.

And isn't it better this way? she asked herself. *Isn't it better to finally leave her behind?* Vera thought the answer was yes. Still, as she felt herself nodding off in her chair, she felt the inner dissonance of one who has lost and gained in equal measure.

Chapter Fourteen

The next two weeks were the lost days, spent in a state of half waking.

This was a time when one day bled into another, a time when sleeping until two or three in the afternoon was commonplace for Vera. A time when little was required of her other than keeping her mother company. She ate her mother's plain New England cooking—everything baked and boiled within an inch of its life—and listened to her complain about the neighbors, who, her mother was sure, were running a brothel out of their house. She picked up smoking cigarettes again—her former habit, and her mother's lifelong one—and she and her mother often sat out on her patio, inhaling tobacco and stubbing their butt ends into a shared ashtray with particular emphasis, as though the extermination of a cigarette were the period at the end of an unspoken sentence.

Vera seldom went outside during these days for fear of running into Peter and his new wife or—worse, in its own way—former high school classmates who might wonder what she was doing back in town. She slept in the same bed she'd had as a child, under the slanted roof with its window that looked out at the barren crab apple trees, until she realized her Dorset apartment wasn't paying for itself and that she would either have to relinquish her rental or go back to it.

She was afraid to go back, she had to admit. She felt safer under her mother's roof. Then again, if Jensen could find her at the volunteer headquarters, she could surely find her at her mother's address. She could find her anywhere.

There was also the question of how Vera would continue to support herself. She had appealed to her former boss at Dorset Community College, asking if there might be some adjunct work she could pick up there, but she'd been told all the sections of English composition were full—and she'd received this message not from the boss himself but from his secretary, which made her think she was unwelcome on campus, just as she was at every other academic institution in Dorset. *Only to be expected,* she thought with a sort of fatalism.

During the fourth week of her unemployment, after she'd returned to her studio, Vera went to the shopping mall in South Portland and walked out with a low-paying job as a sales associate in the junior formals department; she had no retail experience, and she saw this as a dismal step down from teaching. Still, she felt lucky to get this job over the other options—fast-food worker, grocery store carryout girl—that were available to her; at least at the department store she could wear pretty clothes and lipstick and handle garments intended for events Vera herself had never attended: prom, homecoming, spring formal. She spent a great deal of time herding giddy teenagers and their tired mothers into fitting rooms and shooing boyfriends out of them; she zipped zippers and tied sashes and straightened petticoats of dresses.

Tending to these exuberant younger girls, she tried not think of Jensen Willard. Sometimes she was successful. Sometimes not. There were times when she would see a dark-clad girl sulking in the waiting area outside the fitting rooms—usually a younger sister who had been dragged along while the older girl tried on gown after gown—and Vera would stop dead in her tracks, her arms often laden with heavy garments that needed to go back on the sales floor, her mouth a small O of consternation until she realized, as she always did, that the girl she was looking at was not Jensen Willard. Not even close. No matter how many times this happened, she never failed to be surprised by the commingling feelings of relief and disappointment she felt all at once.

One day an older customer came into the department store with a younger one; as the girl browsed the racks, the older woman proudly told Vera that this girl was her granddaughter, looking for a formal dress to wear to "nice events" at Princeton.

"Oh, I went to Princeton," Vera said without even thinking.

"You did?" The older woman looked horrified. "And this was the best job you could get?"

"Well," Vera said, hiding the sense of affront she felt, "I do other things, too."

But this was a lie. She didn't do anything else. She didn't even pretend to work on the Ivan Schlosser book anymore. She hadn't read a real book in months. She hadn't talked to anyone but her mother and her customers—and the customers barely counted, as most of them looked at her as an impersonal "it," a means of getting something they wanted. As for Elliott, even his chiding emails had softened, taking on the pitying tone of one who has assessed his friend as being beyond hope. She couldn't even summon her bright wit in her own email responses, but one day, after crawling out of bed in the late afternoon, she logged on to her email and wrote, *Elliott, you old cabbage. Do you know of any jobs available in New York City right now? Maybe a desk job. A cubicle job. Entry level is okay. I don't really care what it is.*

But Elliott, in his reply, knew of no available work: *Vee, you old Nutter Butter. If I knew of a job in NYC, do you really think I'd continue to write about Crunch 'n Munch vs. Cracker Jack? The pickings are slim.*

Do what you did before and apply to a college program around here—something practical this time, like auto repair. Oh, wait—you don't drive! Maybe library science, then. You'd like that. But don't do it unless you can get a tuition reimbursement and a little stipend on the side. With your credentials, you could probably teach remedial English to the incoming frosh. It's just an idea.

To Vera it wasn't a bad idea at all. She could imagine herself living somewhere in the outer boroughs—Queens, perhaps—and taking the train to night classes after putting in her shifts at some quiet editorial job. She would not mind living modestly, in another cramped space; she could imagine herself walking back from the train at night amid the sound of police sirens and cheerfully drunken Irish immigrants calling to one another outside the neighborhood taverns, and this thought warmed her all through. *As soon as I can,* she thought, *I will request an application from Queens College. Maybe I* could *get a scholarship.* If she could not teach impressionable young minds anymore, then at least recommending books to these same young people might give her some sense of fulfillment. She imagined herself one day working in the young adult section of the library, suggesting titles to those who were betwixt and between—neither adults nor children—as well as to those adults who felt similarly in limbo.

But this would take time. It might be too late even to apply for the fall semester. Nevertheless, this possibility of reinventing herself gave her the fortitude she needed to get up and face her job and her empty life over the next few months.

In the meantime she took a metro bus to South Portland each day, seeing the usual mix of college students, local drunks, and working folks who were either too poor to buy a car or tired of the hassle of finding a place to park in the city. One drizzly morning, as she boarded the bus, she took one of the only empty seats and hoped there would be no new passengers to take the space next to hers—but during a busy, rainy-day commute, this was an unrealistic hope. At the Park Avenue stop near the post office, an entire Latino family, an old man in a motorized wheelchair, and several young professional types waited to get on. Vera guessed that the girl in the sundress and the white linen jacket might ask to share her seat, but she took a seat closer to the back, next to a boy wearing headphones. "Is it okay if I sit here?" said a tall young man at her elbow, a man in a dark-green server's apron, and of course Vera had no choice but to say that it was perfectly okay.

The man settled in beside her, not taking up too much space as men often did, and carefully unfolded a newspaper in his lap, turning to the crosswords page and taking a pen out of his shirt pocket. The crossword was half filled out already, with several scratched-out words that had failed him. Vera glanced at the crossword, then at the light hairs on the man's exposed forearms under his rolled-up shirtsleeves, and then, with a sudden dawning, at the man's profile. His rather sunken cheeks, high forehead, and thinning hair all seemed familiar to her.

She was sitting next to Ritchie Ouelette. She was sure of it. She wanted to say something to him, but she did not know what there was to say.

"Are you good at crosswords?" Ritchie Ouelette suddenly asked without actually looking at her.

"Sometimes," Vera said.

"This one's a bear. Do you know of an eleven-letter word that means 'to lie'? I don't know if they mean it like lying down or if they mean it like telling a lie."

"Try *prevaricate*," Vera said after a moment. "See, that has to be it. The *V* fits with *vermilion*, which is what you've got for fifty-six across."

"Thank you," Ritchie Ouelette said. "I didn't think of that one."

"You're welcome."

He seemed so studious, bent over his puzzle, and had such a gentle, almost shy way about him. He must be working at one of the chain restaurants around the mall, based on the looks of his uniform. The accountant job, the numbers-crunching job, hadn't been there waiting for him when he'd been released from prison. In a way, they'd both been demoted. They had this in common.

For the next fifteen minutes Vera wanted to say something else to him. She wanted to tell him she knew who he was, that he and she had something else in common, too—a close connection to the crimes in Dorset, though both were essentially innocent bystanders who had stepped too close to the flame. She had a feeling that Ritchie would be embarrassed to be recognized, hunched as he was over his newspaper, and that it would be better to say nothing at all. He was wearing a light, woodsy cologne, and she was close enough to see a few small scrapes on his chin where he had shaved himself too closely.

"Have a nice day, now," he said to her, getting up at the stop before the mall.

"You, too," she said, watching him go. The soft cadences of his voice stayed with her, and she smiled to herself as she watched him cross the parking lot toward the restaurant; those cadences were like snow, a gently falling snow that mirrored the soft rain outside the window and something even softer inside her. She thought, *I could have fallen in love with that man's voice,* and she wasn't ashamed. She remembered how she had once told Jensen not to lose sight of the beauty in things. She had been right in giving that advice, whether the girl had taken it to heart or not. It was good to know, after all was said and done, that one could be right about something.

***

As the days and weeks and months passed by, the more stagnant and predictable Vera's existence became. Things continued around her and without her during the quiet days that she later would see as a convalescence of sorts. She read on the Wallace School website that Tim Zabriskie had been promoted to associate dean. She saw a newspaper article saying that *The Catcher in the Rye* was banned in several southern Maine high schools; according to one teacher at Millbank Academy, "It's not so much a question of censoring a book because it's controversial, but honestly, this isn't a book that speaks to teenagers anymore." This would have hurt Vera if she'd still had the capacity to feel hurt by such things.

The only story that remained at a standstill was the story of Jensen Willard.

The search of the river had yielded nothing. And then, gradually, the stories about her stopped altogether. At the six-month mark of her disappearance, the attention had vanished as completely and utterly as Jensen Willard herself; there was one article in the *Journal* telling how her parents still "held out hope" that their daughter was alive, but this sentiment was not echoed by the local police or, it seemed, by anyone else.

Vera did not know if she held out hope. After the first few weeks, she had stopped being entirely afraid and once again allowed herself some curiosity about the girl who had aroused her curiosity from the very beginning.

When she worked on her writing during her favorite predawn hours, her mind would, on occasion, wander back to Jensen Willard. On such occasions she could not help entertaining the possibility that the girl was alive somewhere and poised to come back. As she toiled over the flow of her sentences, she wondered if Jensen was somewhere not so far away, writing works of her own—but who was her audience now, she wondered? Whom could she possibly find to take Vera's place?

She wondered if Jensen would continue her education someday and maybe go on to college. She wondered if she would ever have a teacher who appreciated her talents and handled these as they should be handled. She wondered what the girl would think of herself ten or twenty years down the line, when adolescence had lost some of its sting but none of memory's potency.

If, that is, she lived to remember.

If she was alive—and if she did remember—Vera hoped Jensen would one day see her in a kind light, and as something other than what she now knew Jensen had seen her as: a weak scapegoat serving the girl's temporary purpose. But a time might come when the girl truly *would* see something good of herself in Vera, just as Vera had seen something of herself in the girl.

She hoped, either way, that Jensen Willard might think of her in the future and remember that someone had identified with and cared about her and had not given up so easily—even if that realization was a long time in the making and came without regrets.

Just a few months shy of the one-year anniversary of the day she had first met Jensen Willard, Vera bused home from her evening shift in junior formals and reread the handwritten text in the notebook on her lap. She was putting the finishing touches on her rough draft for the essay portion of her application to the Queens College library science program; the rest of the application was filled out at home, and tonight, she thought, she could put the essay in a Word document and have the whole packet ready to send out in the morning.

It was a wet and foggy walk back to her studio, but Vera didn't mind these things. She felt as though she were taking the first real step to metamorphosing, or perhaps settling in to the self she'd been meant to be all along. *Reinvention—so wonderfully American,* she thought. As music blasted from a car at a nearby stoplight, she tried to hum along to the tuneless hip-hop, bobbing her head a little as she sought out a beat.

Her apartment lobby was empty when she arrived at home. Next to the mailboxes in her lobby, a roach the size of a small mouse lay crushed on the floor, its head missing but its legs still waving. Vera shuddered and took her mail out of her locked mailbox, carrying it up the three flights of stairs to her studio. She let herself in and glanced at the mail with little interest. Her electricity bill. A subscription offer for the *New York Times*. A letter from Princeton's alumni relations coordinator asking for donations. An envelope that looked as if it might contain a greeting card.

She pried at the envelope's seal with her bitten-off fingernails, wondering about the sender of the card; her fortieth birthday had come and gone the month before. She tugged at the edge of the card inside until it came out; as soon as she saw what it was, Vera physically jumped back, and both envelope and card drifted out of her hands.

The card stared faceup from her hardwood living room floor. She looked down at a portrait of Mark Twain, and the quotation produced below his image:

> **No, the romance and beauty were all gone from the river. All the value any feature of it had for me now was the amount of usefulness it could furnish . . . Since those days, I have pitied doctors from my heart. What does the lovely flush in a beauty's cheek mean to a doctor but a "break" that ripples above some deadly disease?**
>
> —Mark Twain, "Two Ways of Seeing a River"

She bent down until she rested on her haunches and lifted the cover of the card with the tip of one finger. The handwritten message inside contained no greeting for Vera at the top, no warm salutation; instead, the text got right to its point, as though the author had no time for niceties.

I told you the next time you'd hear from me I'd write something less gloomy, so here it is: Things are all right. Yes, I said that things are all right. Life is about learning, isn't it? If you're not learning, you're not living, and sometimes part of living is figuring out what your limits are. Have you ever done something just to see what it would feel like and so that you could say you've done it and then not have to worry anymore? And if you've ever done something like that, have you ever decided that it wasn't something you felt like doing again? Even though you sort of have to?

I hope things are okay with you these days. It's too bad you aren't teaching anymore because I think you were pretty good at it. I'm still sorry that I didn't get to finish reading "Catcher" with you, though, of course, I already know how it ends.

I won't be needing this anymore.

Vera had no doubt who had written this card: Jensen Willard, that unhappy being who had long lived in the land of monsters. She looked again at the final line of the unsigned note, wondering what it meant. What was it that Jensen wouldn't be needing—the card? *The Catcher in the Rye*? Life itself? Something occurred to her, and she looked in the envelope that had landed a few feet away from the card. She saw its postmark—California—and as she bent to pick it up, she saw a flash of something folded in the bottom of it—something purple, like a ribbon. But not a ribbon. A shoelace.

She extricated it and held it in her open palm. *Jensen's bootlace,* she thought, but then she remembered that Jensen had never worn purple laces in her combat boots. And this lace was too short, anyway, to be a bootlace. What was the significance of a purple shoelace? Why did she feel as though this were something she should know the answer to?

She sat down on the edge of her bed, still holding the envelope and the shoelace, when it came to her. Angela Galvez with her purple-laced sneakers and their silver detail. *You have to wonder what happened to the other one and why someone would think that was a good trophy to keep, out of all the trophies one could keep.*

Vera looked at the envelope and the shoelace again. *No,* she thought. *No.* The shoelace looked new and clean—even smelled clean; its plastic tips felt cold and hard against her hand. *It could be newly bought,* Vera thought. *It might not mean what I'm meant to think it means.*

But then again, it could.

She sat there for what felt like several long minutes, listening to the sounds outside her window: the wail of police sirens, the conversational voices on the sidewalk below. She got up and opened her closet, took down a shoebox containing office supplies she'd pilfered from work, and picked out a folded manila envelope and a packet of Post-it notes.

On the topmost Post-it note, Vera wrote the following:

Detective Ferreira,

I received the enclosed correspondence in my mailbox at my Dorset address. I ask you to make of it what you will. You'll hear nothing further from me unless you seek me out, but please feel free to do so if you want. I'm still trying to be good.

Sincerely,
Vera Lundy

She looked up the address she wanted, filled out the front of her envelope, affixed what she hoped was the correct postage, and slid the card and its envelope inside it and, last of all, the shoelace, now warmed from the bed of her palm.

Exiting her apartment, she walked down the street until she reached the mailbox on the corner. The hinge of the old mail chute whined as she pulled it open, and she tossed the envelope into this dark mouth, imagining it float down, down, down into the darkness, where it would it would rest on other messages and missives and bills and pleas and snugly enclosed secrets.

She closed the door to the chute and turned back in the direction of her apartment. A breeze had picked up outside; her hair blew into her face, tips of it sticking to the residue of lipstick on her lips, but she did not brush them away. Though the police sirens had died, the foggy neighboring streets of Dorset still showed signs of life. She could hear someone drunkenly singing a soft ballad from an open upper-story window, and on the corner before the mailbox, two young men teased two young women who looked as though they'd all come stumbling from the tavern together. As Vera passed them, they looked up briefly to see who had come and gone, took note of the woman with her straight and determined walk, and then went back to their negotiations and their banter as the last chorus of the window singer caressed them all and disappeared into the mist.

Acknowledgments

I would like to thank my agent, Denise Shannon, for her representation, persistence, and consummate professionalism always. And I would like to thank my editor, Denise Roy, for her brilliant grasp of narrative and for giving me permission to take this novel where I secretly wanted it to go. A great thanks, too, is extended to all of the folks at Dutton who had a hand in bringing *What Has Become of You* to life.

This novel is partly a detective story, but the idea for it sprang from my love of teaching and from my love for many teachers—some of whom are no longer with us, and many of whom are very much alive—who have inspired me and encouraged my writing along the way. Specifically, I would like to acknowledge Helen Jackson, Deborah Barnes Carey, Lillian Huntington, Lewis Hillier, Yvonne Farnsworth, Wesley McNair, Patricia O'Donnell, Bill Roorbach, Elizabeth Cooke, Joyce Johnson, Rebecca Goldstein, Helen Shulman, and Mary Gordon. An equal thank-you is owed to my teaching colleagues, past and present, for their support.

Finally, I'd like to thank my mother, Corris Cammack, and my stepfather, the late Robert P. Cammack, for not dissuading me when I told them, at age six, that I wanted to be a novelist.